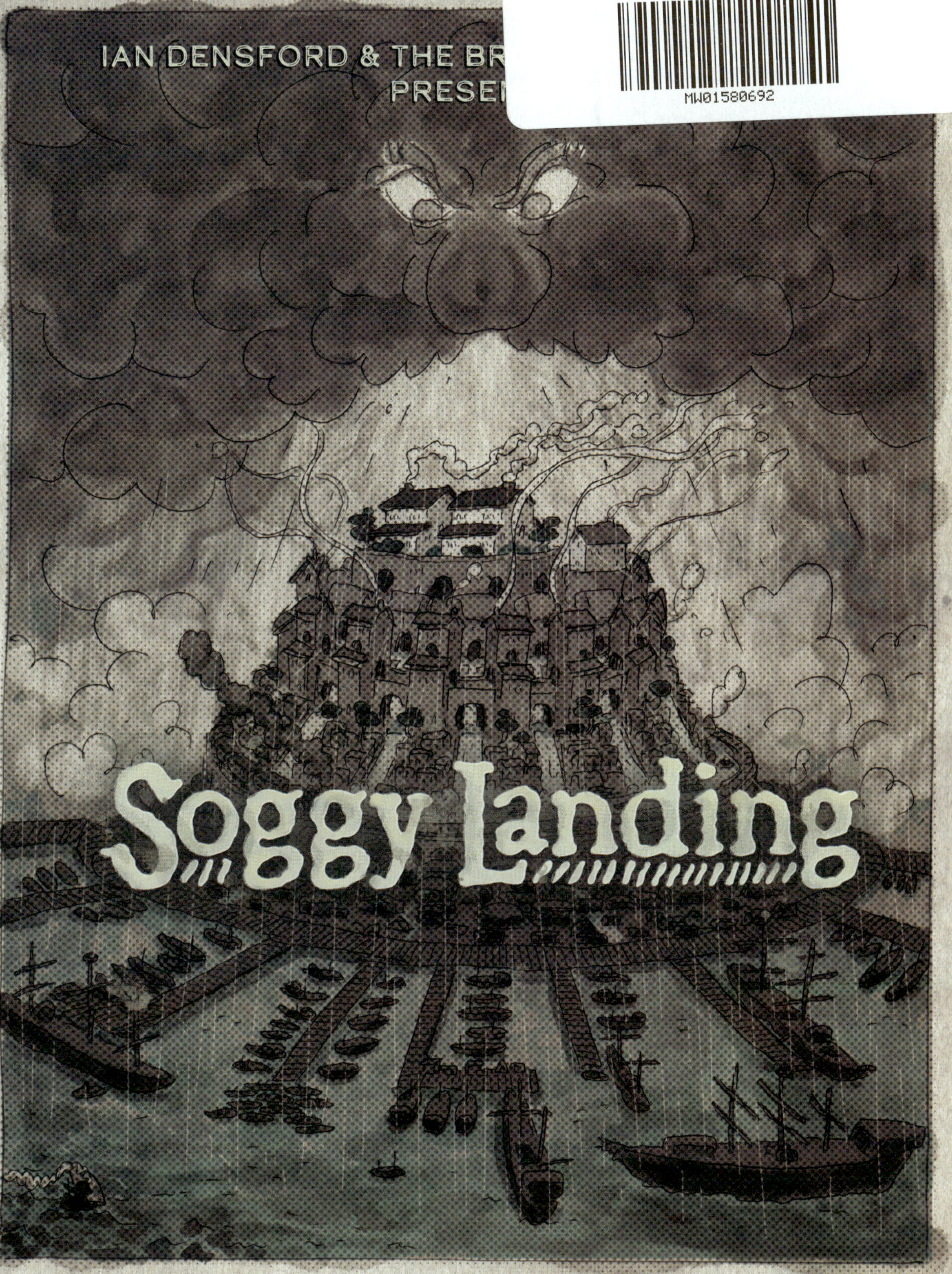
IAN DENSFORD & THE BR
PRESE
Soggy Landing

—DESIGNED BY—
SARAH ROCKWELL

—EDITED BY—
ZACK SOTO

PUBLISHED BY ONI-LION FORGE PUBLISHING GROUP, LLC.

Hunter Gorinson, *president & publisher* • Sierra Hahn, *editor in chief* • Troy Look, *vp of publishing services* • Katie Sainz, *director of marketing* • Angie Knowles, *director of design & production* • Michael Torma, *senior sales manager* • Desiree Rodriguez, *digital marketing manager* • Sarah Rockwell, *senior graphic designer* • Carey Soucy, *senior graphic designer* • Matt Harding, *digital prepress technician* • Chris Cerasi, *managing editor* • Bess Pallares, *senior editor* • Grace Scheipeter, *senior editor* • Gabriel Granillo, *editor* • Zack Soto, *editor* • Sara Harding, *executive assistant* • Jung Hu Lee, *logistics coordinator & editorial assistant* • Kuian Kellum, *warehouse assistant*

Joe Nozemack, *publisher emeritus*

First Edition: August 2023

ISBN 978-1-63715-224-9
eISBN 978-1-63715-585-1

1 3 5 7 9 10 8 6 4 2

Library of Congress Control Number 2023931975

ONIPRESS.COM @ONIPRESS
IANDENSFORD.COM @IANDENSFORD
STUFFYREYESWITHWONDER.TUMBLR.COM

SOGGY LANDING, August 2023. Published by Oni-Lion Forge Publishing Group, LLC., 1319 SE Martin Luther King Jr. Blvd., Suite 240, Portland, OR 97214. Soggy Landing is ™ & © 2023 Ian Densford, Alec McGovern & Andrew McGovern. All rights reserved. Oni Press logo and icon are ™ & © 2023 Oni-Lion Forge Publishing Group, LLC. All rights reserved. Oni Press logo and icon artwork created by Keith A. Wood. The events, institutions, and characters presented in this book are fictional. Any resemblance to actual persons, living or dead, is purely coincidental. No portion of this publication may be reproduced, by any means, without the express written permission of the copyright holders. Printed in China.

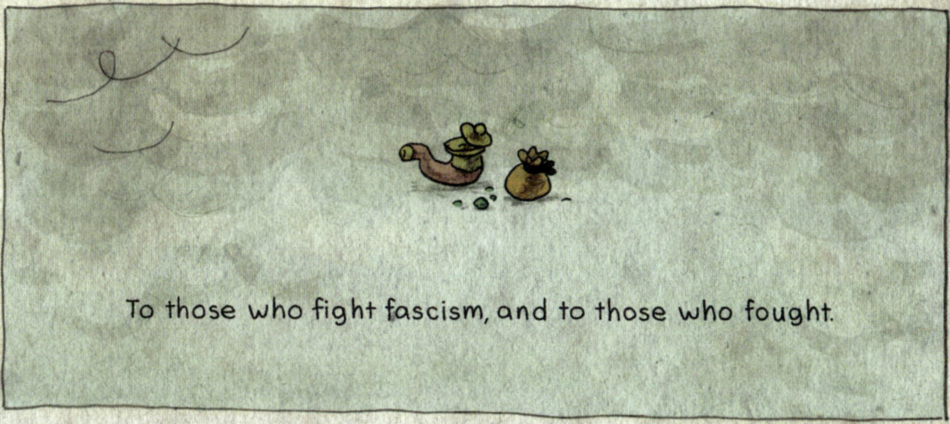
To those who fight fascism, and to those who fought.

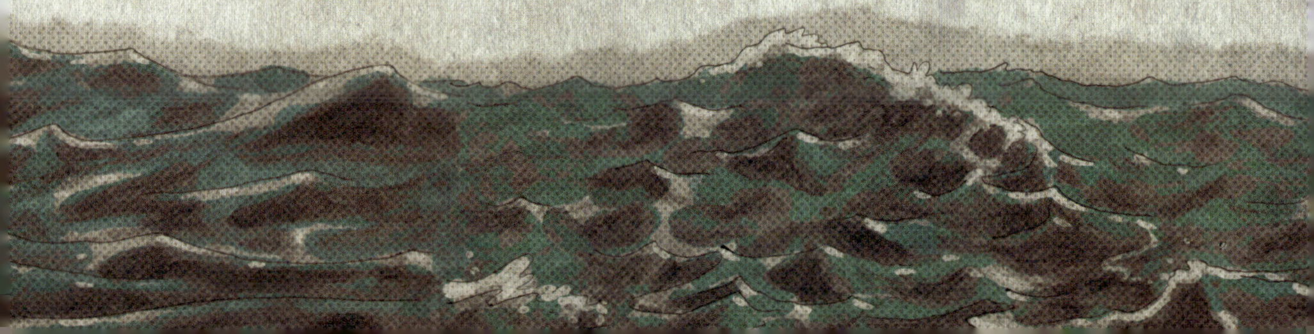

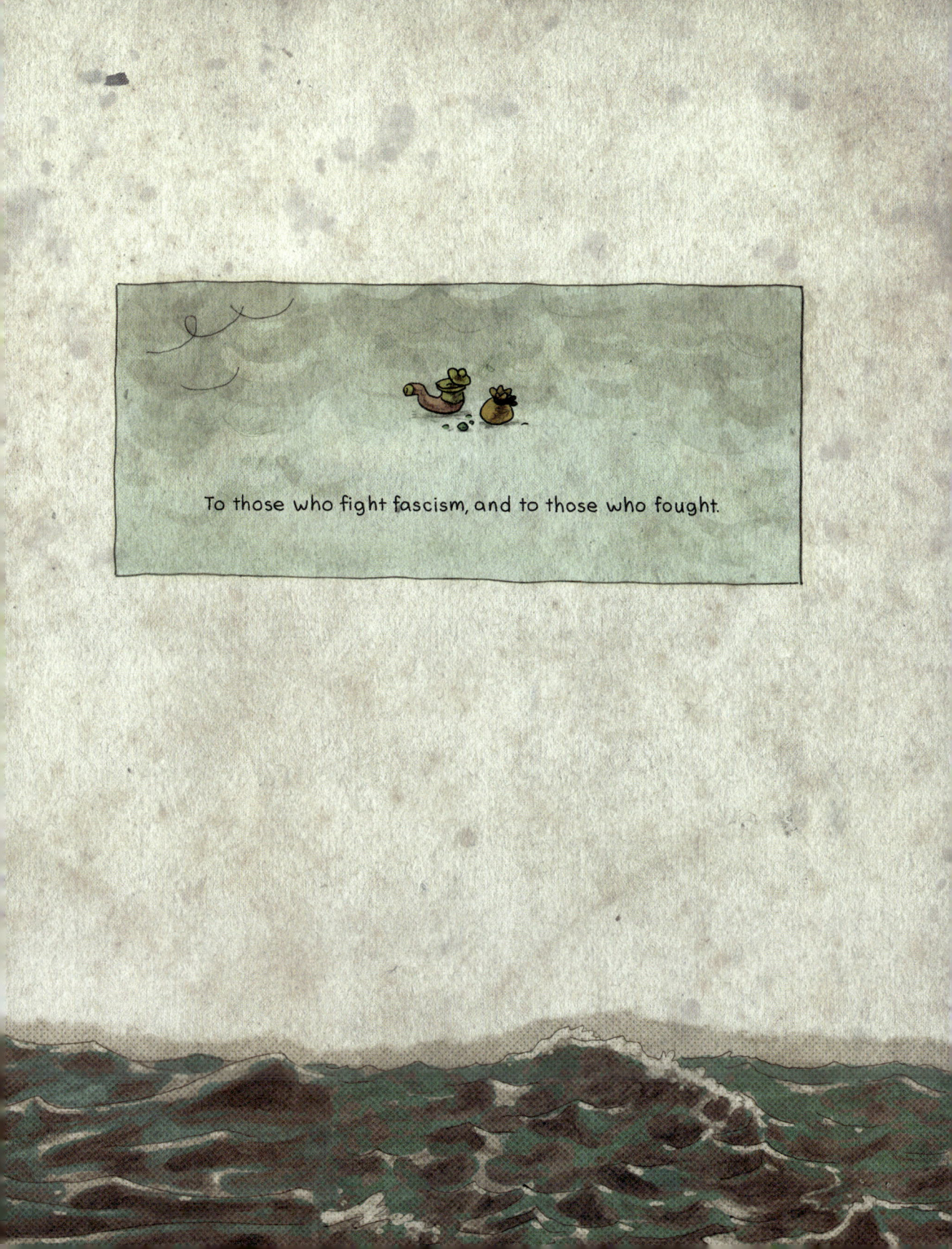

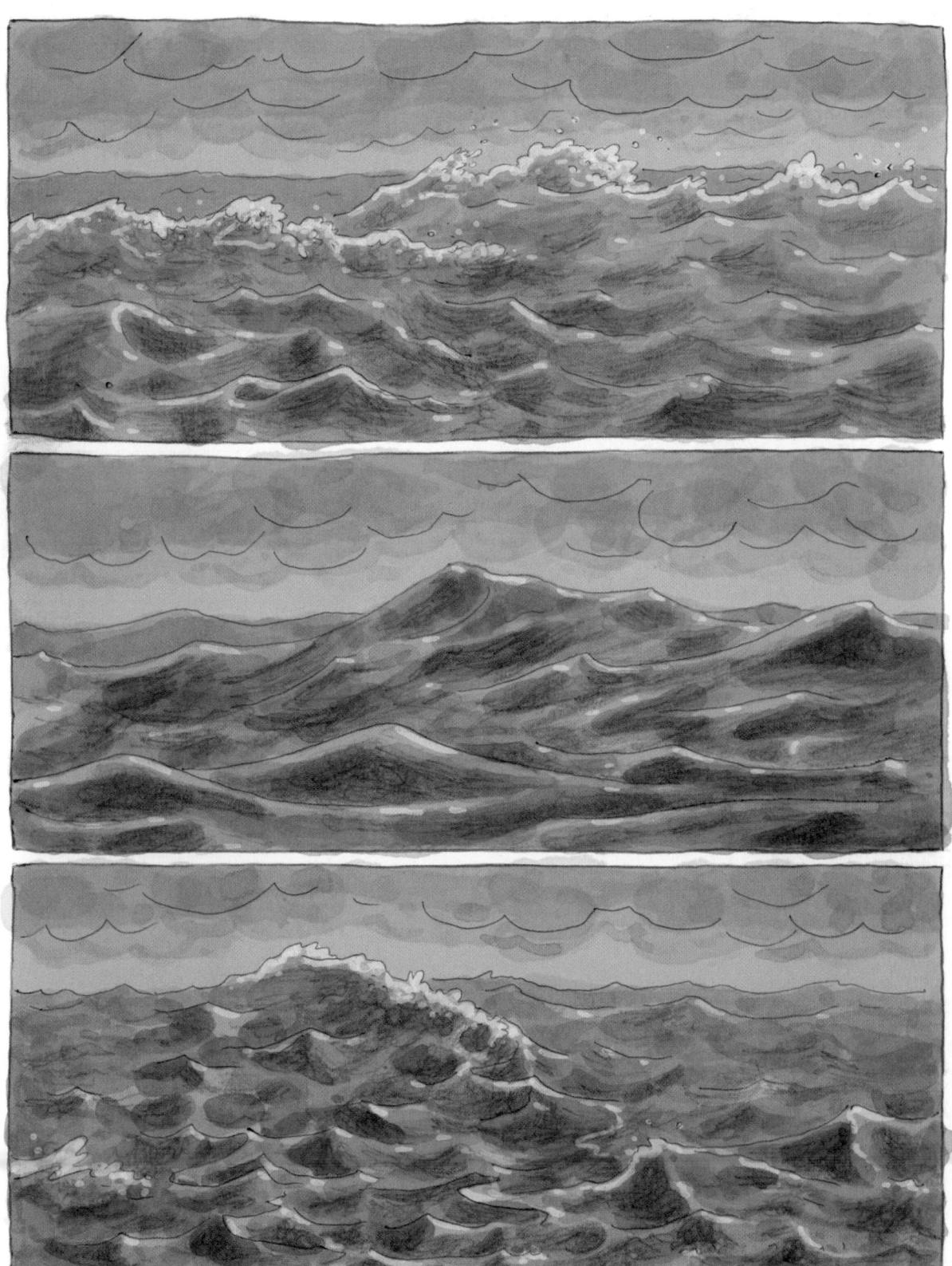

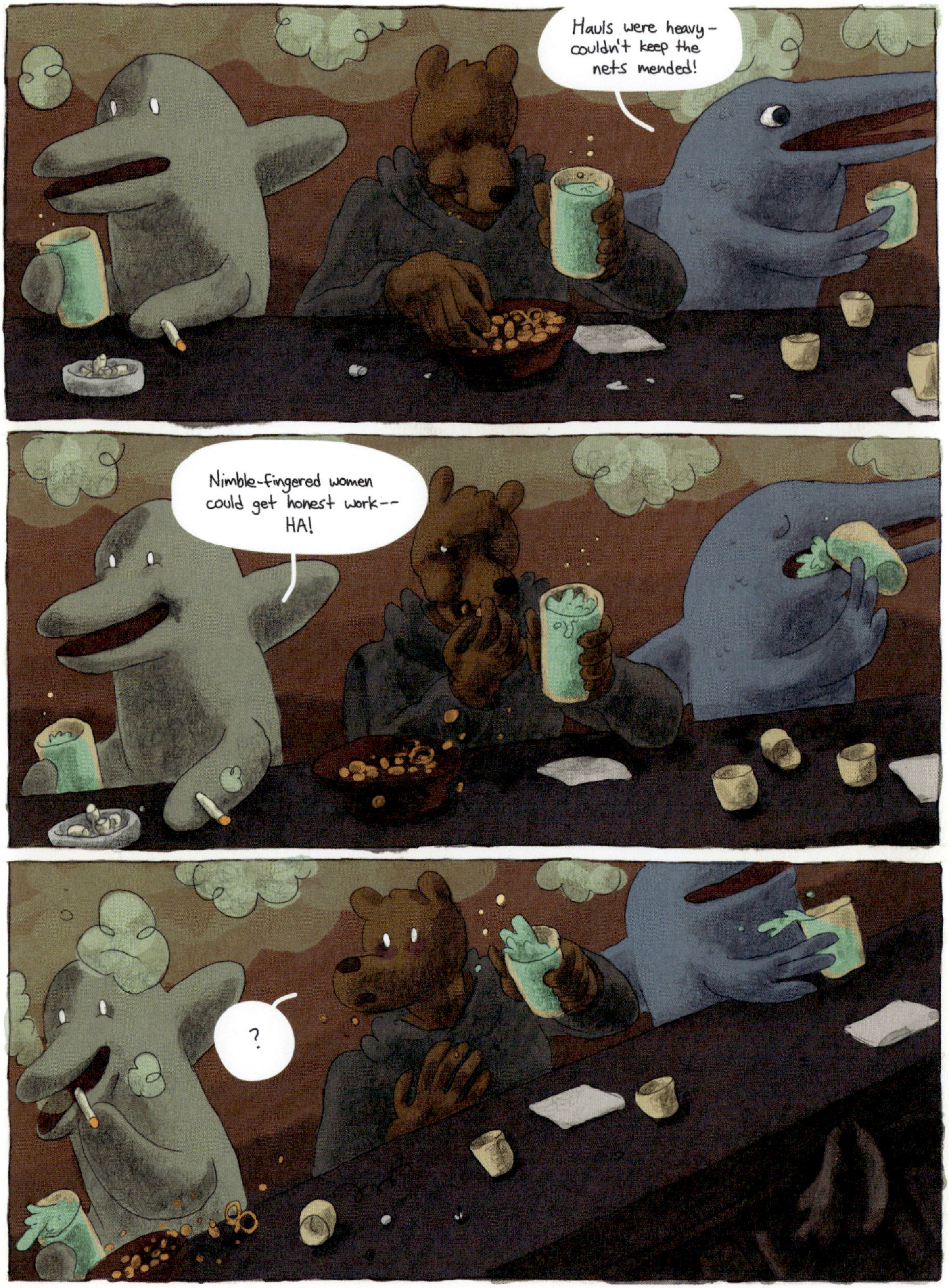
Hauls were heavy- couldn't keep the nets mended!
Nimble-fingered women could get honest work-- HA!
?

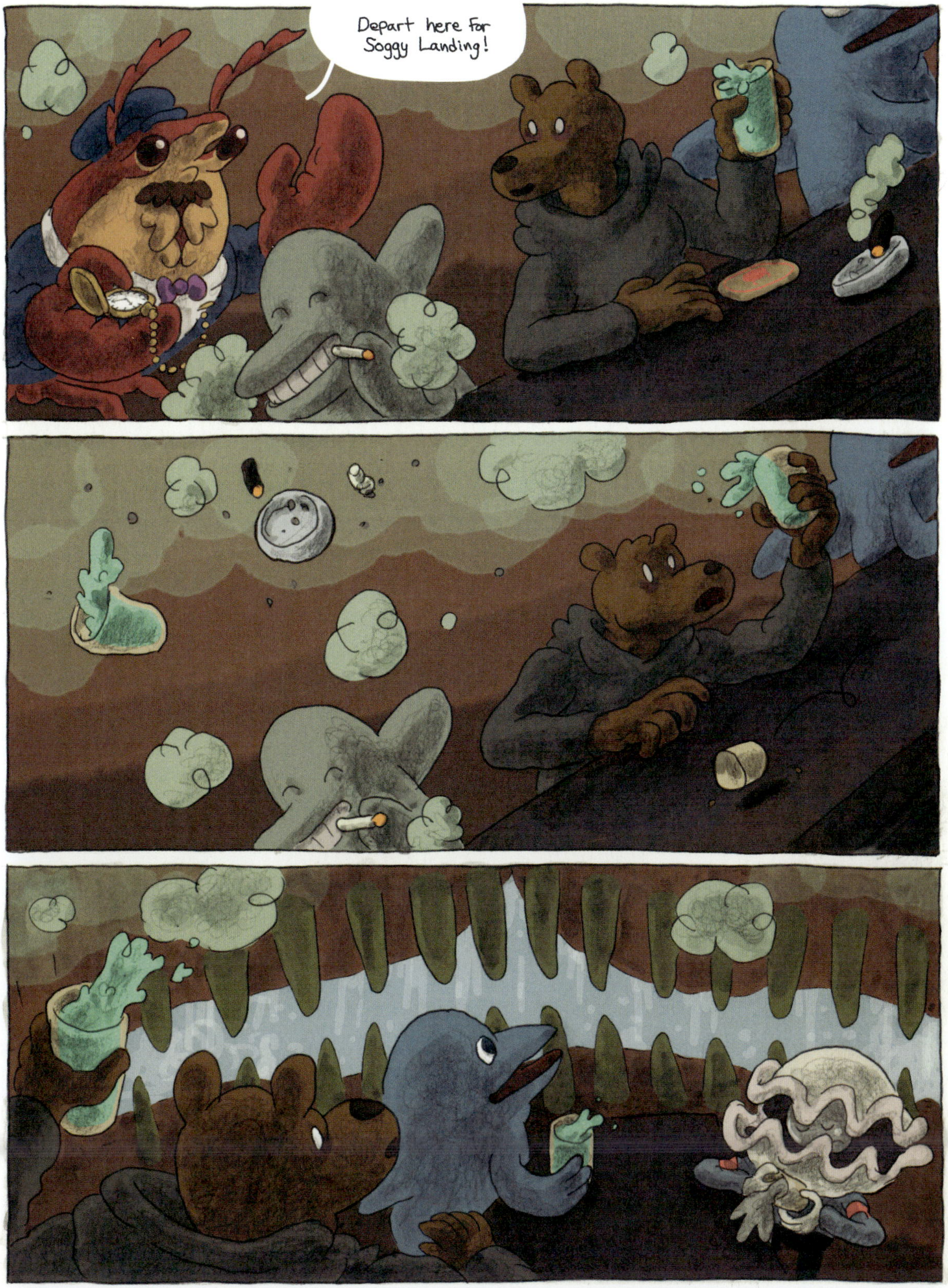
Depart here for Soggy Landing!

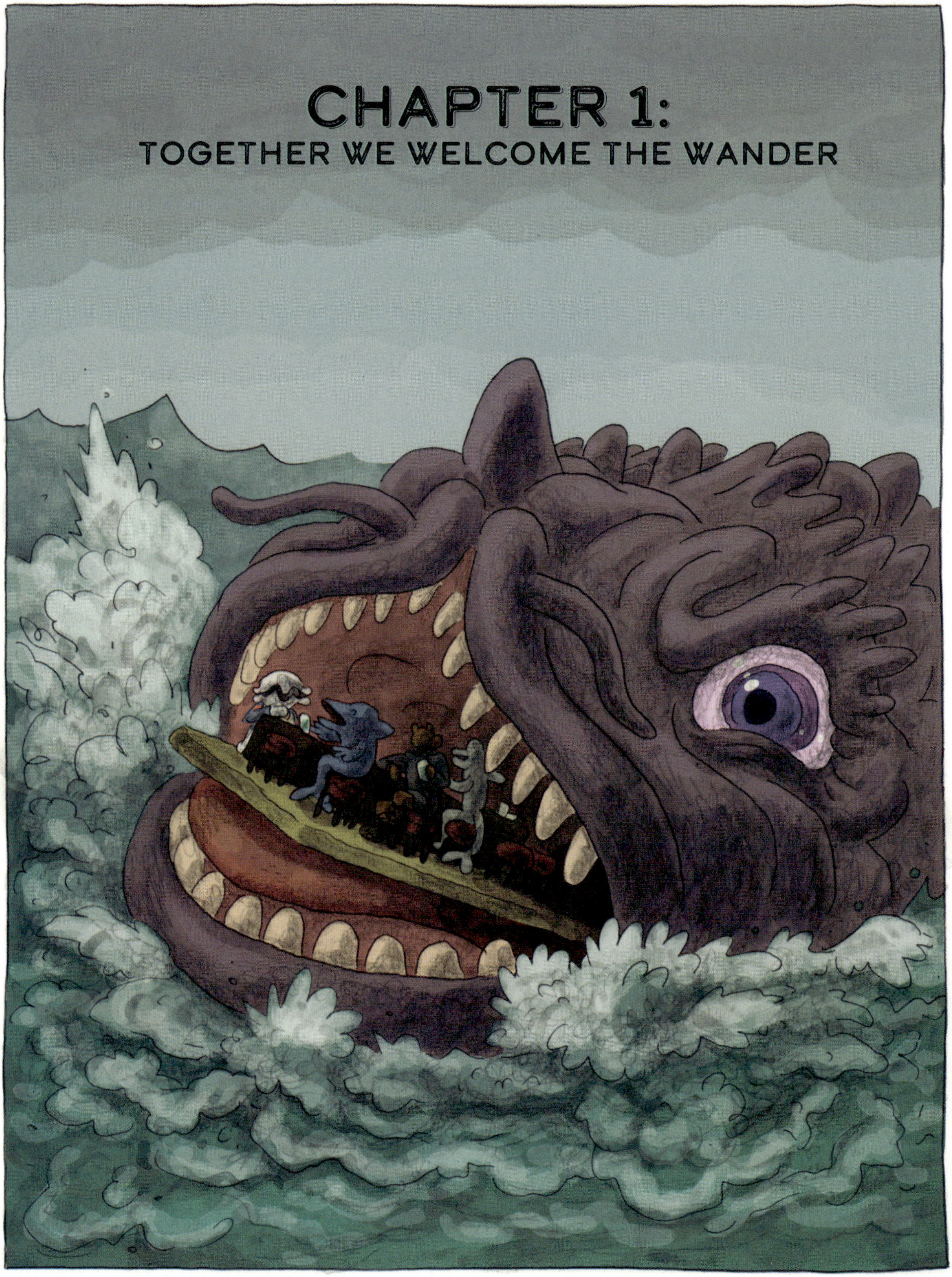
CHAPTER 1:
TOGETHER WE WELCOME THE WANDER

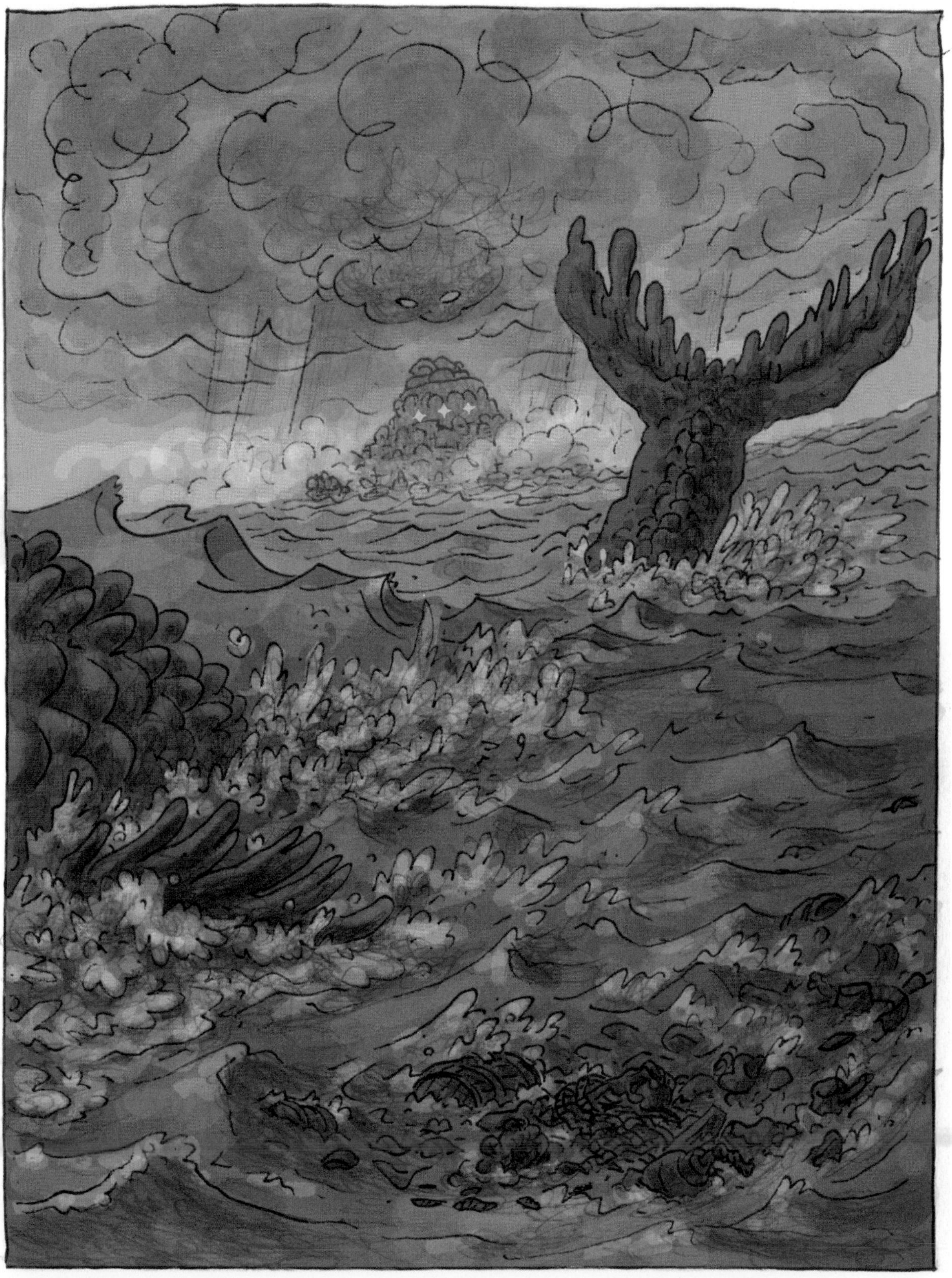

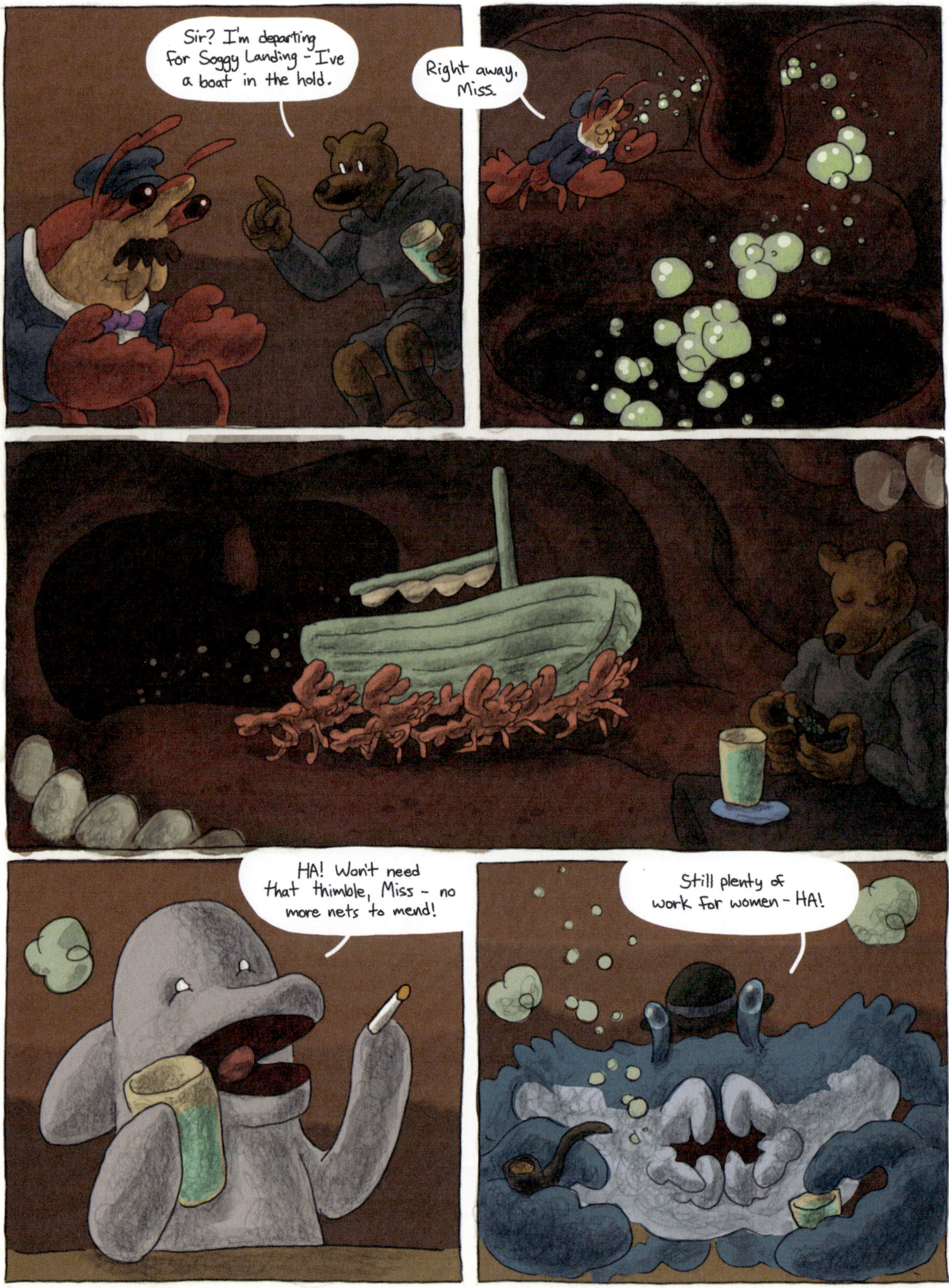
Sir? I'm departing for Soggy Landing - I've a boat in the hold.
Right away, Miss.
HA! Won't need that thimble, Miss - no more nets to mend!
Still plenty of work for women - HA!

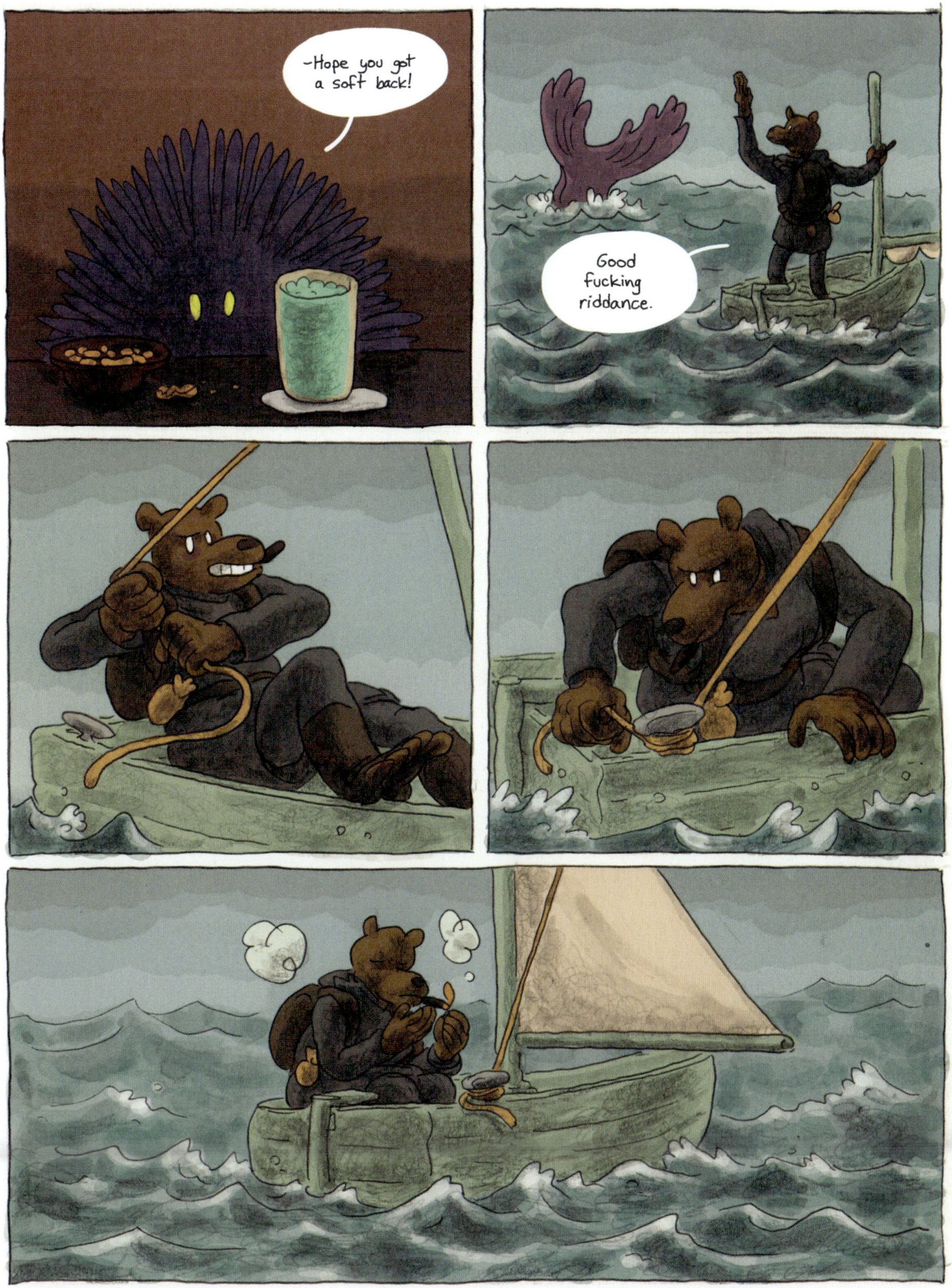
-Hope you got a soft back!
Good fucking riddance.

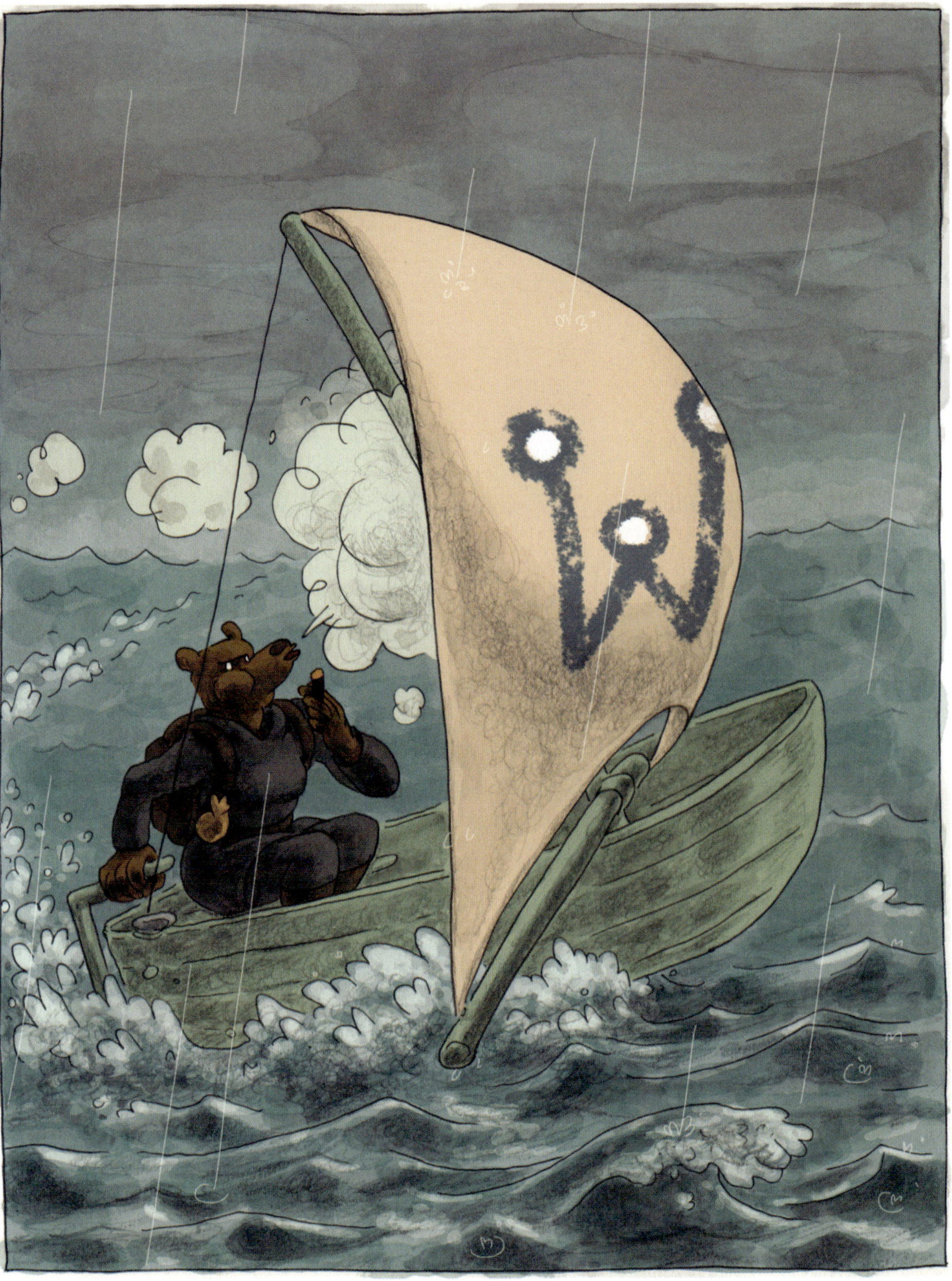

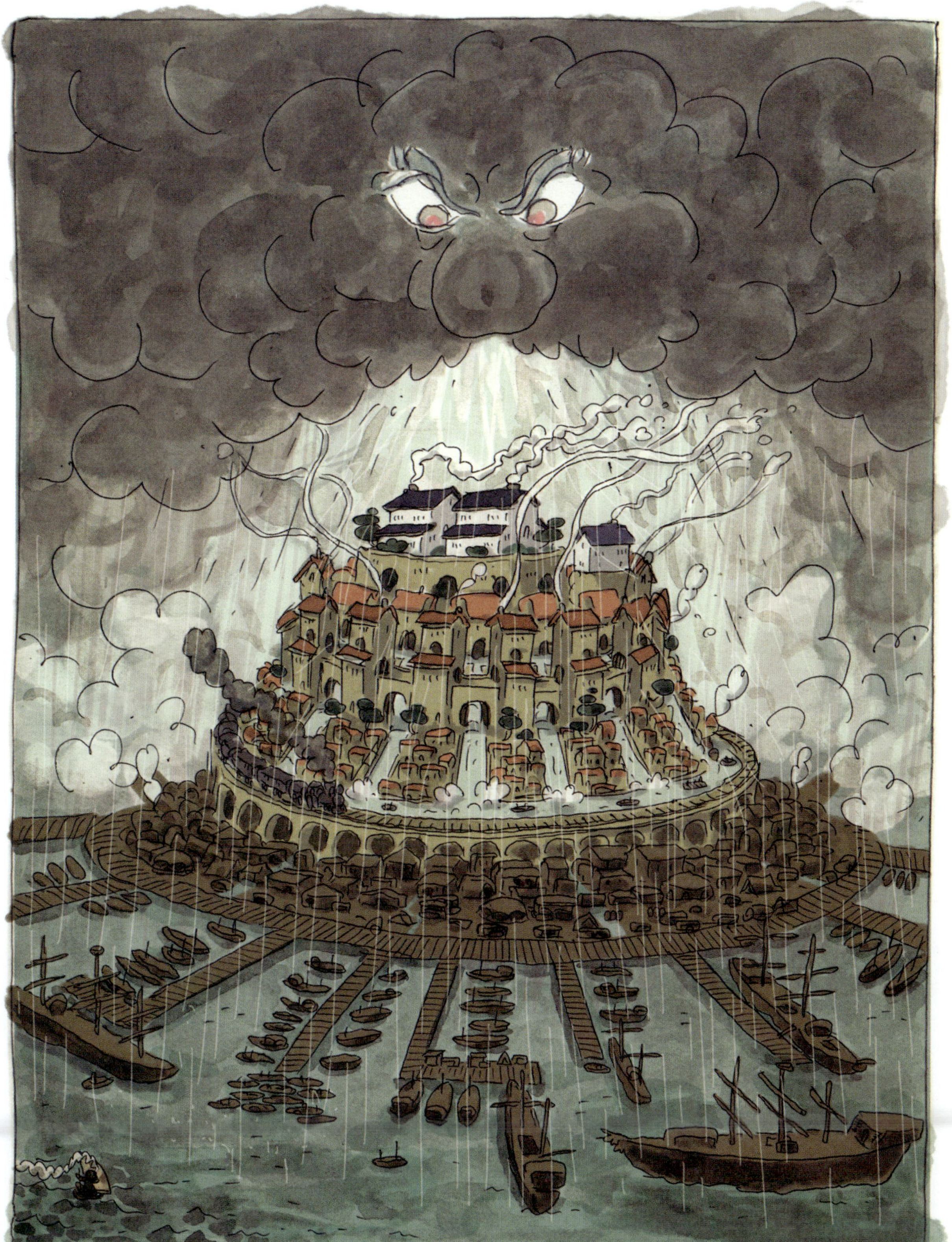

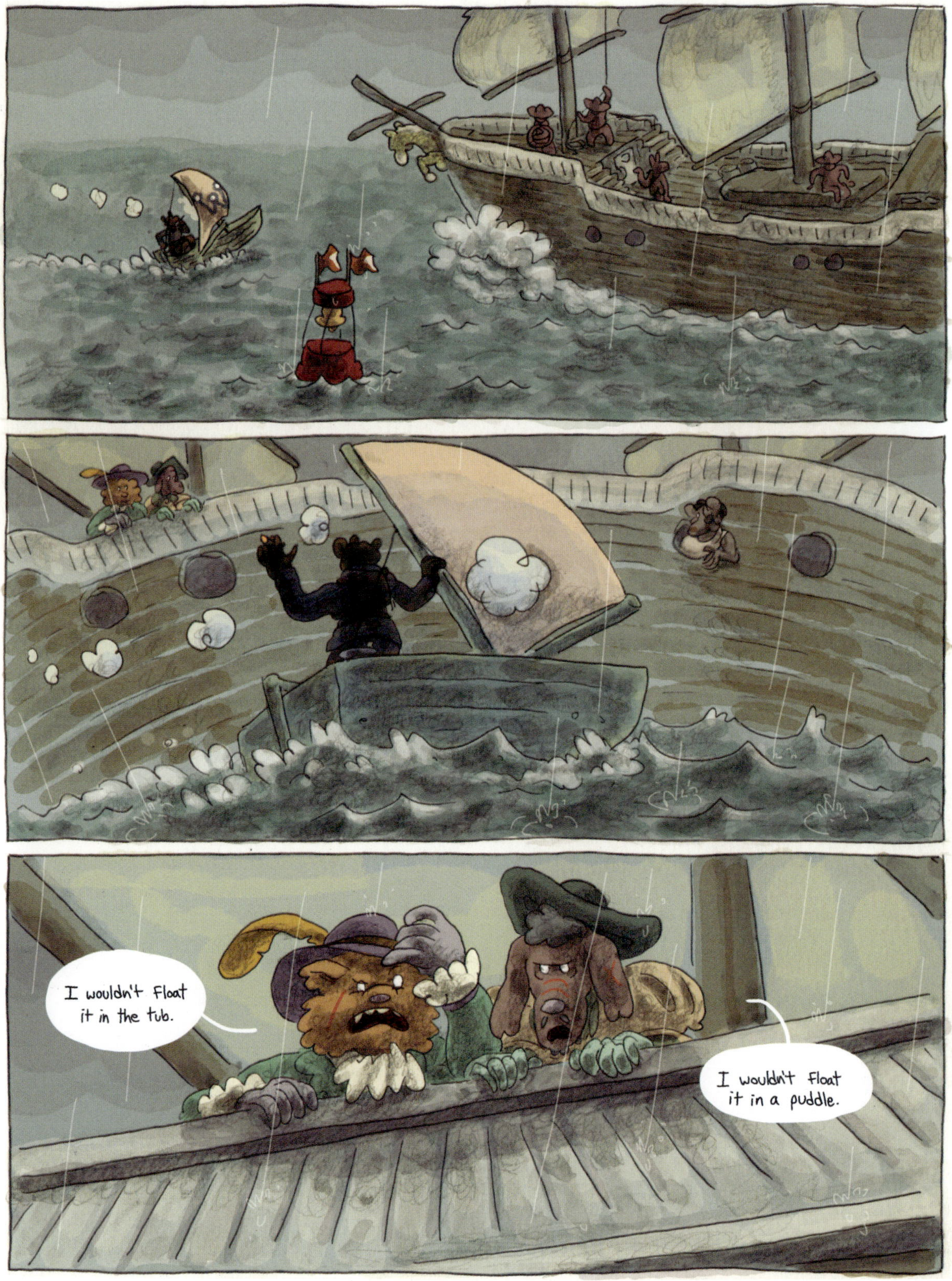
I wouldn't float it in the tub.
I wouldn't float it in a puddle.

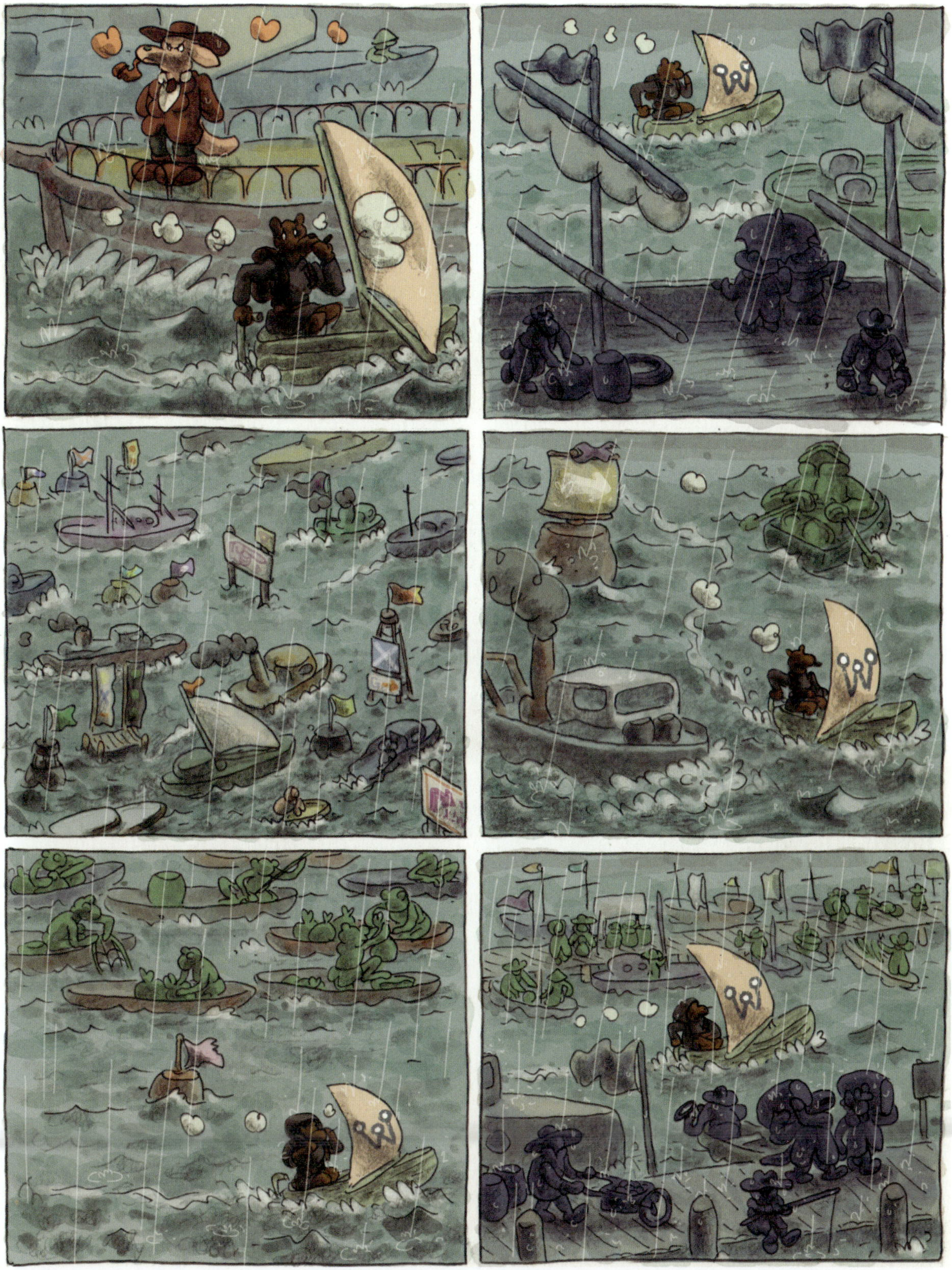

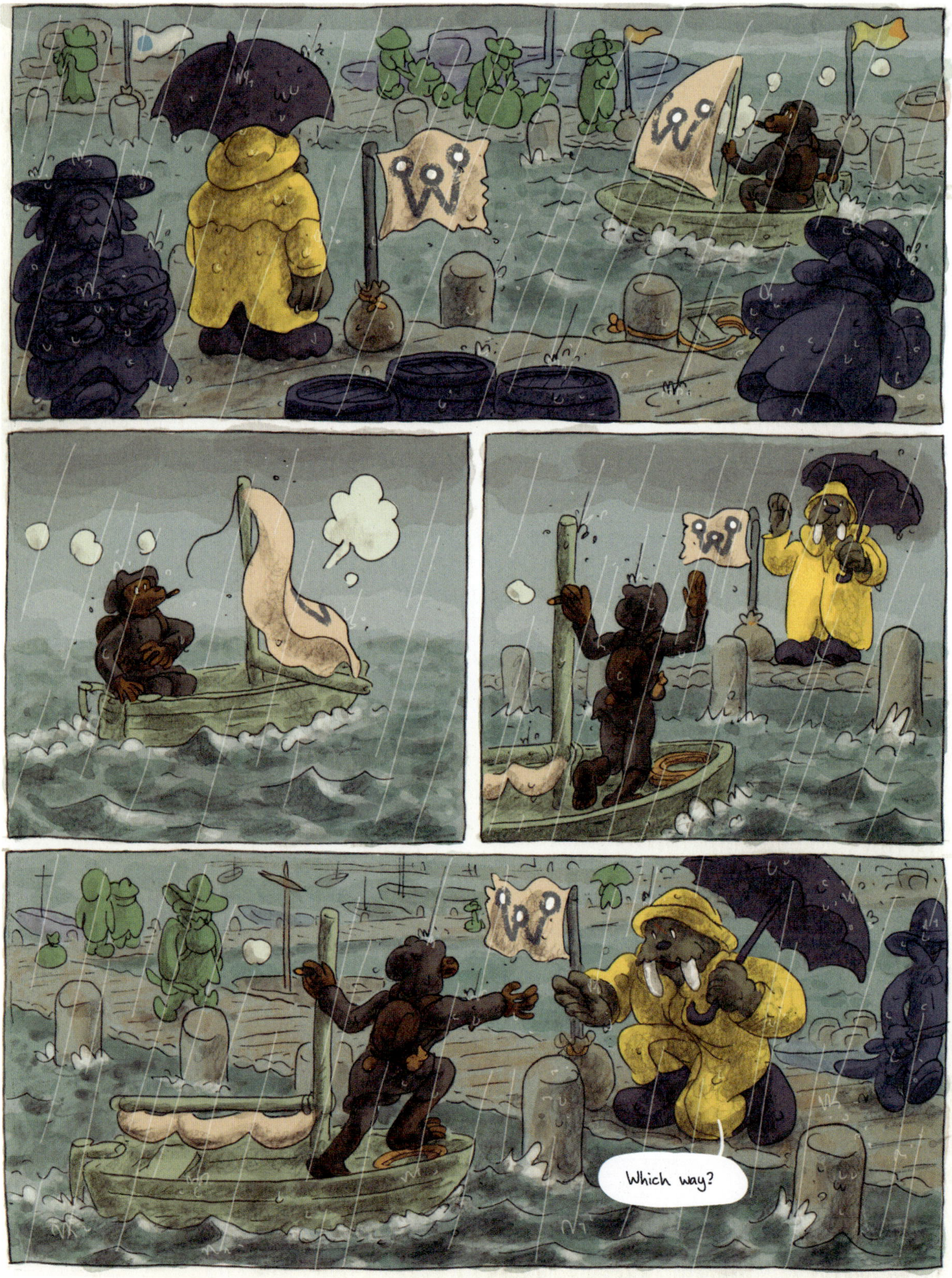
Which way?

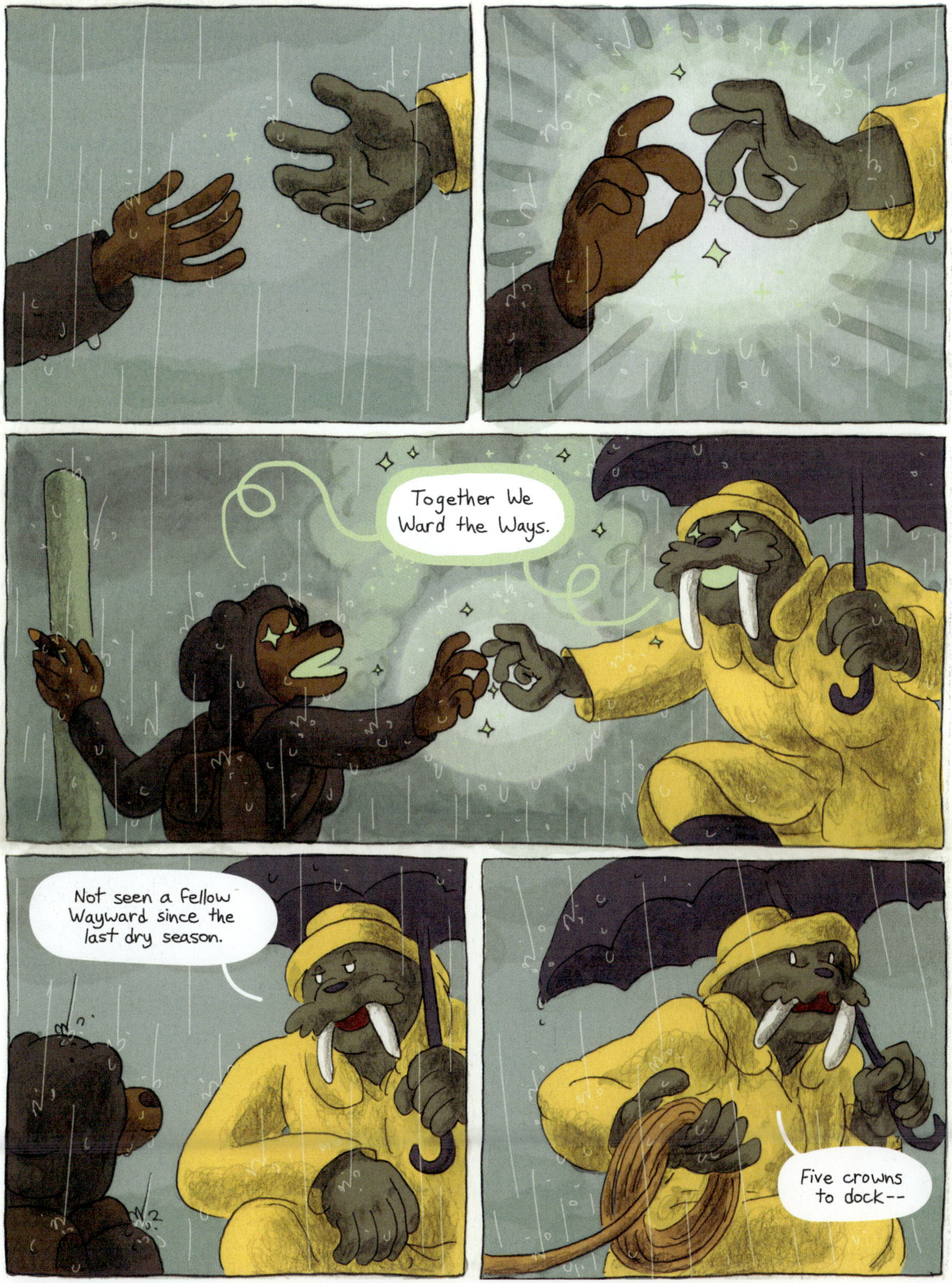
Together We
Ward the Ways.
Not seen a fellow
Wayward since the
last dry season.
Five crowns
to dock--

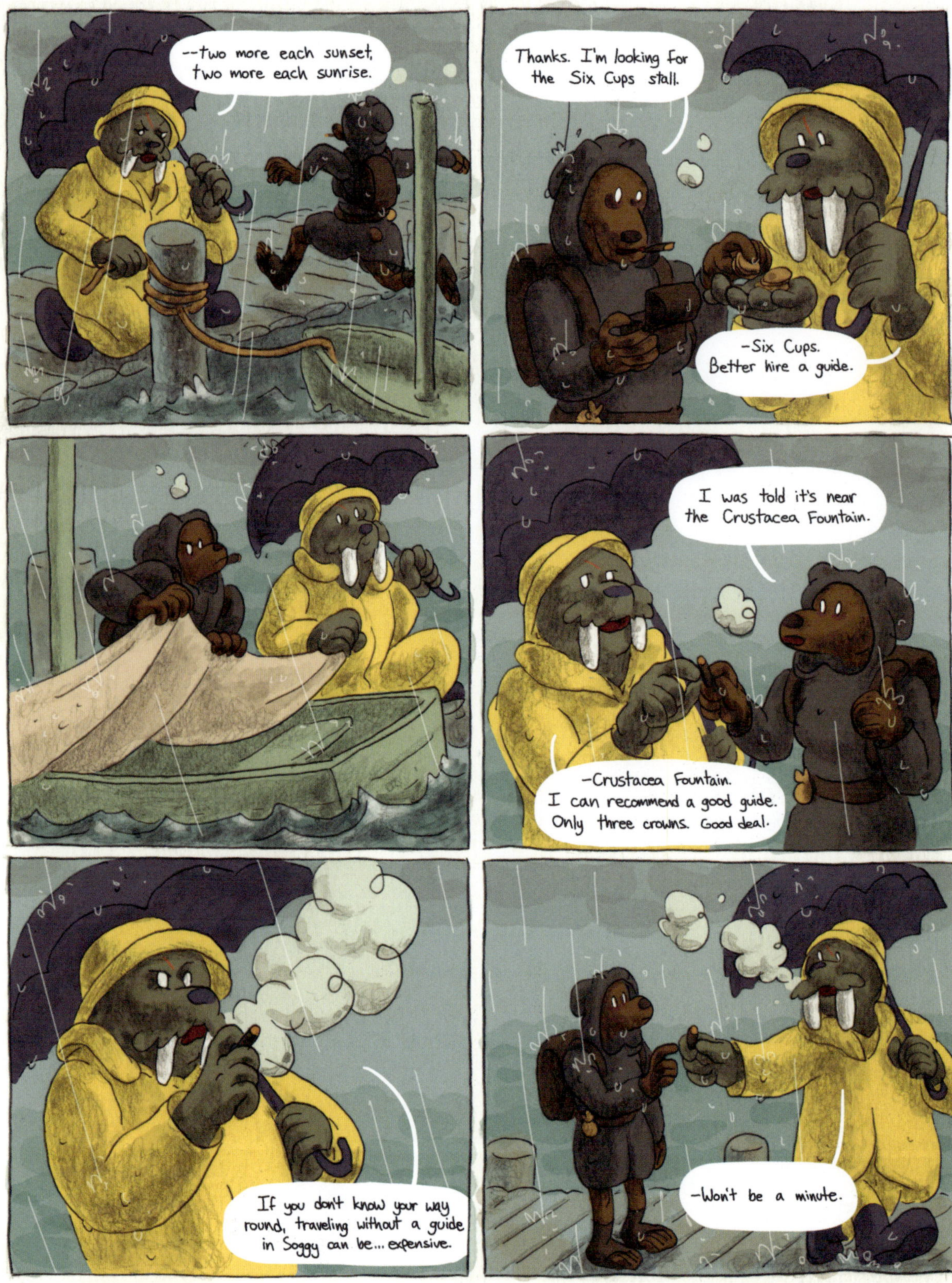
--two more each sunset, two more each sunrise.
Thanks. I'm looking for the Six Cups stall.
-Six Cups. Better hire a guide.
I was told it's near the Crustacea Fountain.
-Crustacea Fountain. I can recommend a good guide. Only three crowns. Good deal.
If you don't know your way round, traveling without a guide in Soggy can be... expensive.
-Won't be a minute.

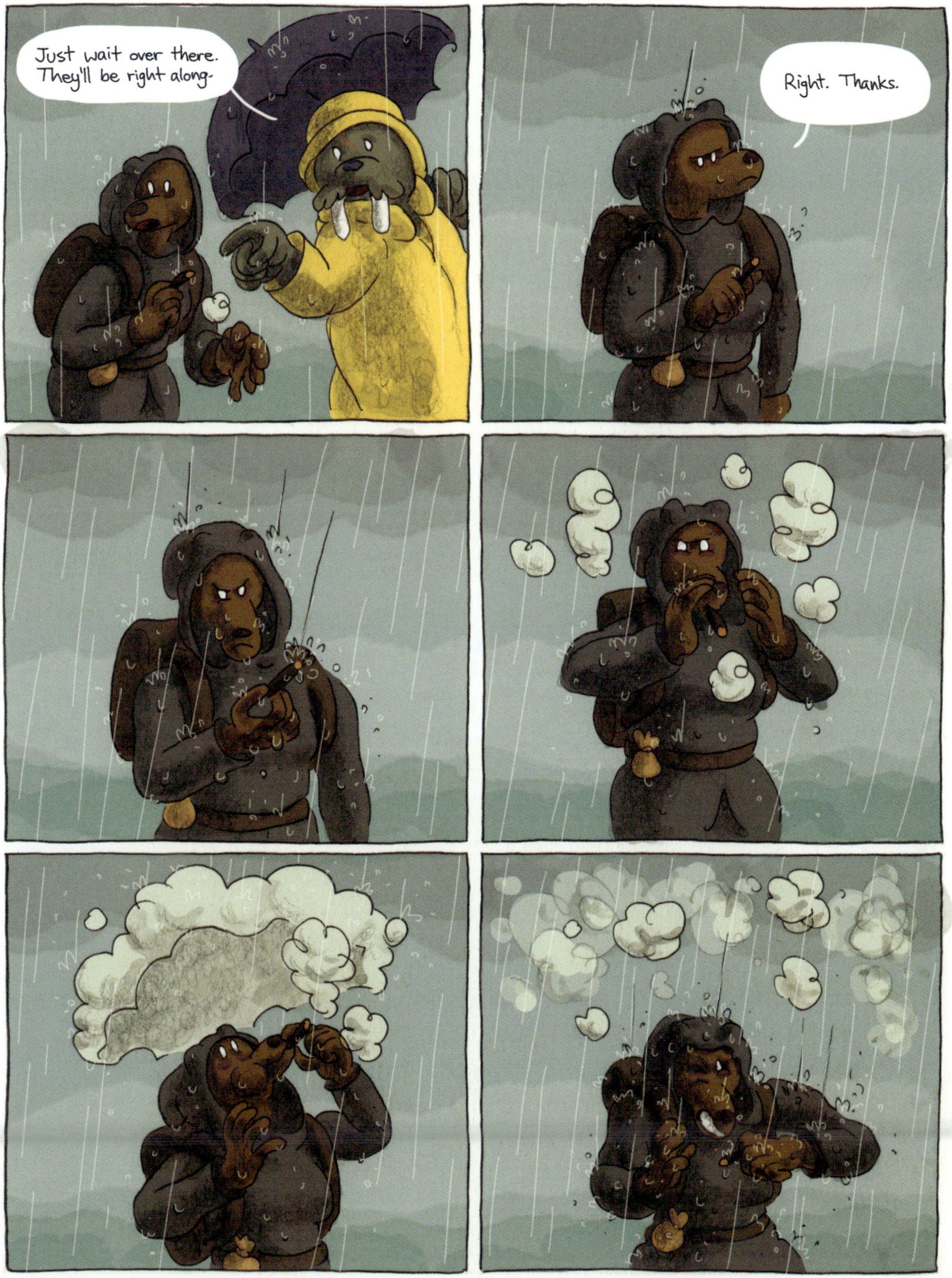
Just wait over there. They'll be right along.
Right. Thanks.

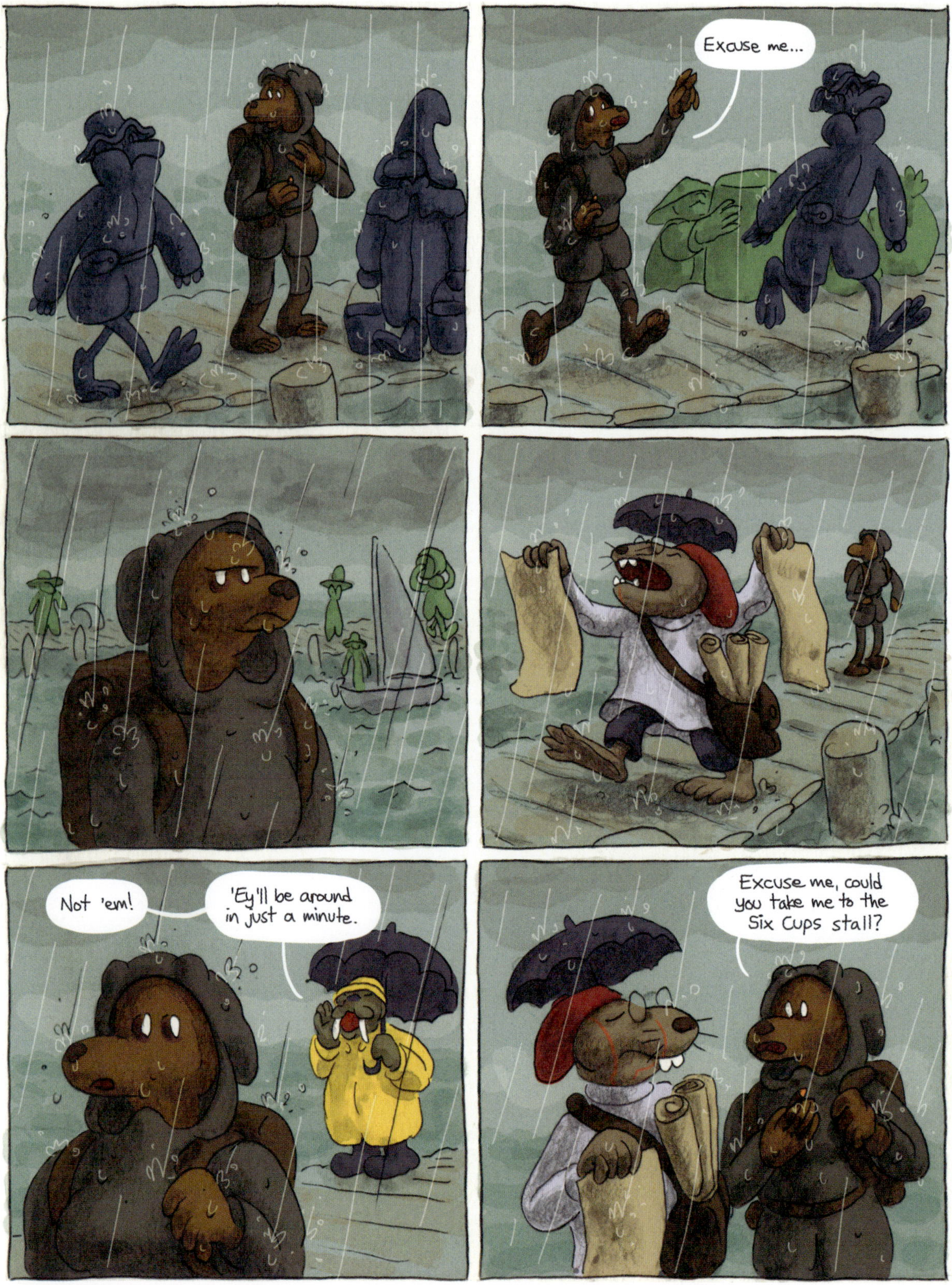
Excuse me...
Not 'em!
'Ey'll be around in just a minute.
Excuse me, could you take me to the Six Cups stall?

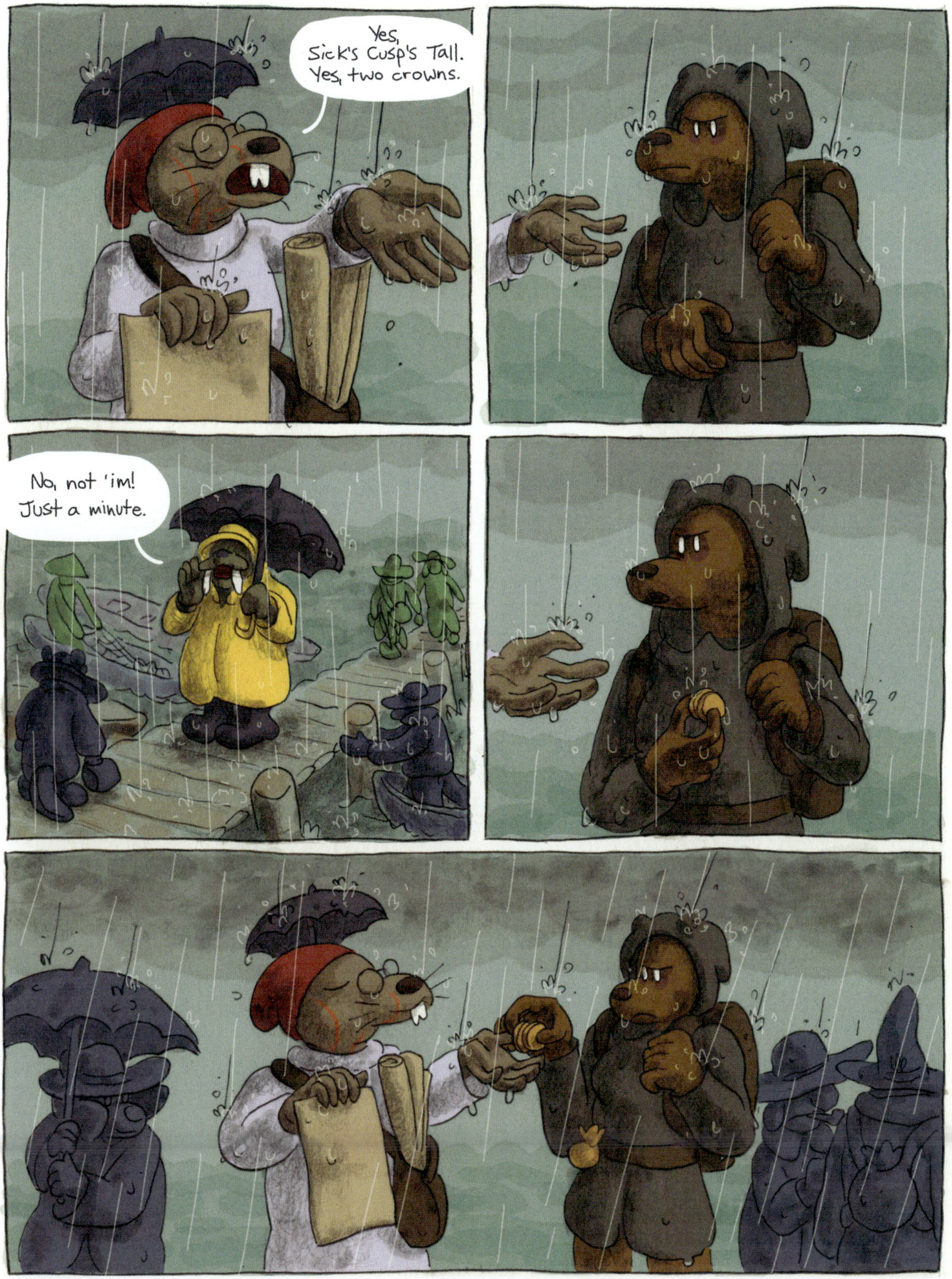
Yes, Sick's Cusp's Tall. Yes, two crowns.
No, not 'im! Just a minute.

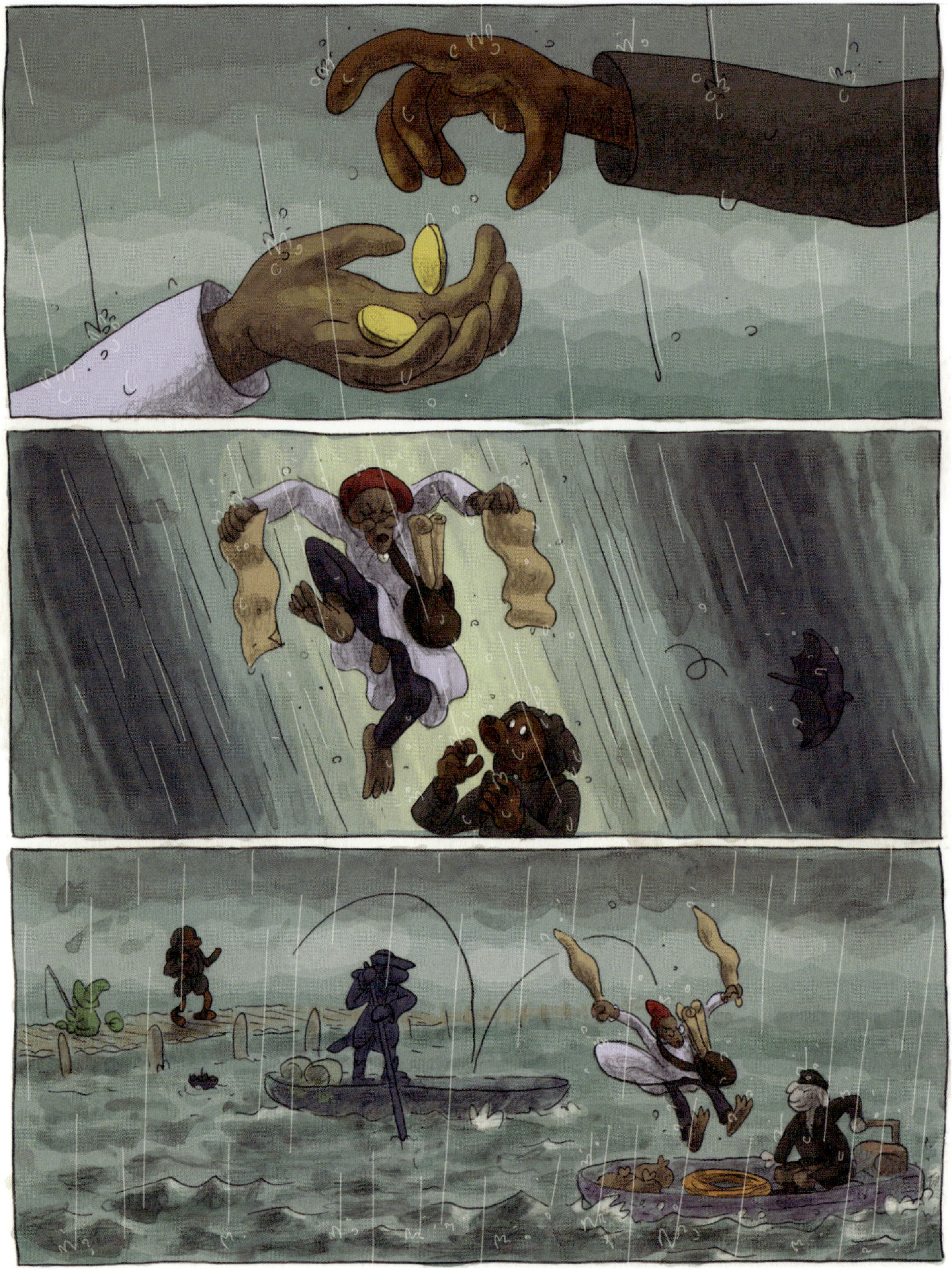

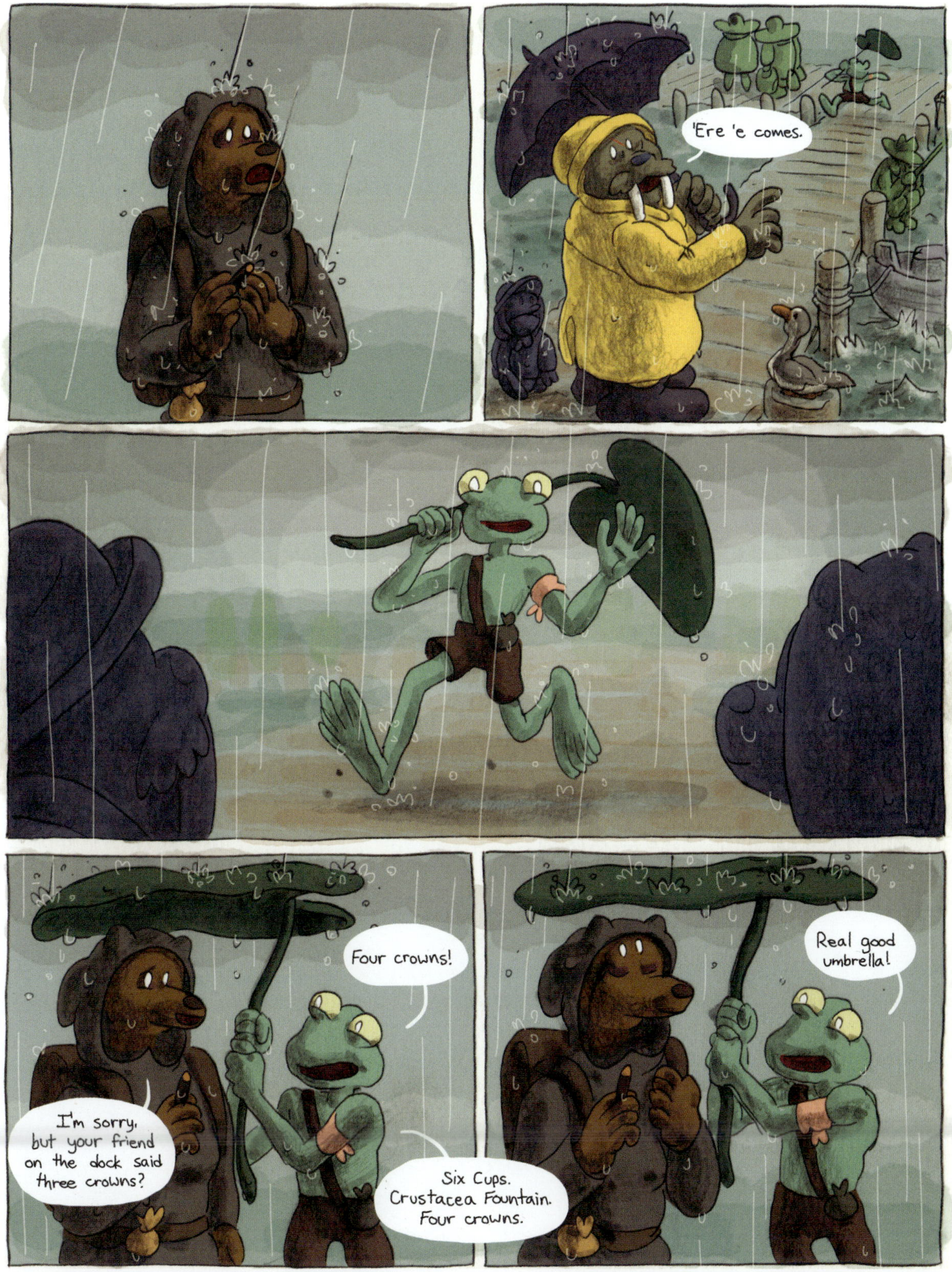
'Ere 'e comes.
Four crowns!
I'm sorry, but your friend on the dock said three crowns?
Six Cups. Crustacea Fountain. Four crowns.
Real good umbrella!

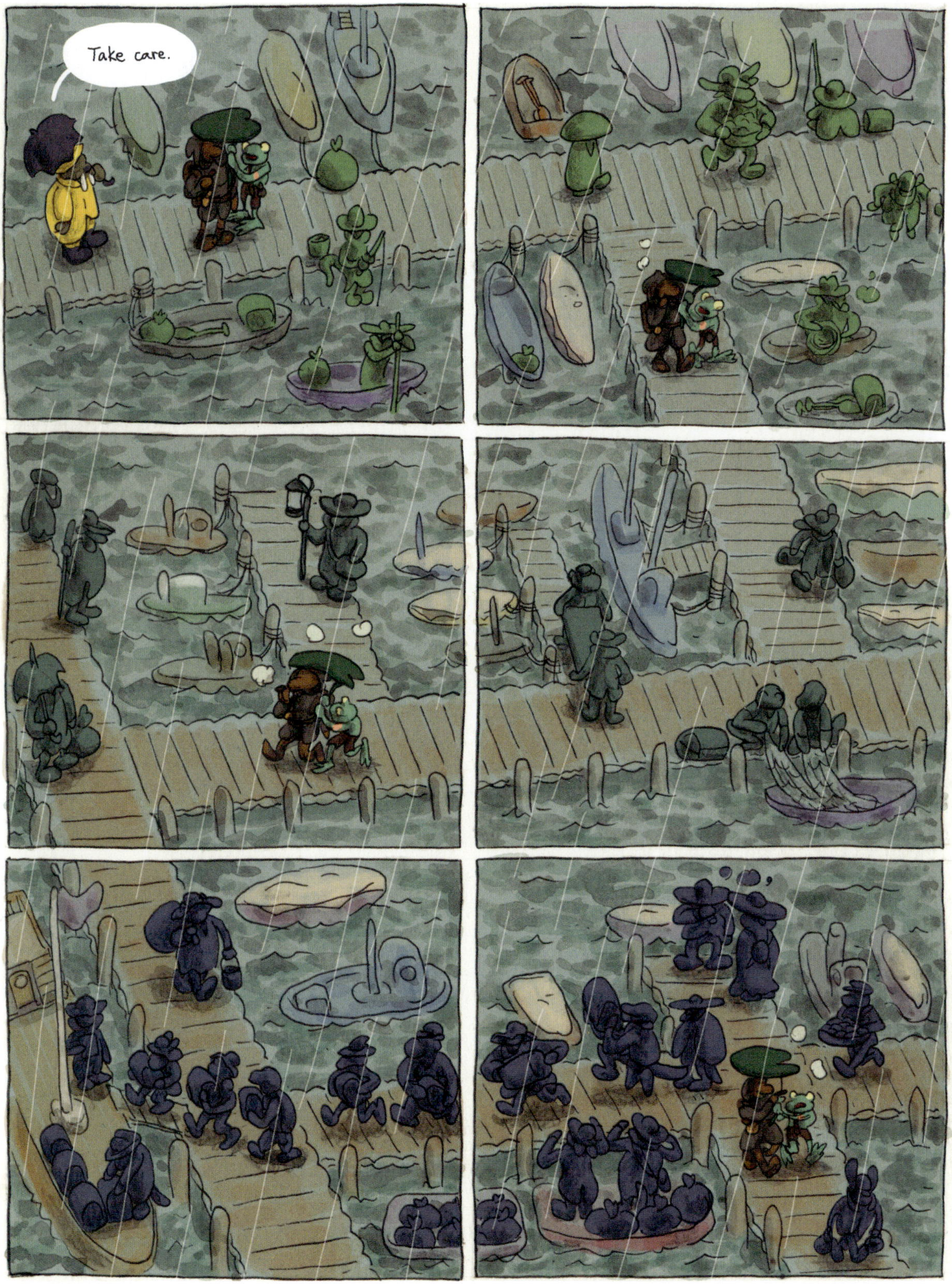
Take care.

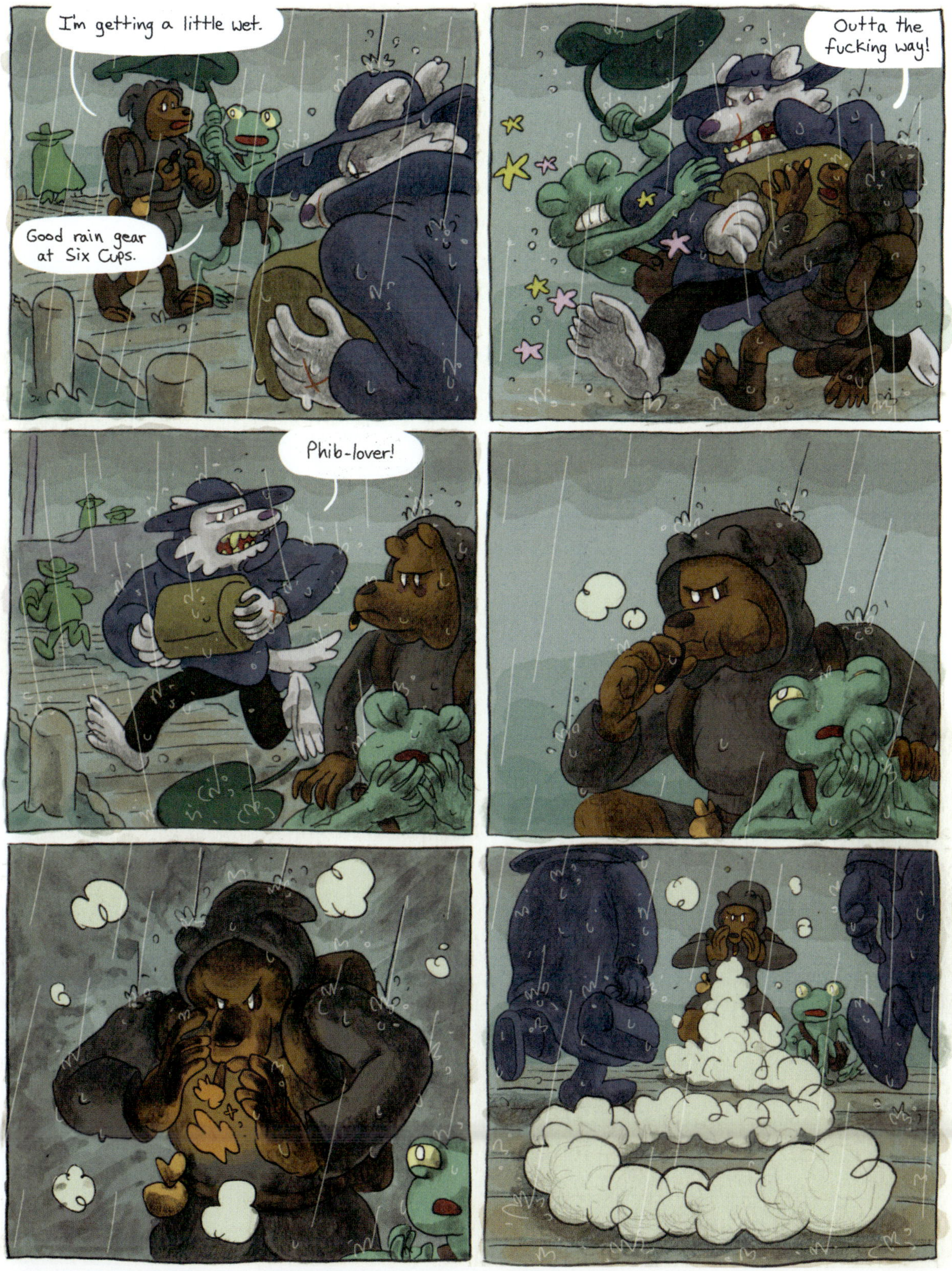
I'm getting a little wet.
Good rain gear at Six Cups.
Outta the fucking way!
Phib-lover!

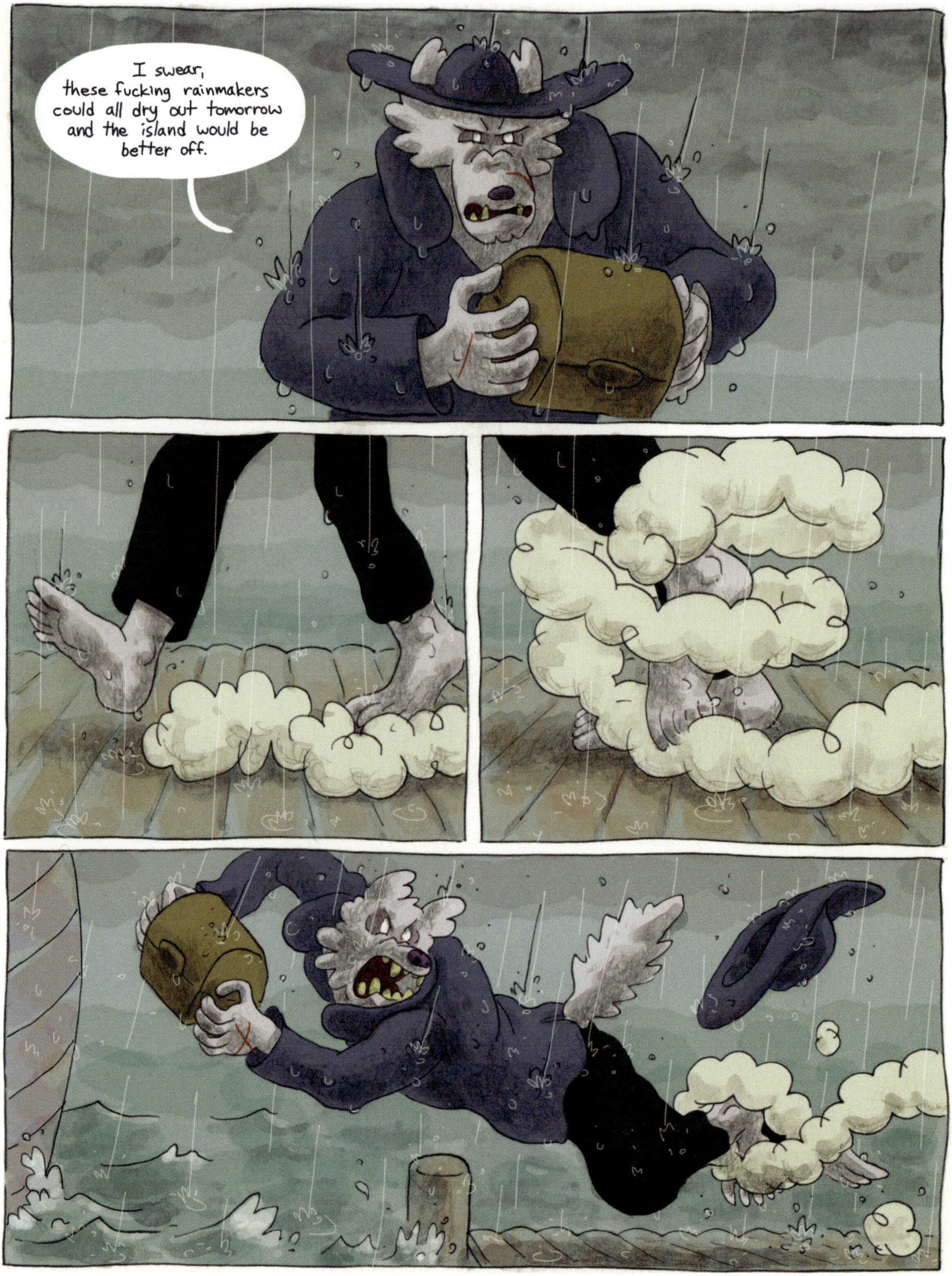
I swear, these fucking rainmakers could all dry out tomorrow and the island would be better off.

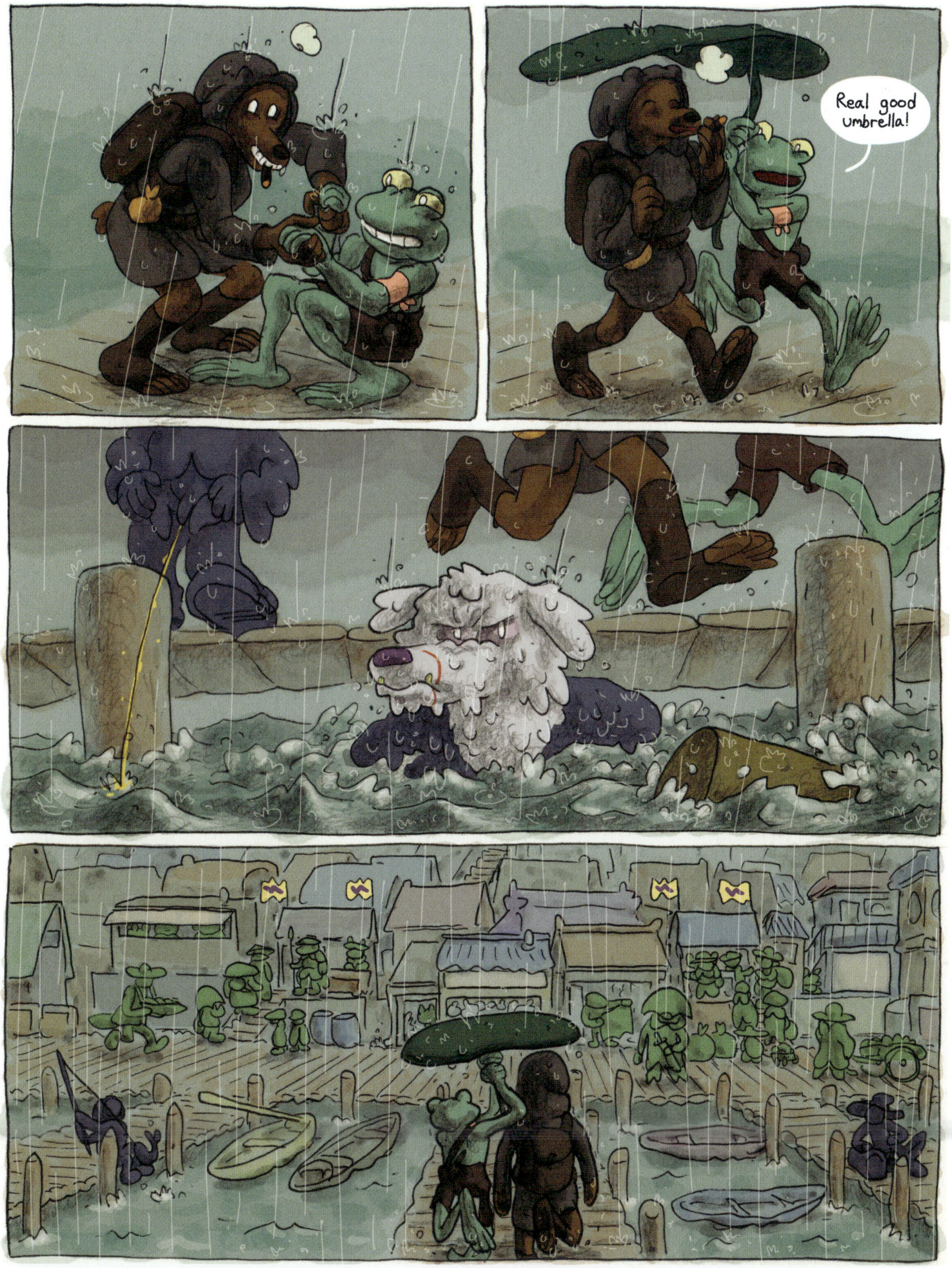
Real good umbrella!

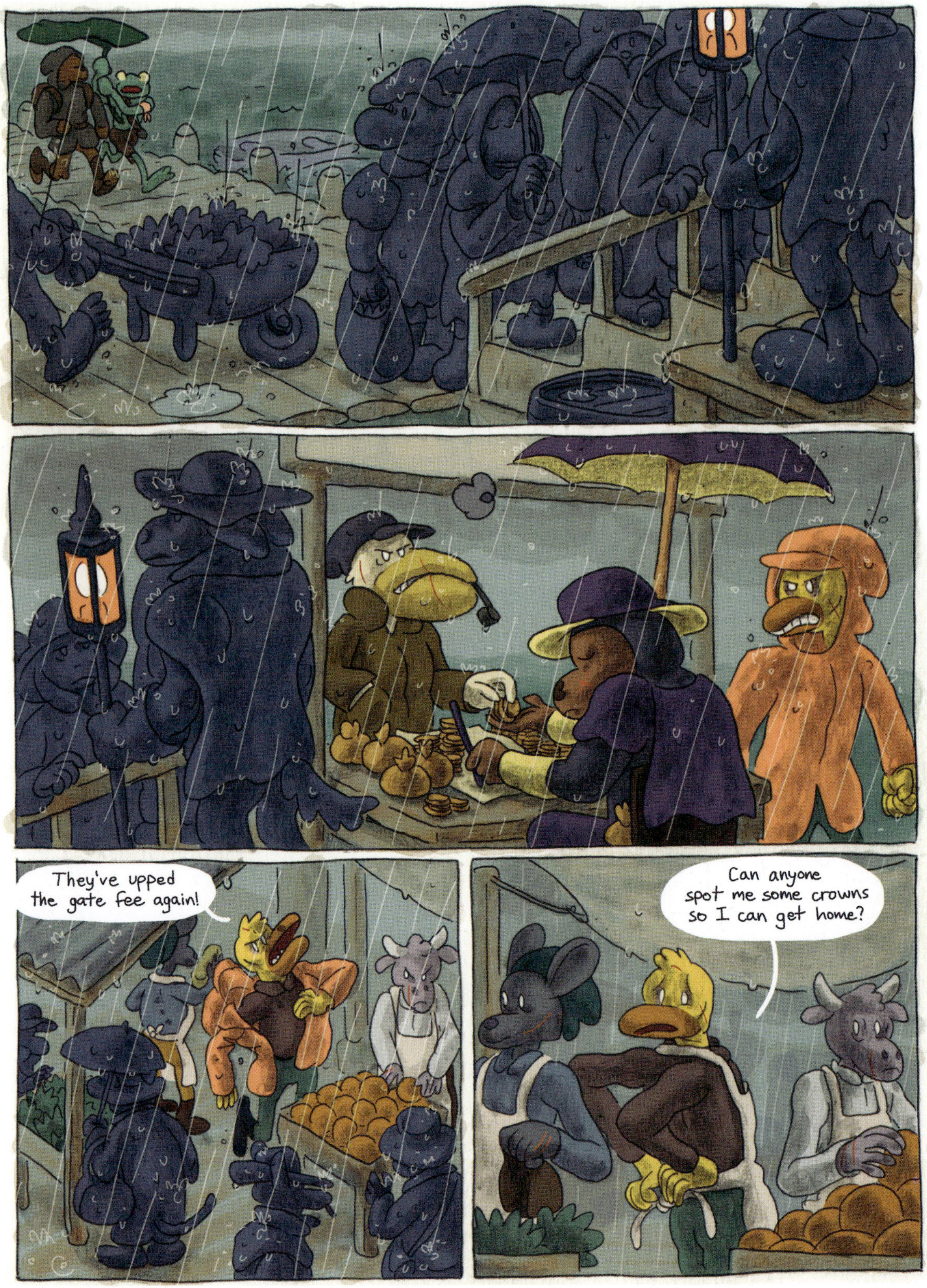
They've upped the gate fee again!
Can anyone spot me some crowns so I can get home?

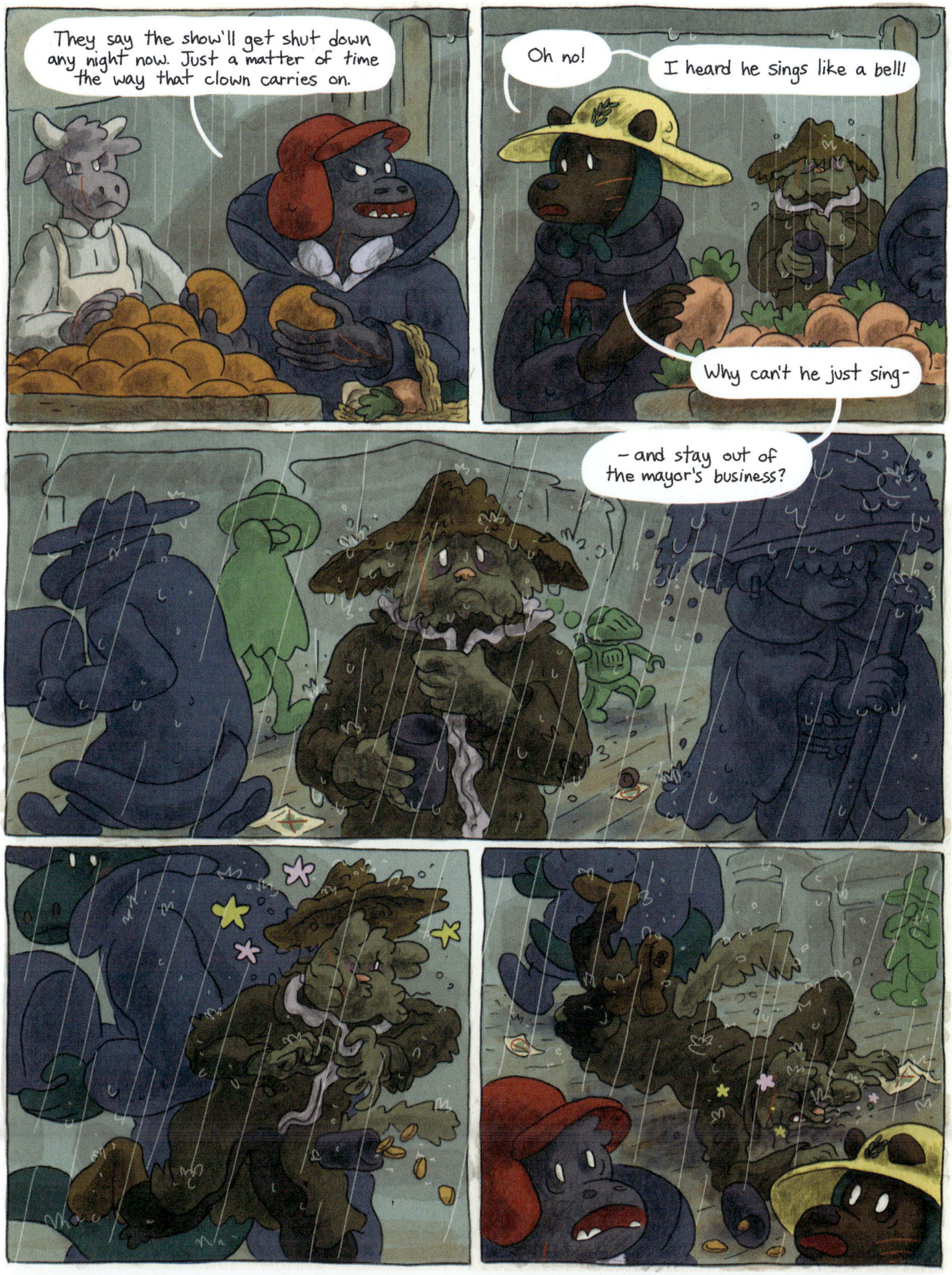

They say the show'll get shut down any night now. Just a matter of time the way that clown carries on.
Oh no!
I heard he sings like a bell!
Why can't he just sing-
- and stay out of the mayor's business?

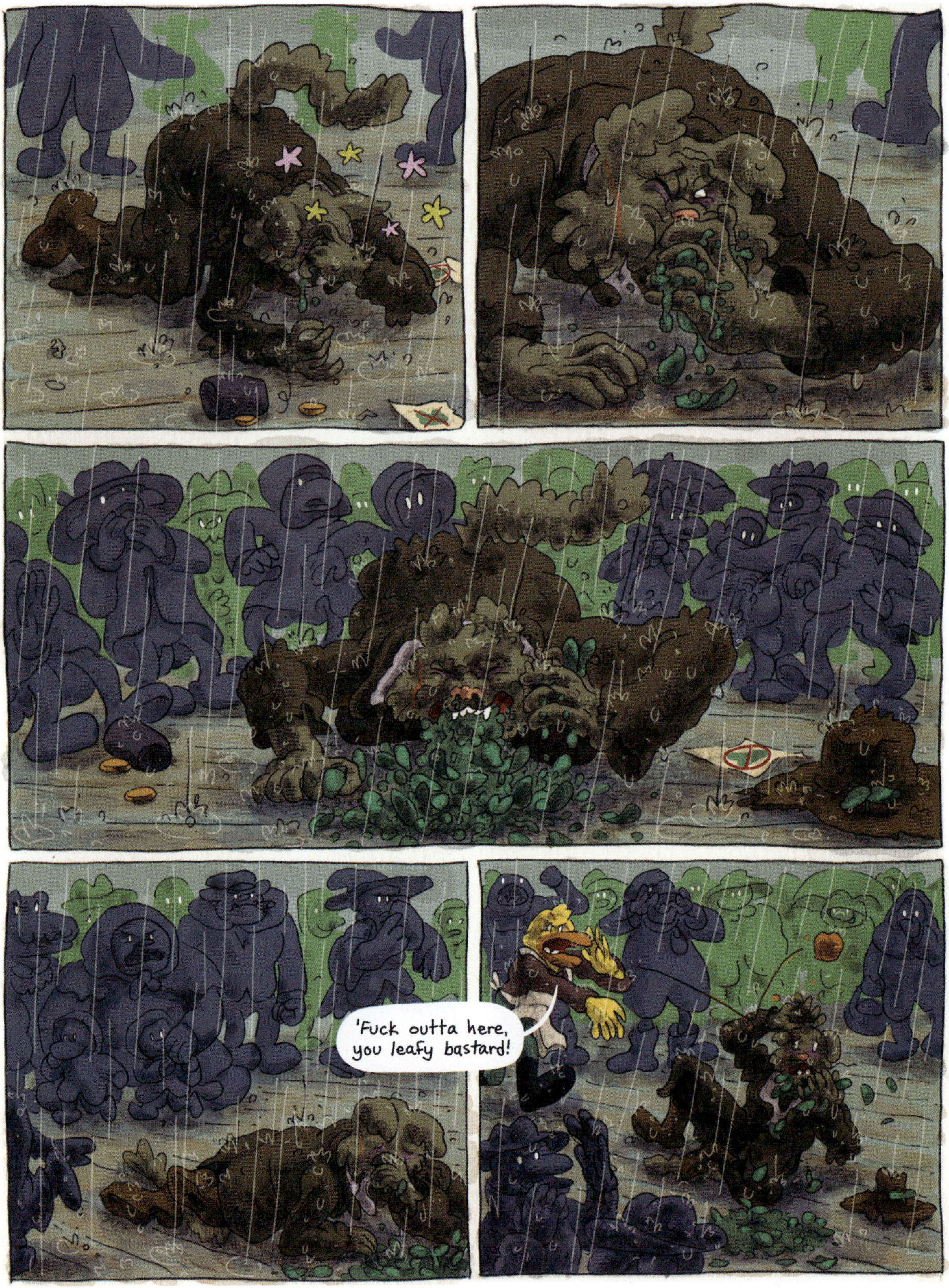
'Fuck outta here, you leafy bastard!

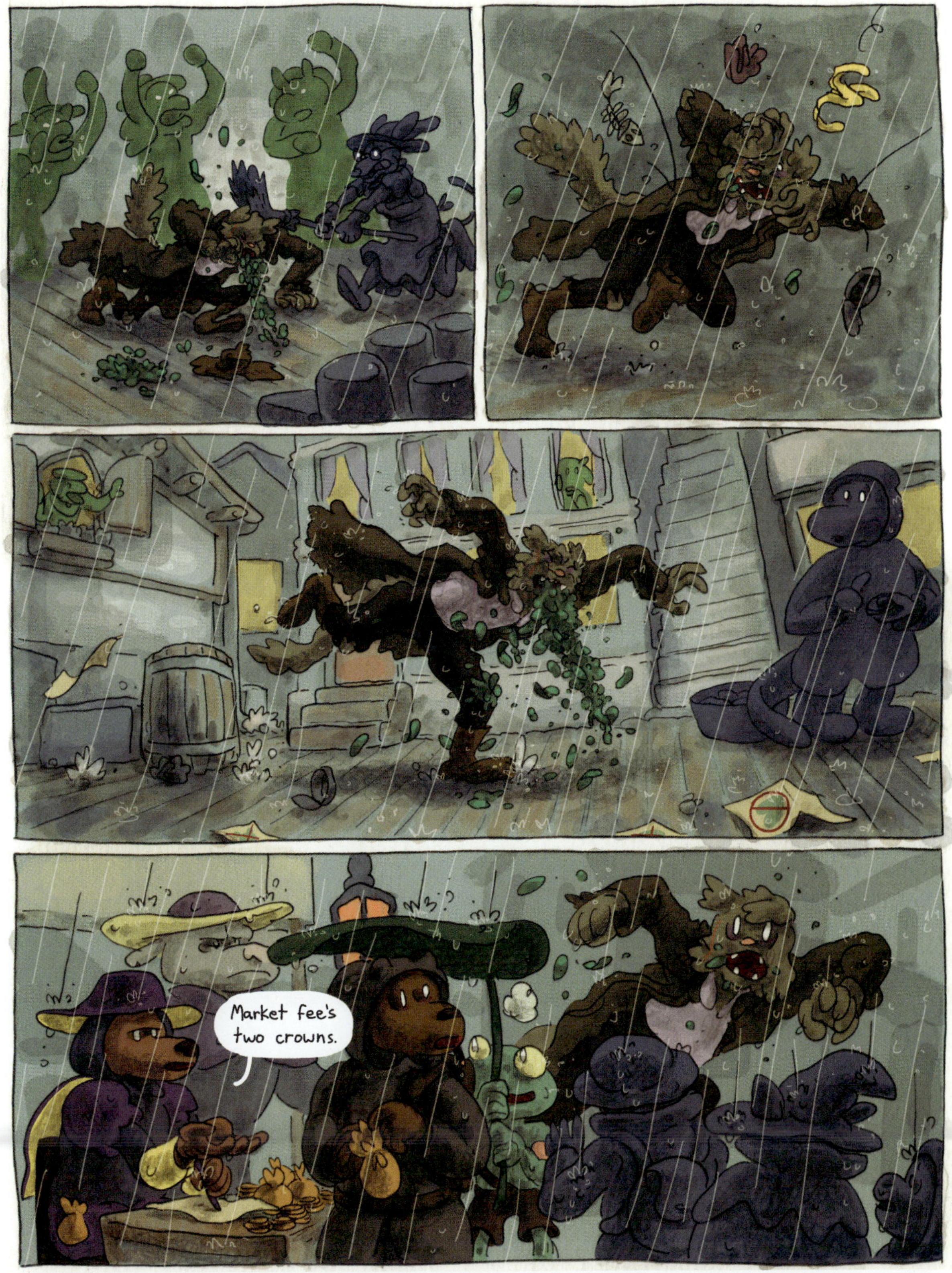
Market fee's two crowns.

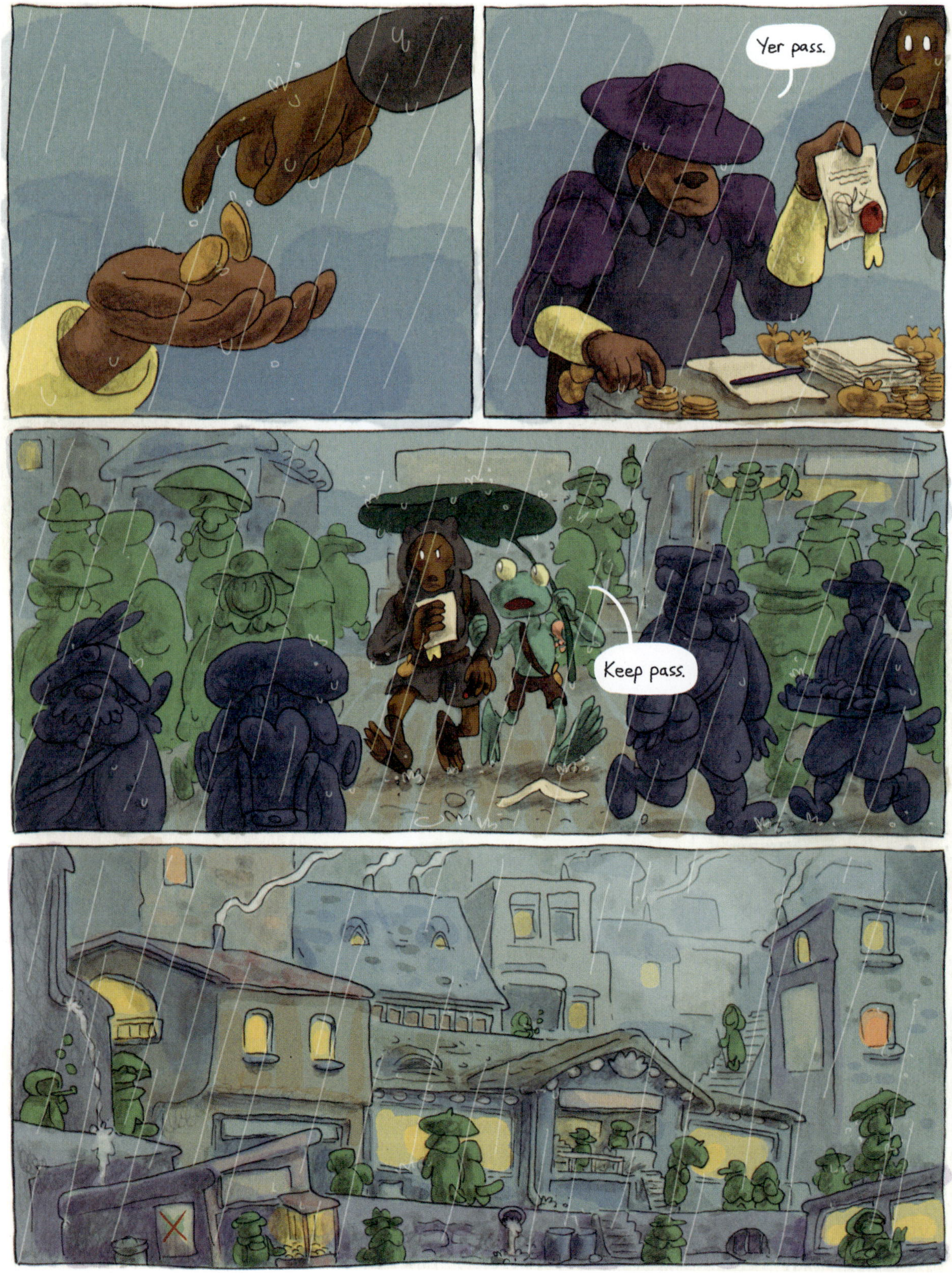
Yer pass.
Keep pass.

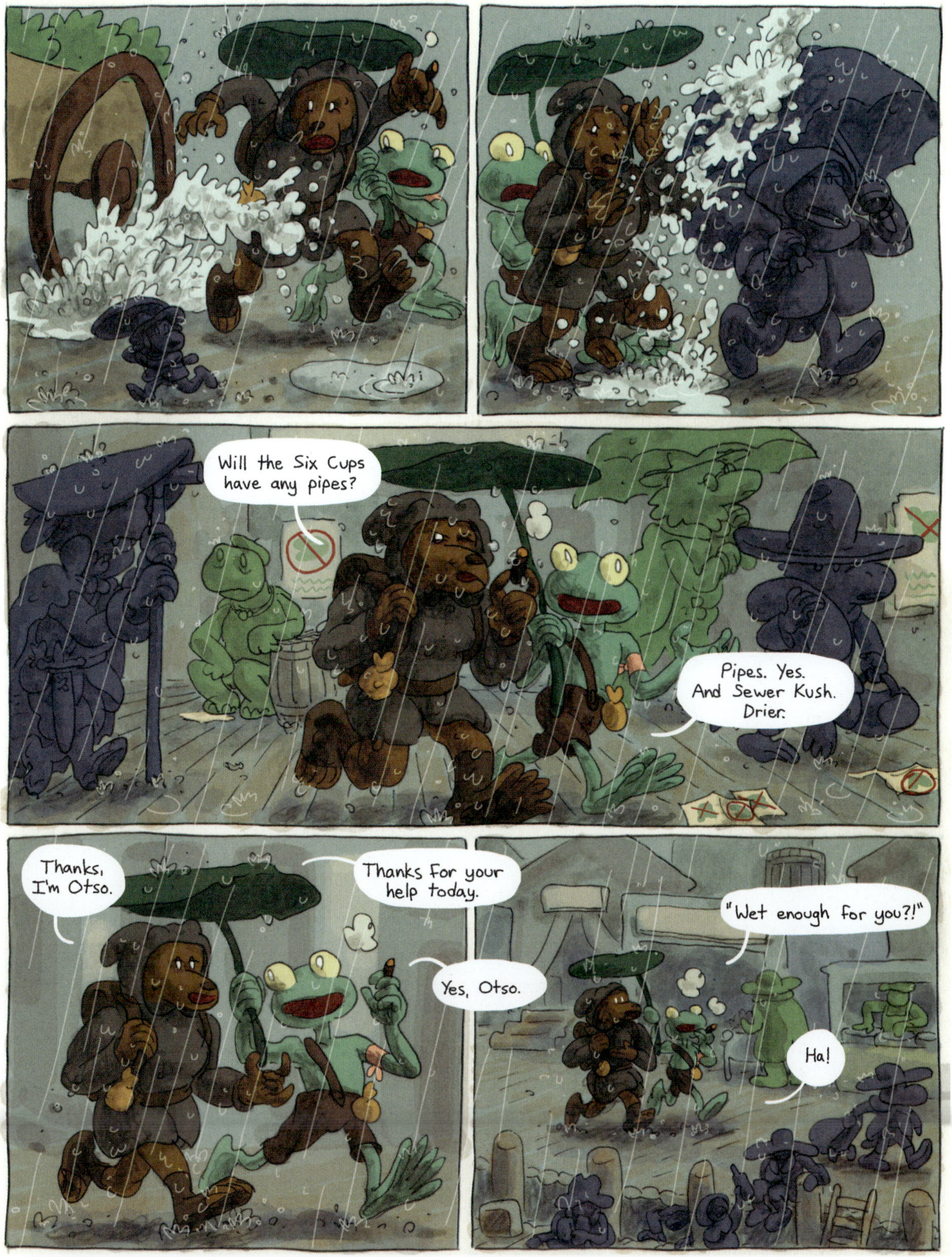
Will the Six Cups have any pipes?
Pipes. Yes. And Sewer Kush. Drier.
Thanks, I'm Otso.
Thanks for your help today.
Yes, Otso.
"Wet enough for you?!"
Ha!

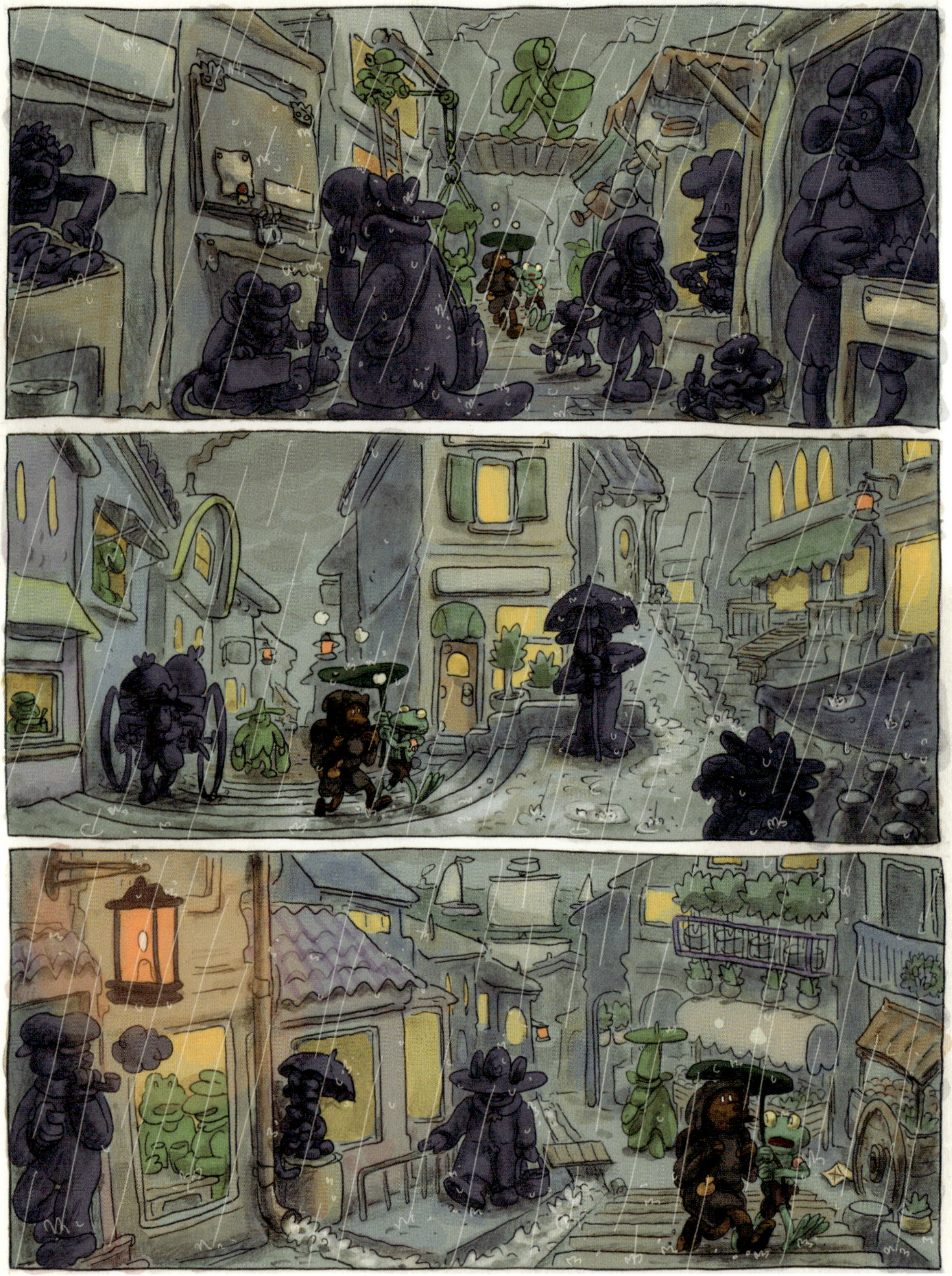

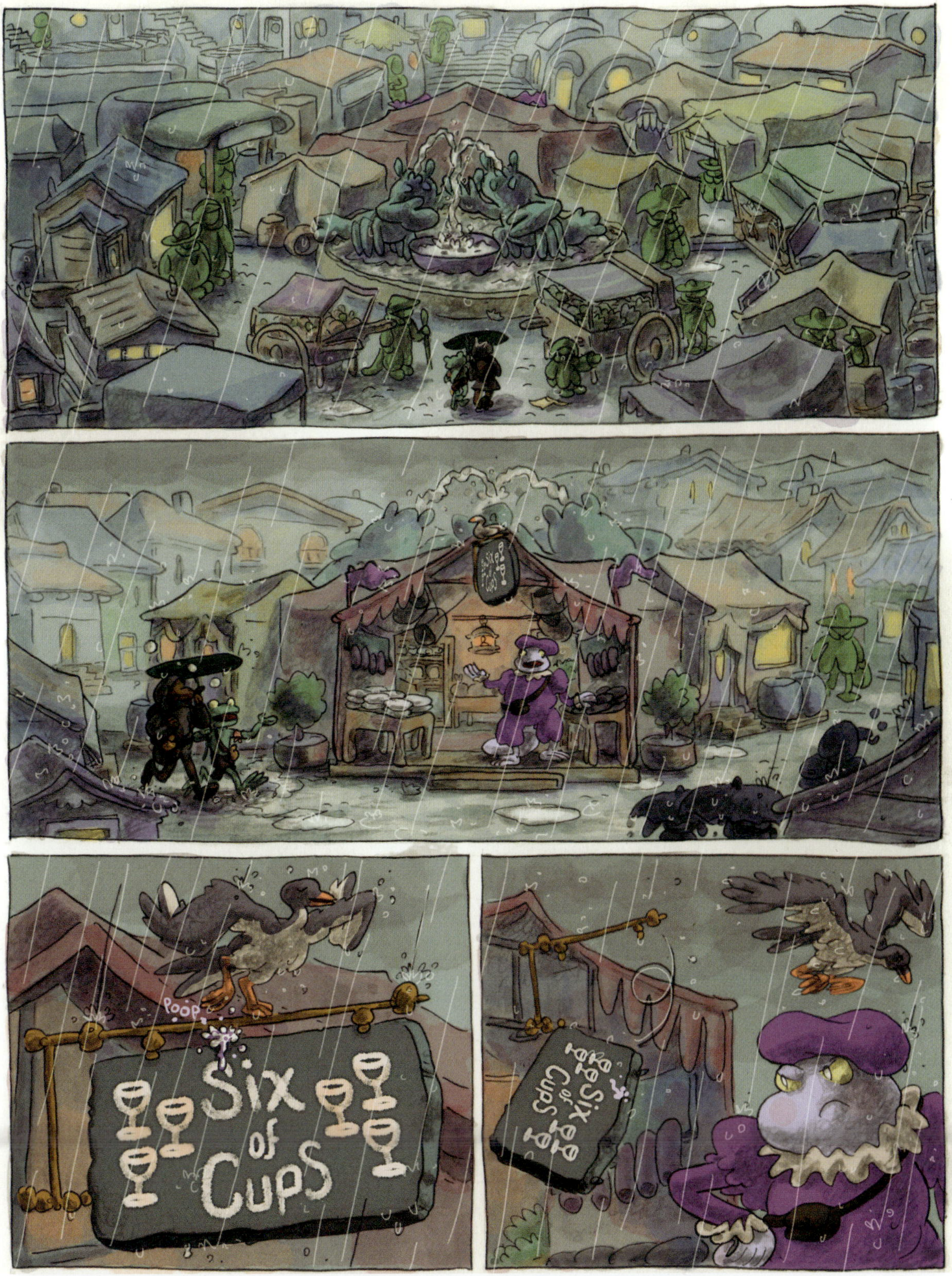
POOP
Six of Cups

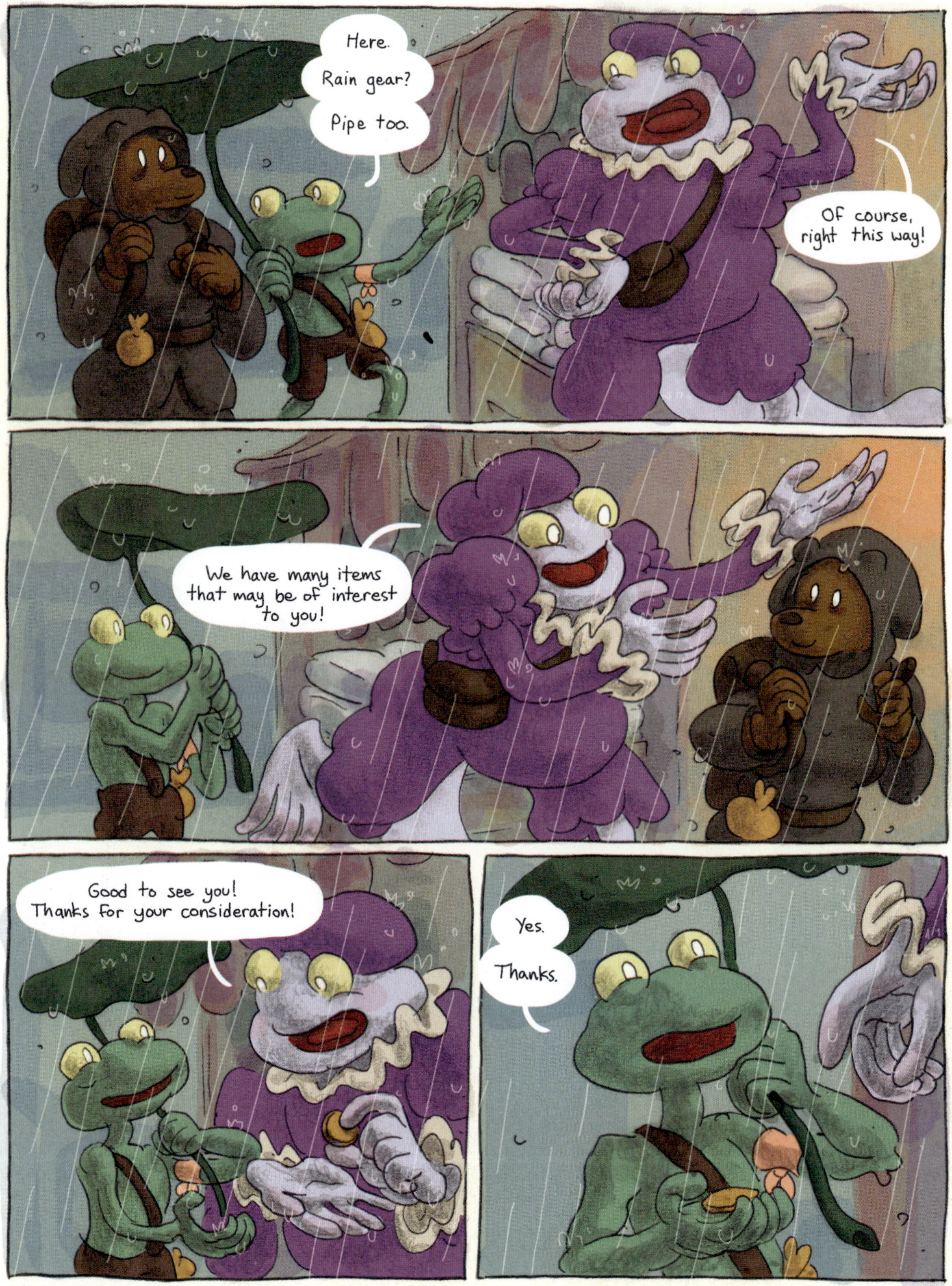
Here.
Rain gear?
Pipe too.
Of course, right this way!
We have many items that may be of interest to you!
Good to see you! Thanks for your consideration!
Yes.
Thanks.

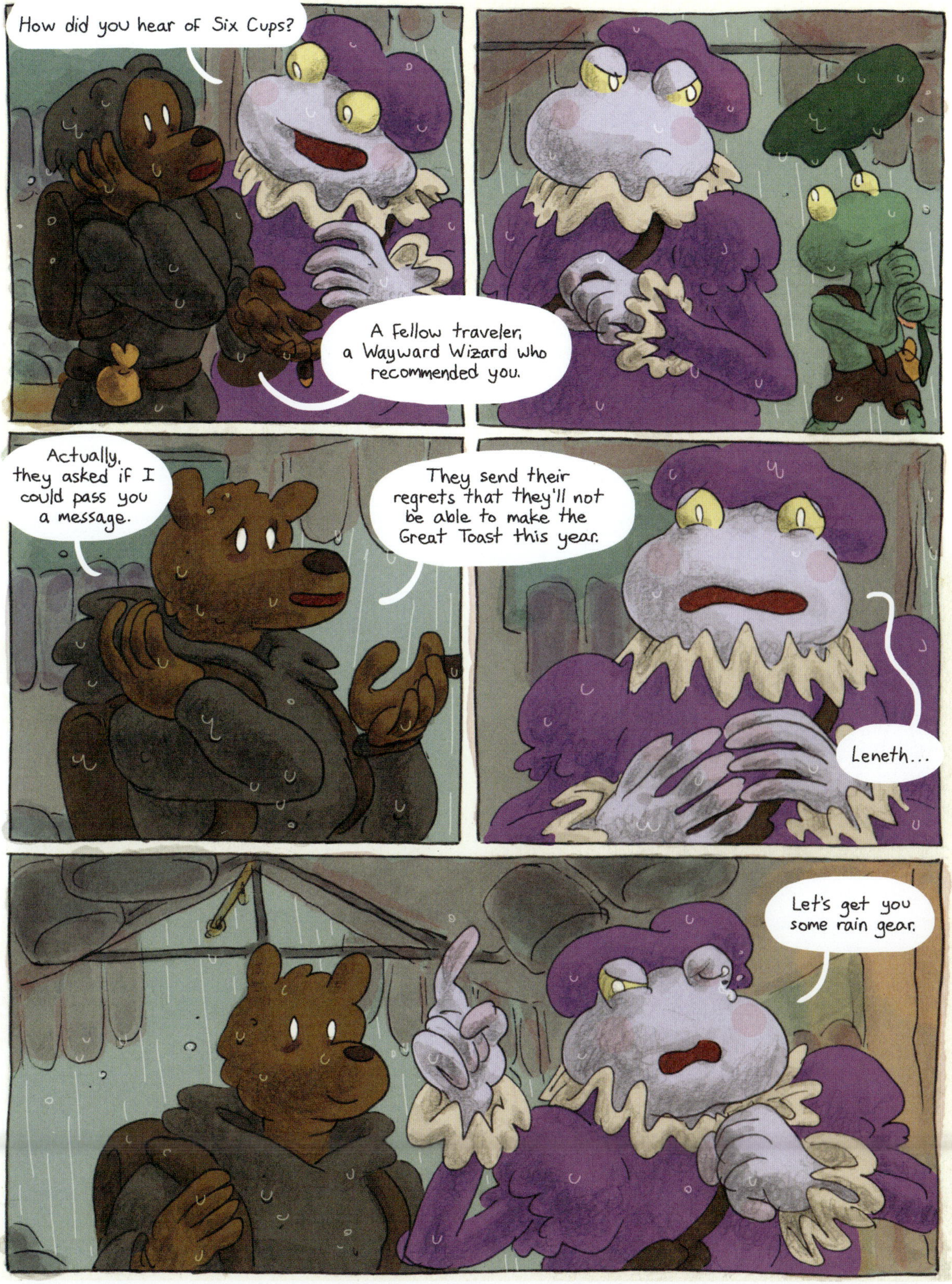
How did you hear of Six Cups?
A fellow traveler, a Wayward Wizard who recommended you.
Actually, they asked if I could pass you a message.
They send their regrets that they'll not be able to make the Great Toast this year.
Leneth...
Let's get you some rain gear.

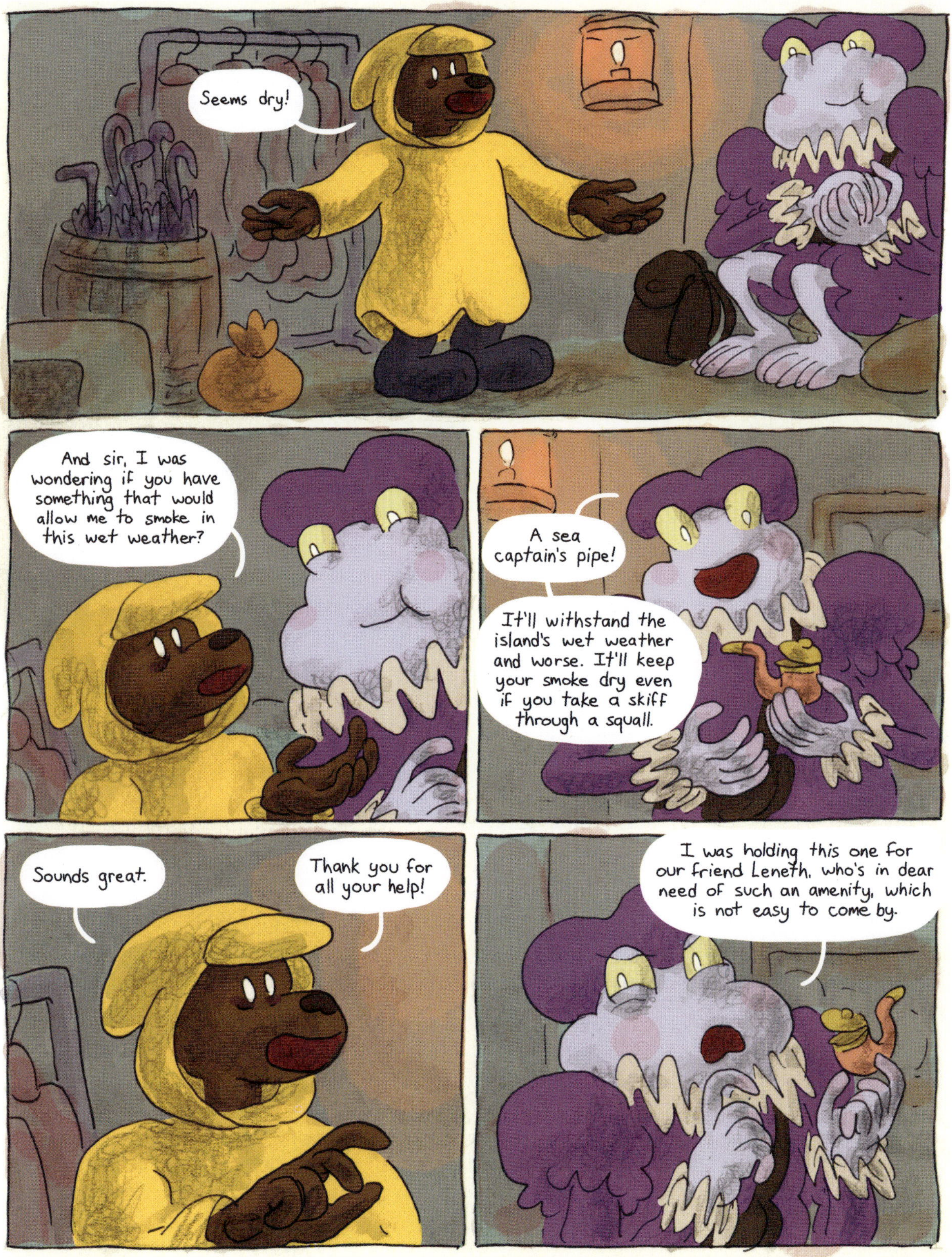
Seems dry!
And sir, I was wondering if you have something that would allow me to smoke in this wet weather?
A sea captain's pipe!
It'll withstand the island's wet weather and worse. It'll keep your smoke dry even if you take a skiff through a squall.
Sounds great.
Thank you for all your help!
I was holding this one for our friend Leneth, who's in dear need of such an amenity, which is not easy to come by.

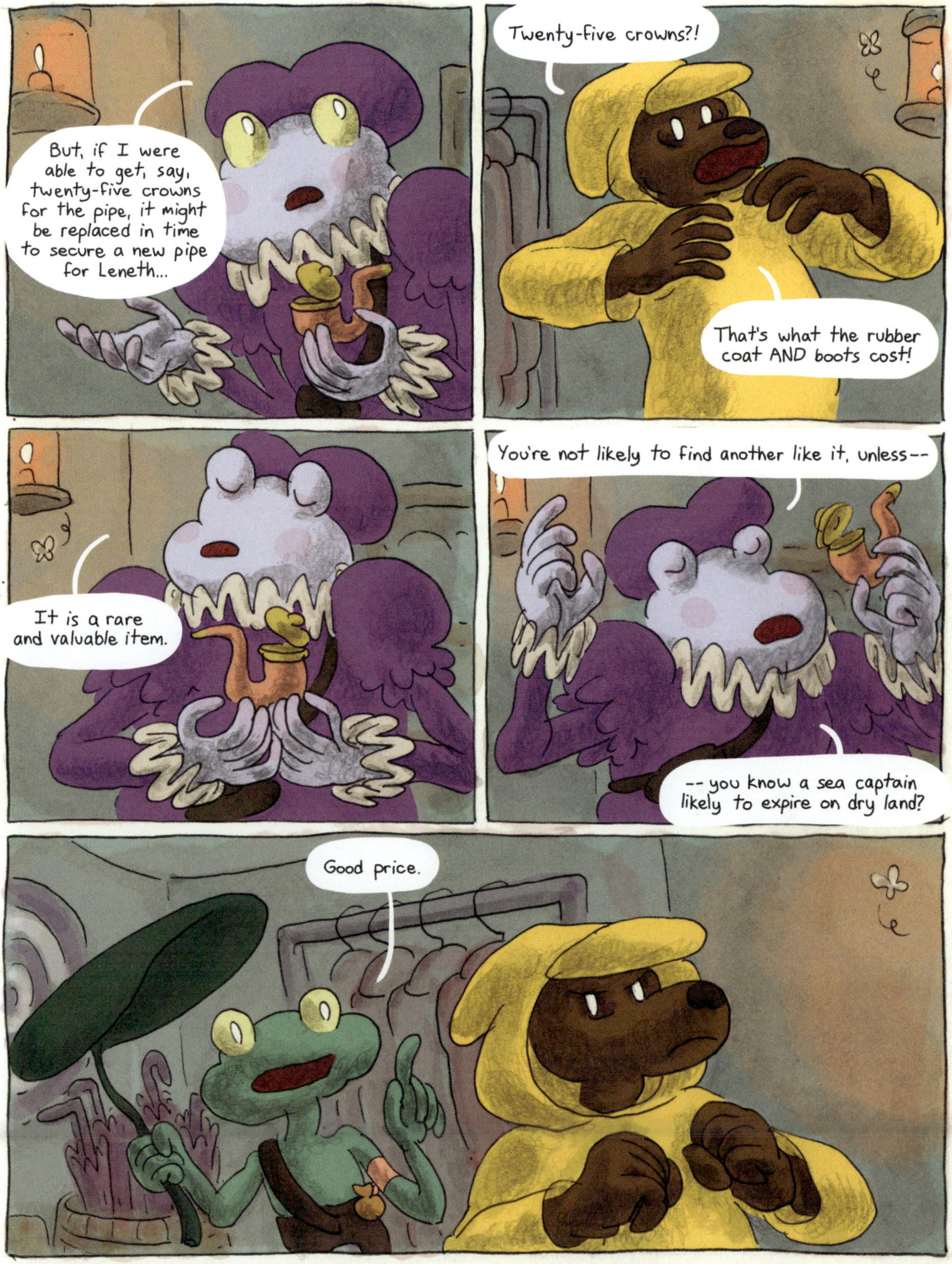

But, if I were able to get, say, twenty-five crowns for the pipe, it might be replaced in time to secure a new pipe for Leneth...
Twenty-five crowns?!
That's what the rubber coat AND boots cost!
It is a rare and valuable item.
You're not likely to find another like it, unless--
-- you know a sea captain likely to expire on dry land?
Good price.

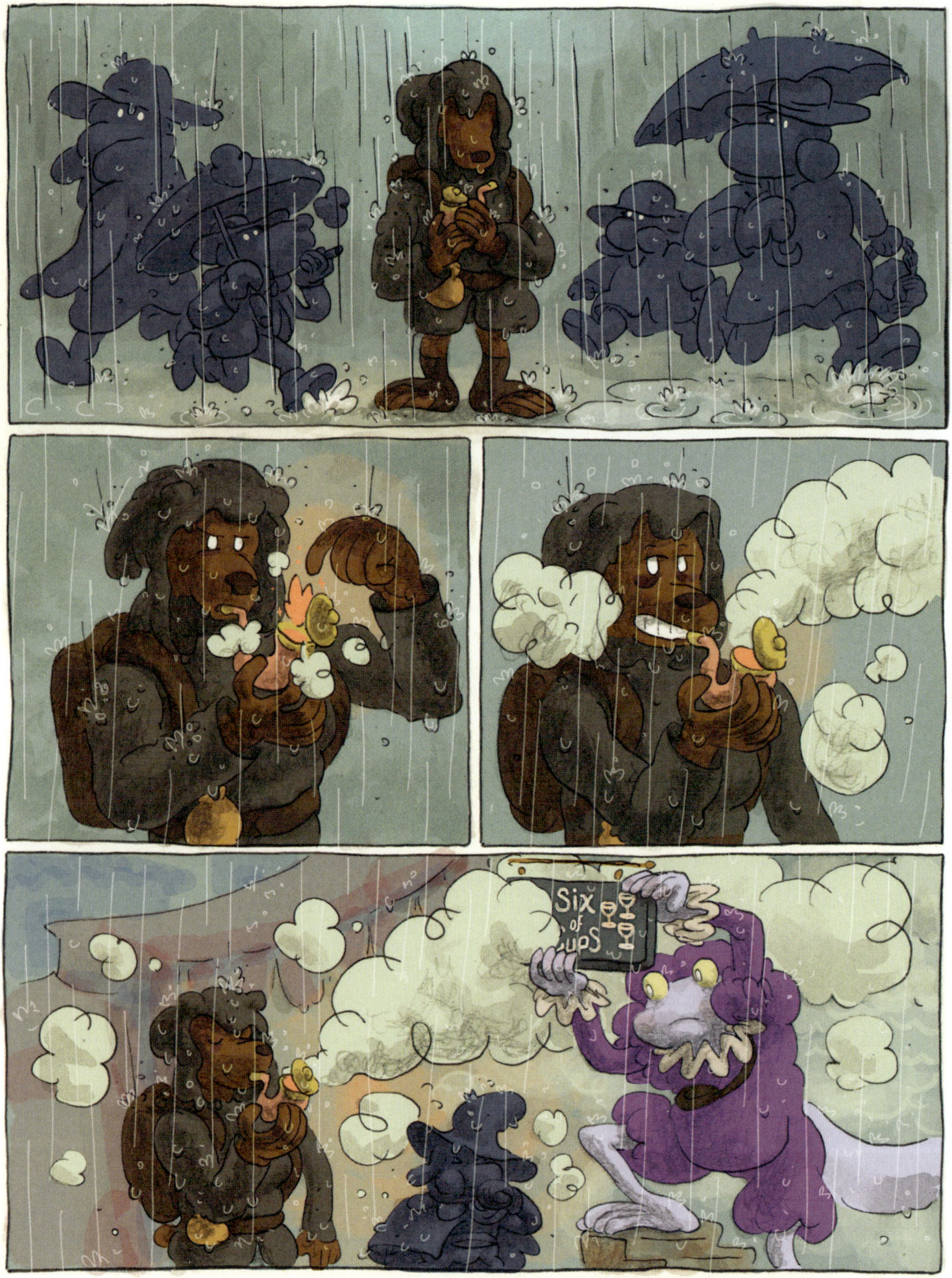
Six of Cups

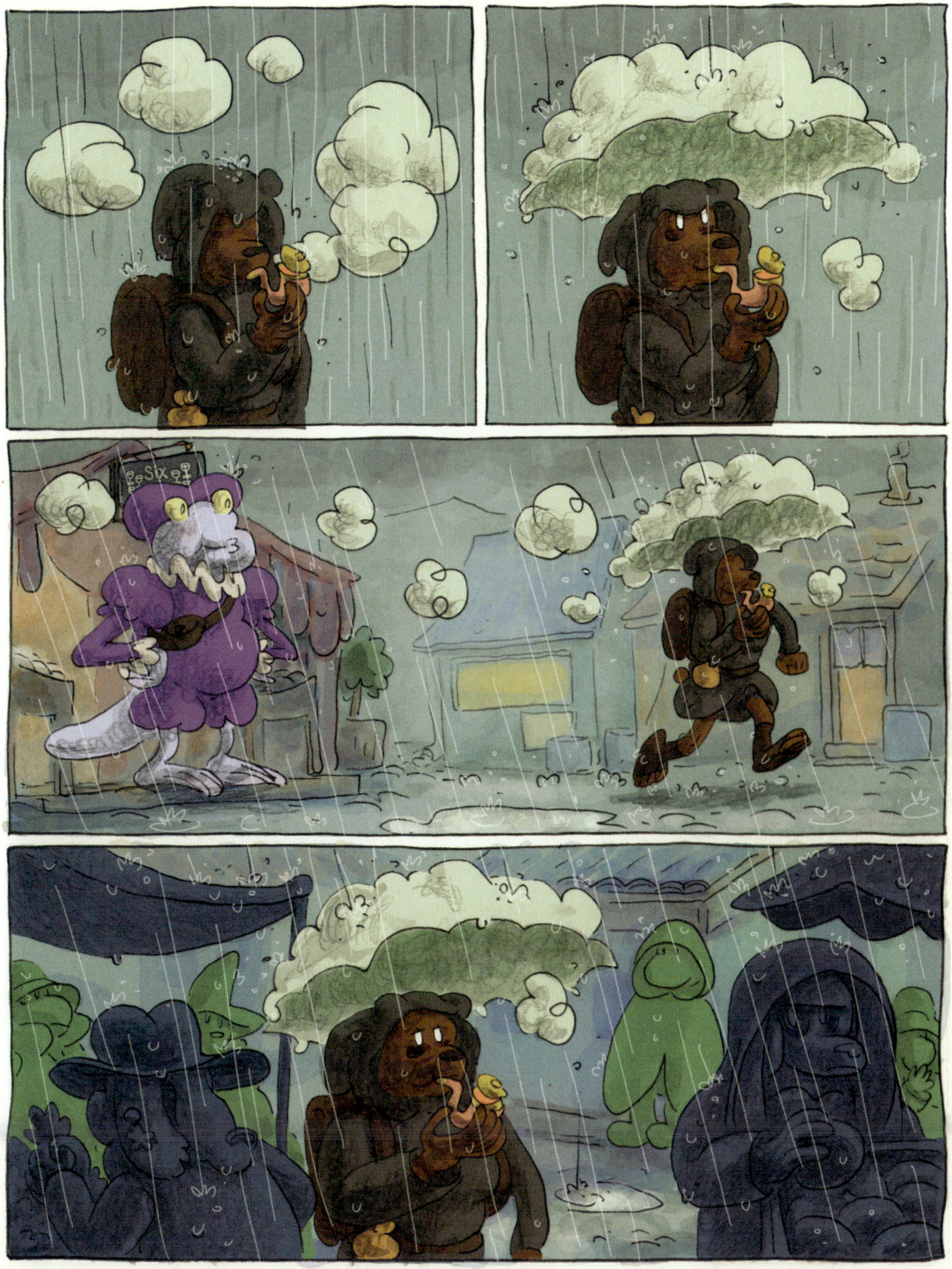
Six

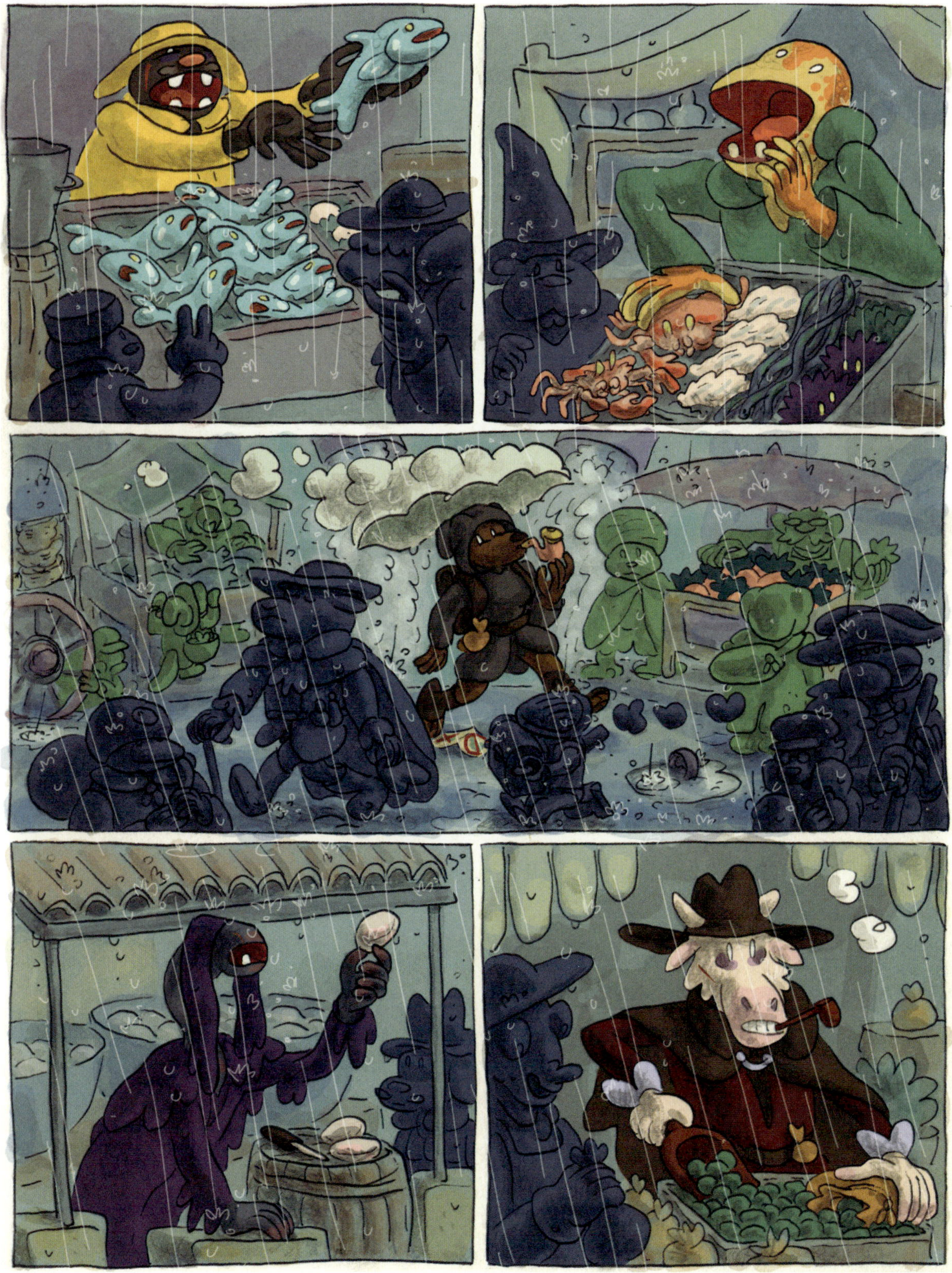

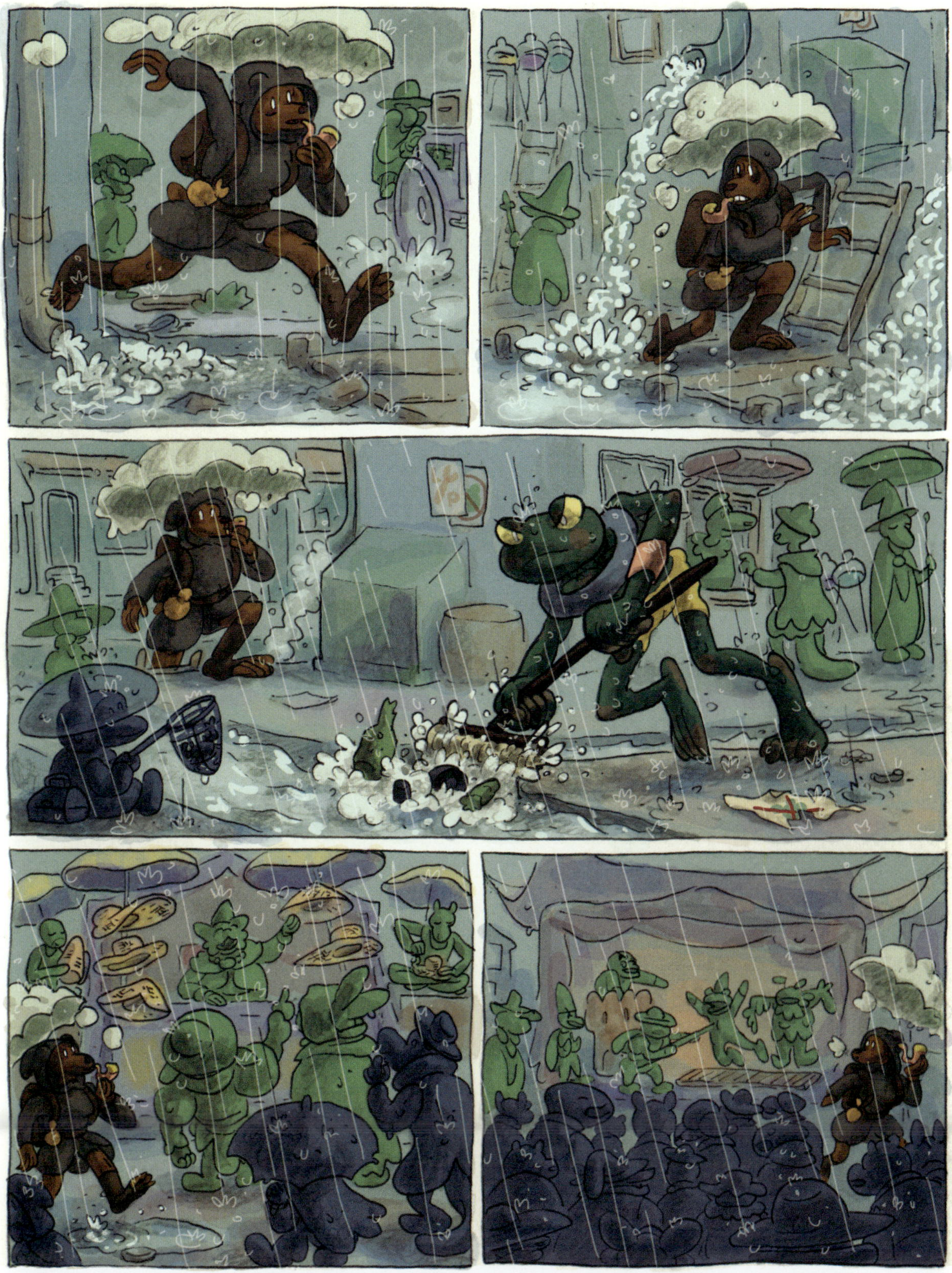

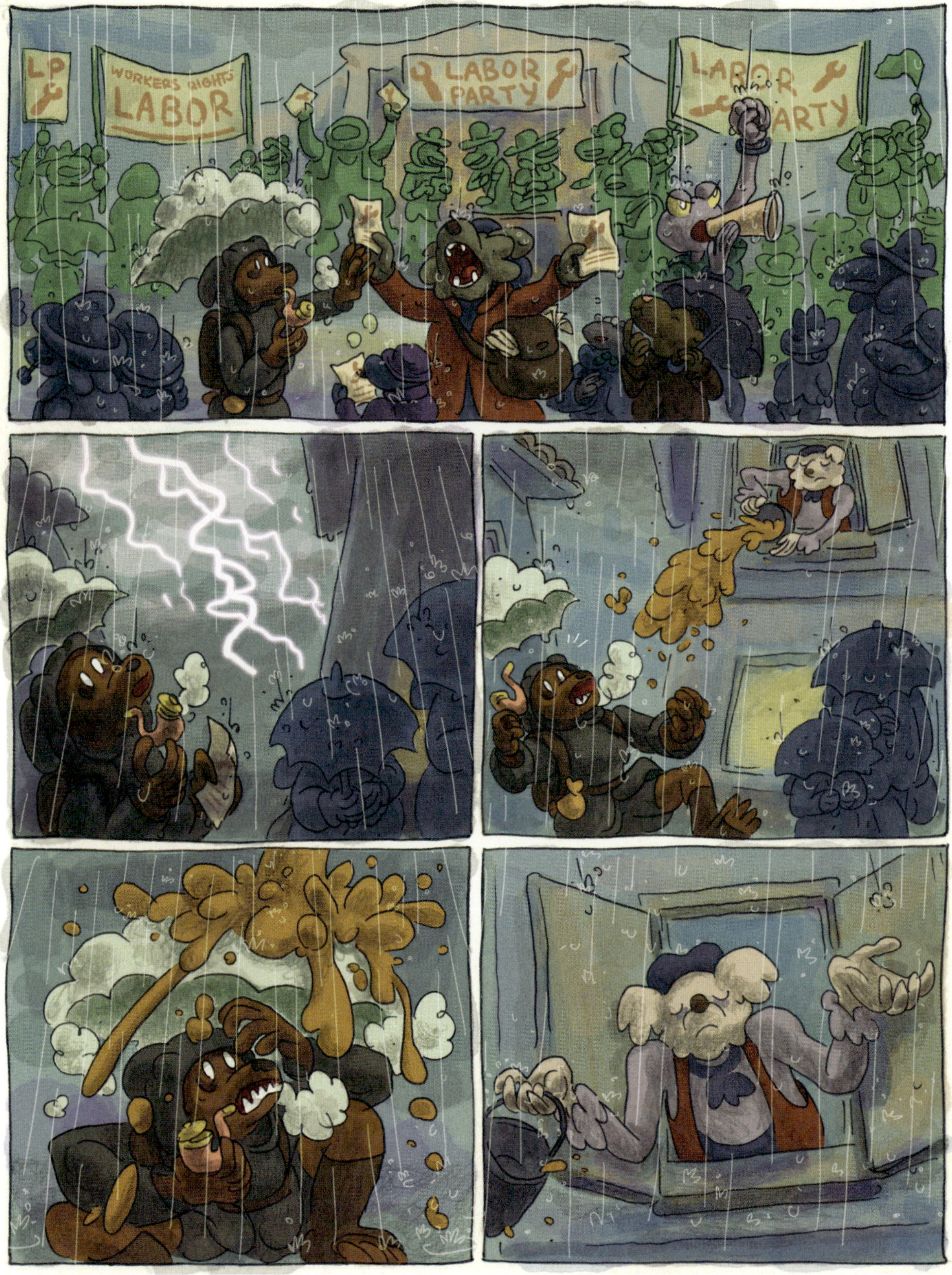
LP
WORKERS RIGHTS
LABOR
LABOR PARTY

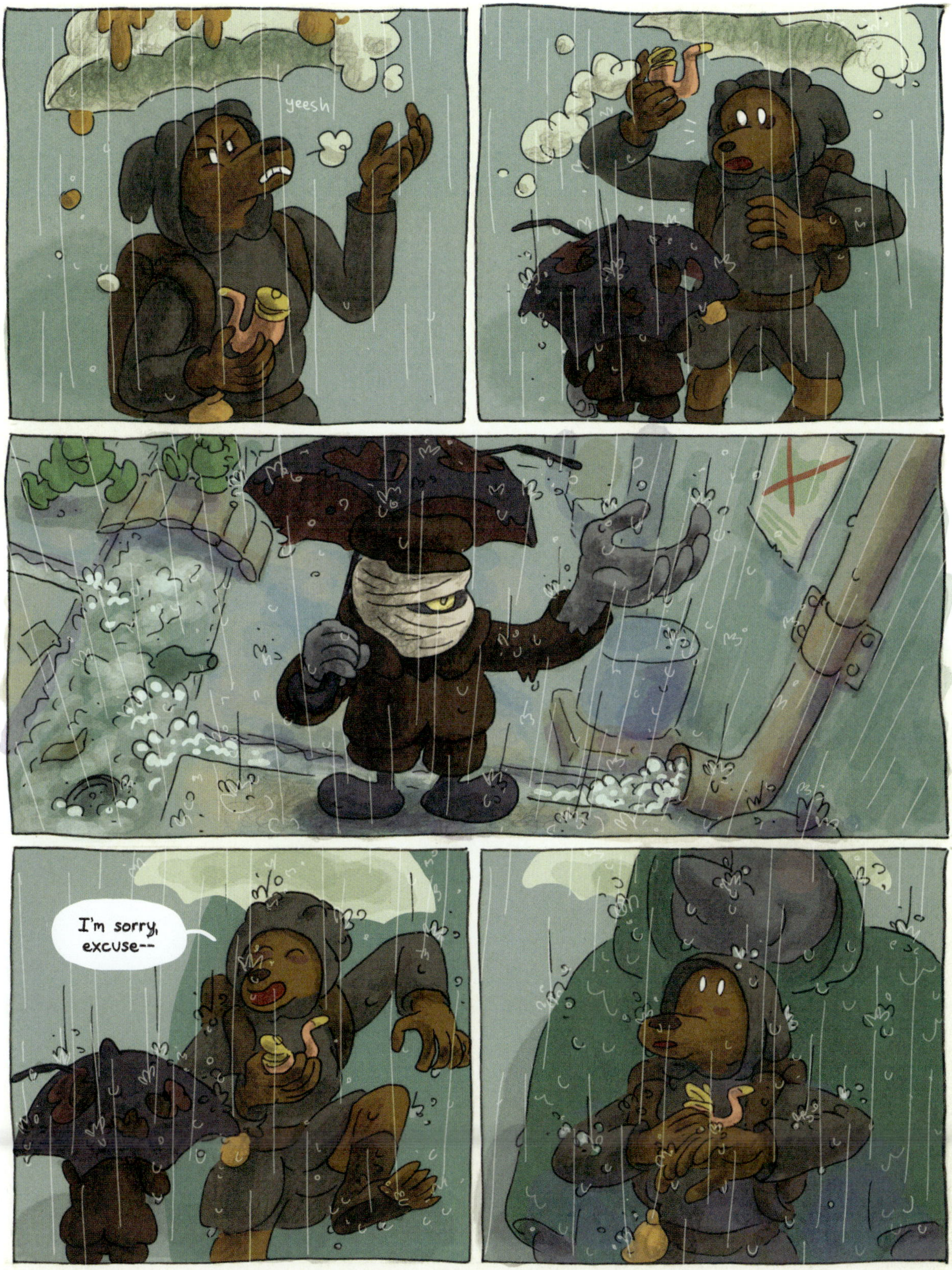
yeesh
I'm sorry, excuse--

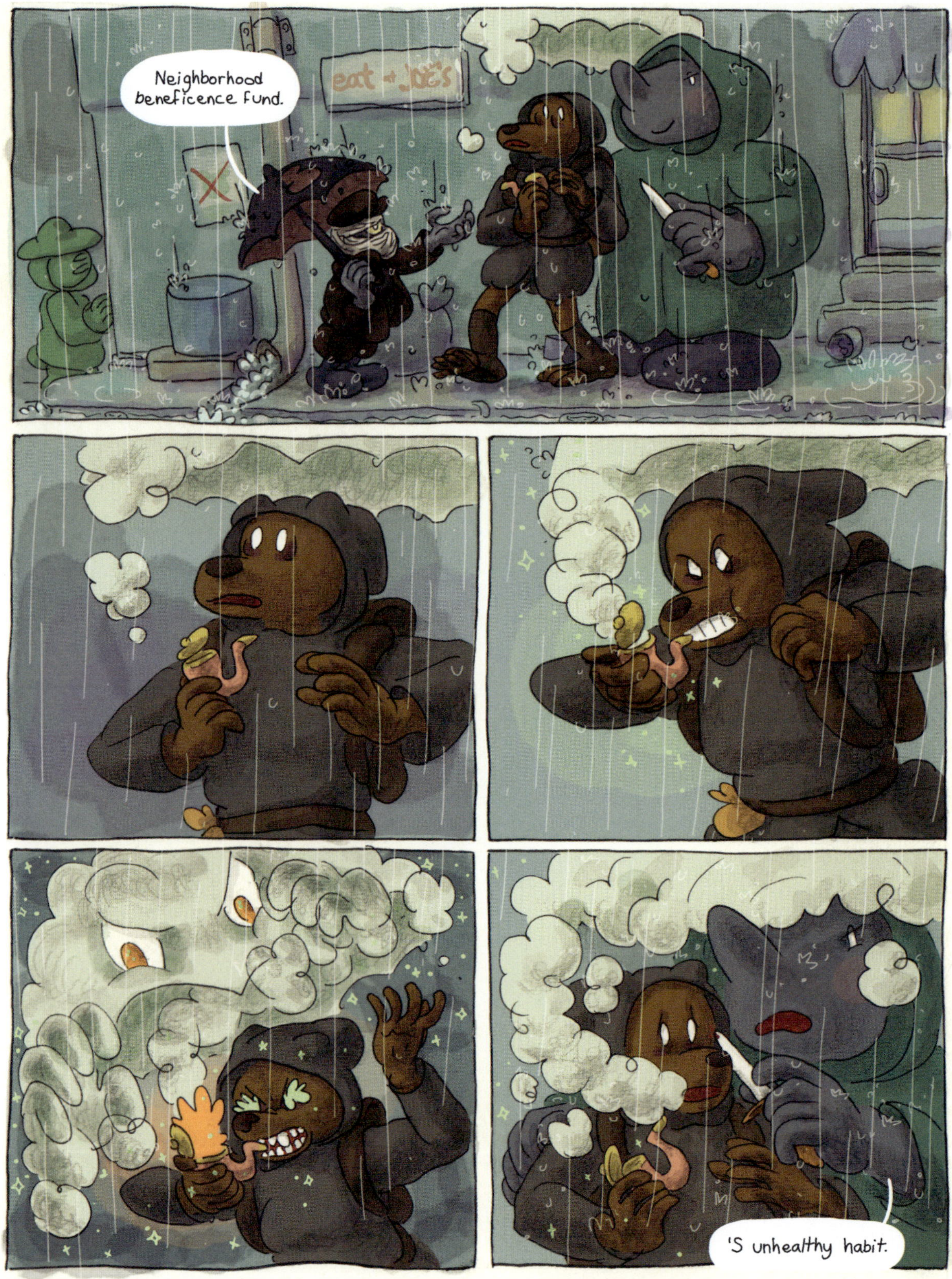
Neighborhood beneficence fund.
eat at JOE'S
'S unhealthy habit.

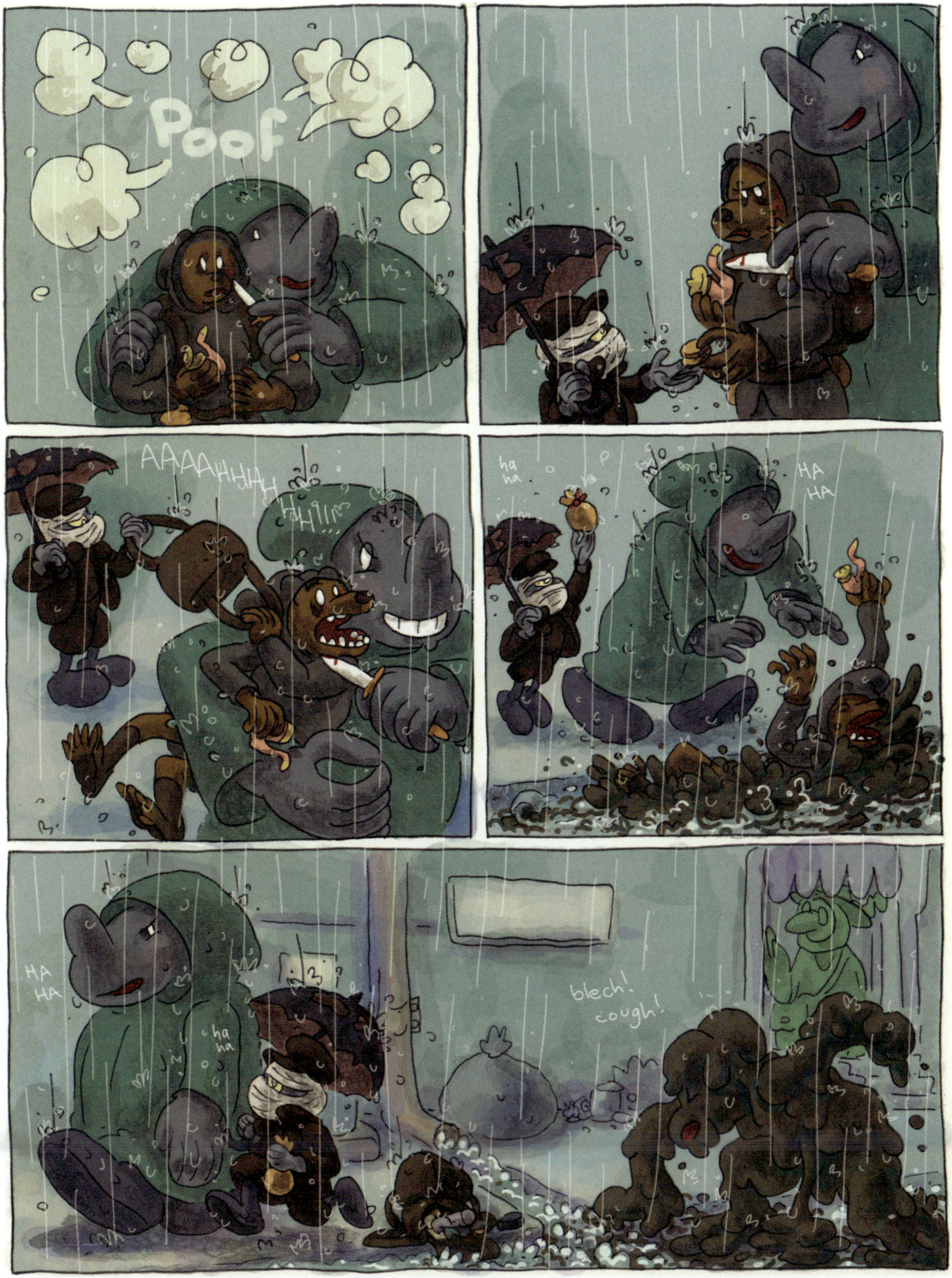
Poof
AAAAHHHHH
HHH!!!
ha ha
HA HA
HA HA
ha ha
blech!
cough!

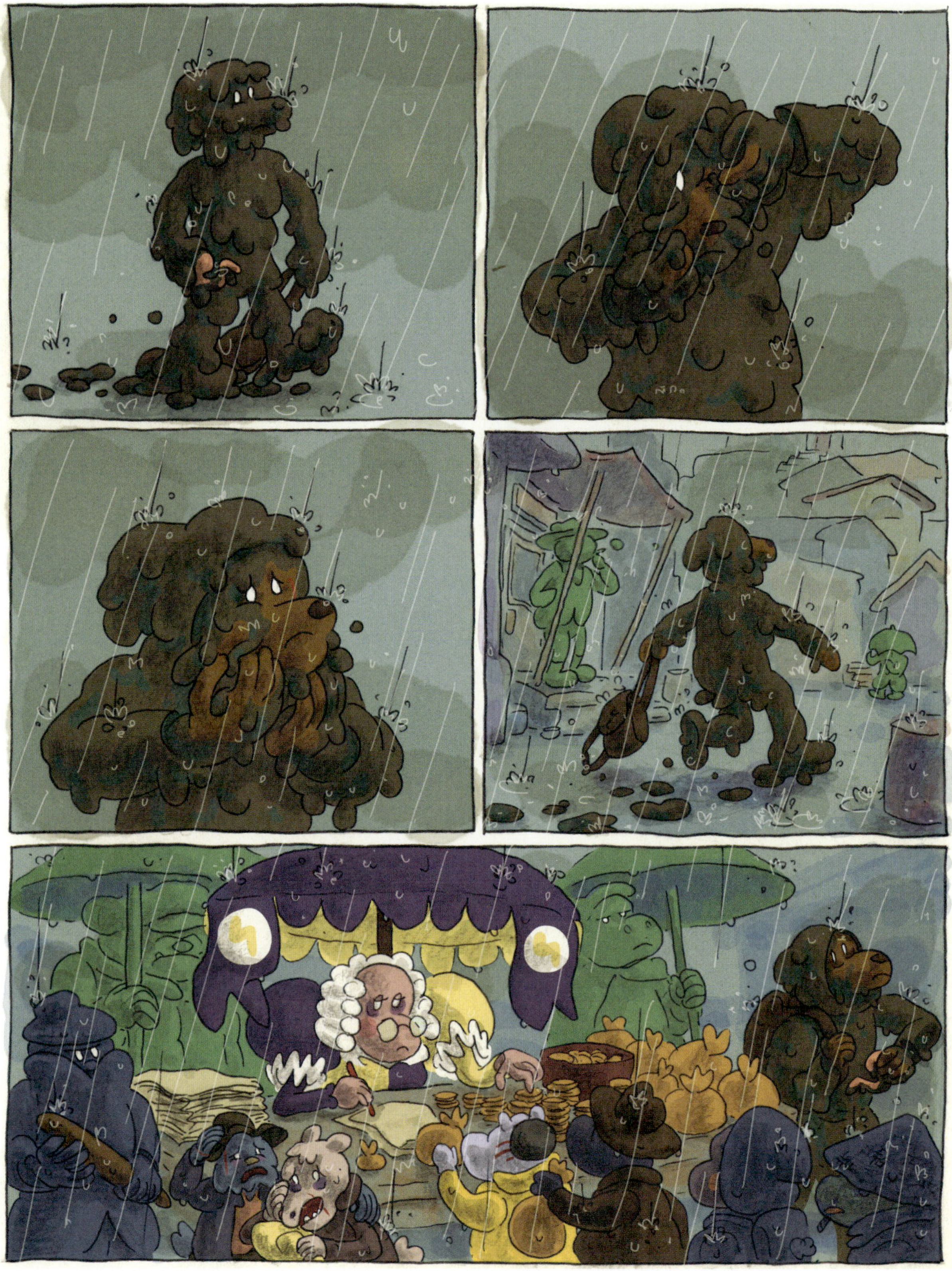

— IAN DENSFORD & THE BROTHERS McGOVERN —

Soggy Landing is created by a stablehand from Shropshire named Ian Densford. His employer, Master Mudge, says the lad wastes his hours scratching away with pen and ink in the hayloft, sometimes through the night, without the benefit of candle or lantern! Densford claims the work, a piece of fancy as depraved as it is imaginative, is written not by him but by two mysterious collaborators he calls the Brothers McGovern. According to the stablehand's telling, one brother is tall and rough, the other small and fine, and neither shows sign of having missed his share of the stirabout. Their existence is to be doubted. Densford claims to be visited only when finding himself alone, almost always in the night. They advise him on his masterpiece and quarrel viscously about the great work's form and direction.

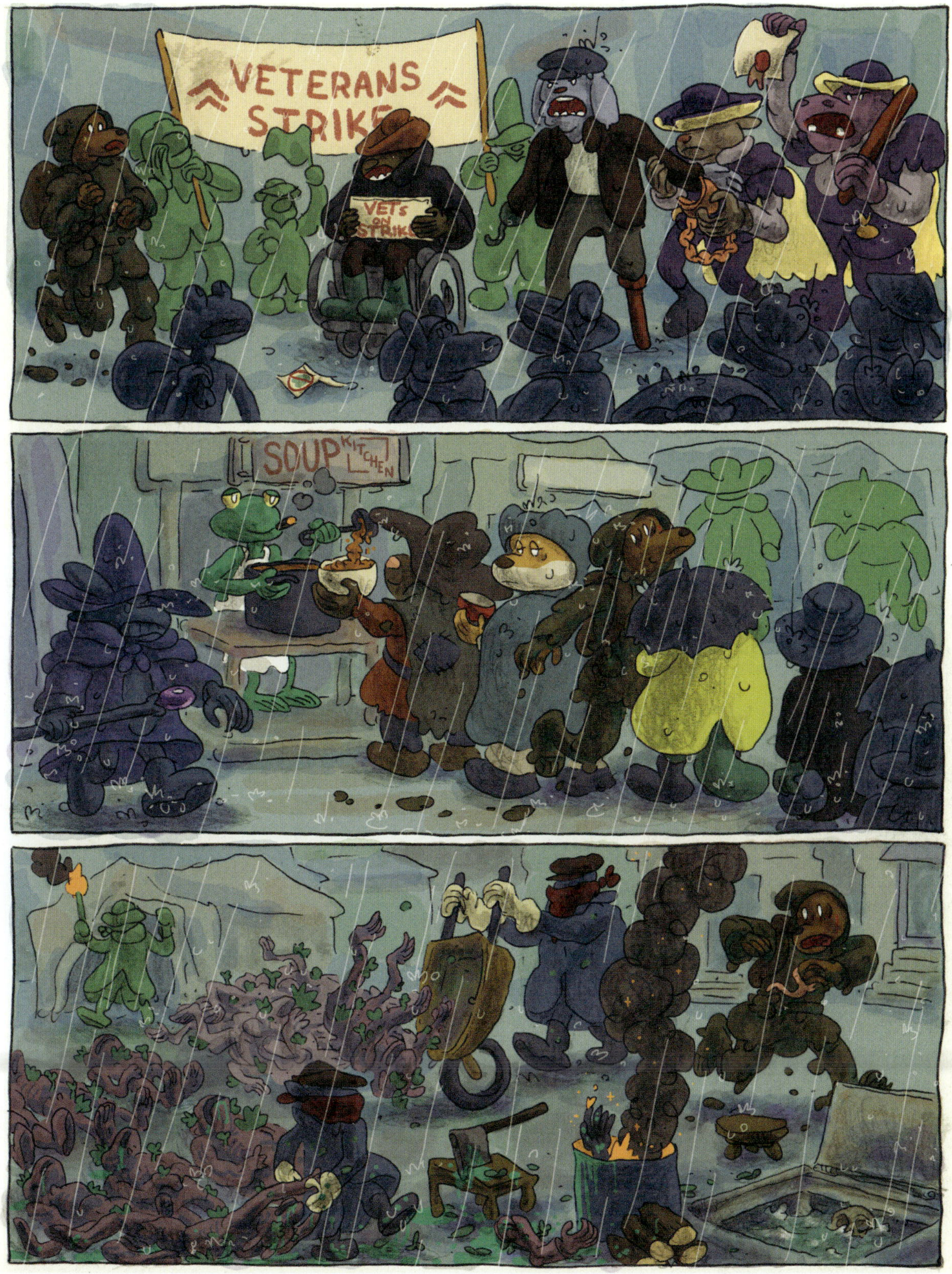
VETERANS STRIKE
VETS ON STRIKE
SOUP KITCHEN

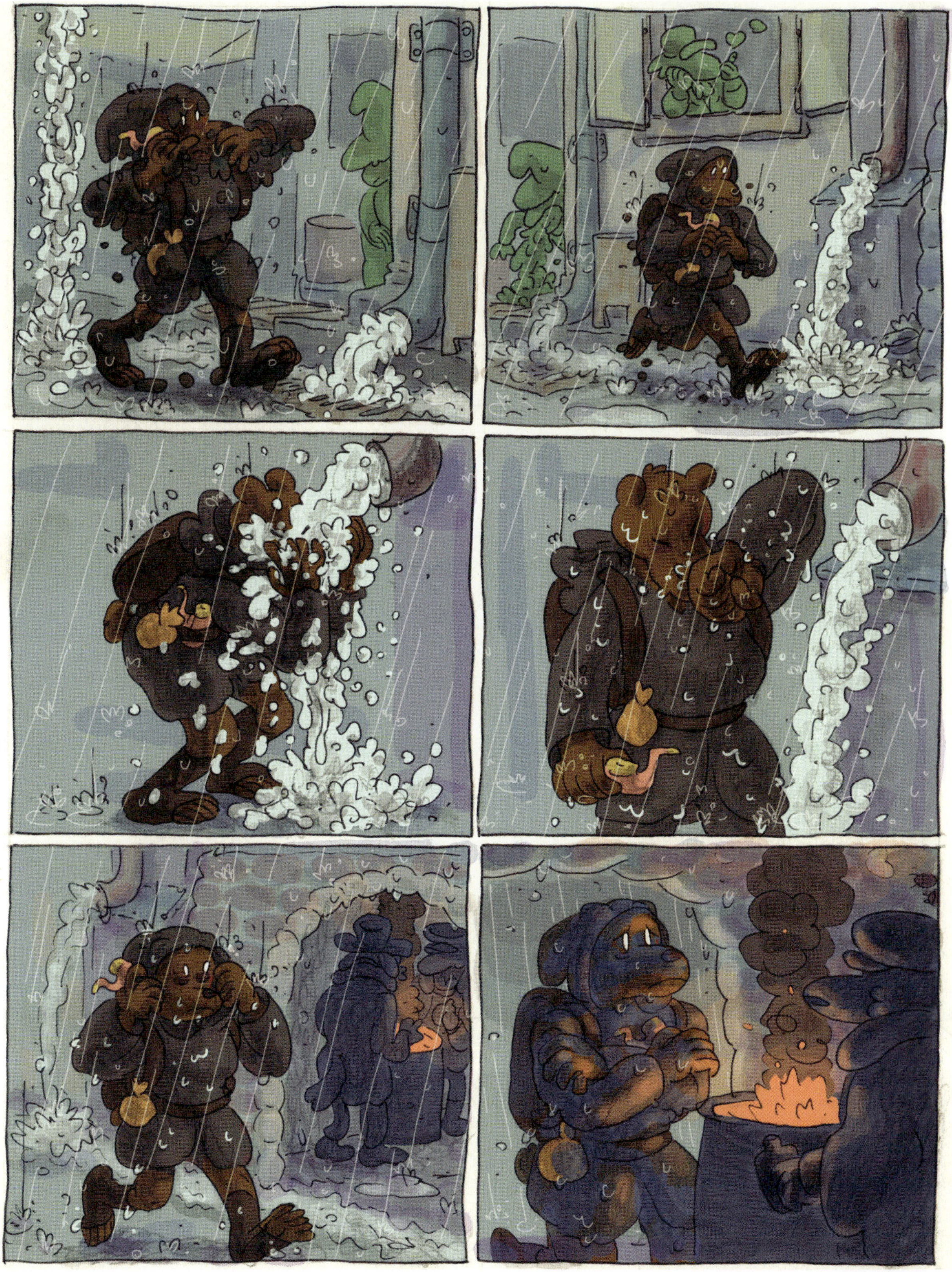

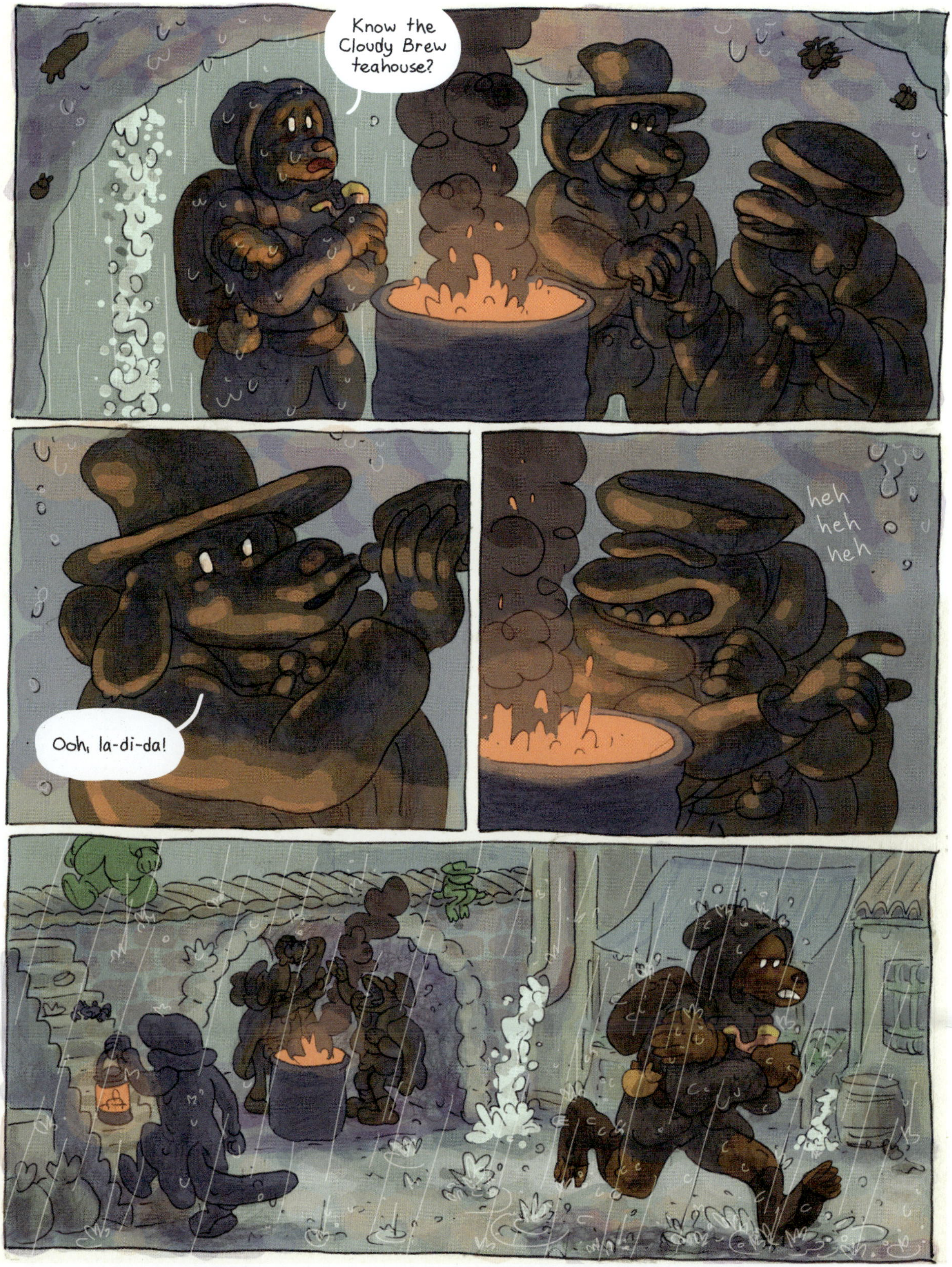
Know the Cloudy Brew teahouse?
Ooh, la-di-da!
heh heh heh

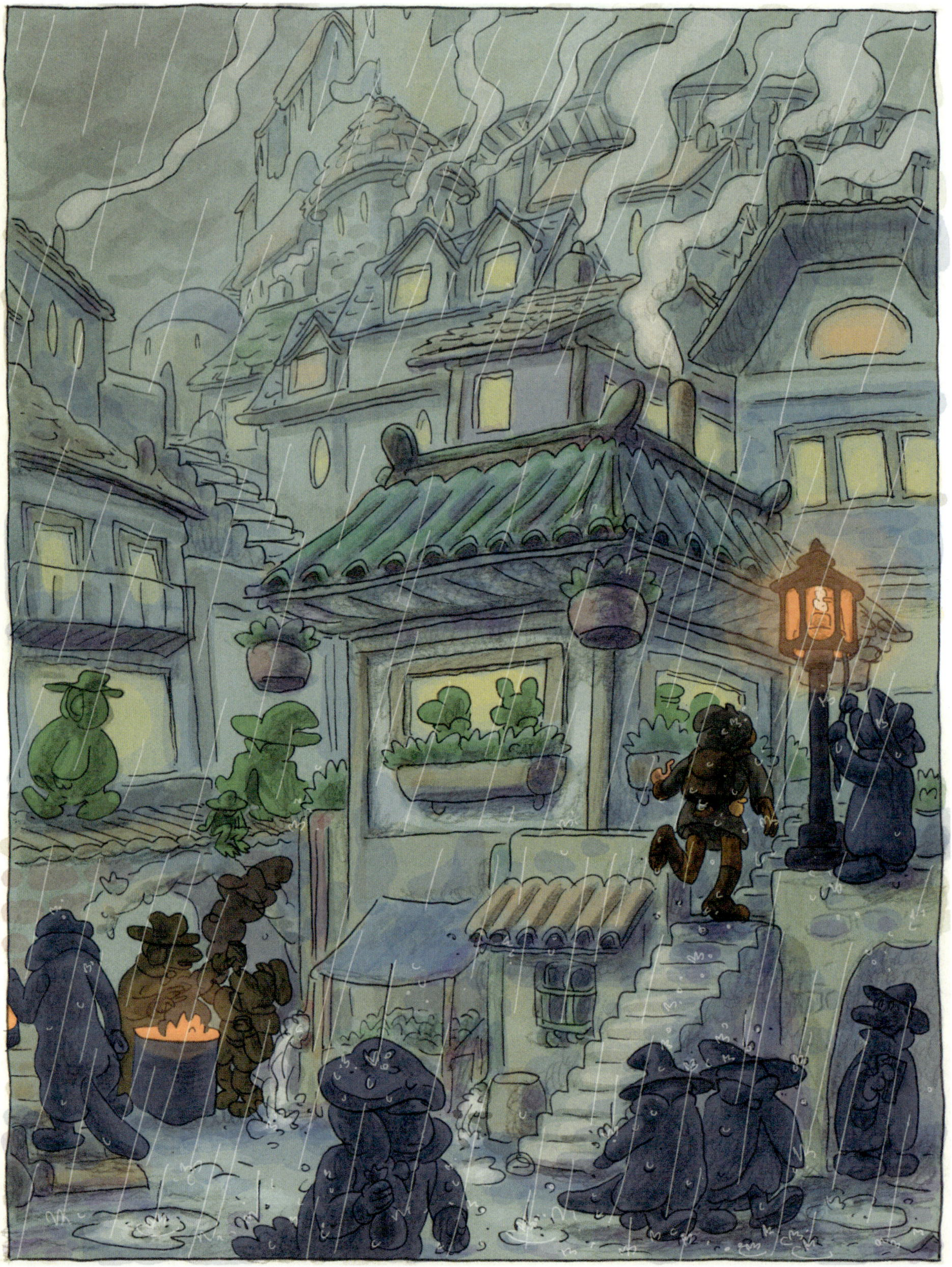

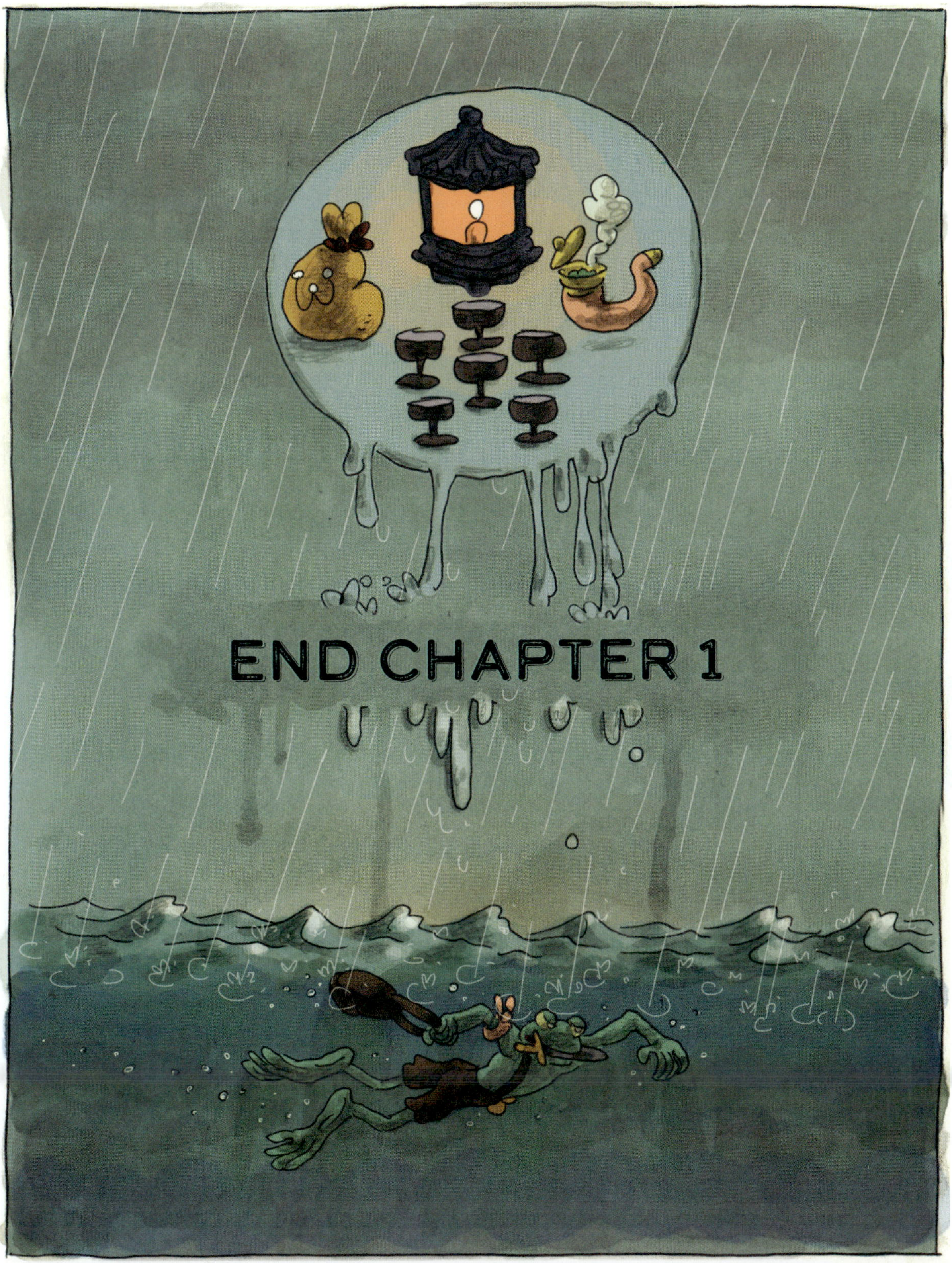
END CHAPTER 1

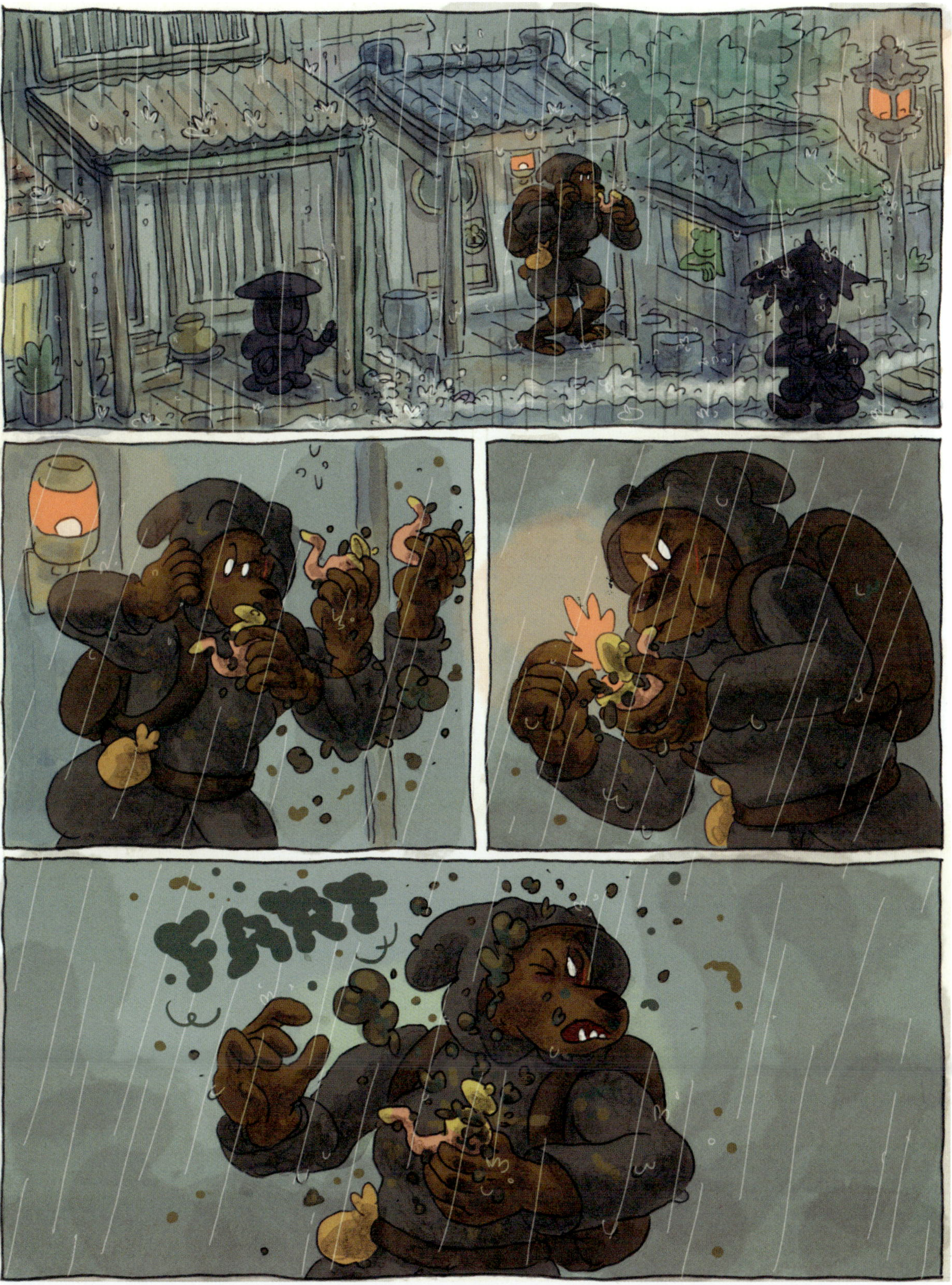
FART

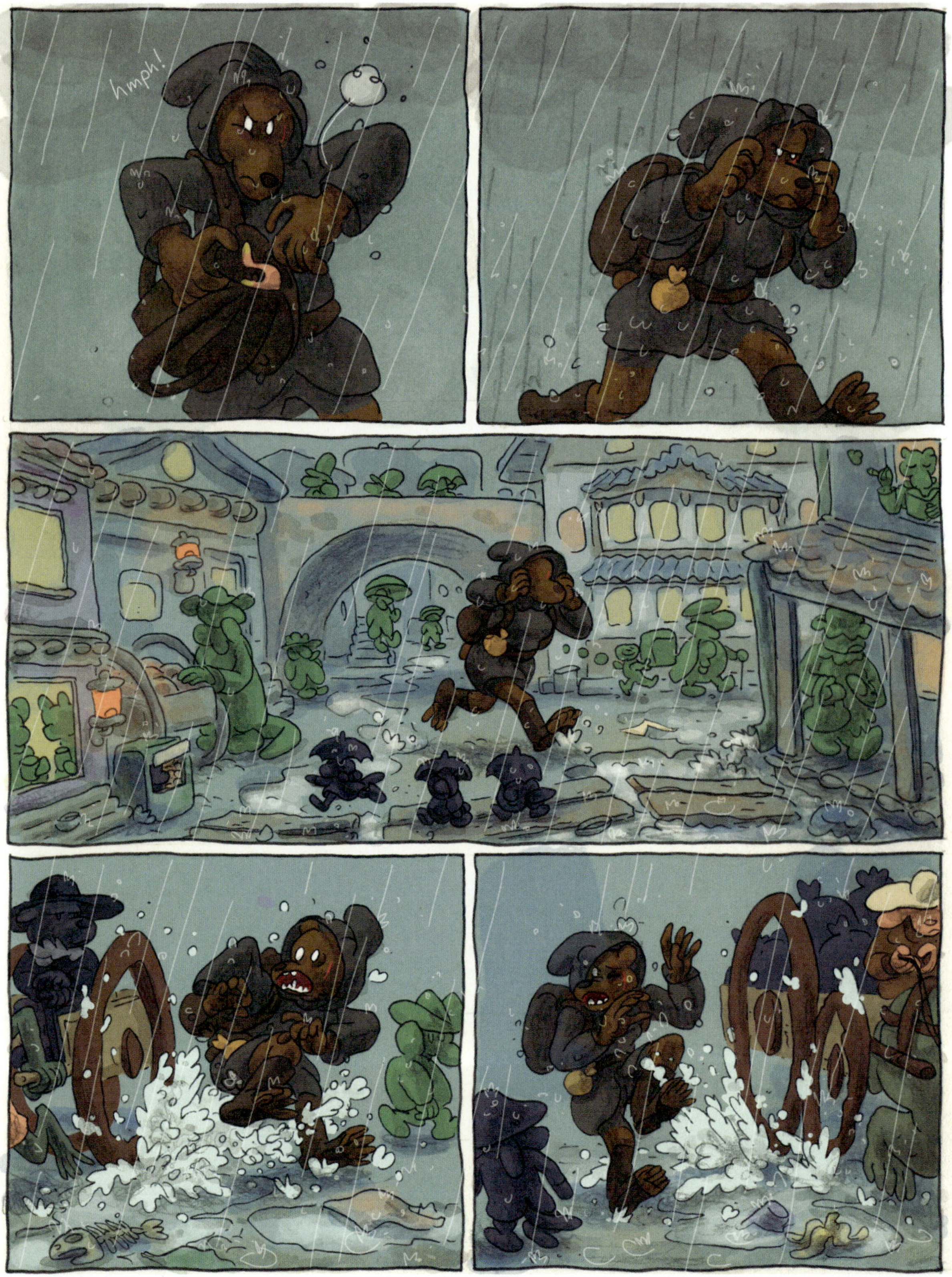
hmph!

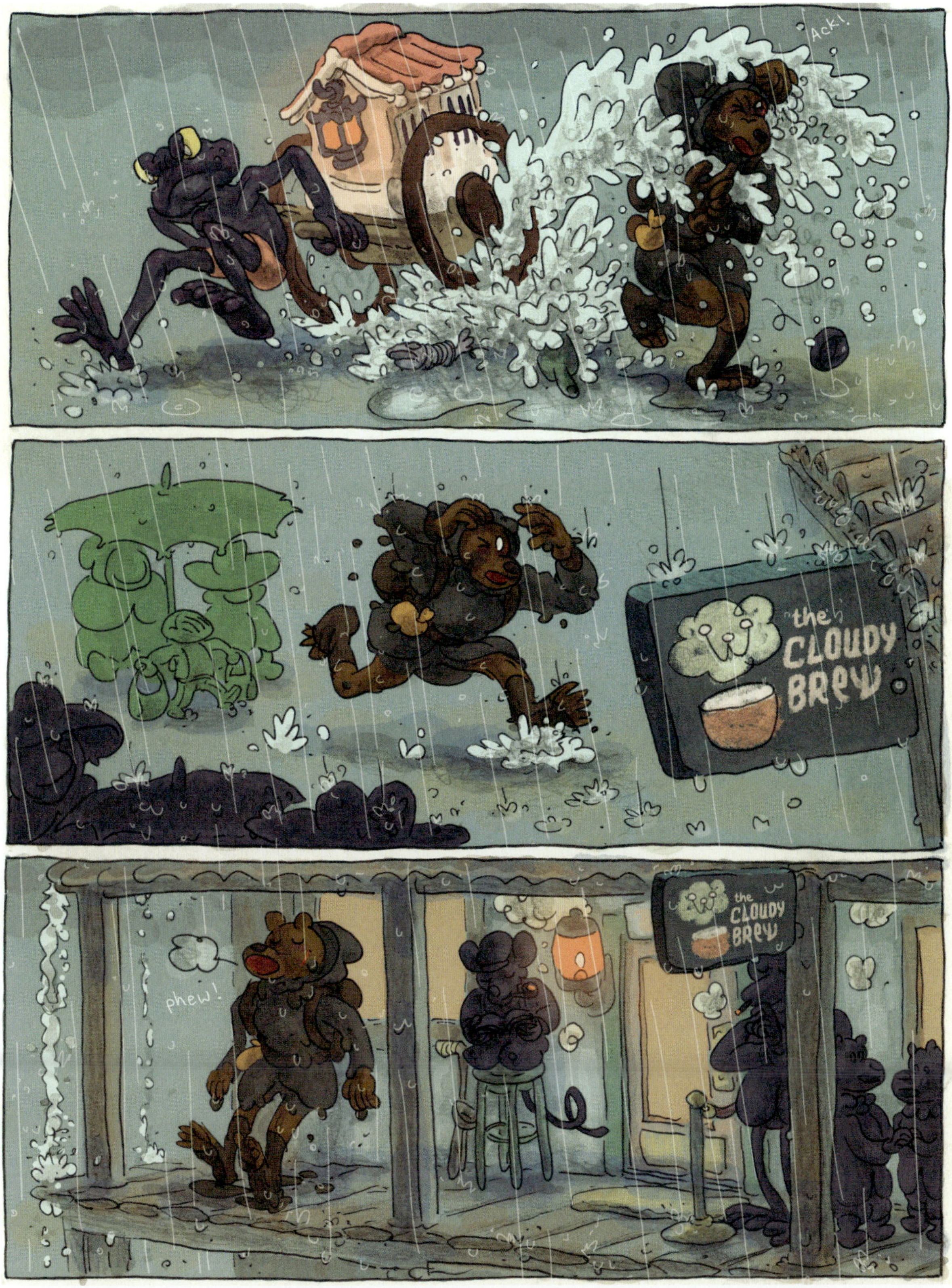
Ack!
the CLOUDY BREW
phew!
the CLOUDY BREW

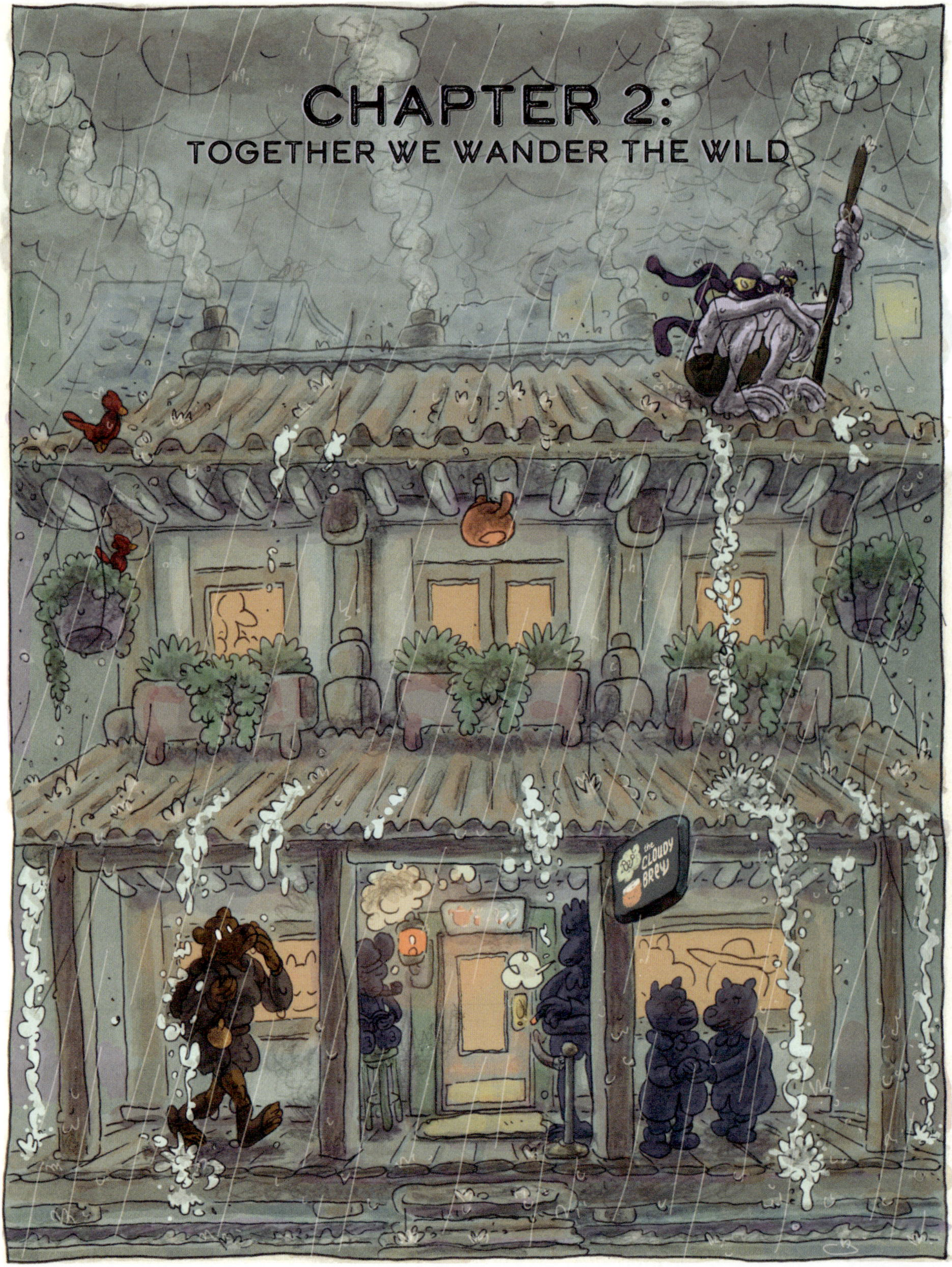
CHAPTER 2:
TOGETHER WE WANDER THE WILD
the CLOUDY BREW

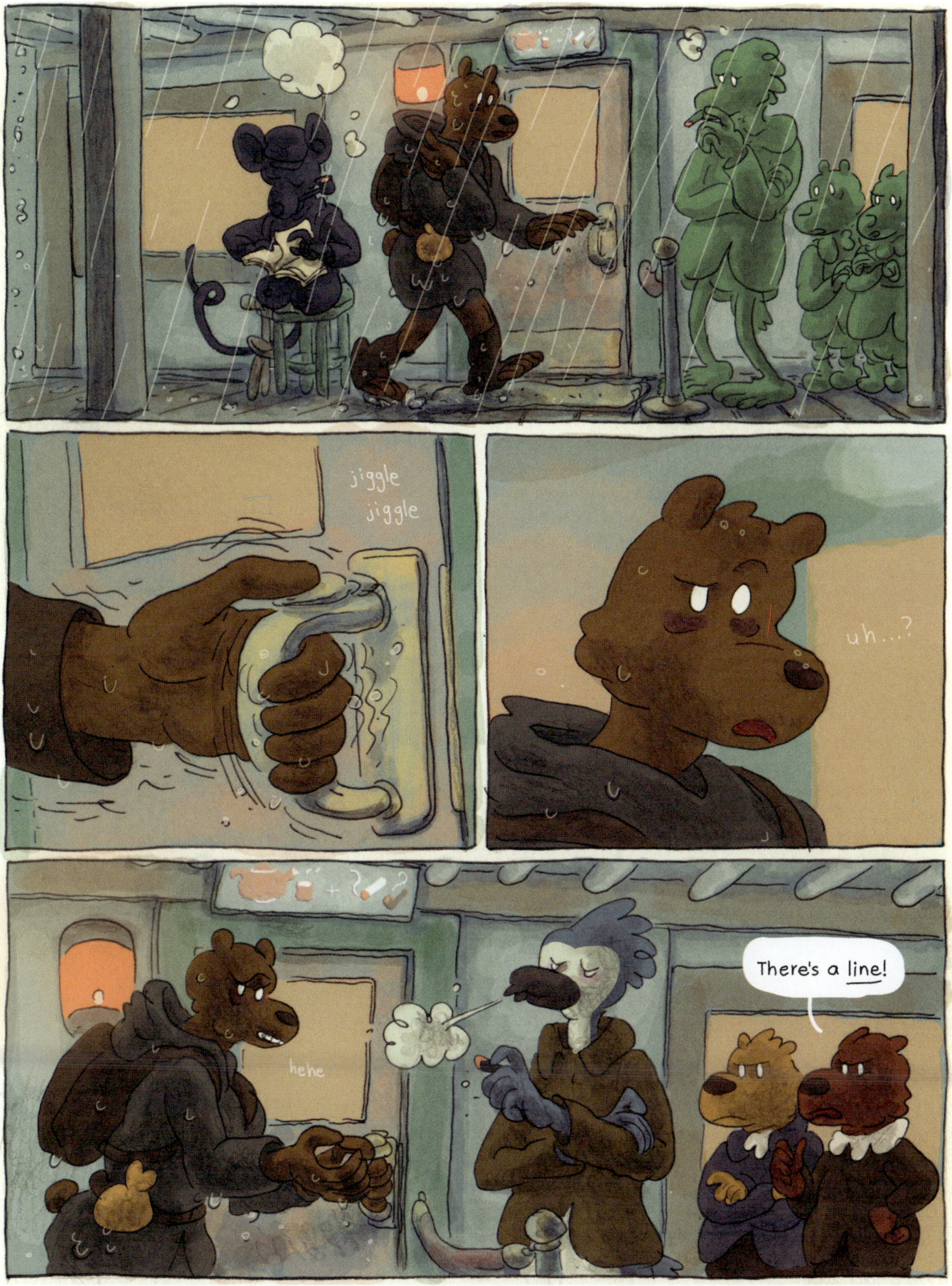
jiggle
jiggle
uh...?
hehe
There's a line!

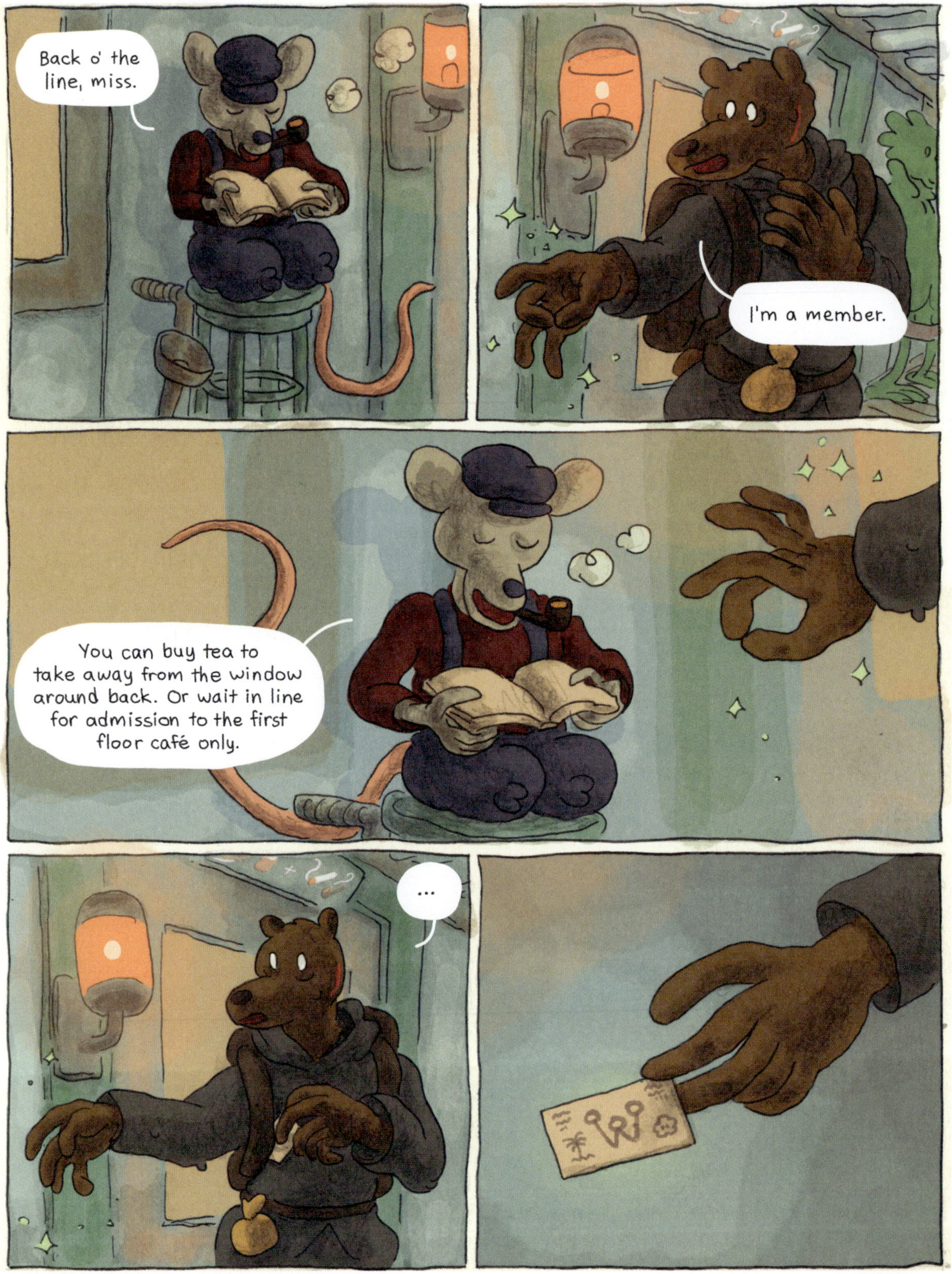
Back o' the line, miss.
I'm a member.
You can buy tea to take away from the window around back. Or wait in line for admission to the first floor café only.
...

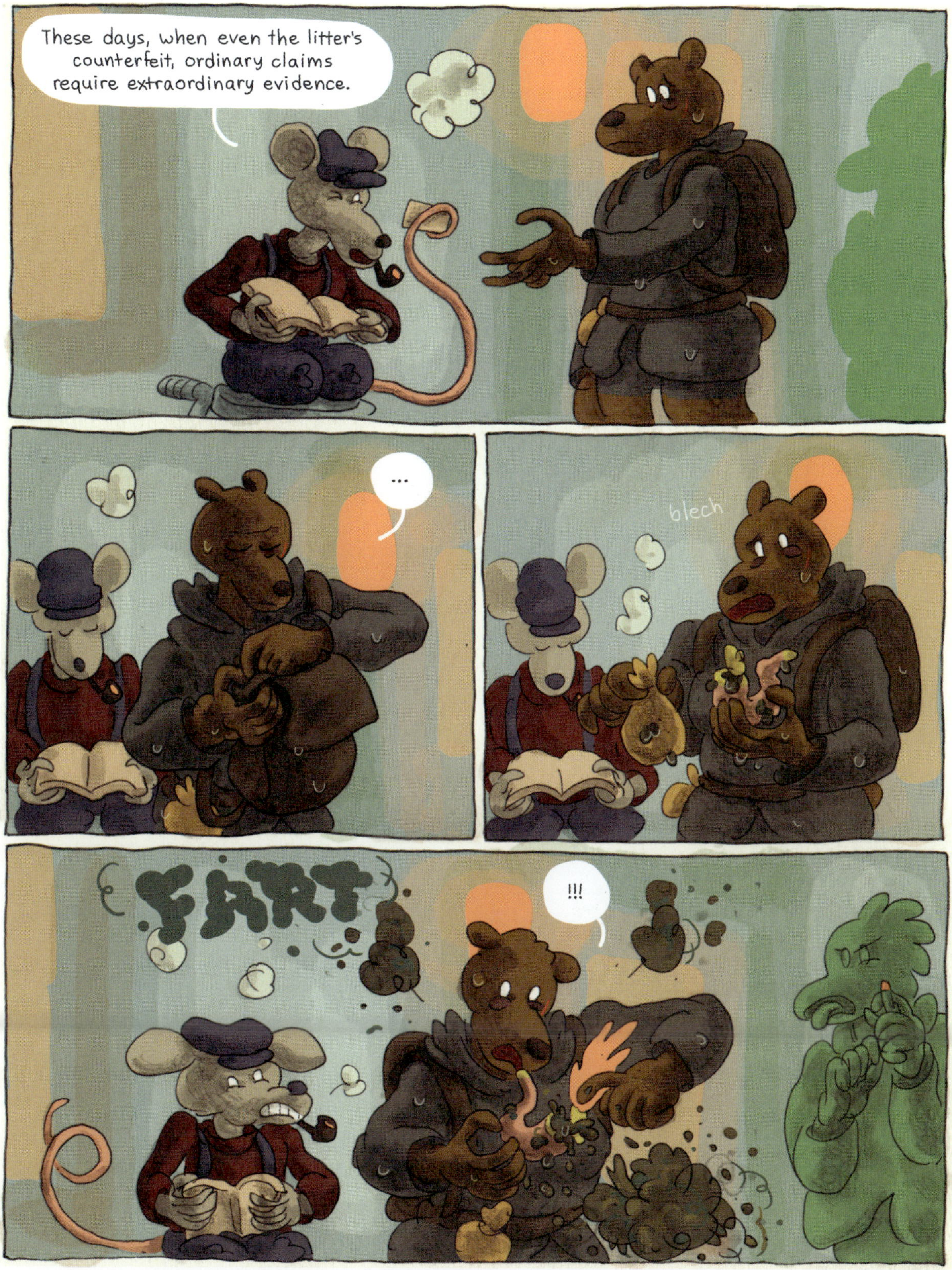
These days, when even the litter's counterfeit, ordinary claims require extraordinary evidence.
...
blech
FART
!!!

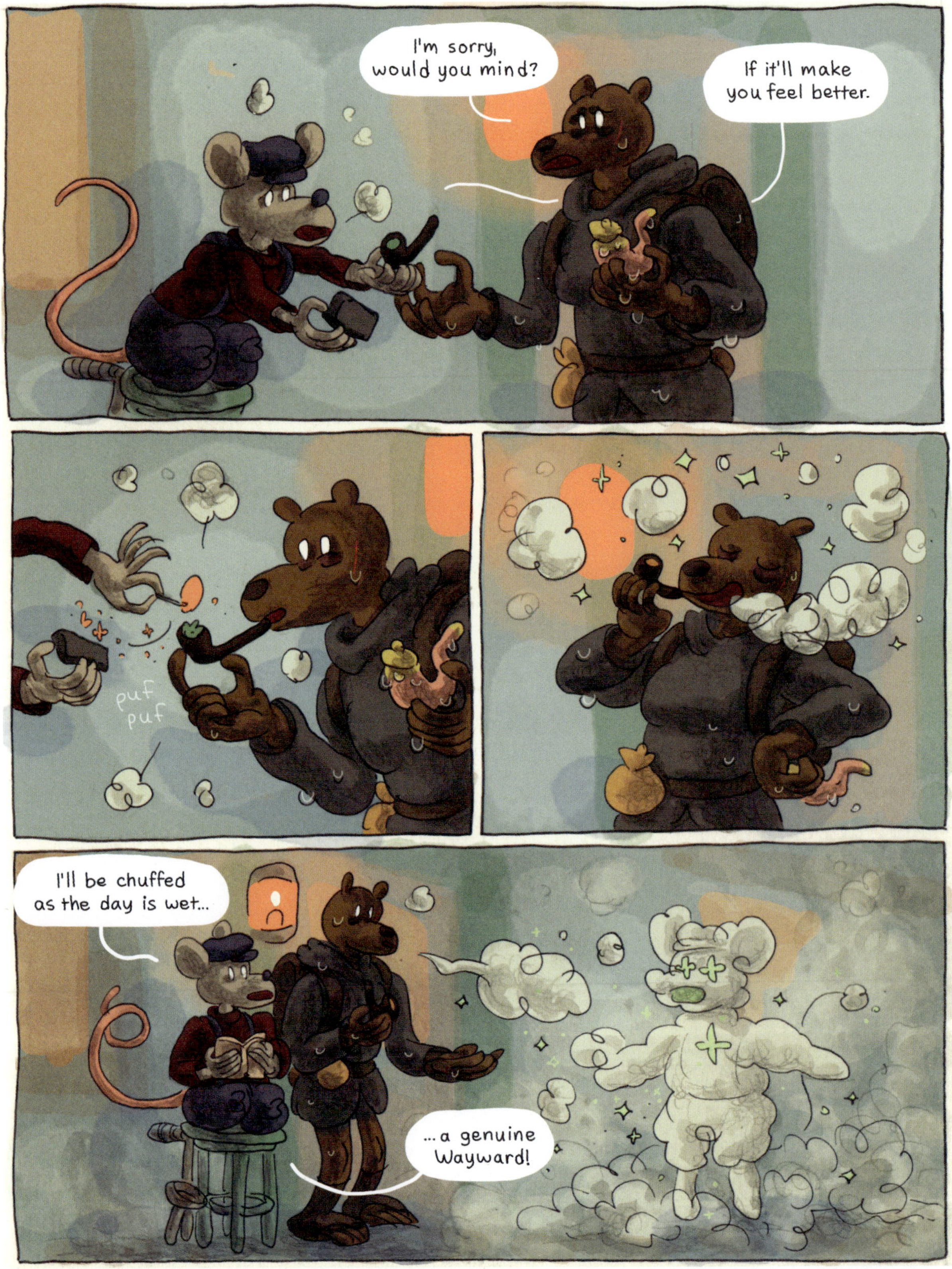
I'm sorry, would you mind?
If it'll make you feel better.
puf puf
I'll be chuffed as the day is wet...
...a genuine Wayward!

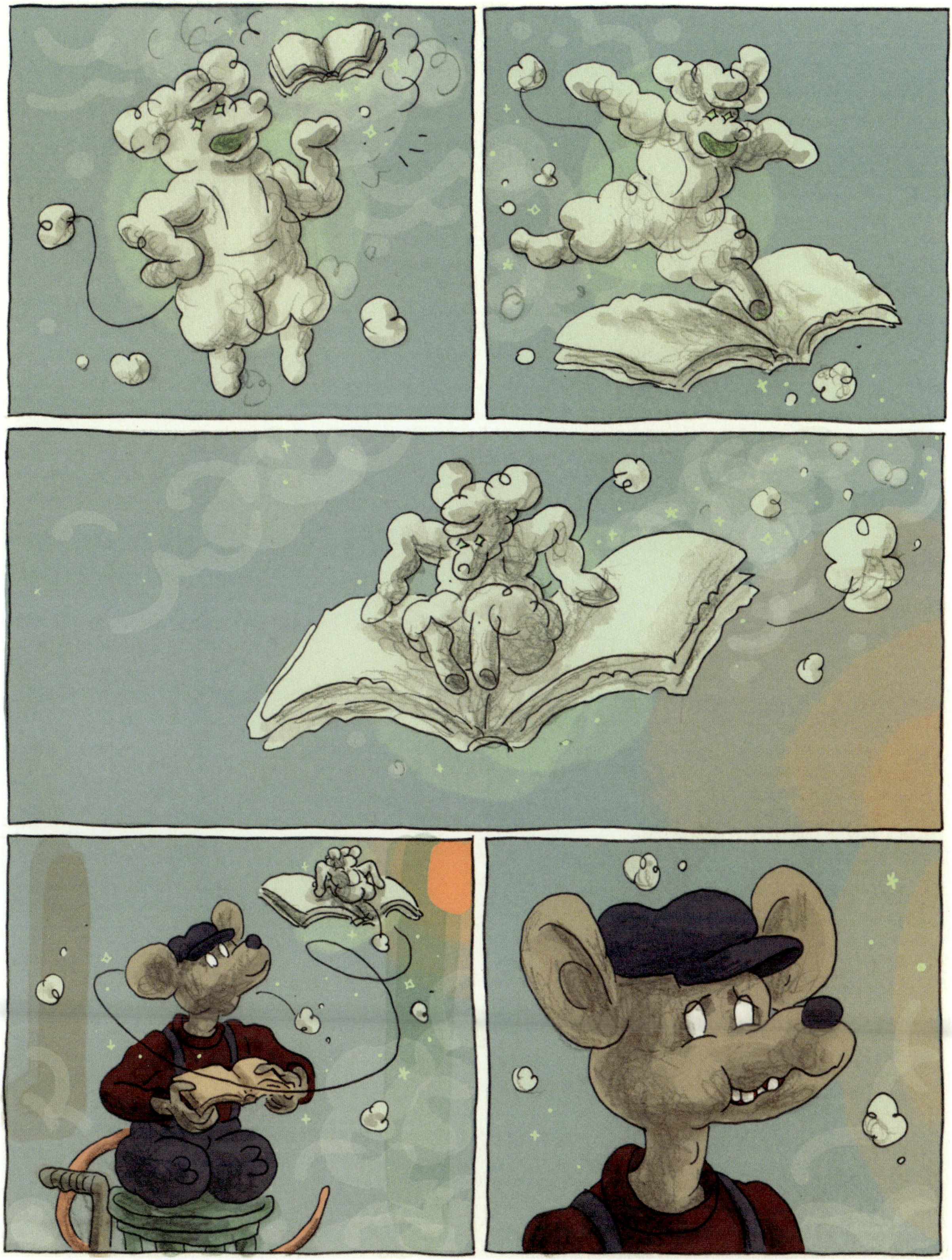

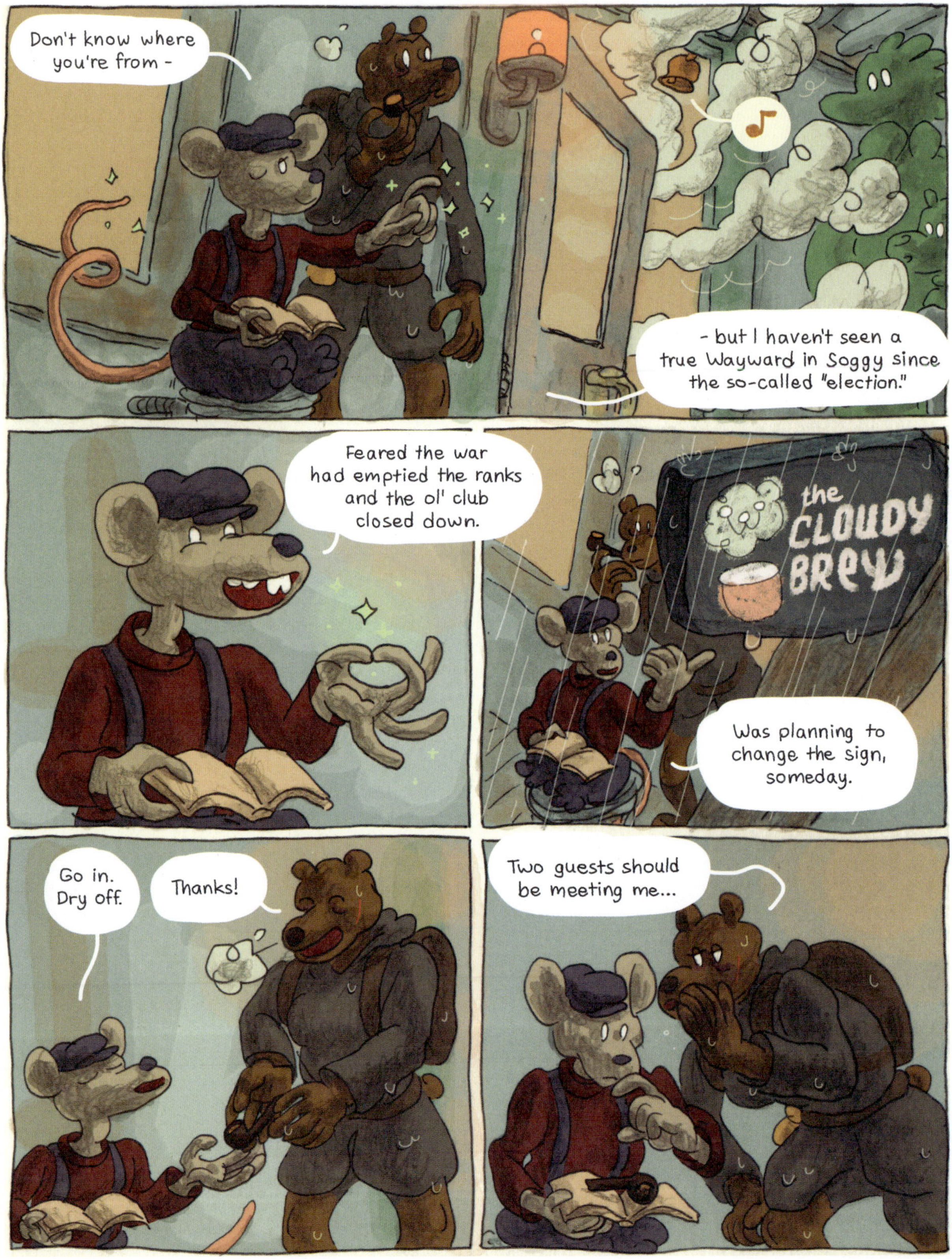
Don't know where you're from -
- but I haven't seen a true Wayward in Soggy since the so-called "election."
Feared the war had emptied the ranks and the ol' club closed down.
the CLOUDY BREW
Was planning to change the sign, someday.
Go in. Dry off.
Thanks!
Two guests should be meeting me...

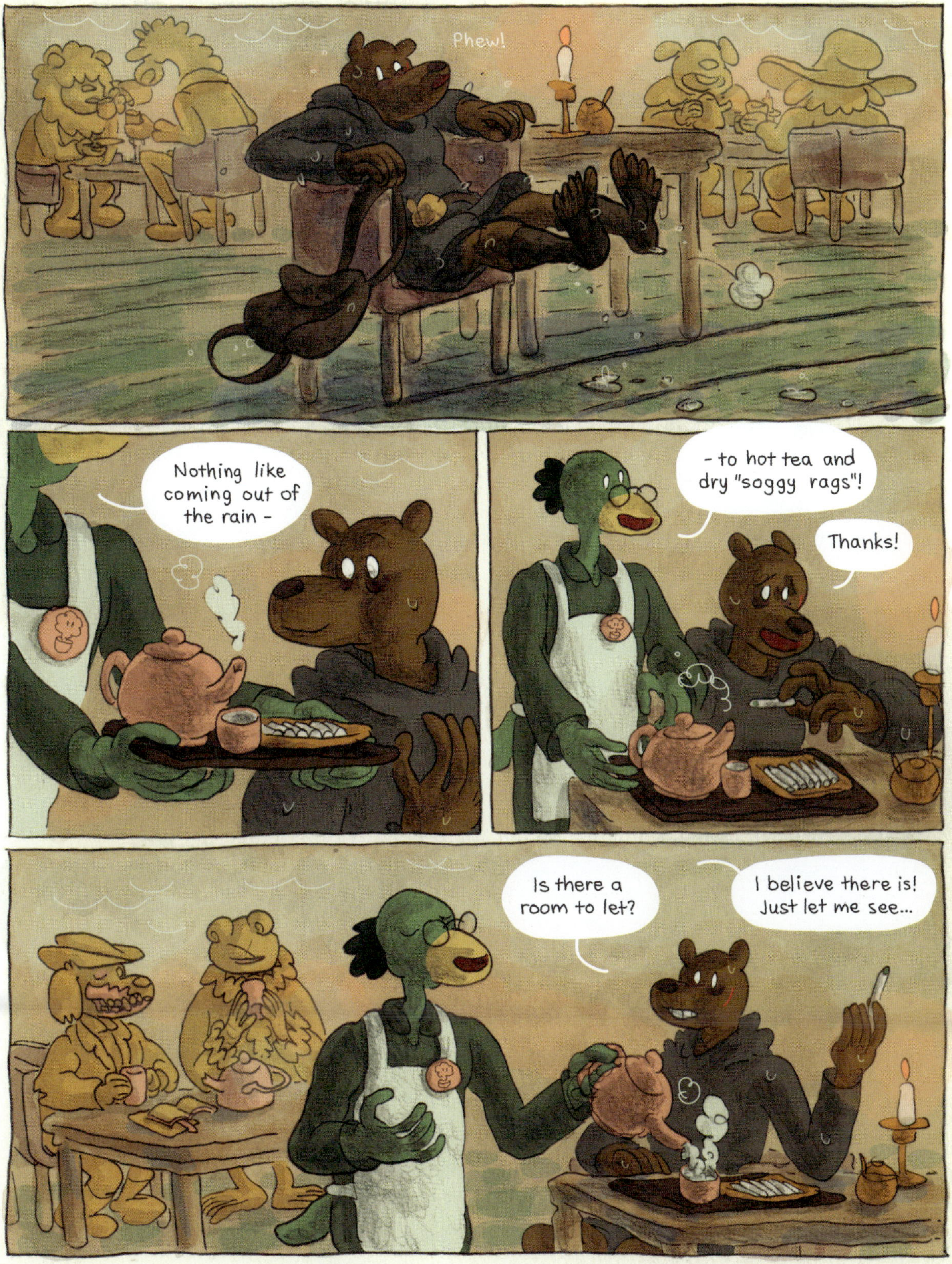
Phew!
Nothing like coming out of the rain -
- to hot tea and dry "soggy rags"!
Thanks!
Is there a room to let?
I believe there is! Just let me see...

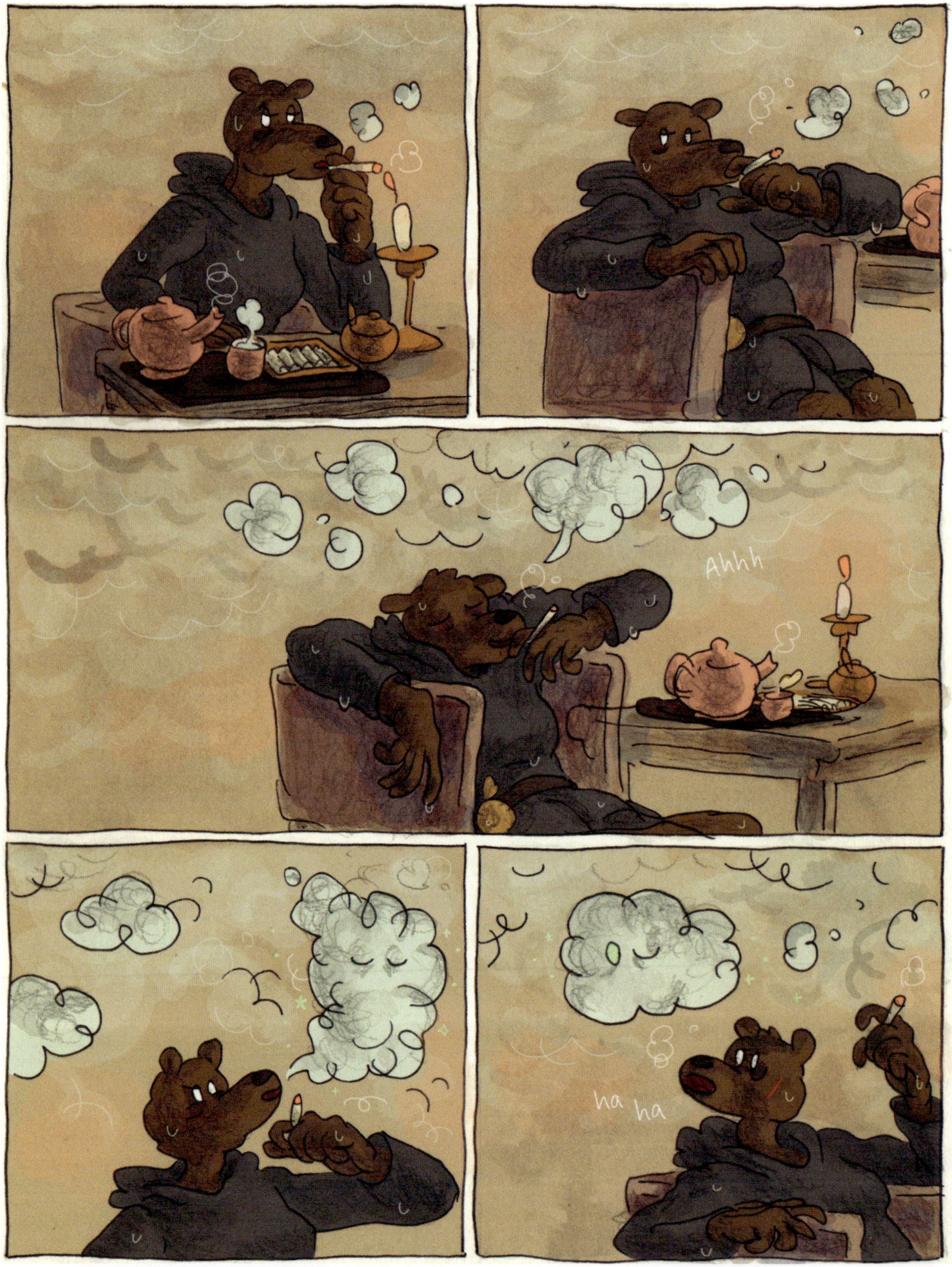
Ahhh
ha ha

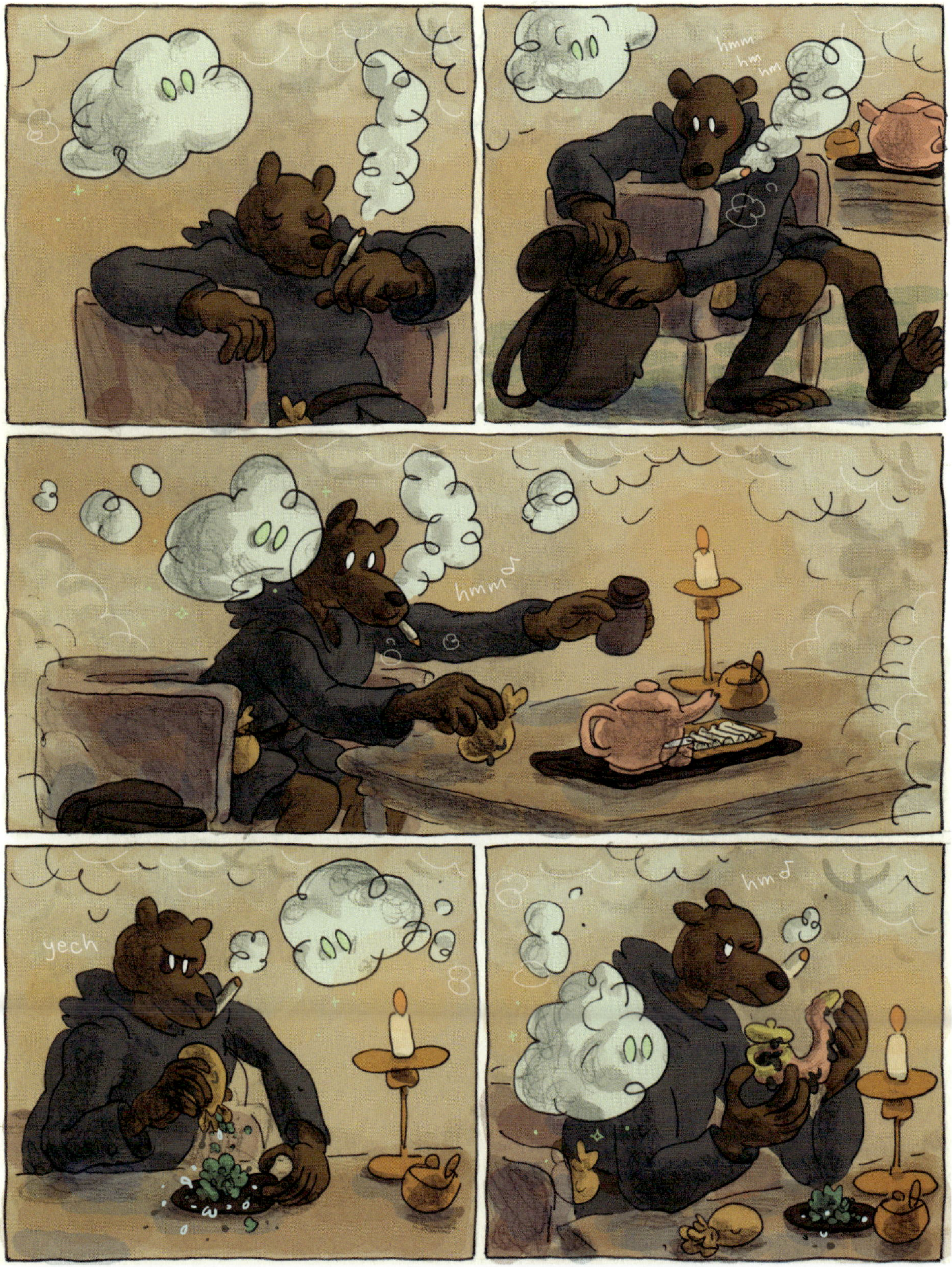
hmm
hm
hm
hmm♪
yech
hm♪

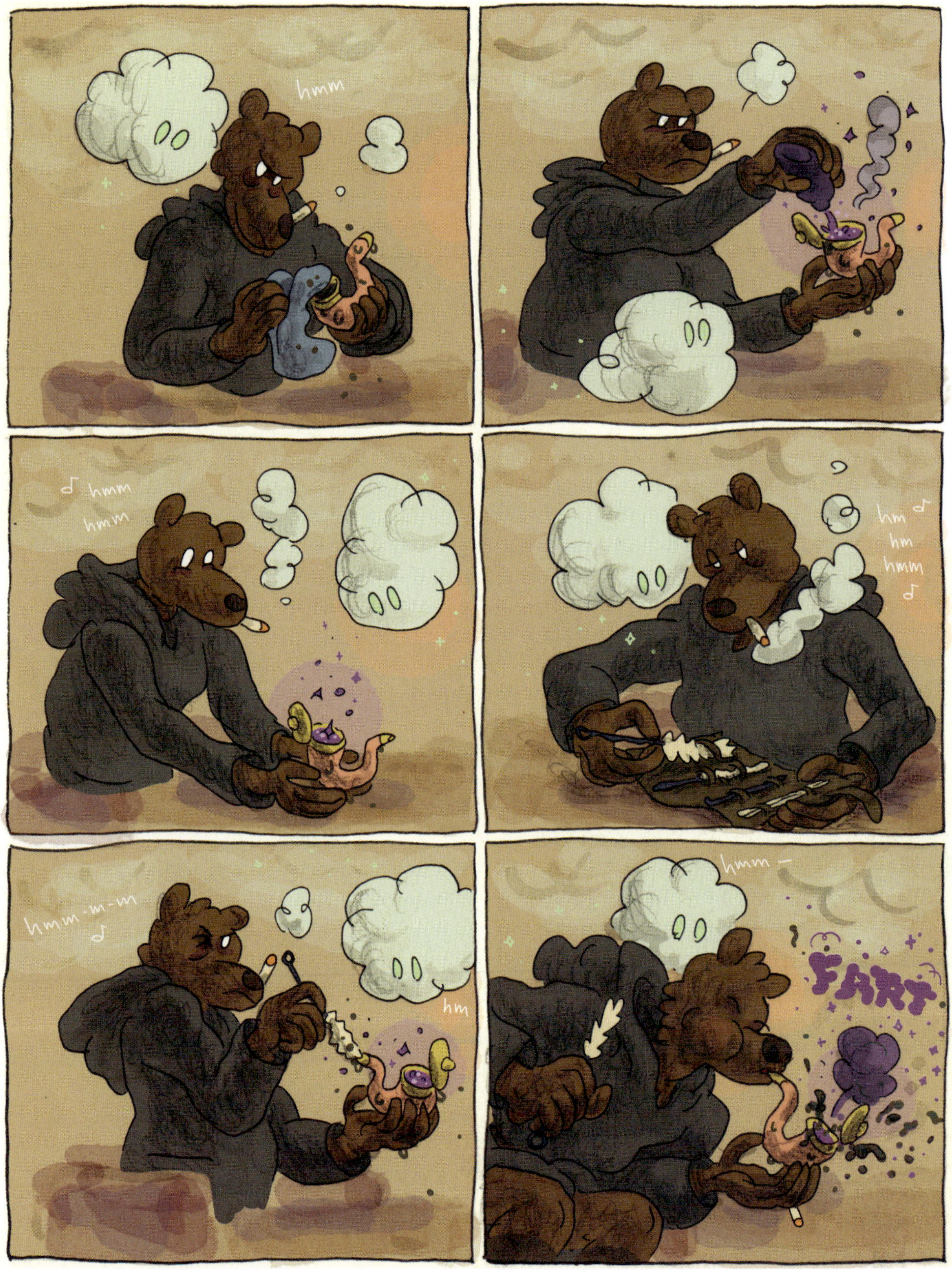
hmm
hmm
hmm
hm
hm
hmm
hmm-m-m
hm
hmm –
FART

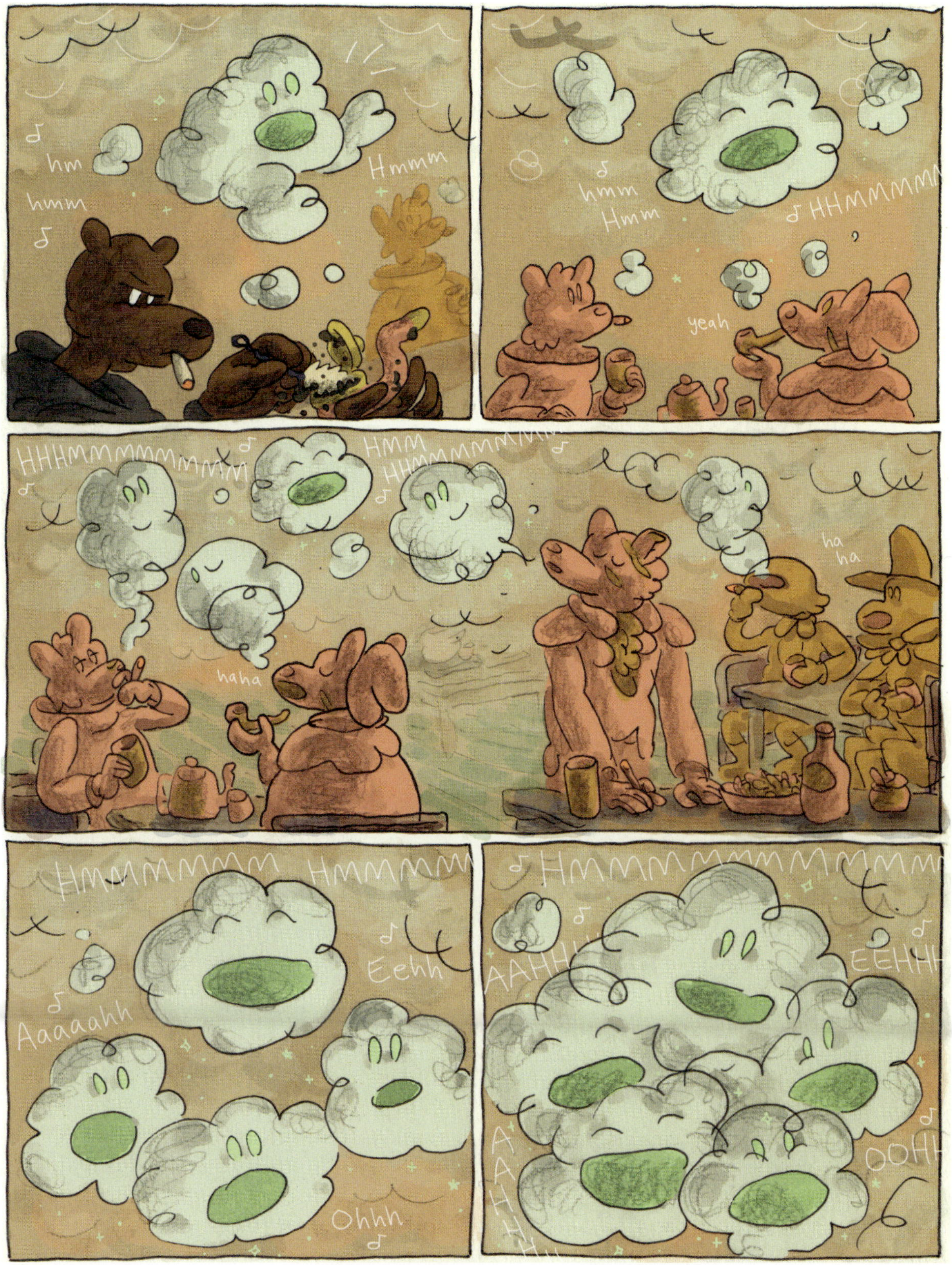
hm
hmm
Hmmm
hmm
Hmm
HHMMMMMM
yeah
HHHMMMMMMMMM
HMM
HHMMMMMMMM
haha
ha
ha
HMMMMMMM
HMMMMM
Eehh
Aaaaahh
Ohhh
HMMMMMMMMMMMMM
AAHH
EEHH
AAHHH
OOHH

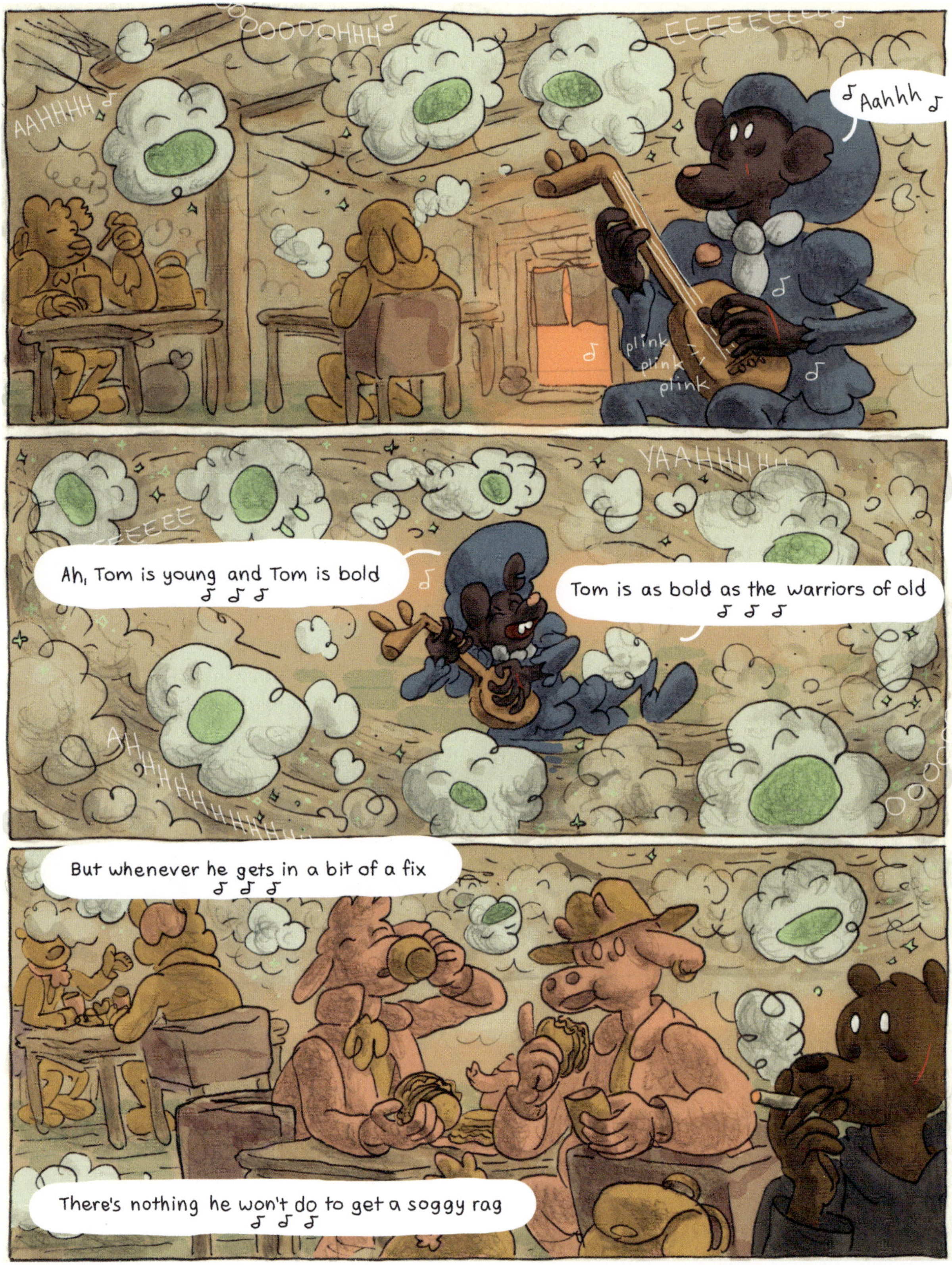
OOOOOOHHH
AAHHHH
EEEEEEEEE
Aahhh
plink plink plink
YAAHHHH
EEEEE
Ah, Tom is young and Tom is bold
Tom is as bold as the warriors of old
AHHHHHHH
But whenever he gets in a bit of a fix
There's nothing he won't do to get a soggy rag

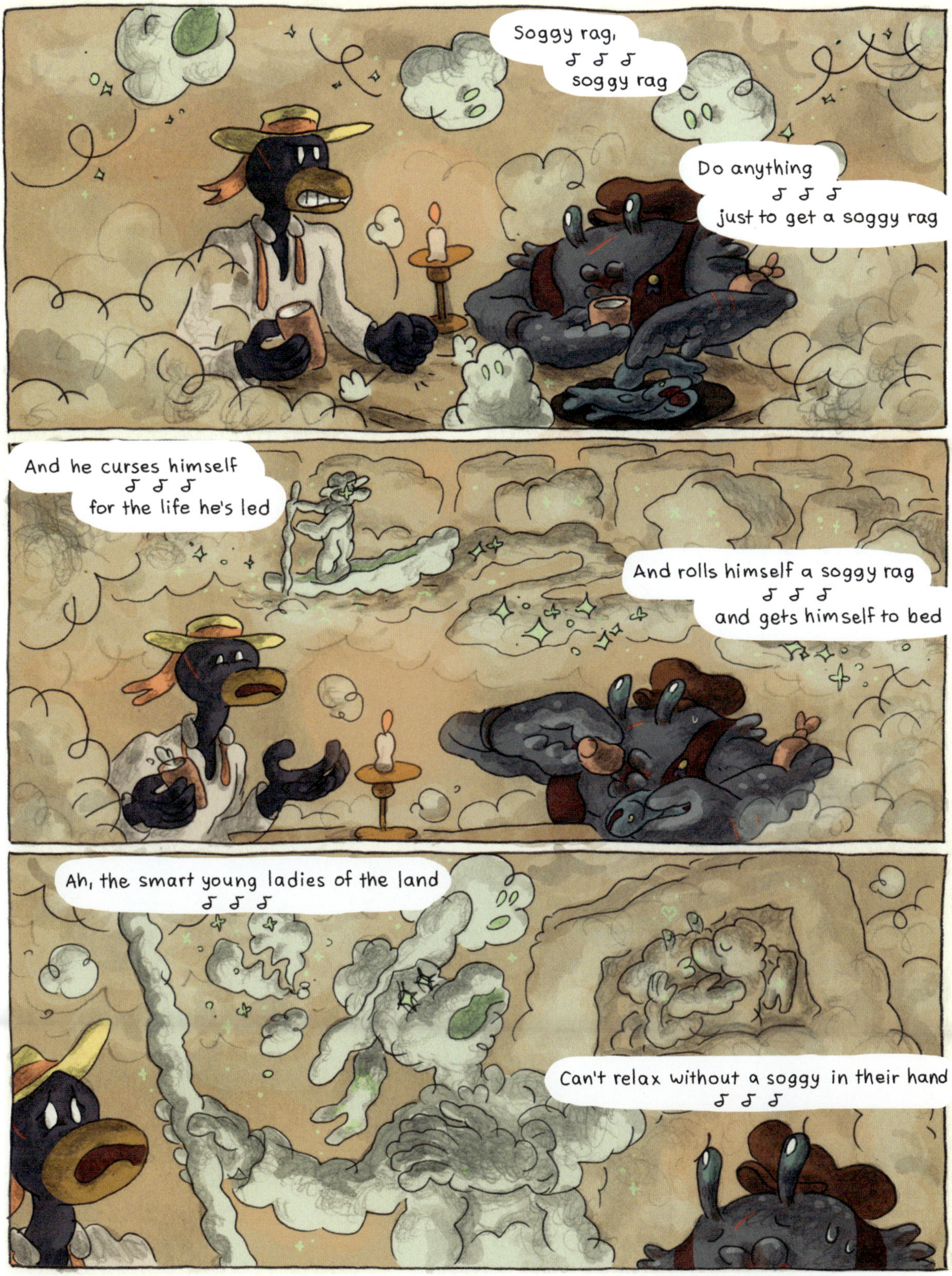
Soggy rag, ♪ ♪ ♪ soggy rag
Do anything ♪ ♪ ♪ just to get a soggy rag
And he curses himself ♪ ♪ ♪ for the life he's led
And rolls himself a soggy rag ♪ ♪ ♪ and gets himself to bed
Ah, the smart young ladies of the land ♪ ♪ ♪
Can't relax without a soggy in their hand ♪ ♪ ♪

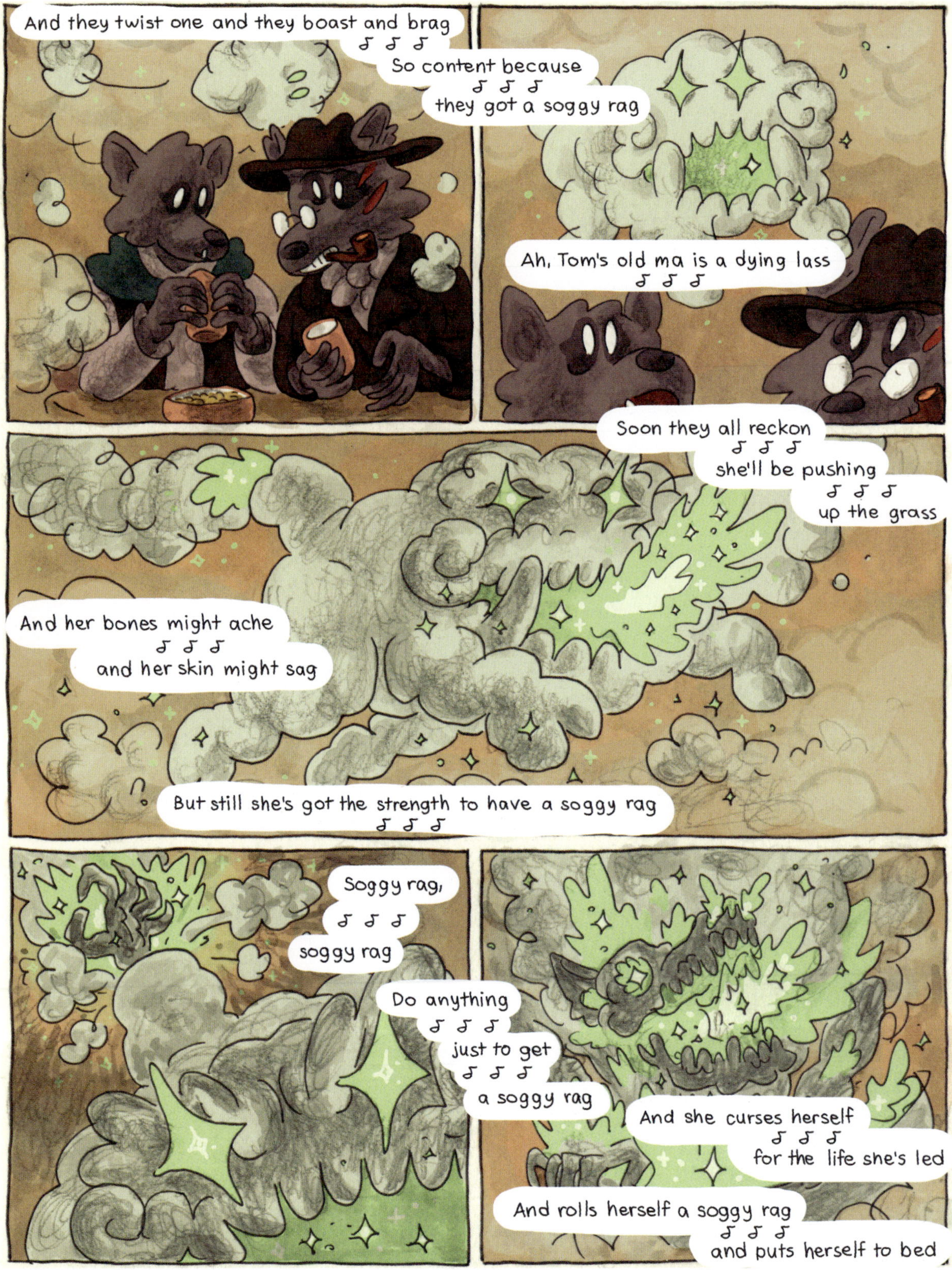
And they twist one and they boast and brag
So content because
they got a soggy rag
Ah, Tom's old ma is a dying lass
Soon they all reckon
she'll be pushing
up the grass
And her bones might ache
and her skin might sag
But still she's got the strength to have a soggy rag
Soggy rag,
soggy rag
Do anything
just to get
a soggy rag
And she curses herself
for the life she's led
And rolls herself a soggy rag
and puts herself to bed

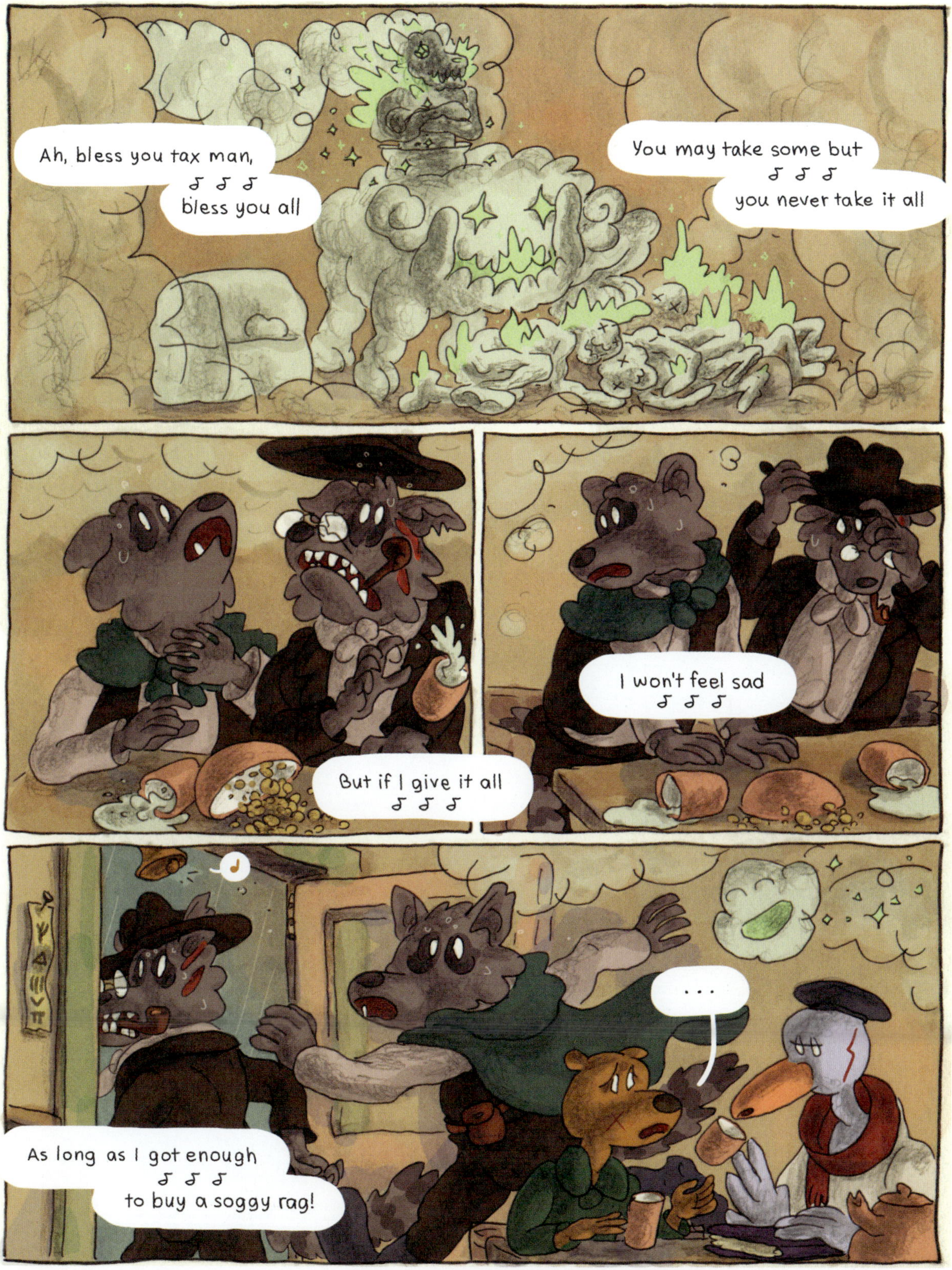
Ah, bless you tax man,
♪ ♪ ♪
bless you all
You may take some but
♪ ♪ ♪
you never take it all
But if I give it all
♪ ♪ ♪
I won't feel sad
♪ ♪ ♪
As long as I got enough
♪ ♪ ♪
to buy a soggy rag!
...

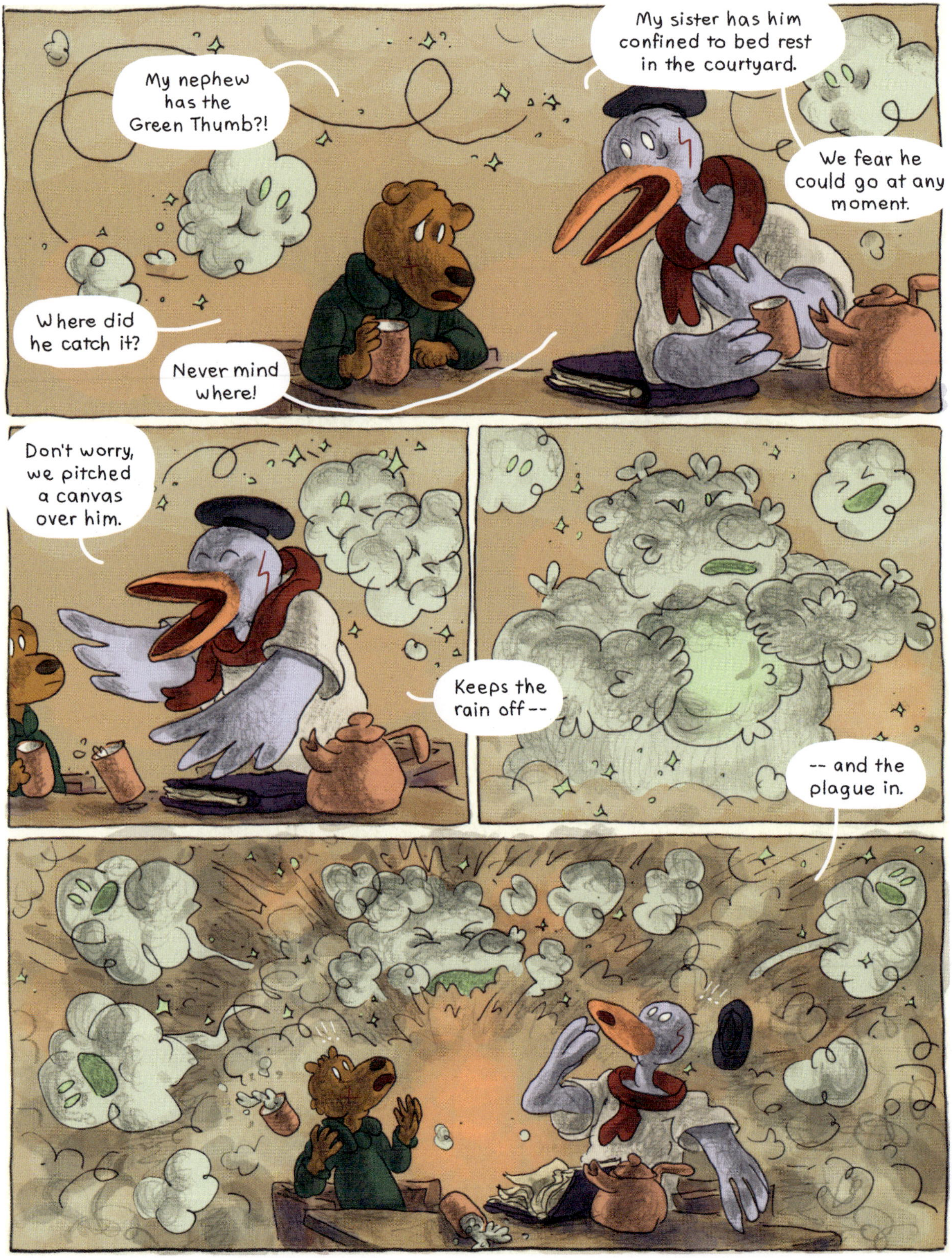
My nephew has the Green Thumb?!
My sister has him confined to bed rest in the courtyard.
We fear he could go at any moment.
Where did he catch it?
Never mind where!
Don't worry, we pitched a canvas over him.
Keeps the rain off--
-- and the plague in.

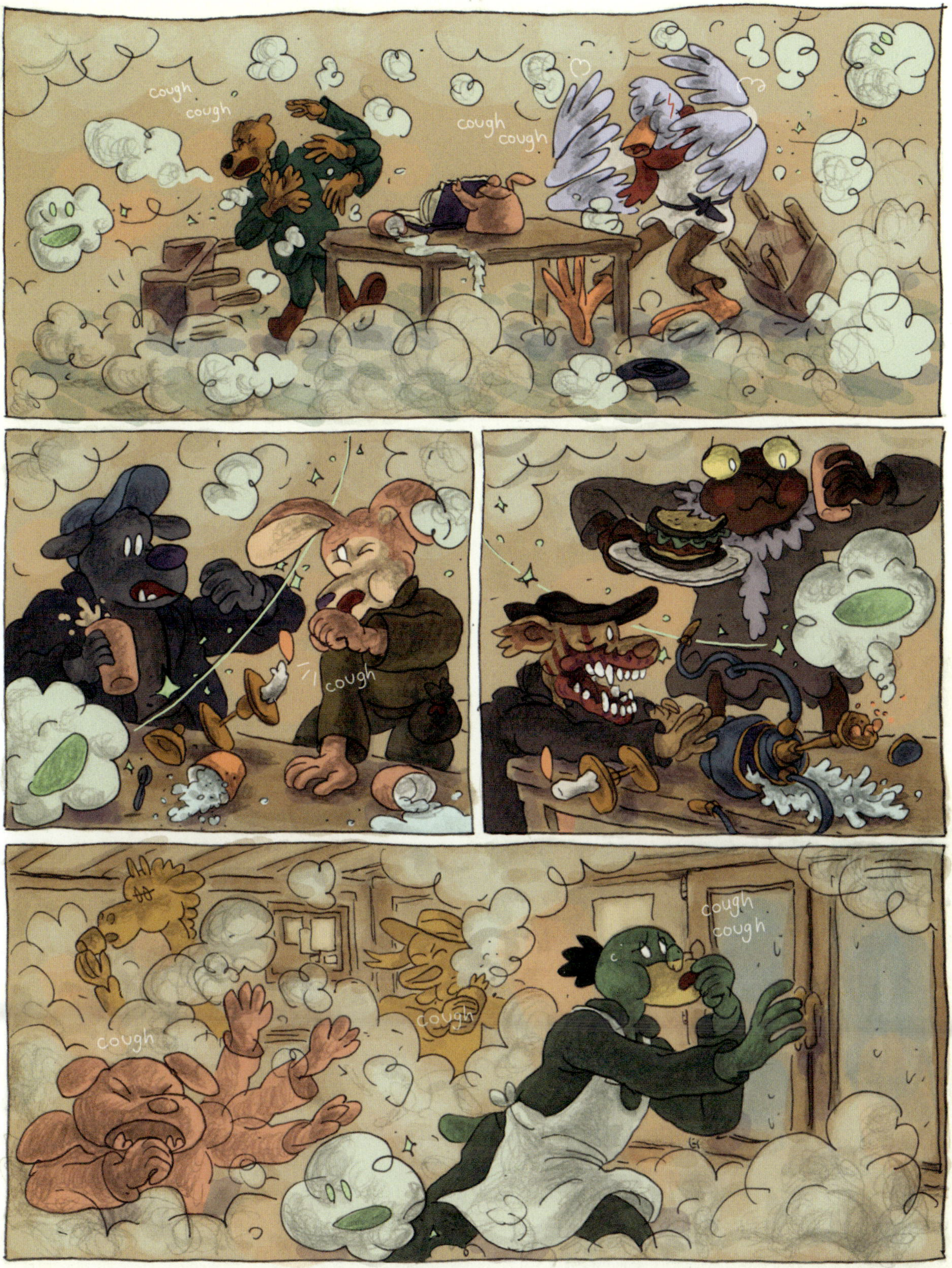
cough
cough
cough
cough
cough
cough
cough
cough
cough

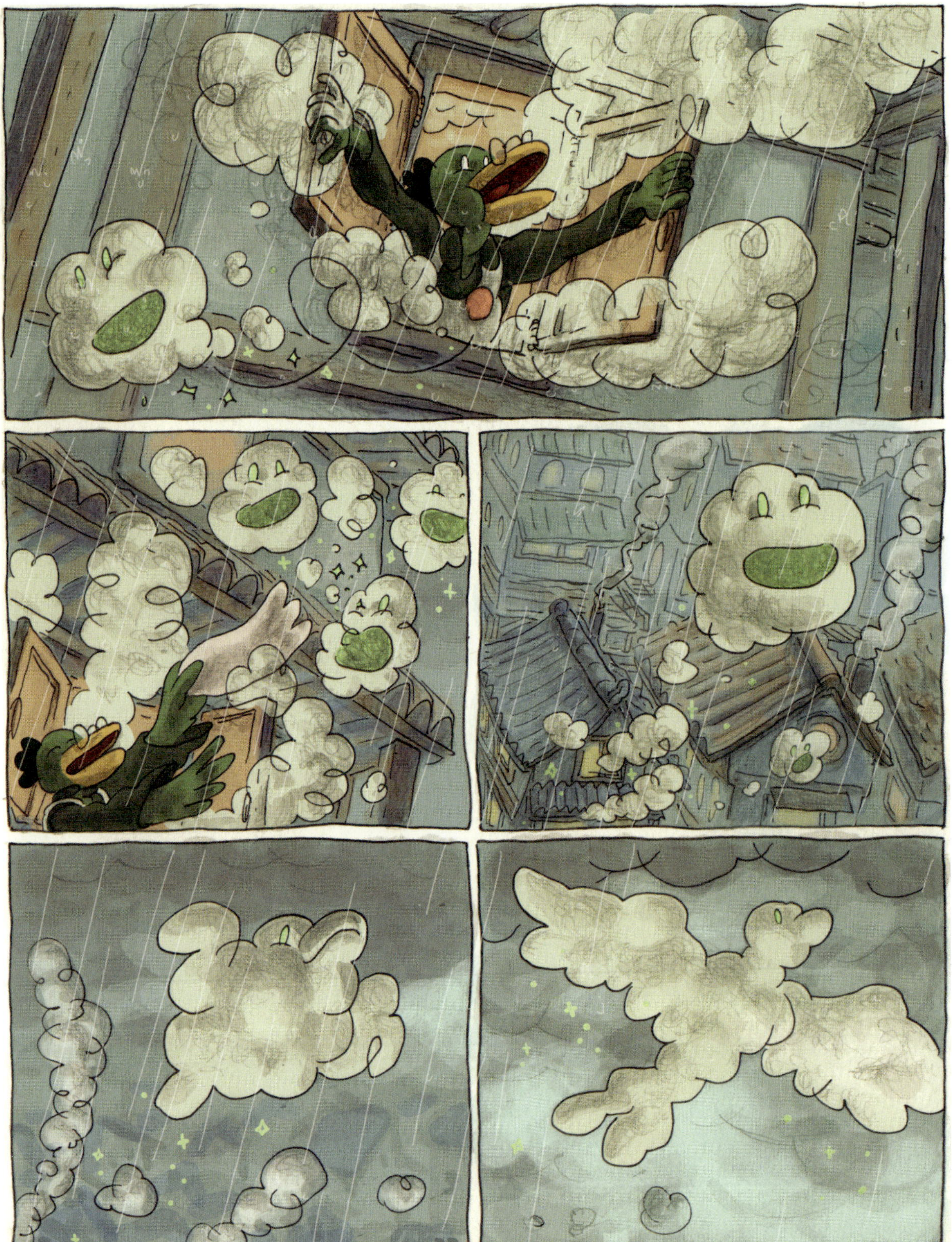

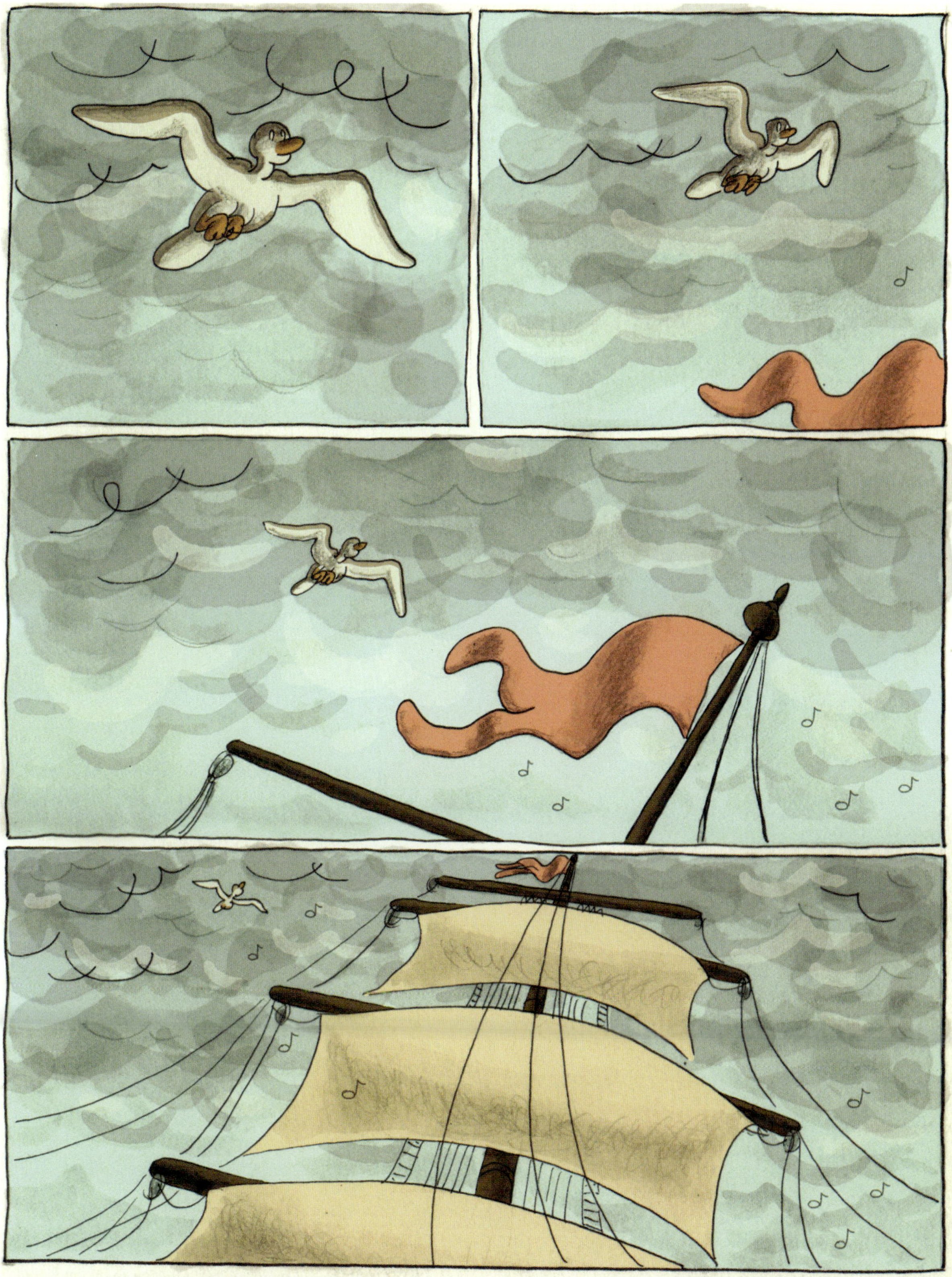

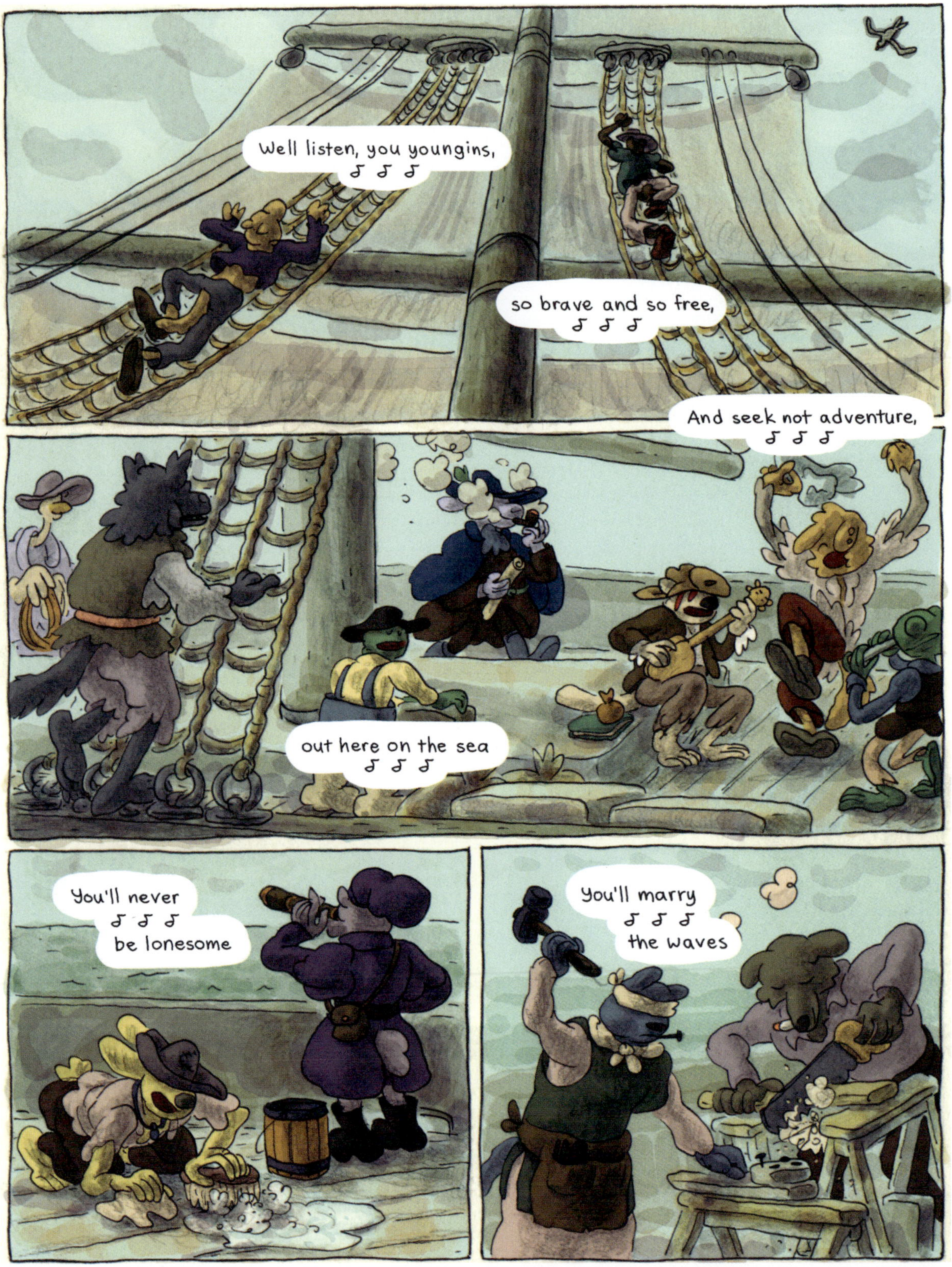
Well listen, you youngins, ♪ ♪ ♪
so brave and so free, ♪ ♪ ♪
And seek not adventure, ♪ ♪ ♪
out here on the sea ♪ ♪ ♪
You'll never ♪ ♪ ♪ be lonesome
You'll marry ♪ ♪ ♪ the waves

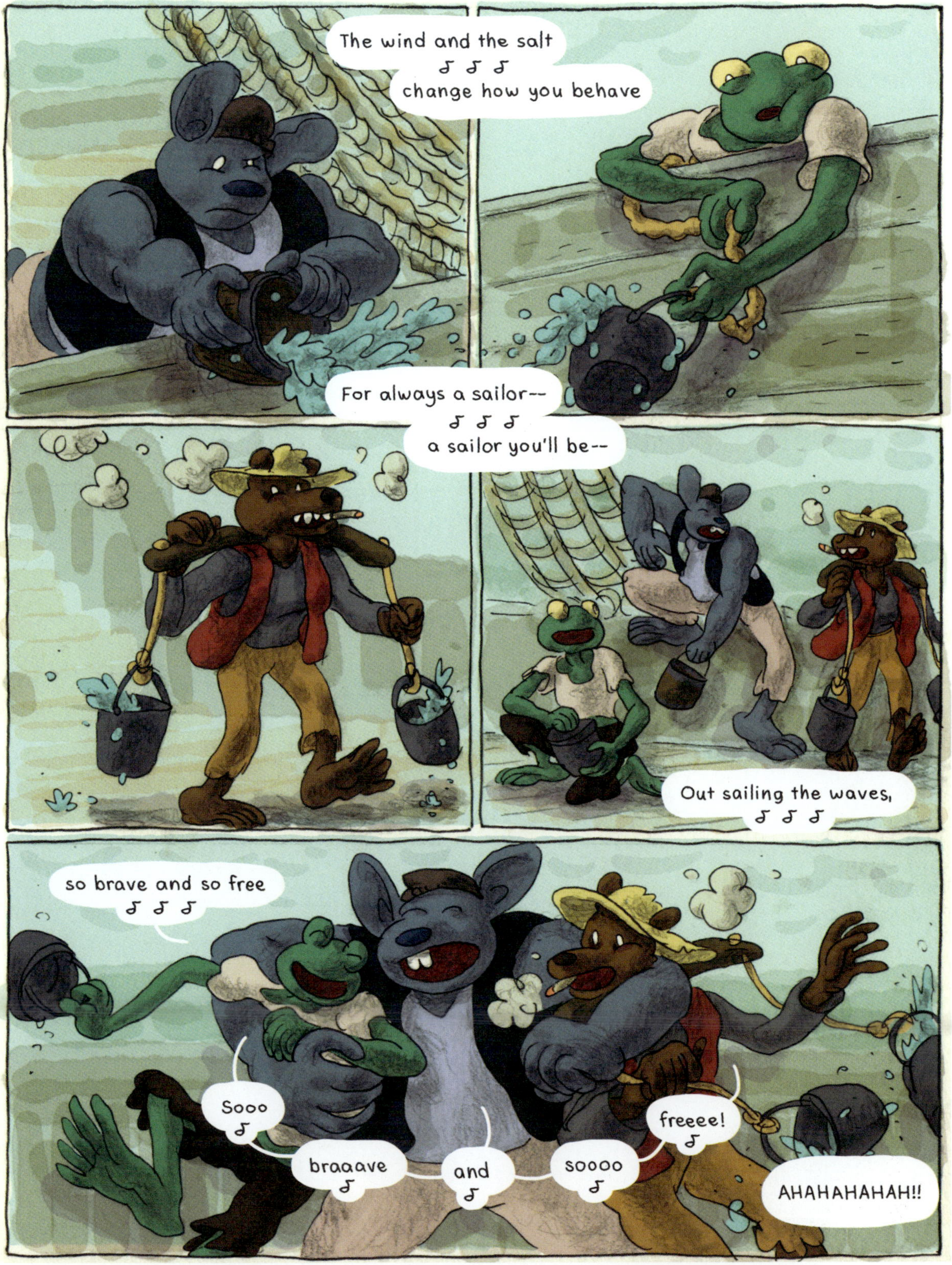
The wind and the salt
♪ ♪ ♪
change how you behave
For always a sailor--
♪ ♪ ♪
a sailor you'll be--
Out sailing the waves,
♪ ♪ ♪
so brave and so free
♪ ♪ ♪
Sooo
♪
braaave
♪
and
♪
soooo
♪
freeee!
♪
AHAHAHAHAH!!

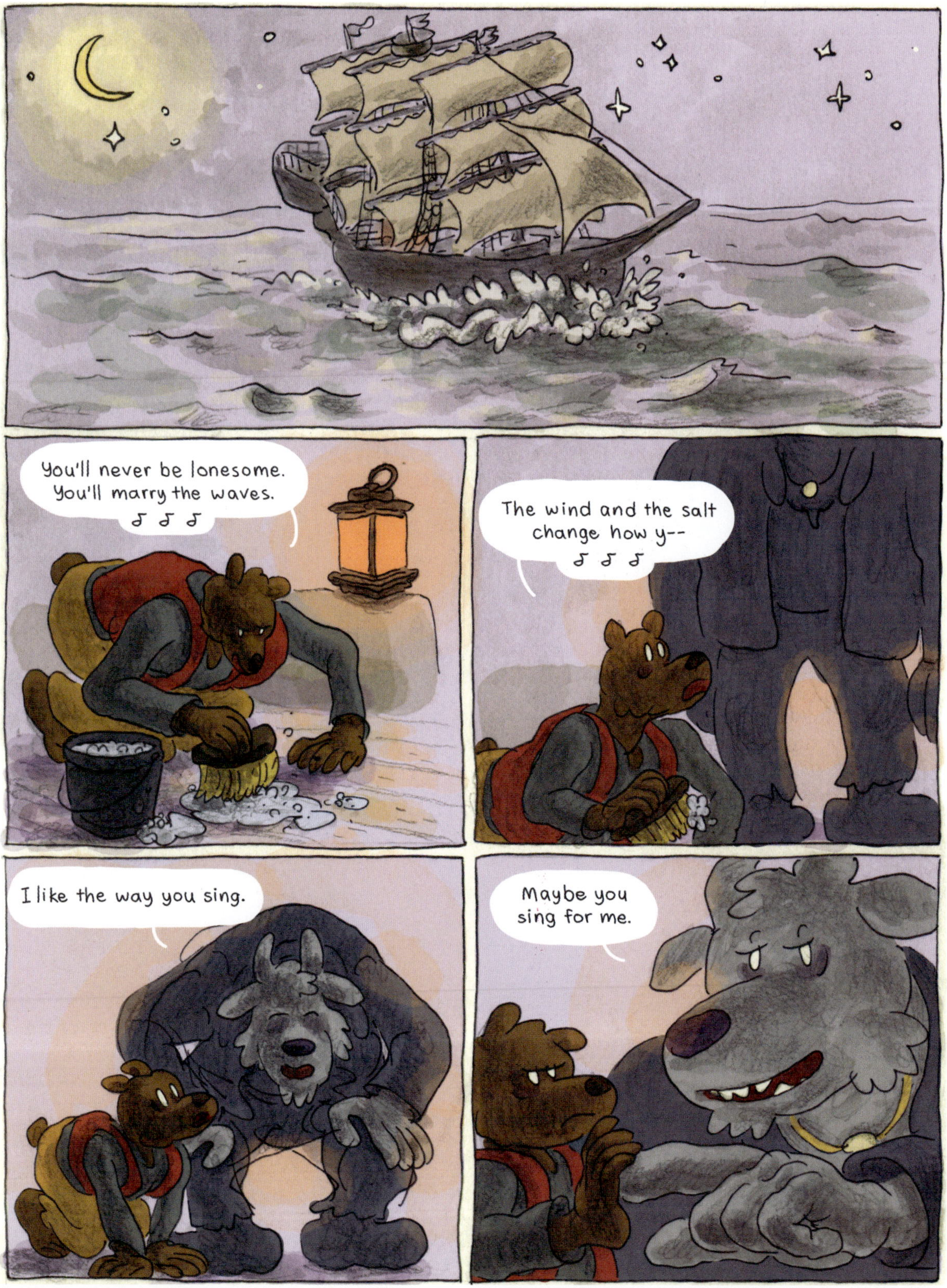
You'll never be lonesome. You'll marry the waves.
♪ ♪ ♪
The wind and the salt change how y--
♪ ♪ ♪
I like the way you sing.
Maybe you sing for me.

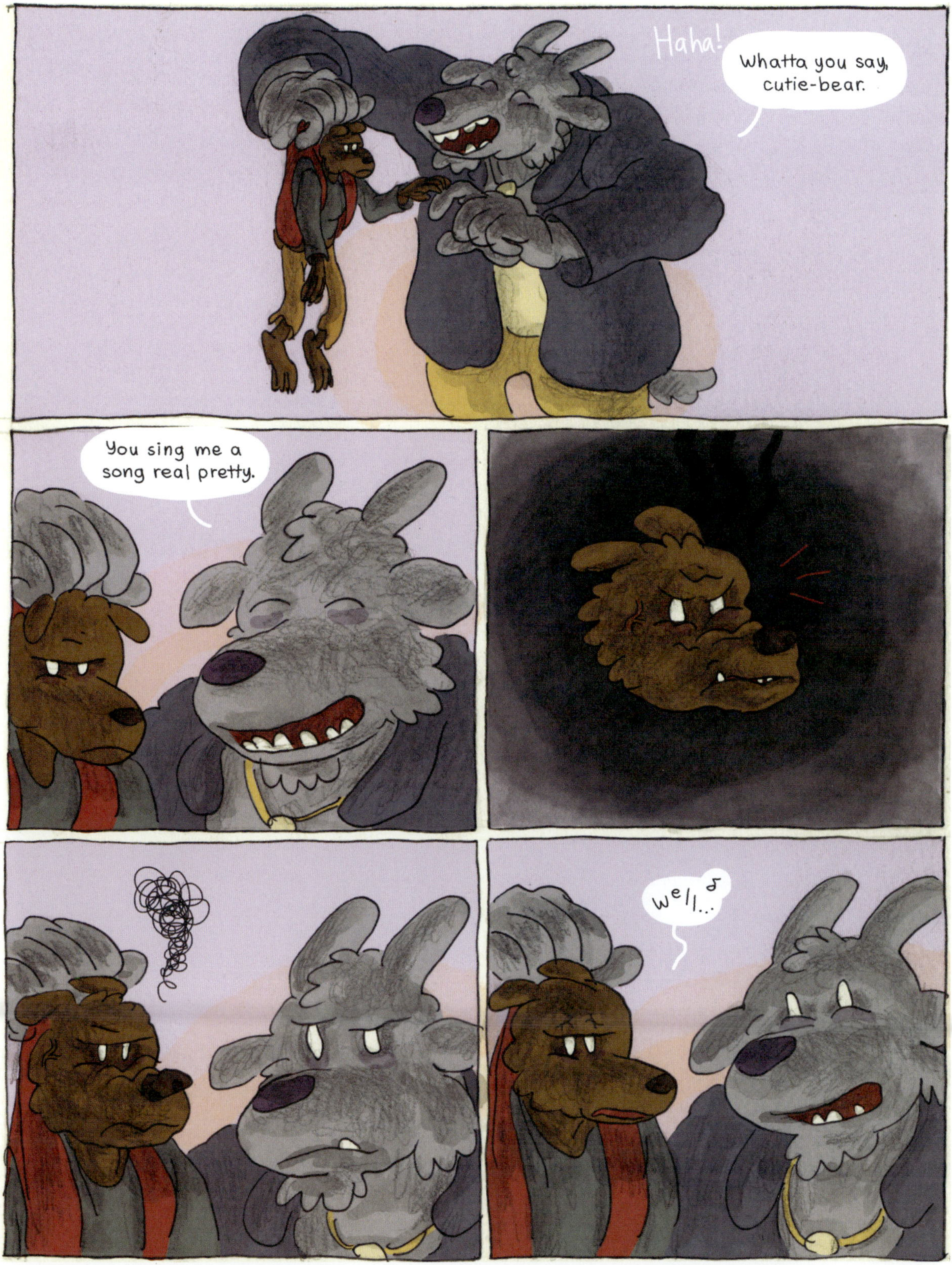
Haha!
Whatta you say, cutie-bear.
You sing me a song real pretty.
well...

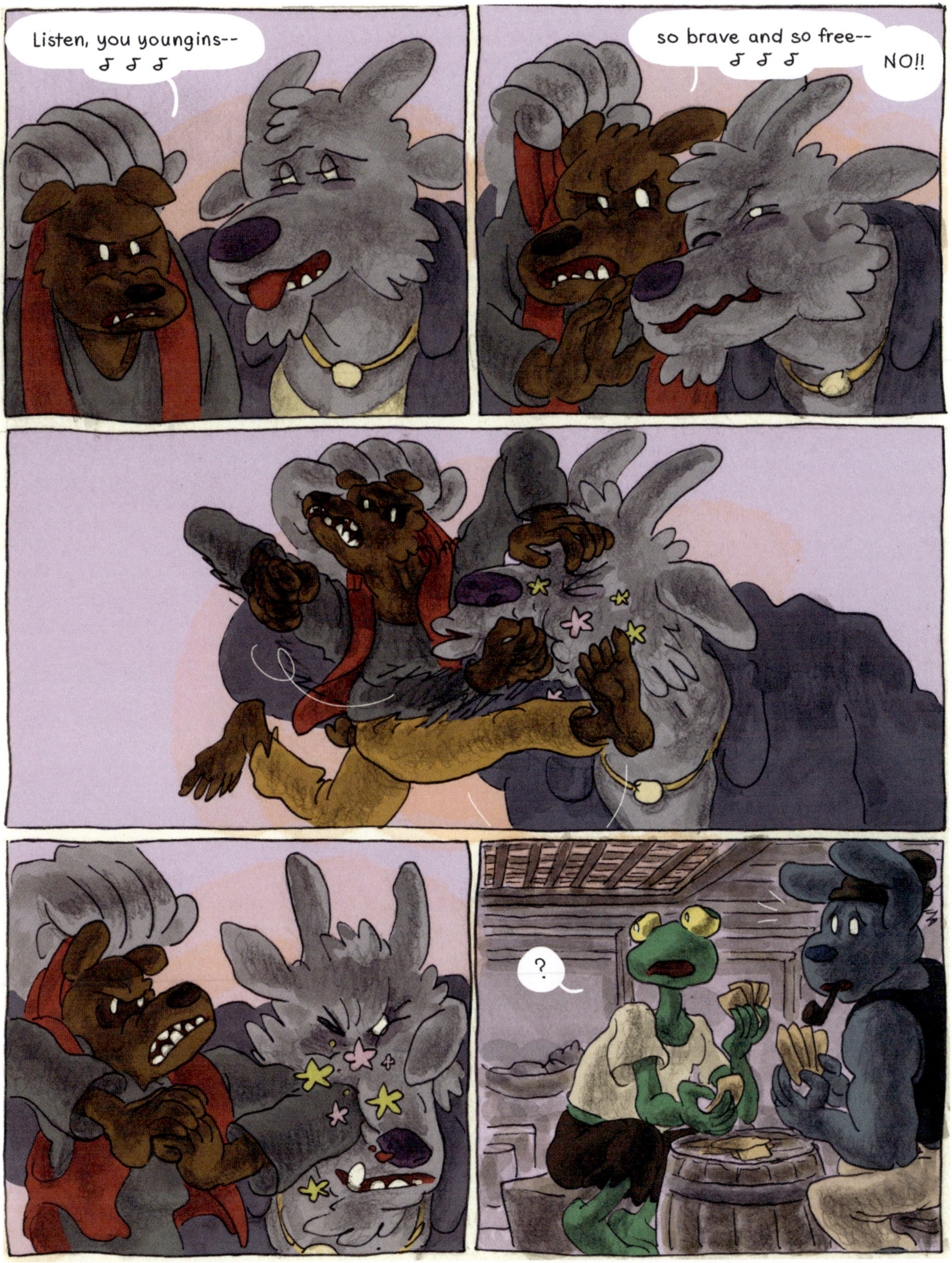

Listen, you youngins--
♪ ♪ ♪
so brave and so free--
♪ ♪ ♪
NO!!
?

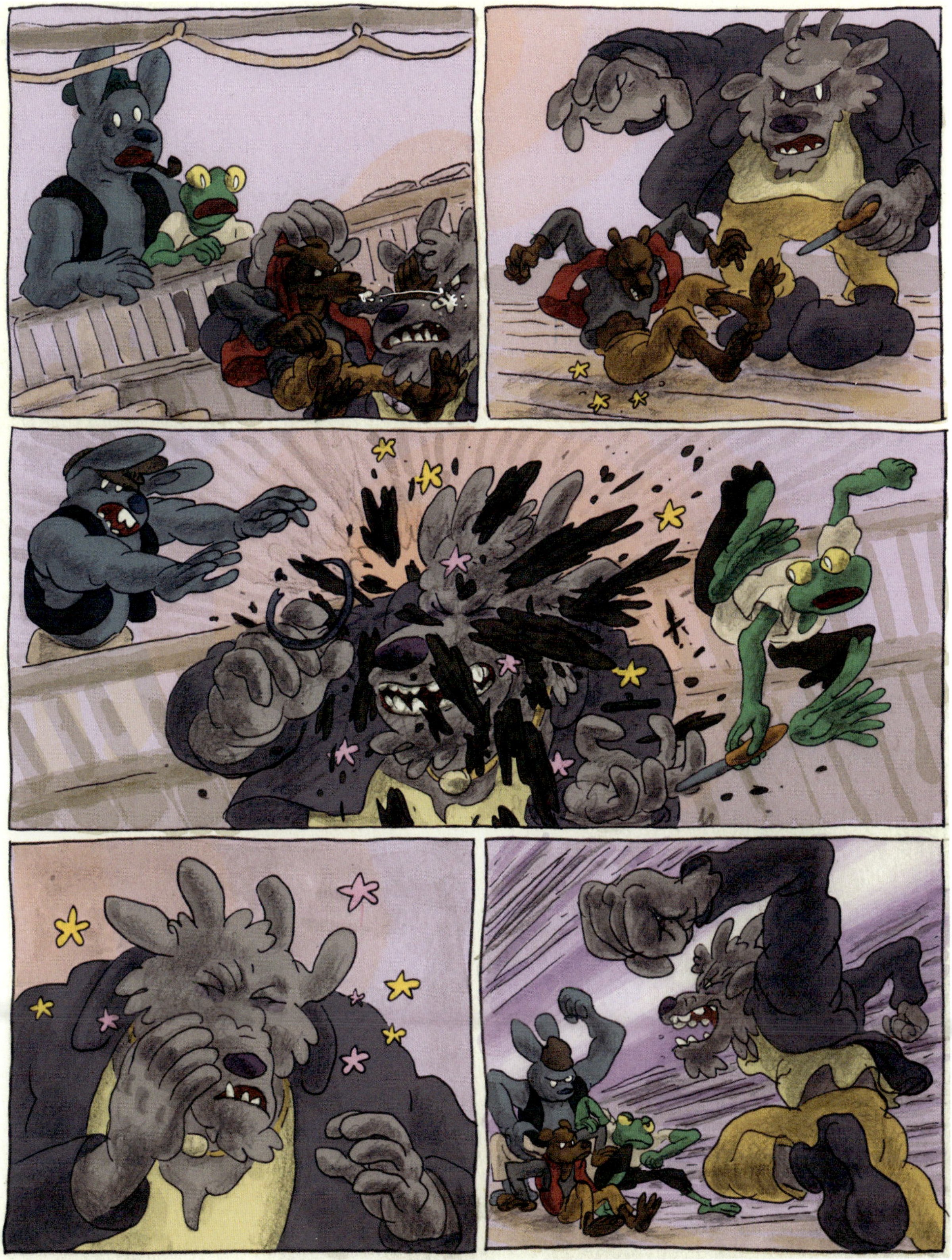

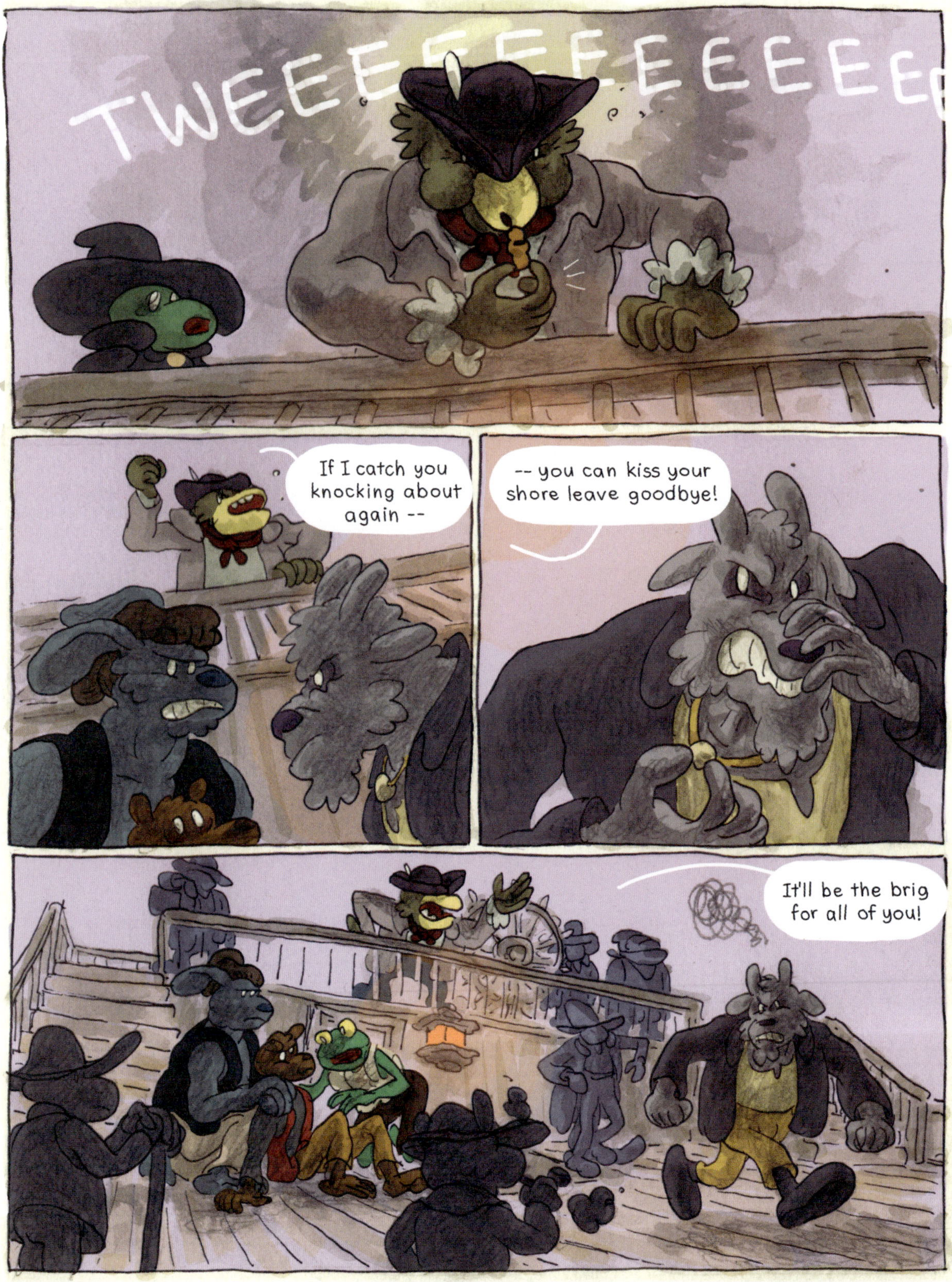
TWEEEEEEEEEEEEEE
If I catch you knocking about again --
-- you can kiss your shore leave goodbye!
It'll be the brig for all of you!

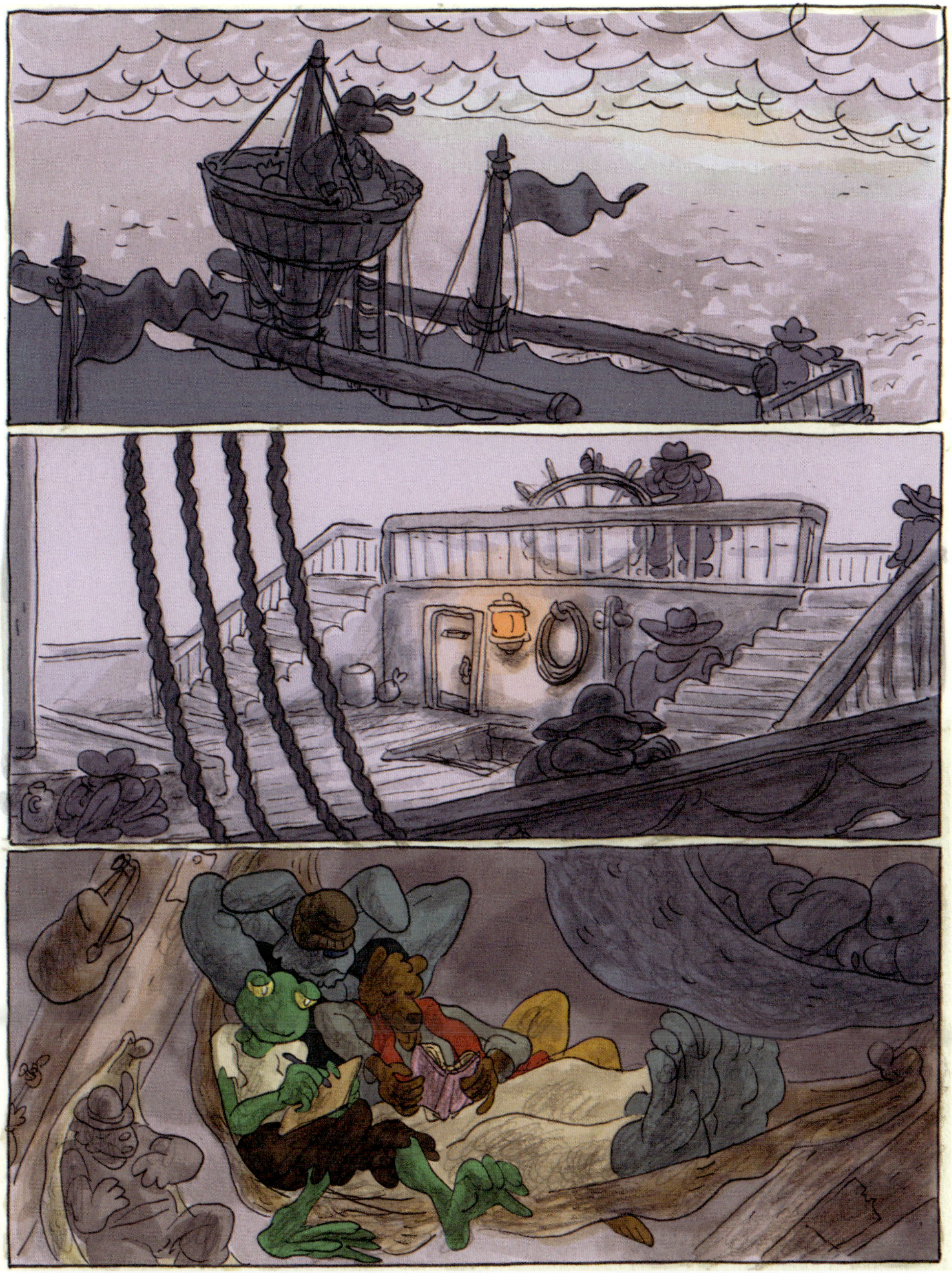

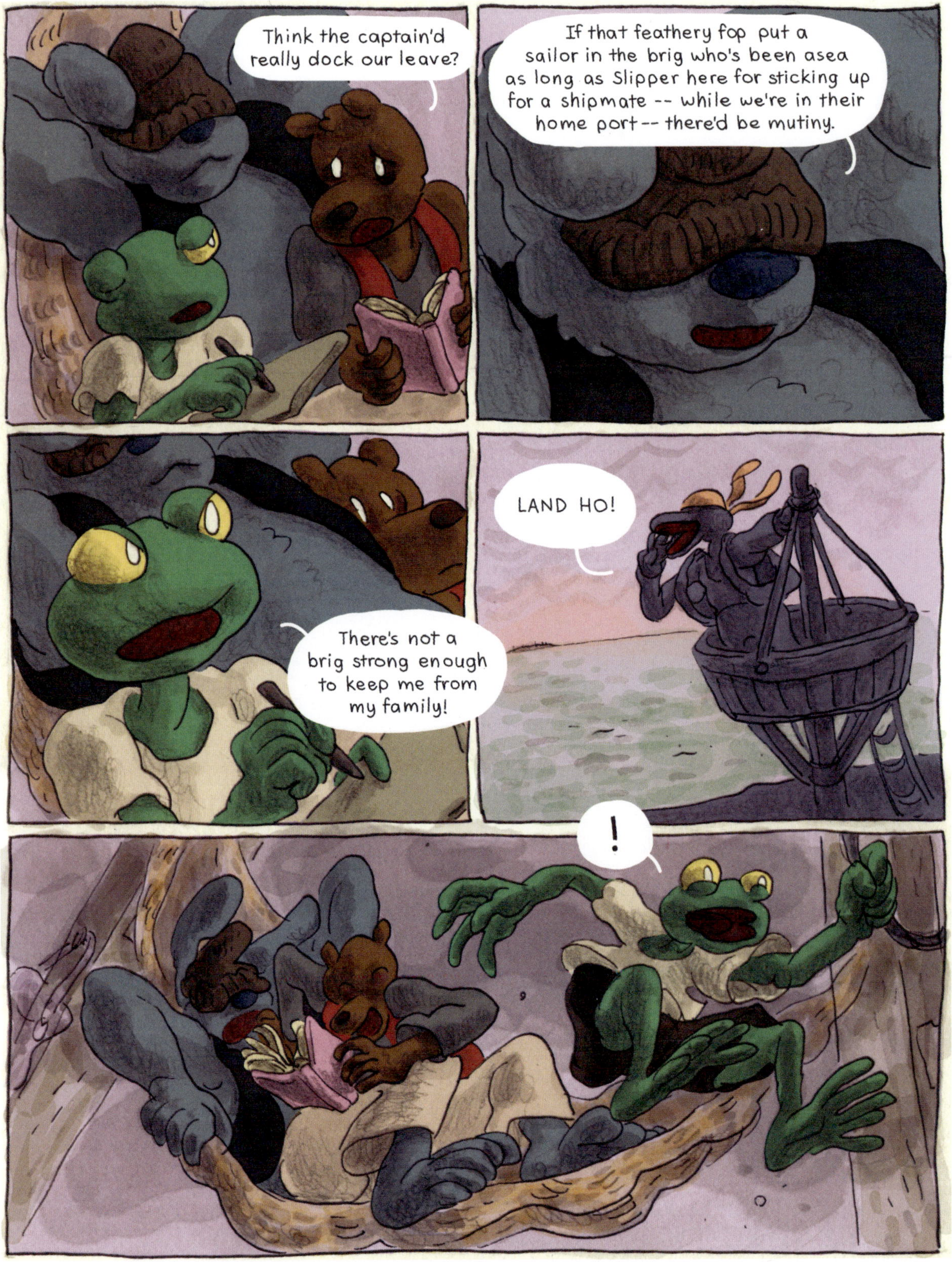
Think the captain'd really dock our leave?
If that feathery fop put a sailor in the brig who's been asea as long as Slipper here for sticking up for a shipmate -- while we're in their home port -- there'd be mutiny.
There's not a brig strong enough to keep me from my family!
LAND HO!
!

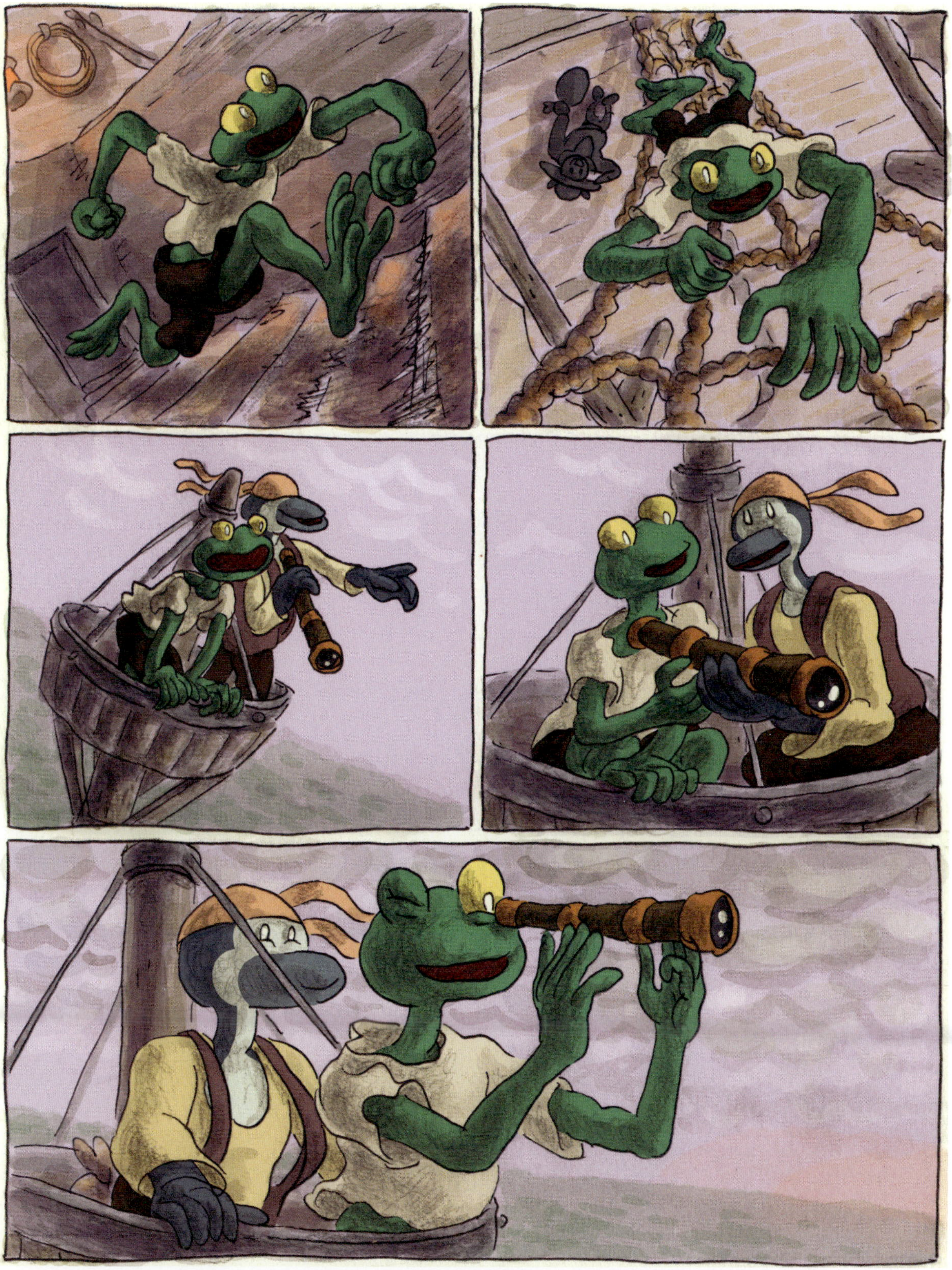

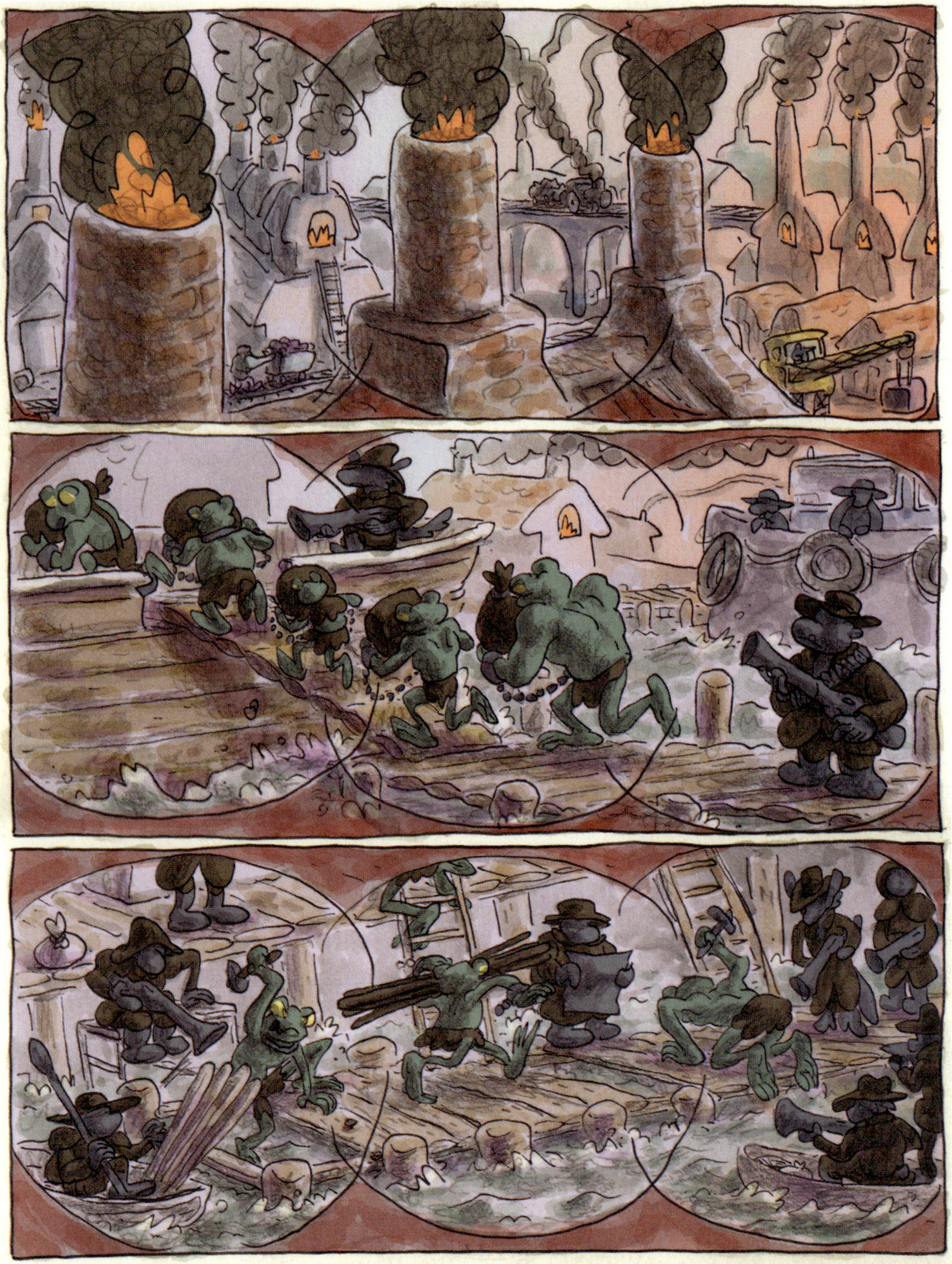

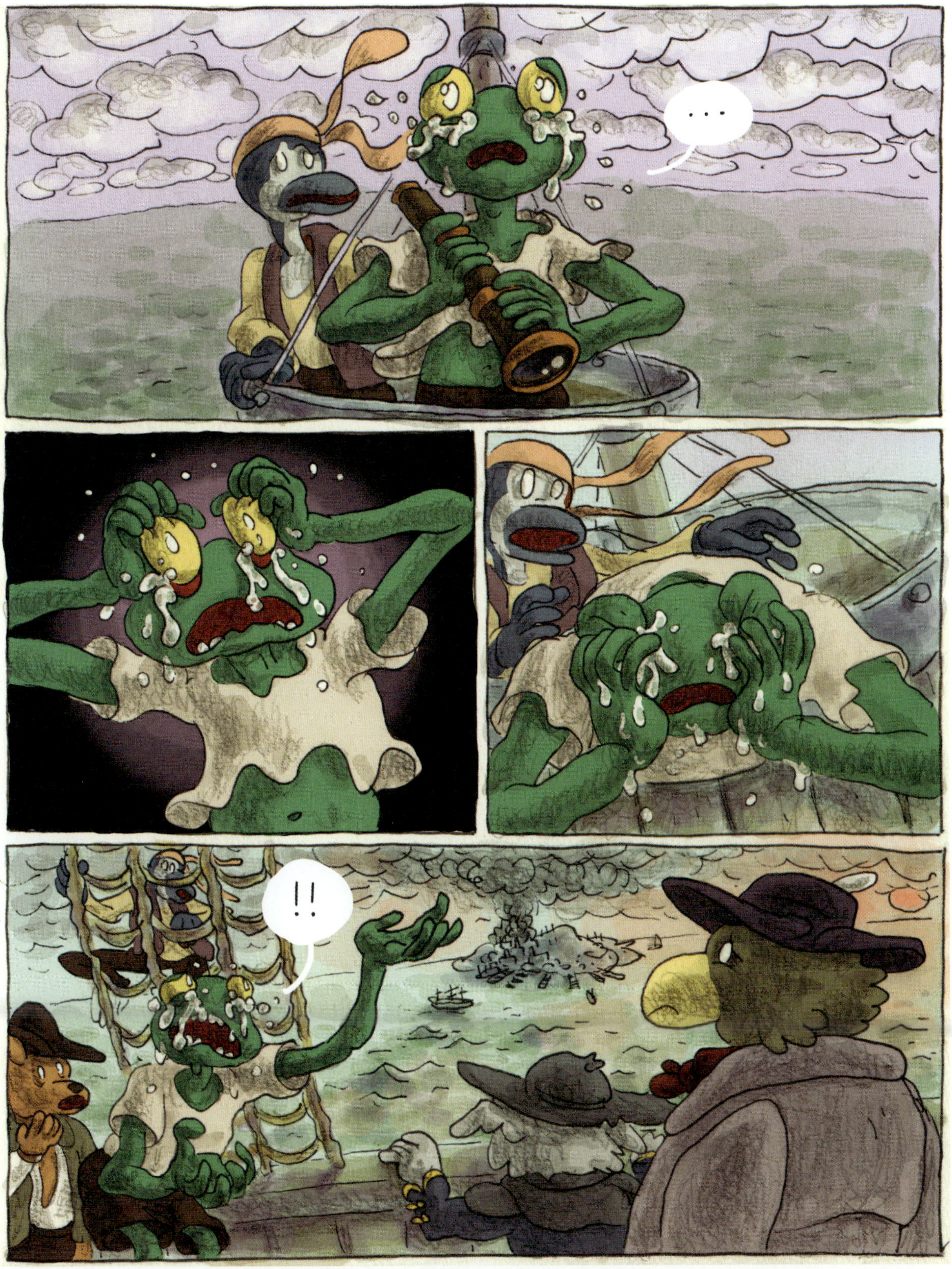
...
!!

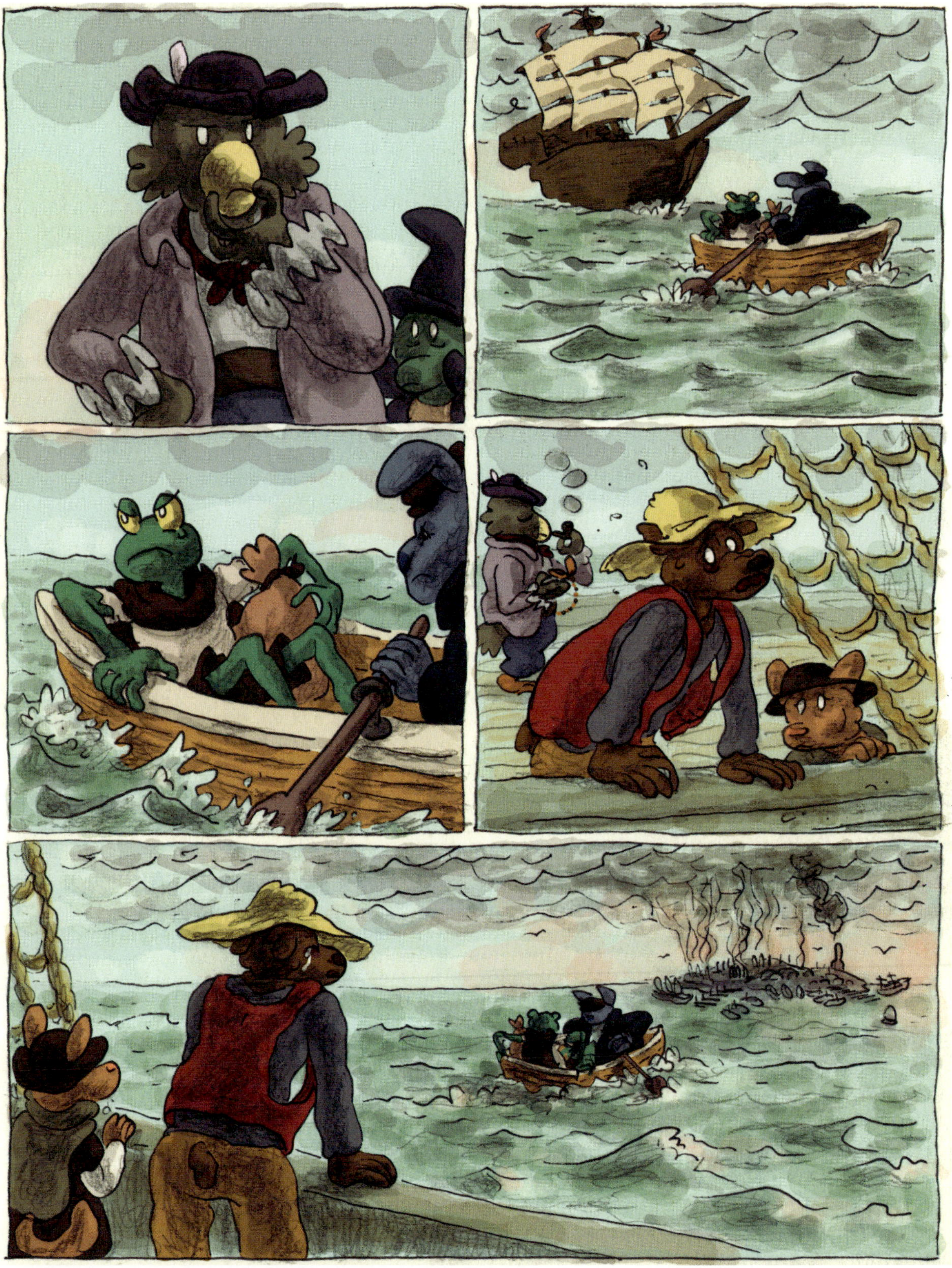

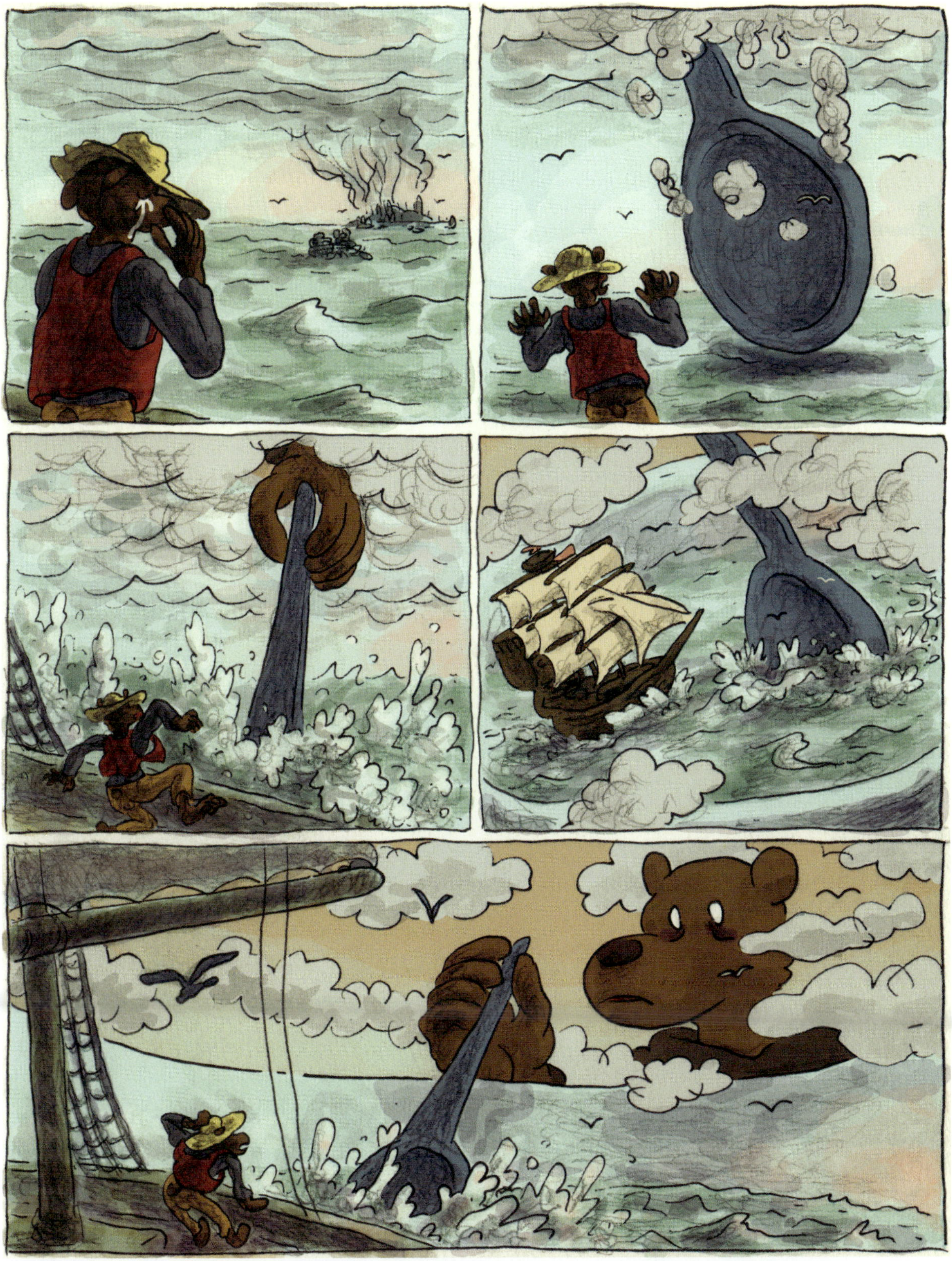

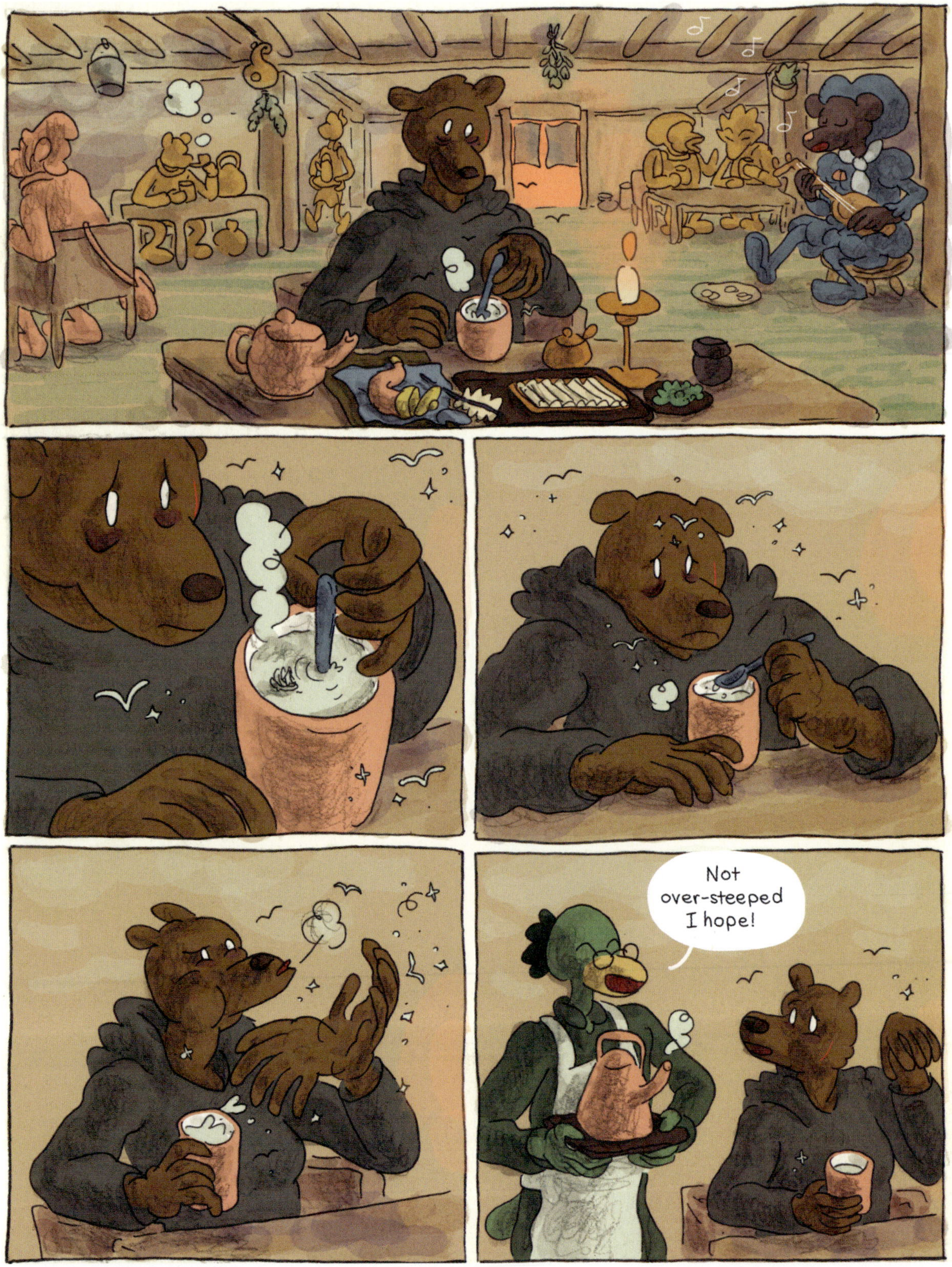
Not over-steeped I hope!

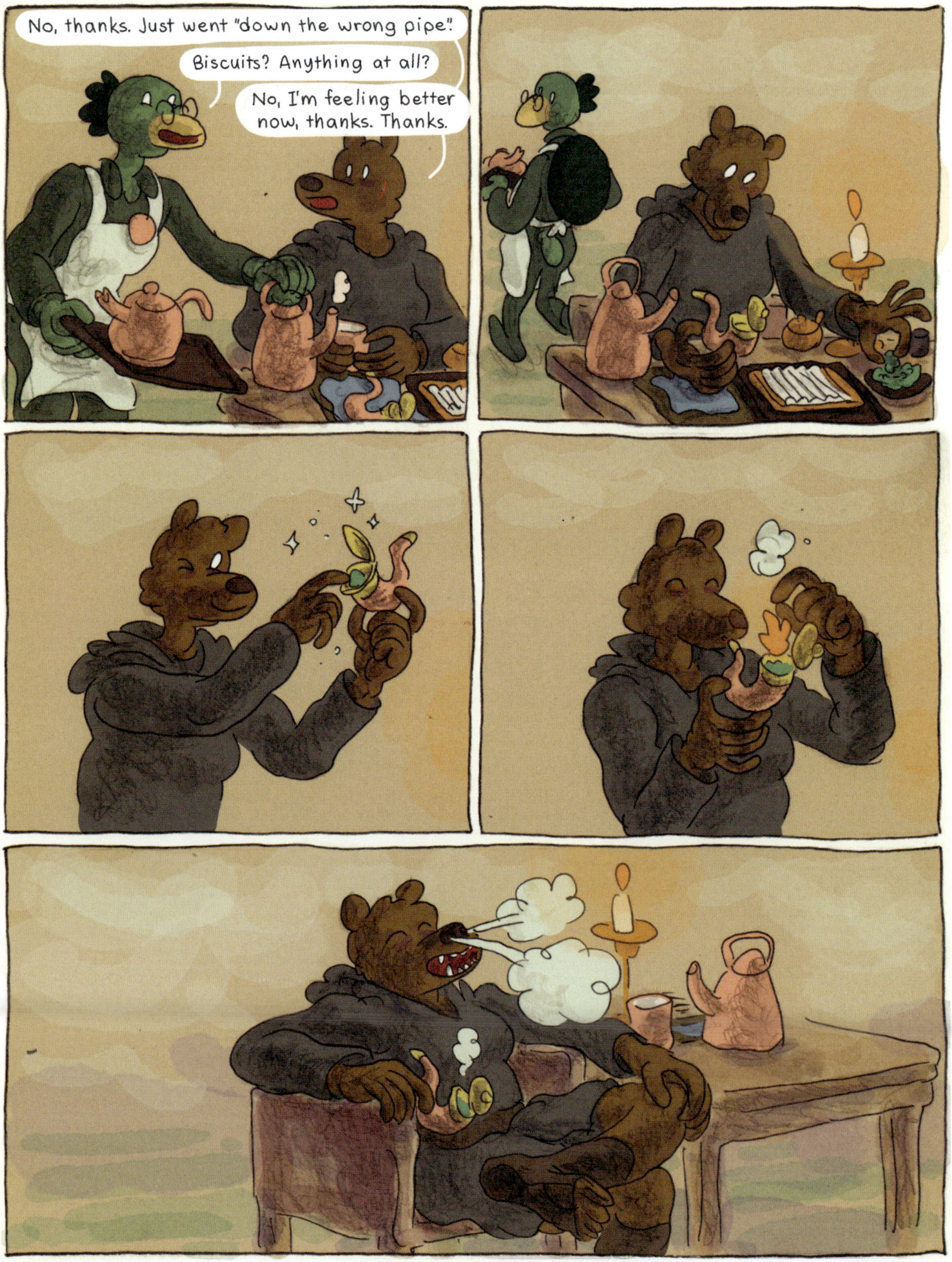
No, thanks. Just went "down the wrong pipe."
Biscuits? Anything at all?
No, I'm feeling better now, thanks. Thanks.

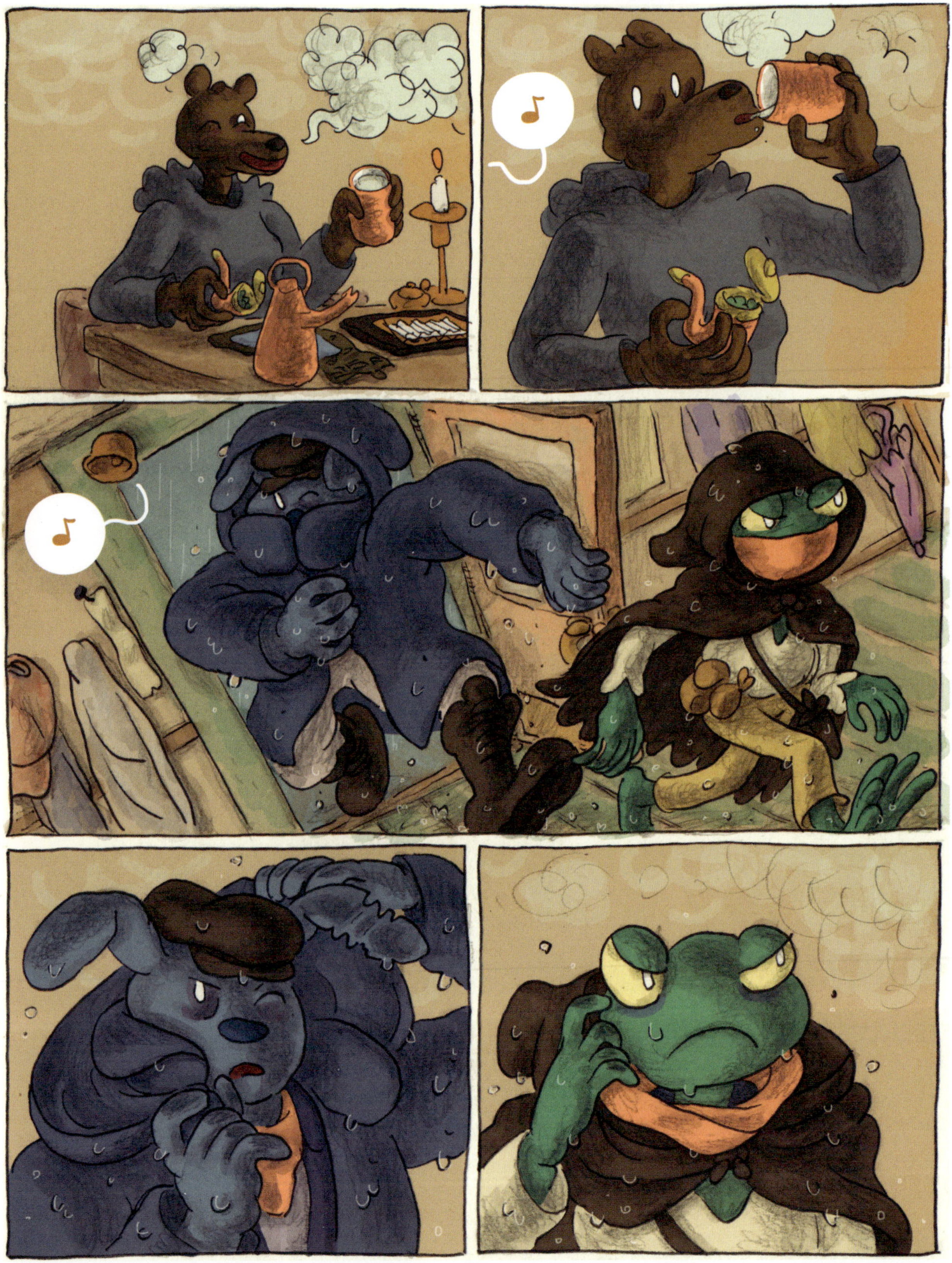

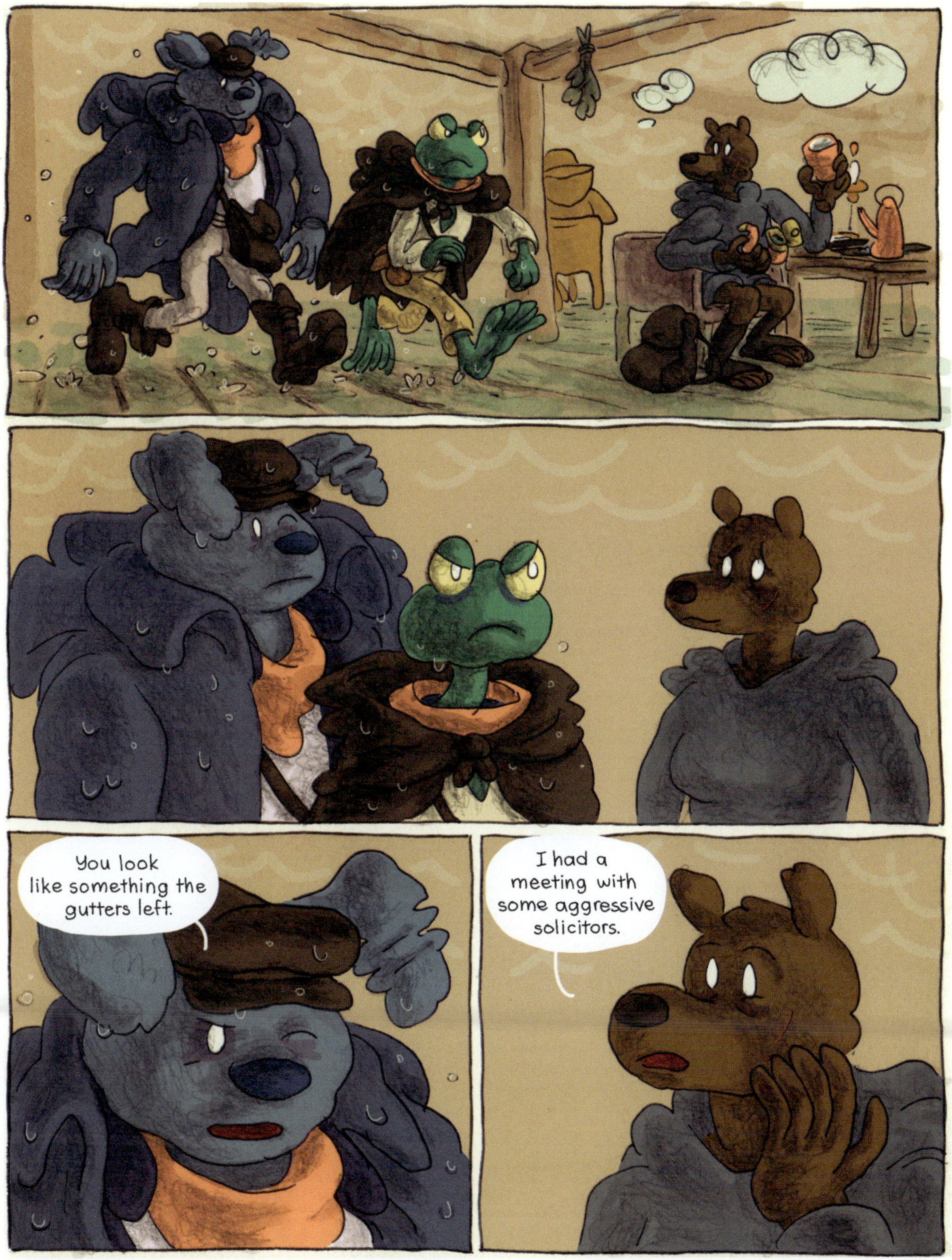
You look like something the gutters left.
I had a meeting with some aggressive solicitors.

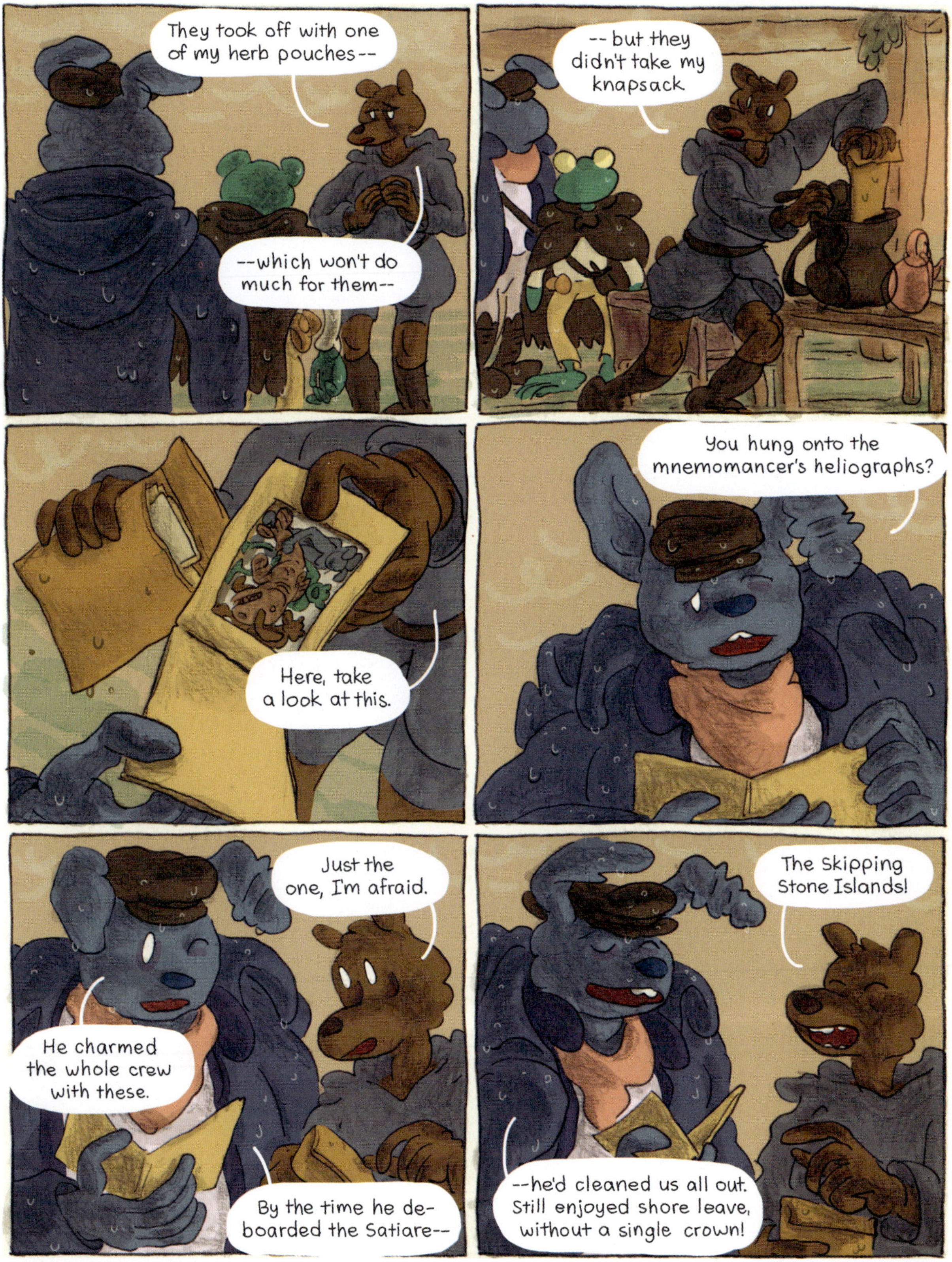
They took off with one of my herb pouches--
--which won't do much for them--
-- but they didn't take my knapsack
Here, take a look at this.
You hung onto the mnemomancer's heliographs?
Just the one, I'm afraid.
He charmed the whole crew with these.
By the time he de-boarded the Satiare--
The Skipping Stone Islands!
--he'd cleaned us all out. Still enjoyed shore leave, without a single crown!

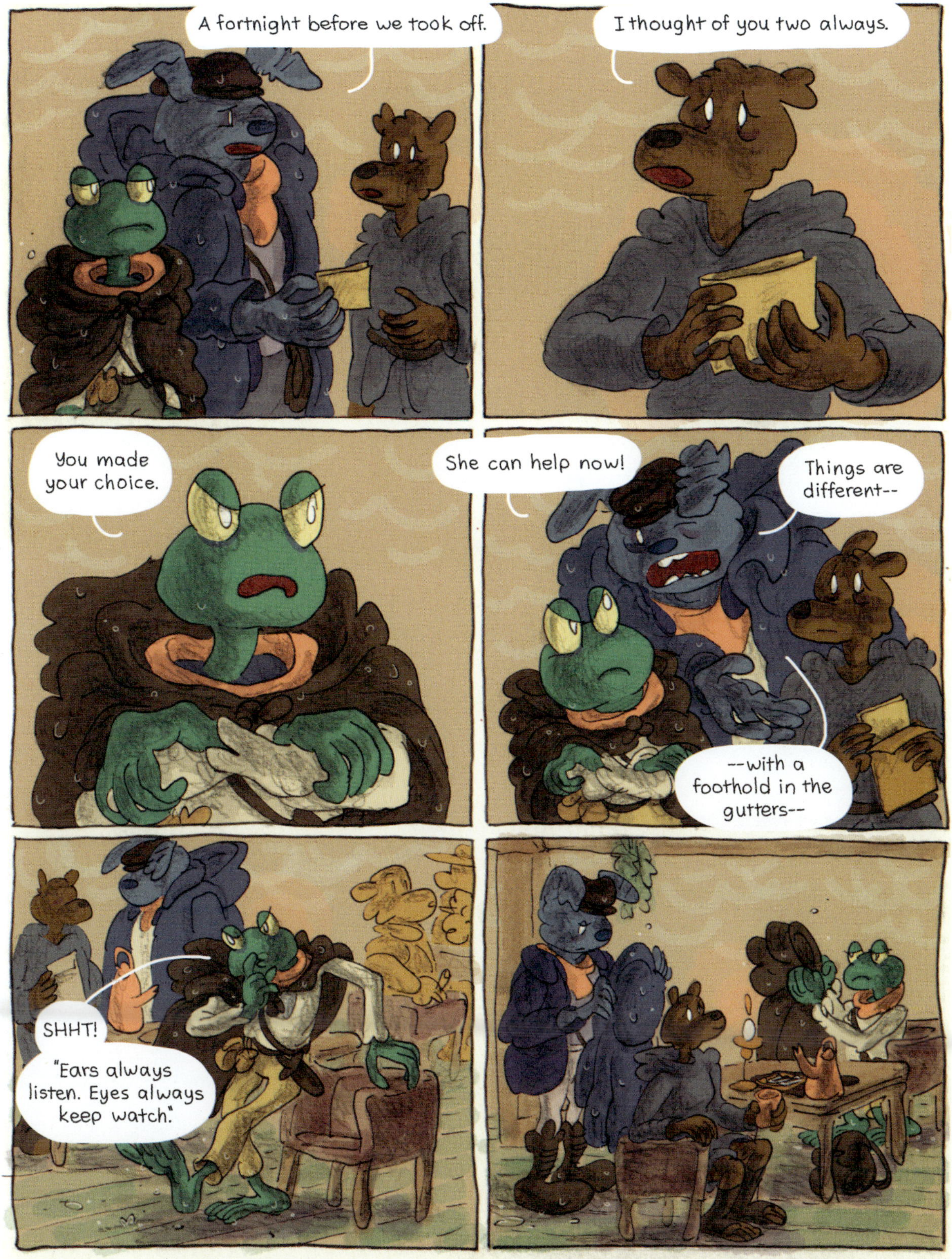
A fortnight before we took off.
I thought of you two always.
You made your choice.
She can help now!
Things are different--
--with a foothold in the gutters--
SHHT!
"Ears always listen. Eyes always keep watch."

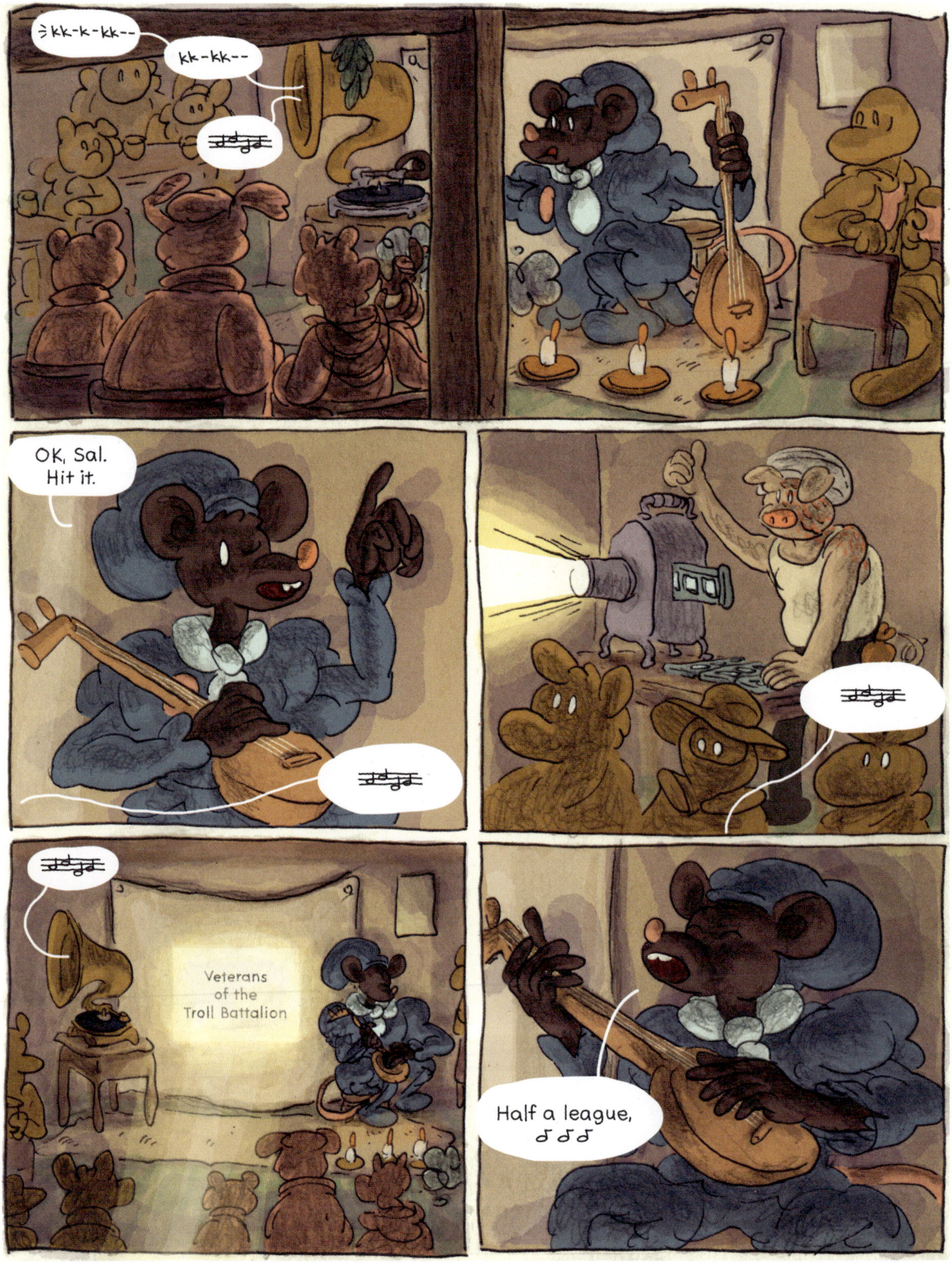
kk-k-kk--
kk-kk--
OK, Sal. Hit it.
Veterans of the Troll Battalion
Half a league,

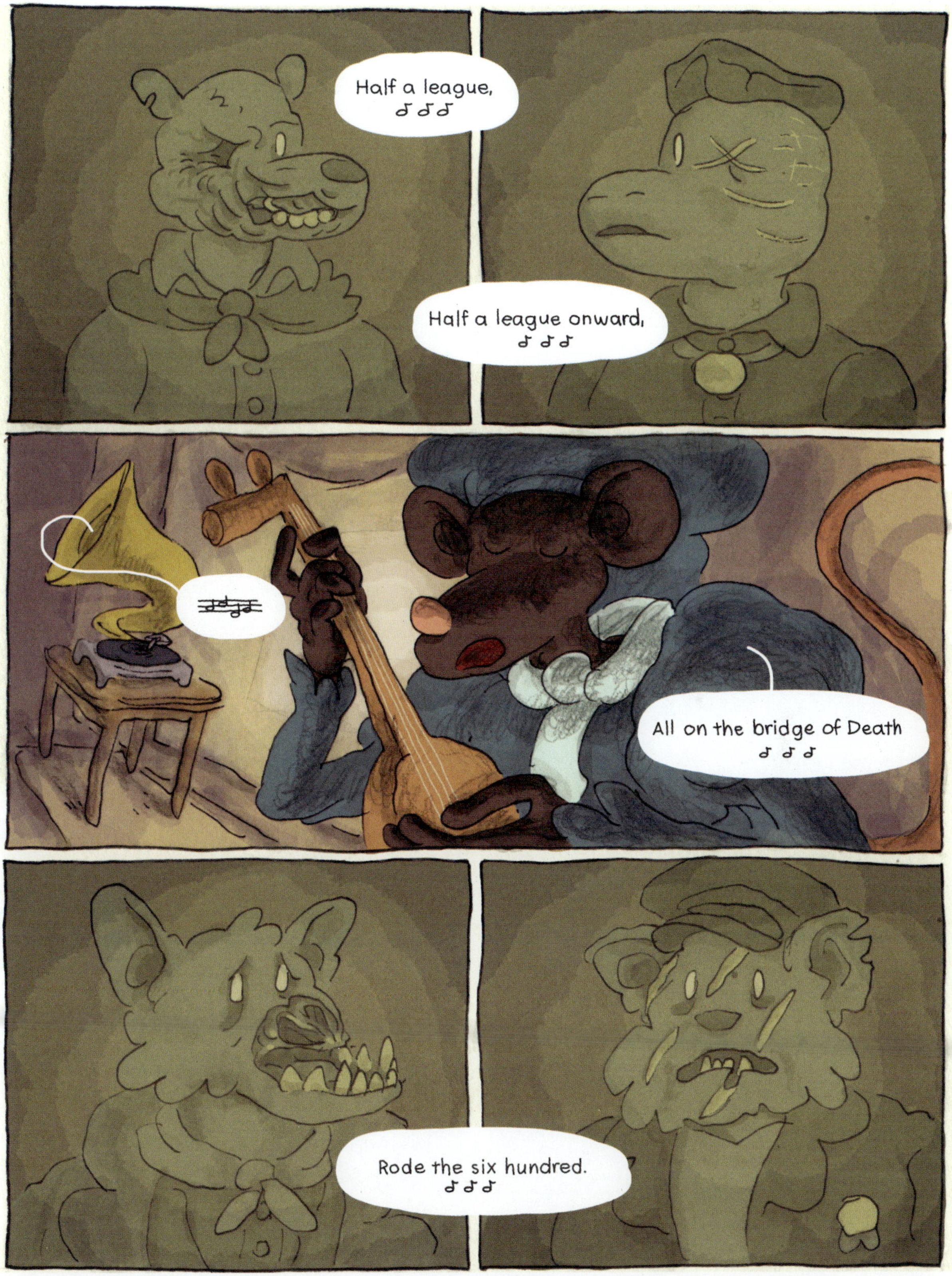
Half a league,
Half a league onward,
All on the bridge of Death
Rode the six hundred.

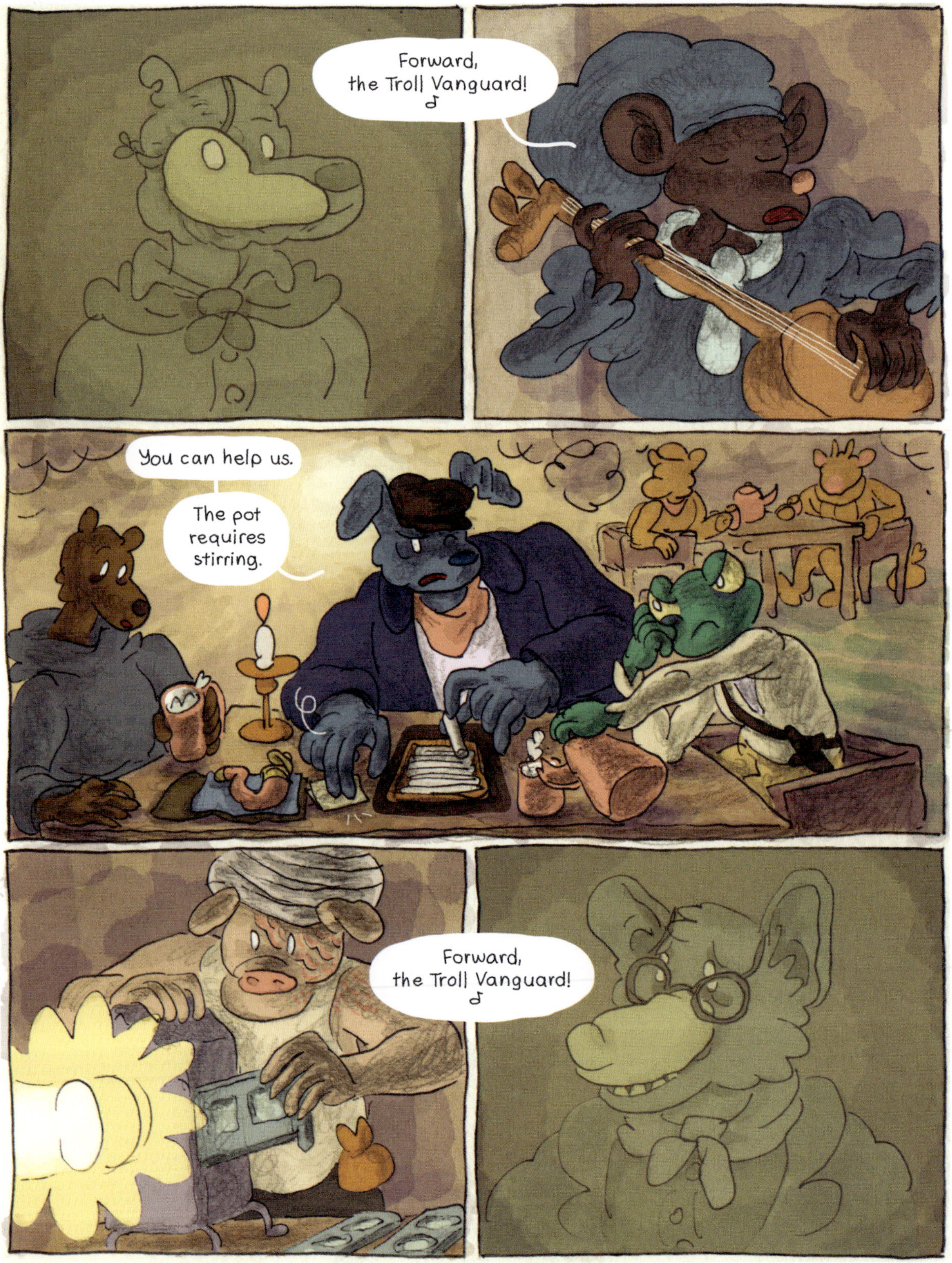
Forward, the Troll Vanguard!
You can help us.
The pot requires stirring.
Forward, the Troll Vanguard!

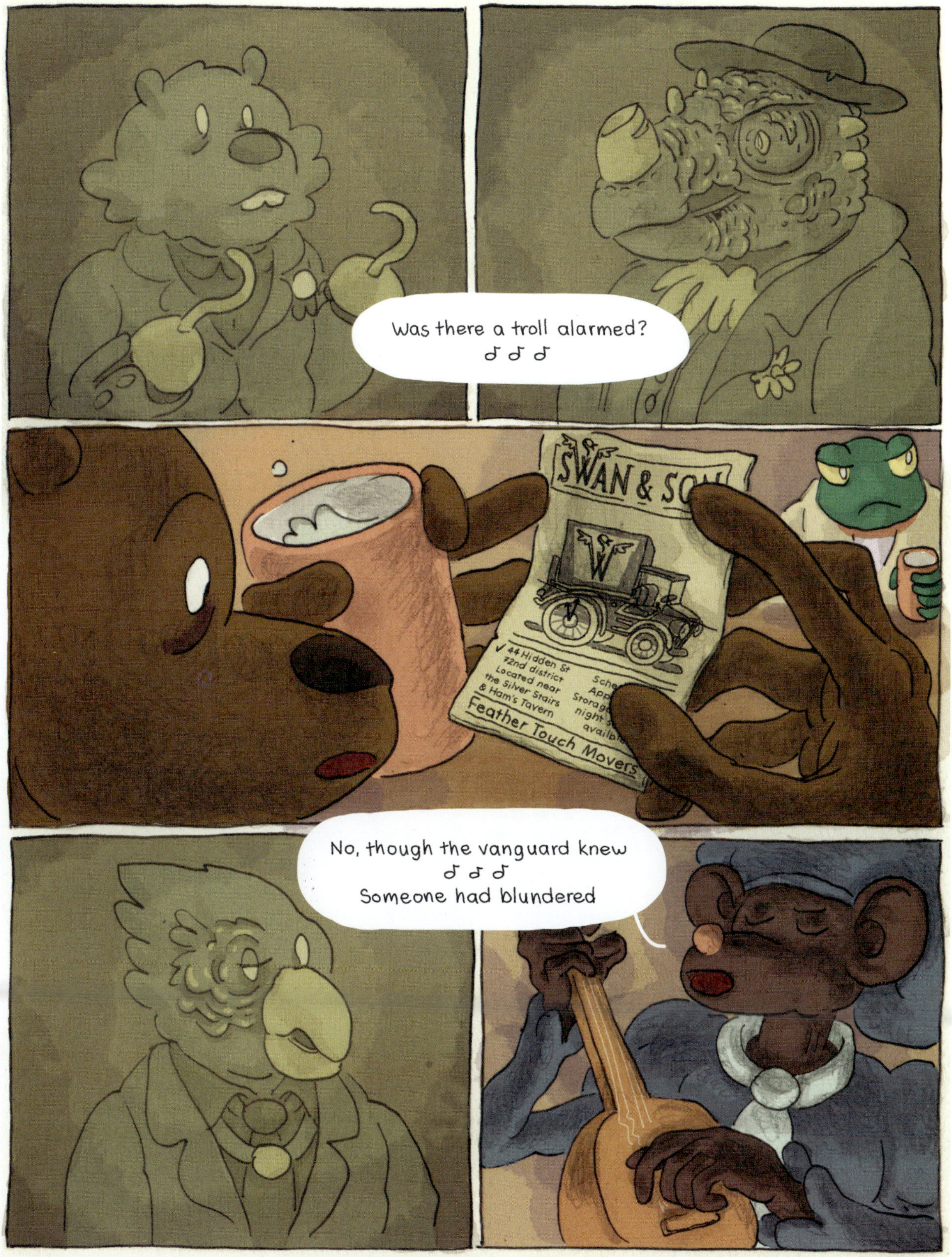
Was there a troll alarmed?
♪ ♪ ♪
44 Hidden St
72nd district
Located near
the Silver Stairs
& Ham's Tavern
Feather Touch Movers
No, though the vanguard knew
♪ ♪ ♪
Someone had blundered

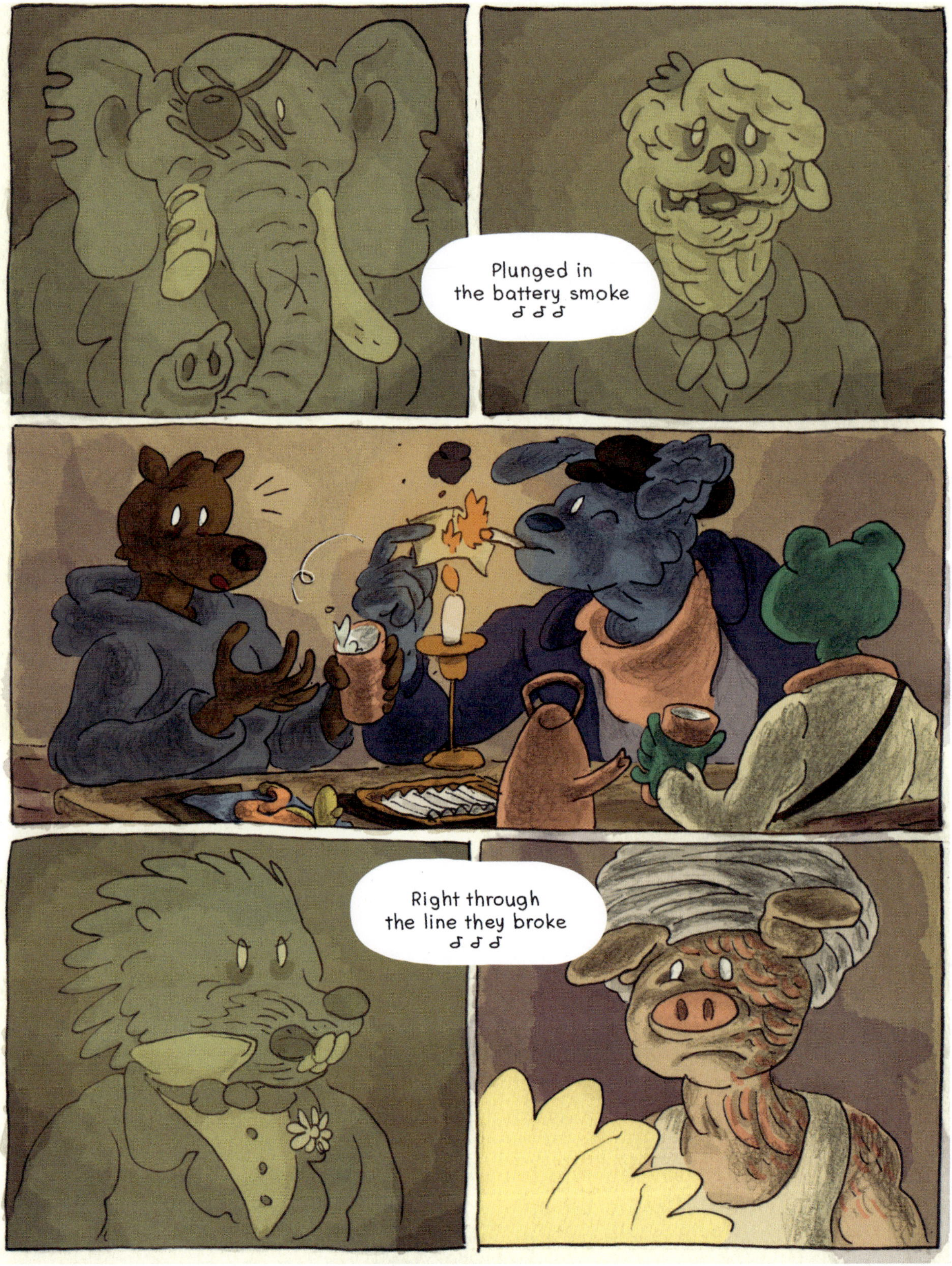
Plunged in
the battery smoke
♩♩♩
Right through
the line they broke
♩♩♩

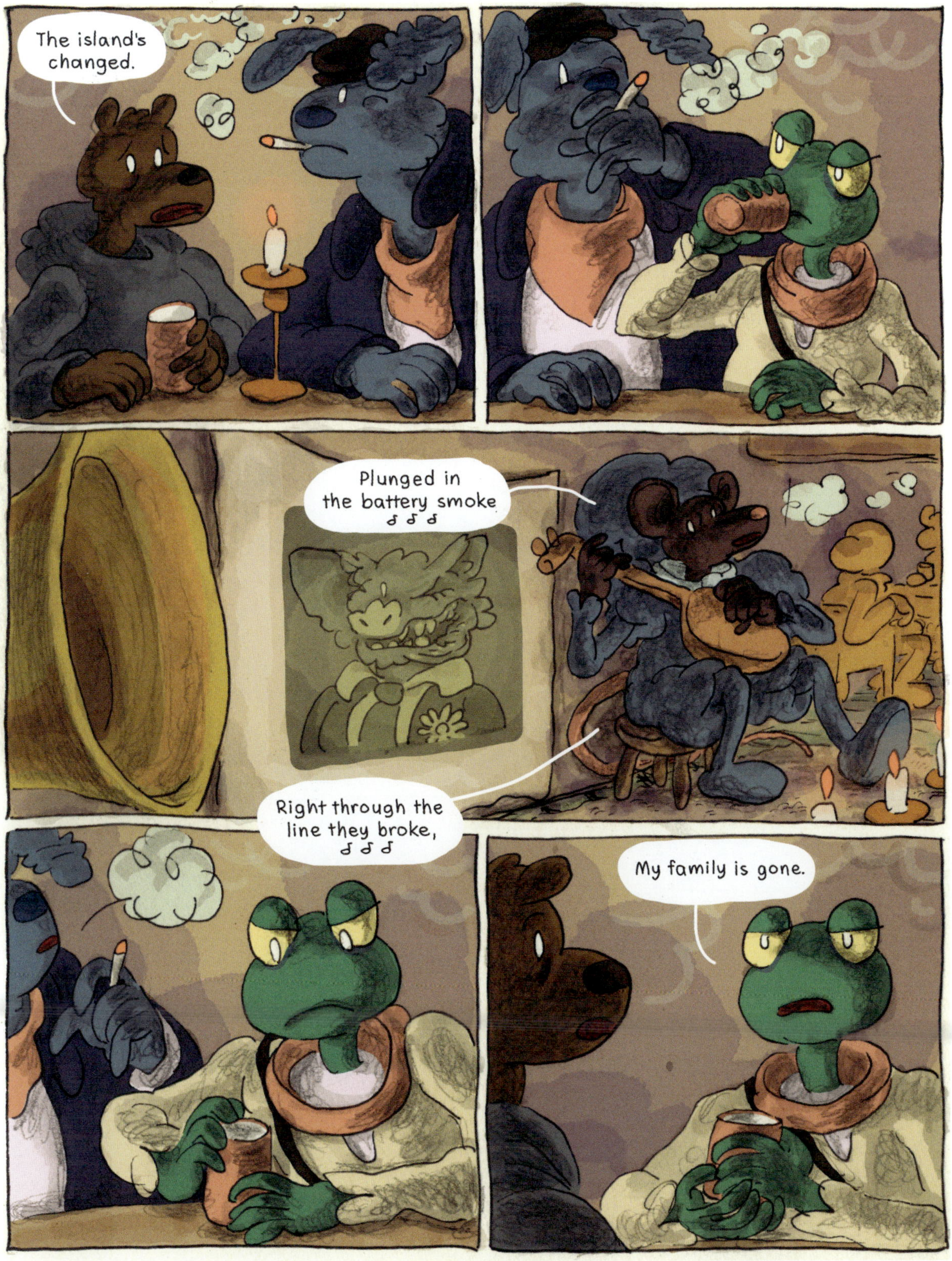
The island's changed.
Plunged in the battery smoke ♪♪♪
Right through the line they broke, ♪♪♪
My family is gone.

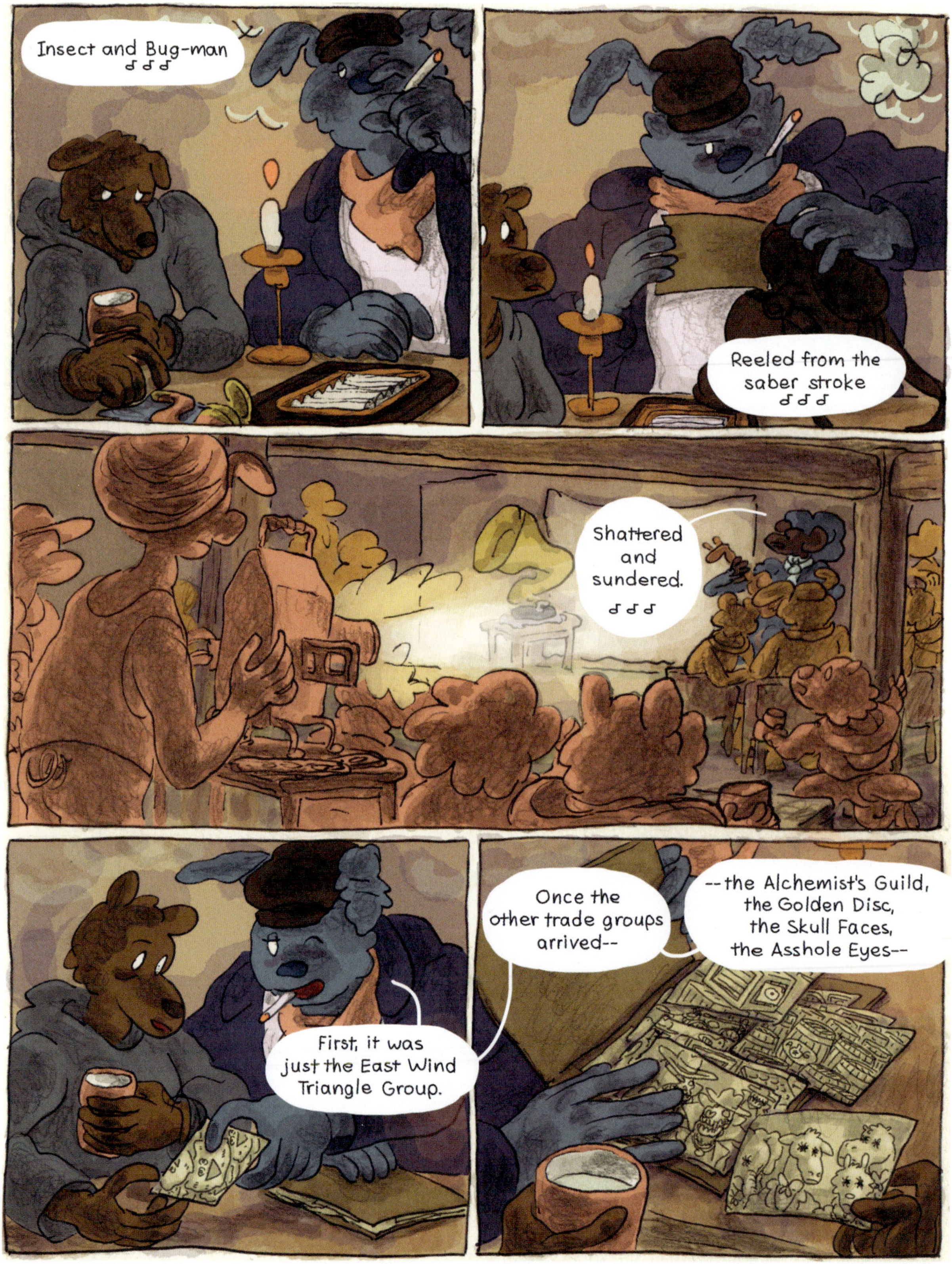
Insect and Bug-man
Reeled from the saber stroke
Shattered and sundered.
First, it was just the East Wind Triangle Group.
Once the other trade groups arrived--
--the Alchemist's Guild, the Golden Disc, the Skull Faces, the Asshole Eyes--

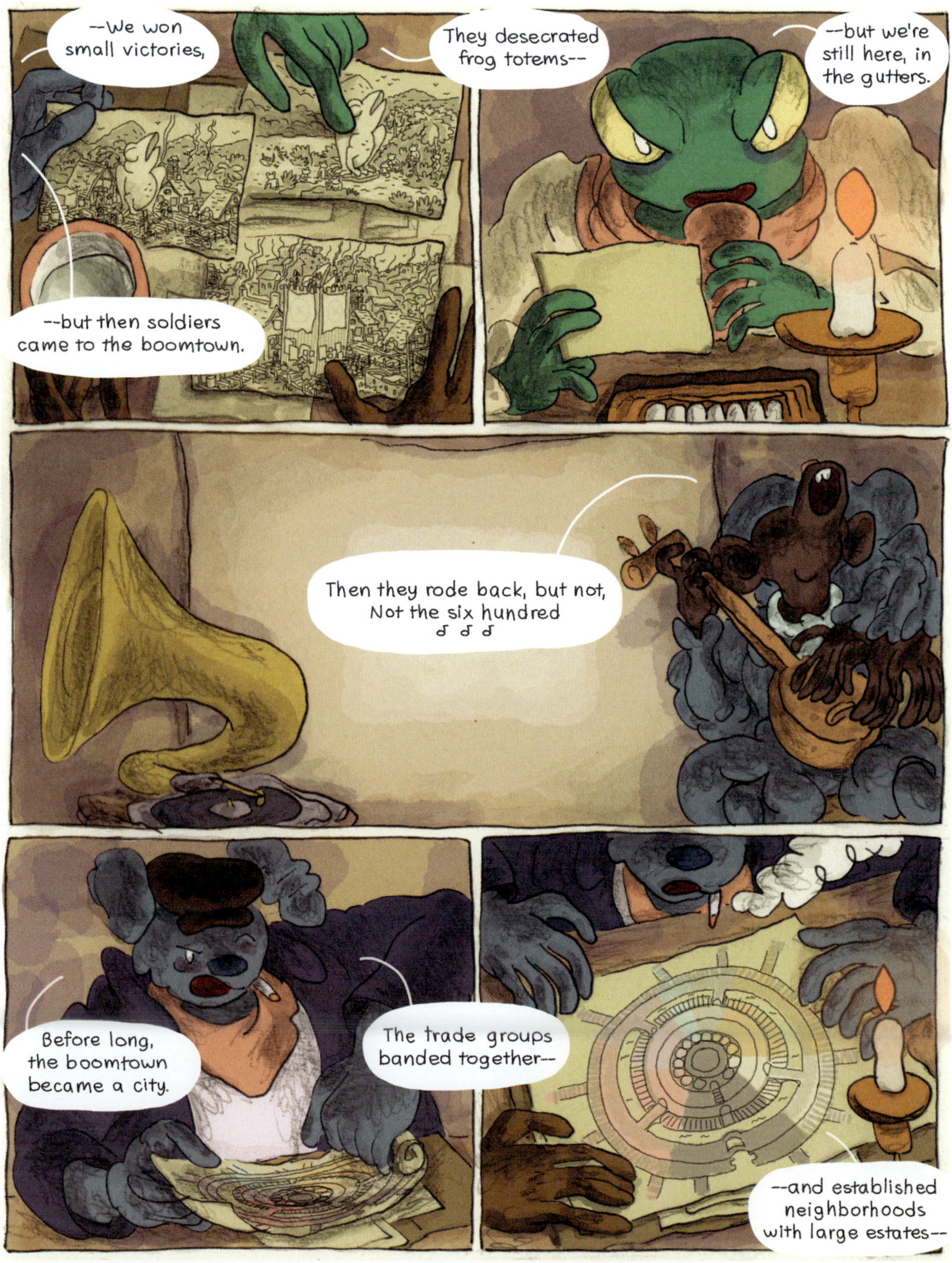
--We won small victories,
They desecrated frog totems--
--but then soldiers came to the boomtown.
--but we're still here, in the gutters.
Then they rode back, but not, Not the six hundred
Before long, the boomtown became a city.
The trade groups banded together--
--and established neighborhoods with large estates--

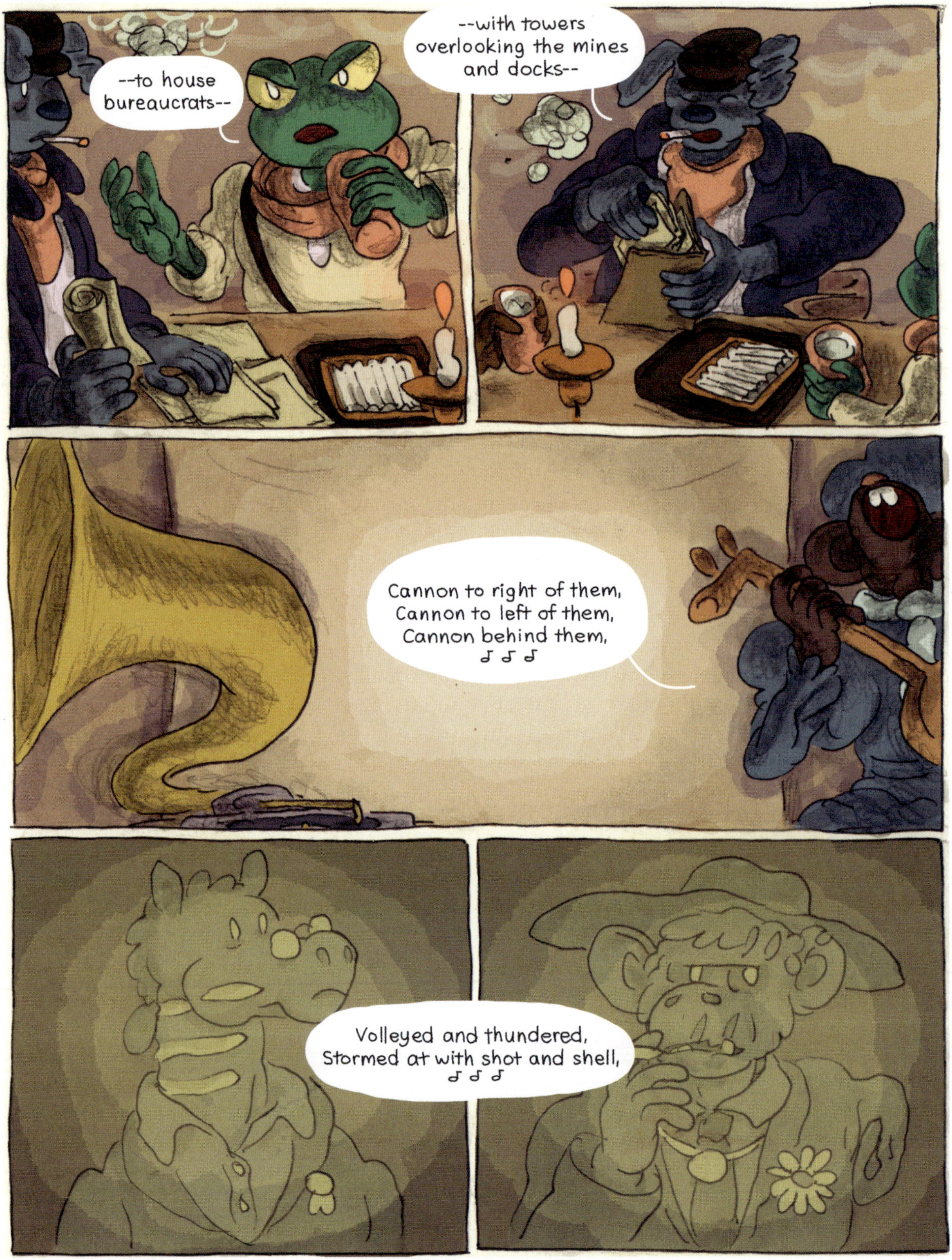
--to house bureaucrats--
--with towers overlooking the mines and docks--
Cannon to right of them, Cannon to left of them, Cannon behind them, ♪ ♪ ♪
Volleyed and thundered, Stormed at with shot and shell, ♪ ♪ ♪

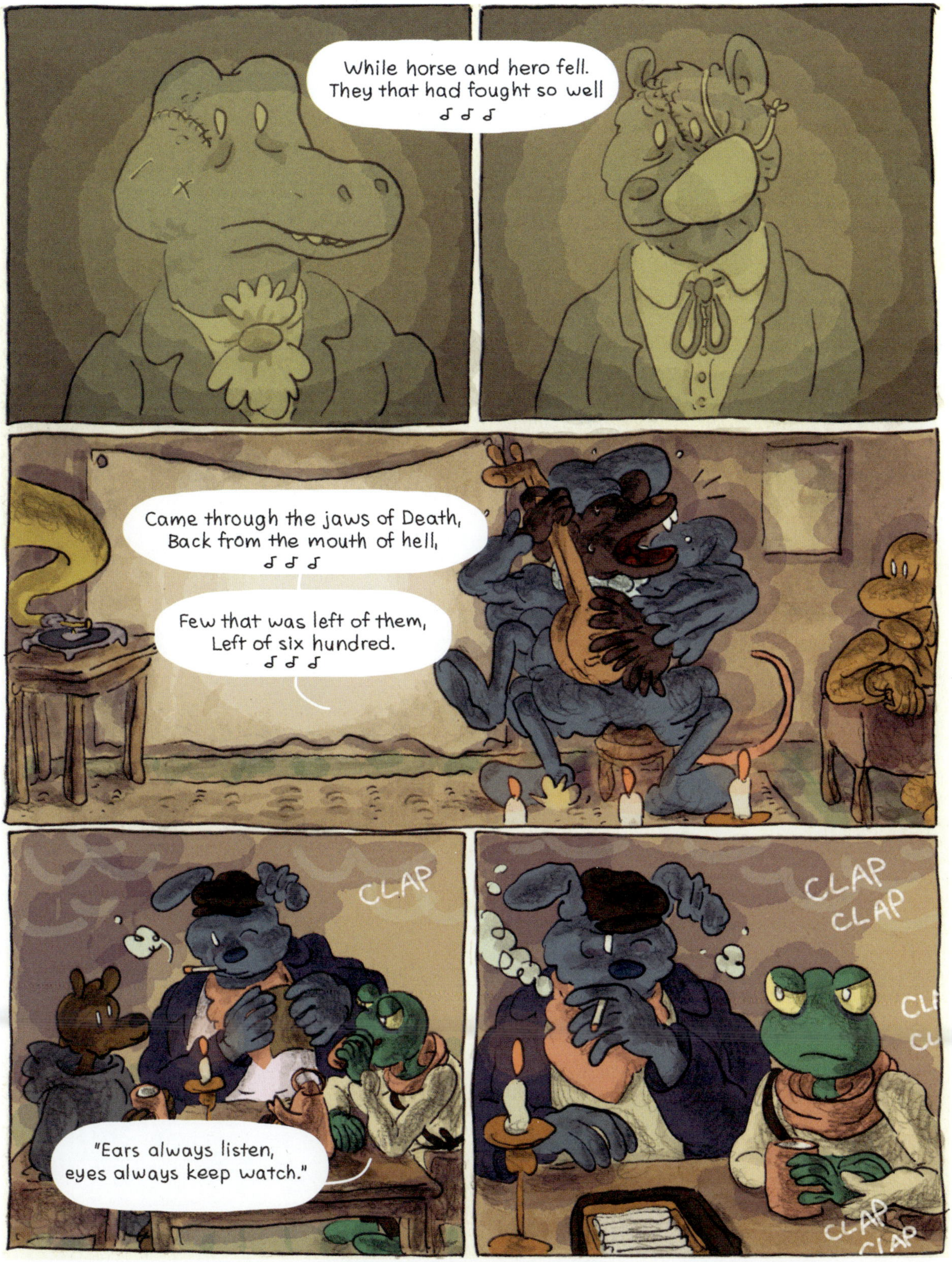
While horse and hero fell. They that had fought so well ♩♩♩
Came through the jaws of Death, Back from the mouth of hell, ♩♩♩
Few that was left of them, Left of six hundred. ♩♩♩
CLAP
"Ears always listen, eyes always keep watch."
CLAP CLAP
CLAP CLAP

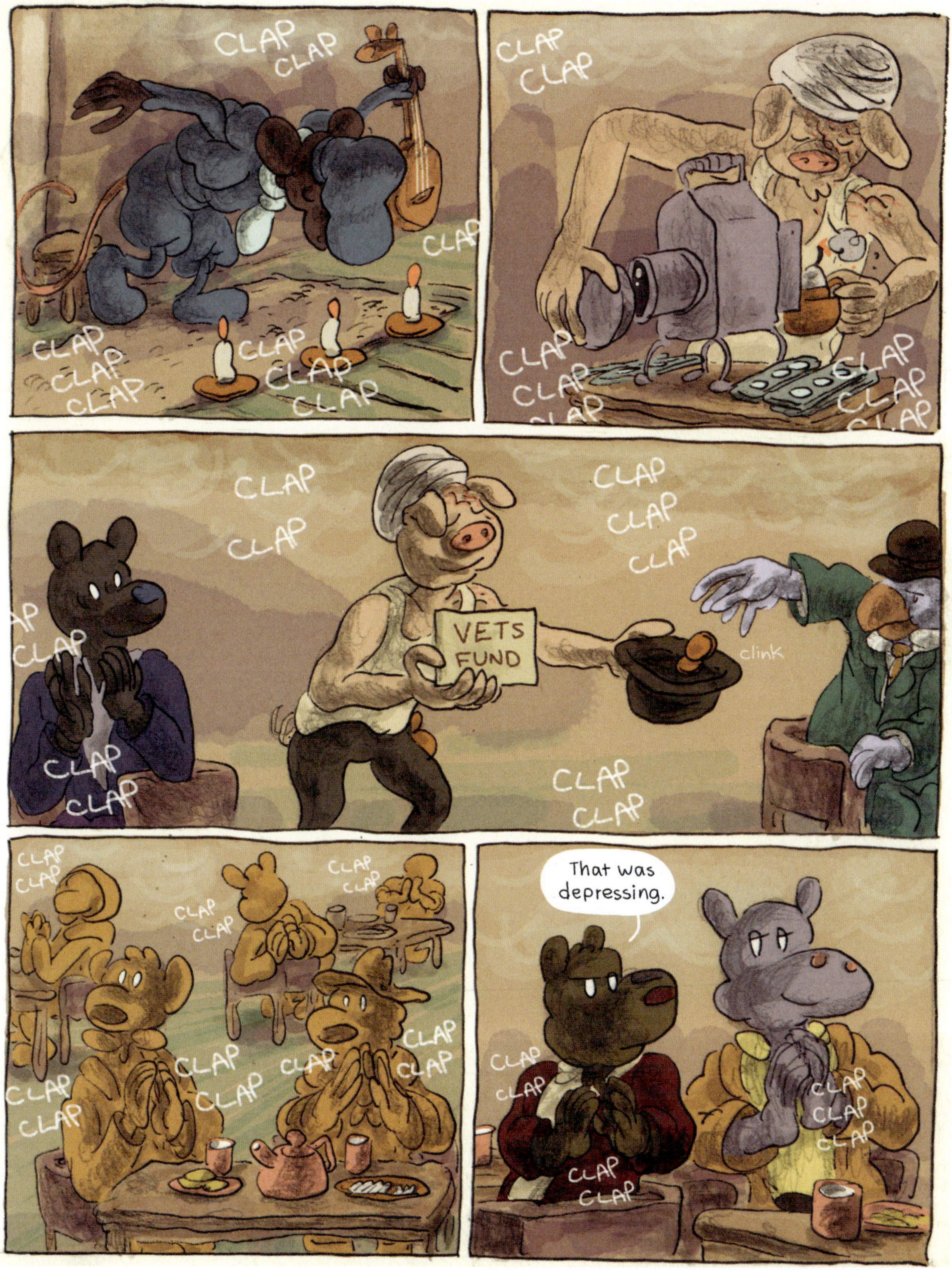
CLAP
CLAP
CLAP
CLAP
CLAP
CLAP
CLAP
CLAP
CLAP
CLAP
CLAP
CLAP
CLAP
CLAP
CLAP
CLAP
CLAP
CLAP
VETS FUND
clink
CLAP
CLAP
CLAP
CLAP
CLAP
CLAP
That was depressing.
CLAP
CLAP
CLAP
CLAP
CLAP
CLAP

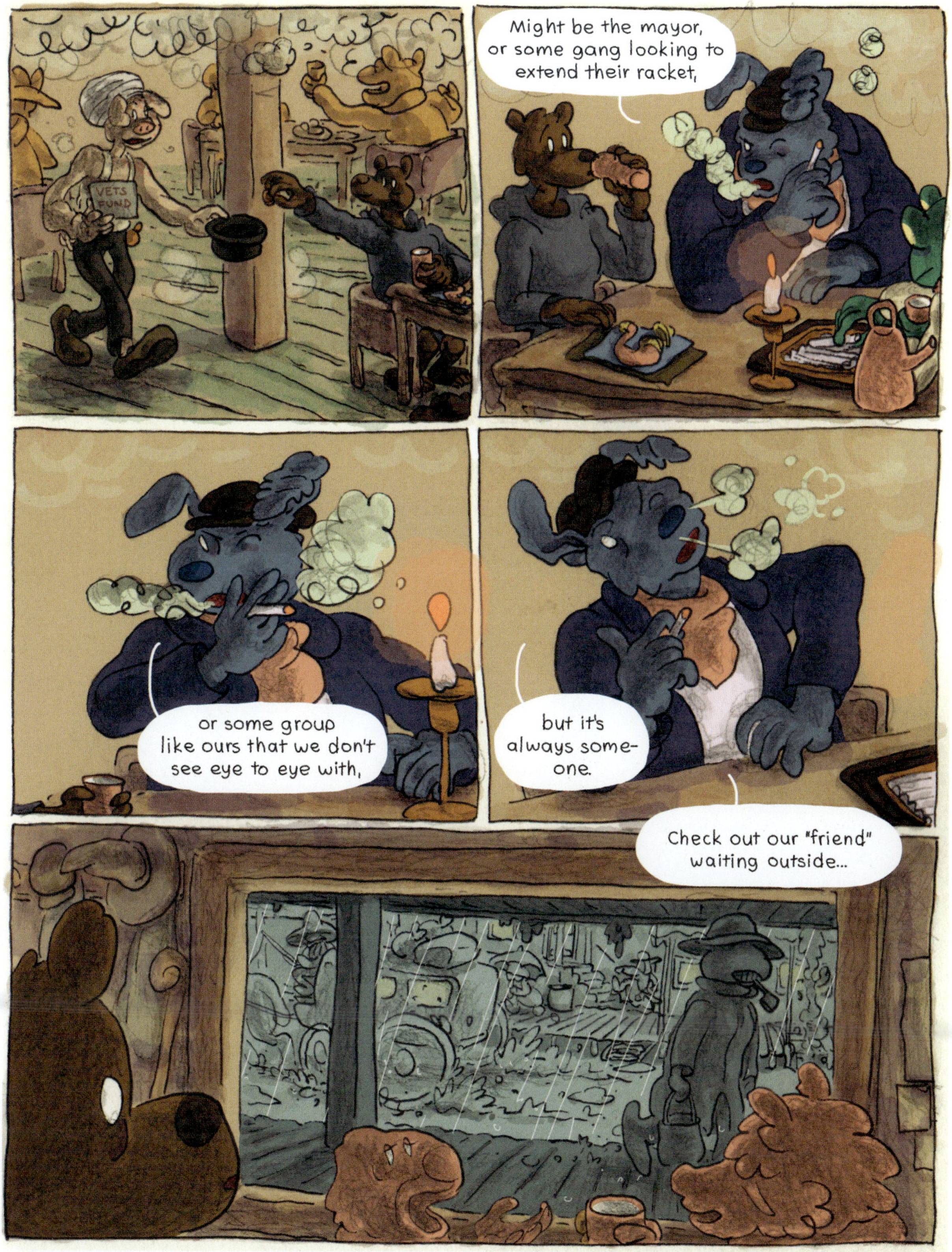
VETS FUND
Might be the mayor, or some gang looking to extend their racket,
or some group like ours that we don't see eye to eye with,
but it's always some-one.
Check out our "friend" waiting outside...

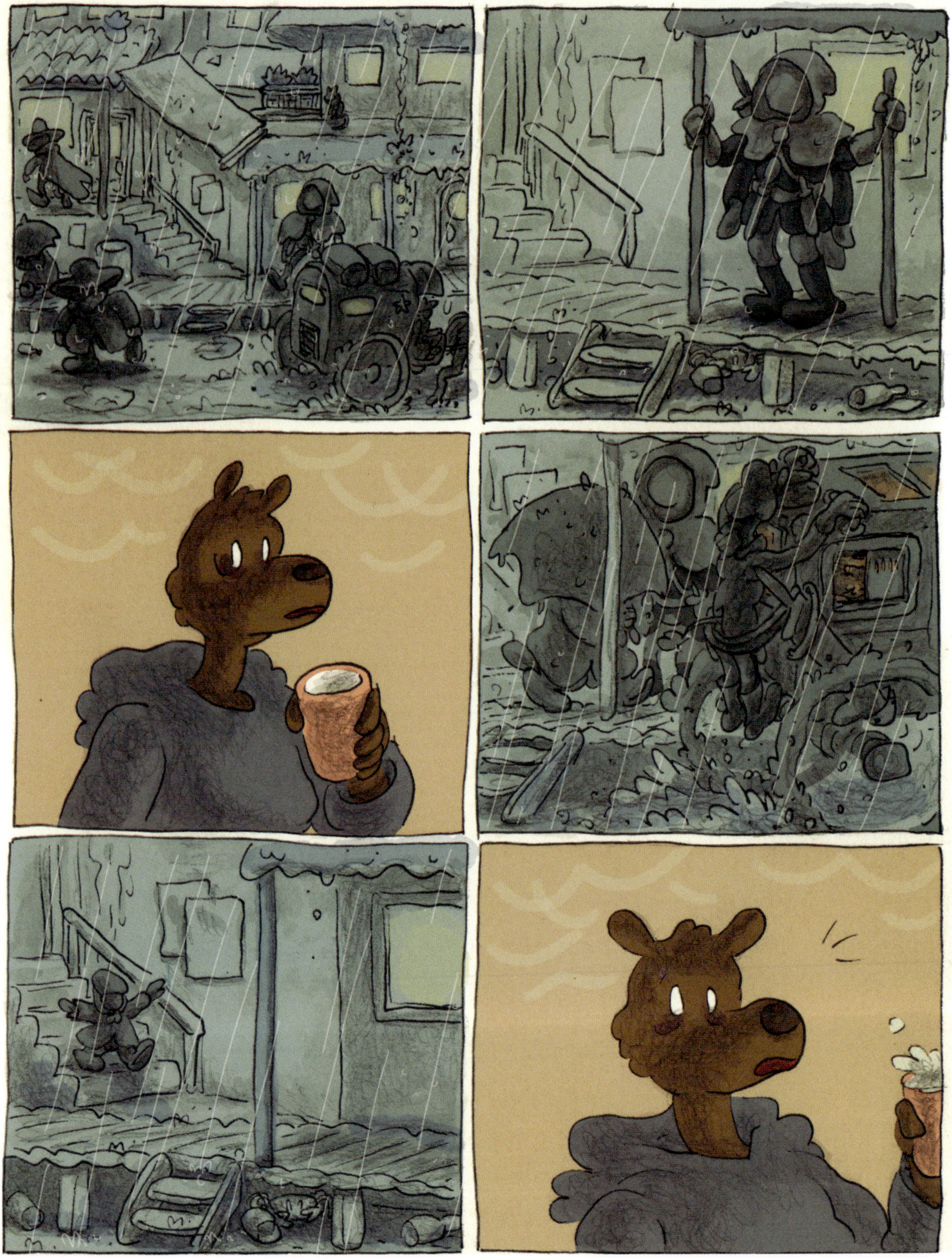

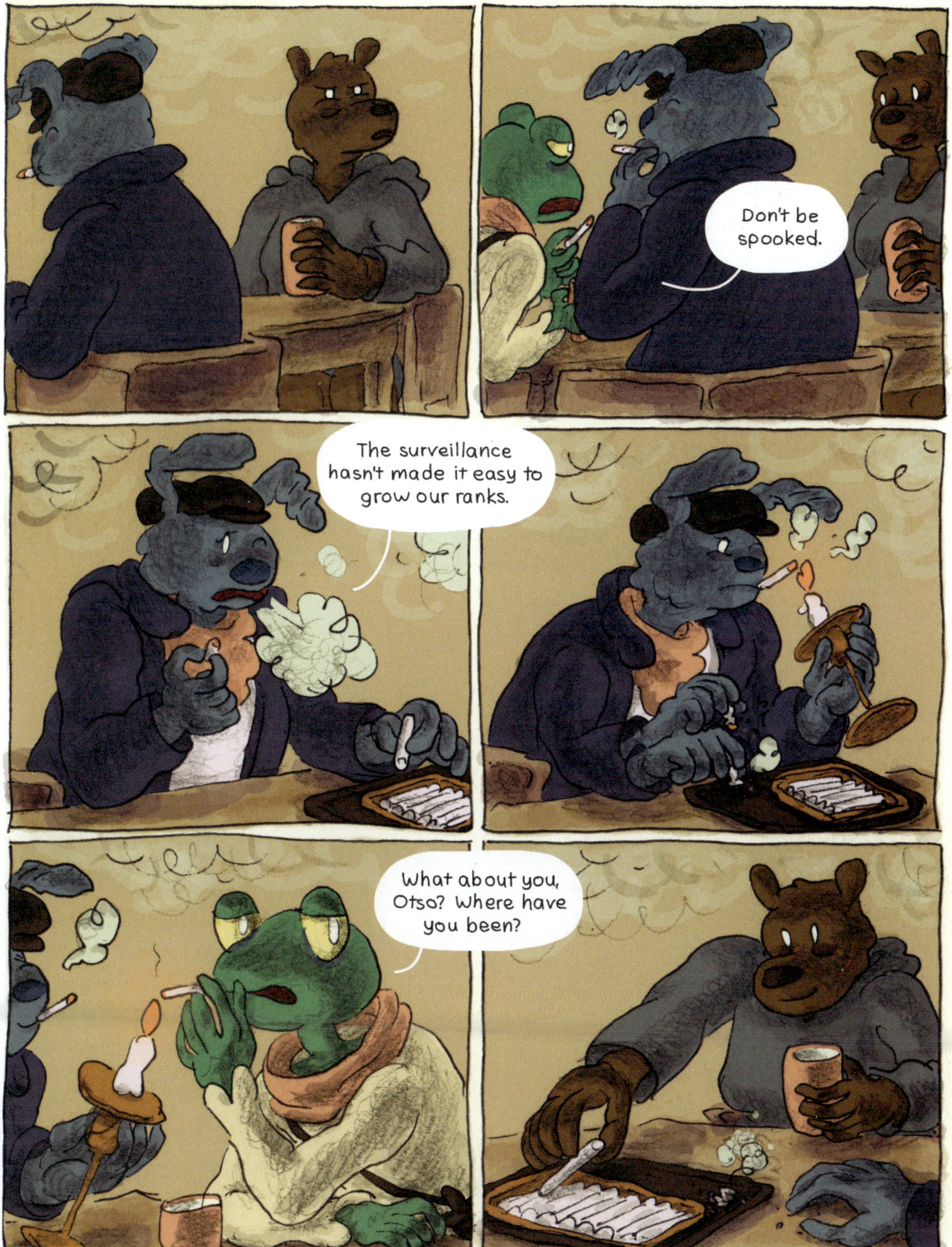

Don't be spooked.
The surveillance hasn't made it easy to grow our ranks.
What about you, Otso? Where have you been?

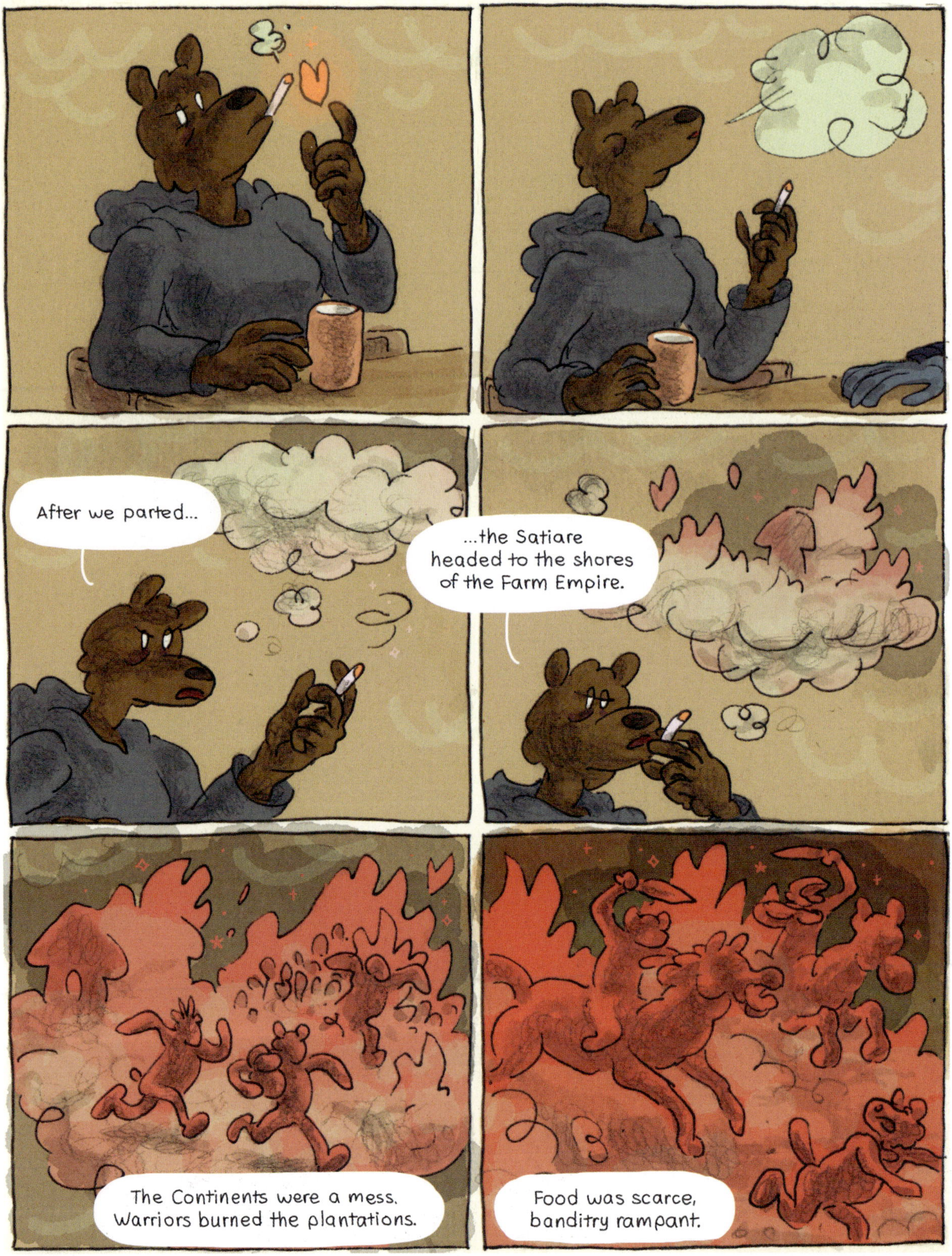
After we parted...
...the Satiare headed to the shores of the Farm Empire.
The Continents were a mess. Warriors burned the plantations.
Food was scarce, banditry rampant.

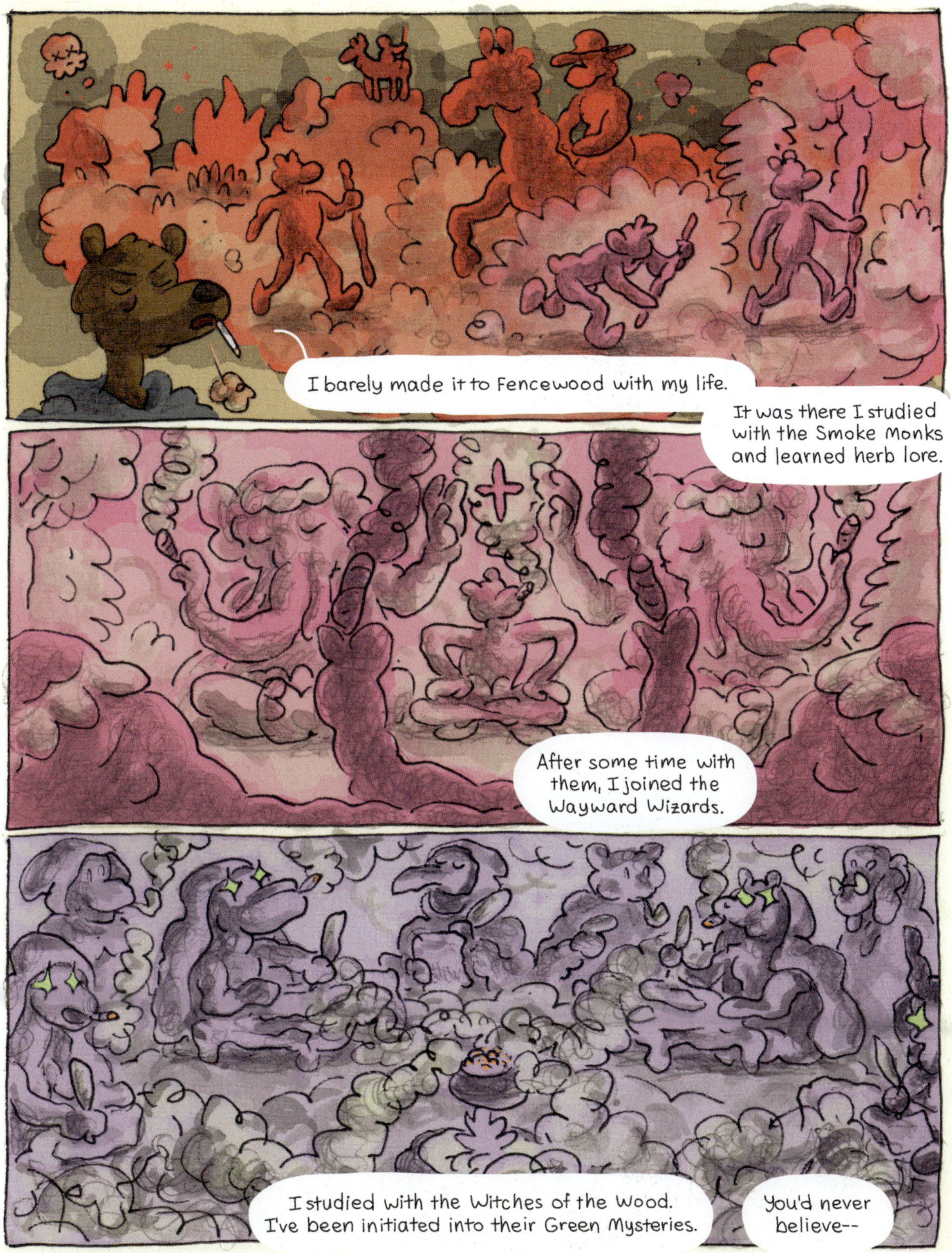
I barely made it to Fencewood with my life.
It was there I studied with the Smoke Monks and learned herb lore.
After some time with them, I joined the Wayward Wizards.
I studied with the Witches of the Wood. I've been initiated into their Green Mysteries.
You'd never believe--

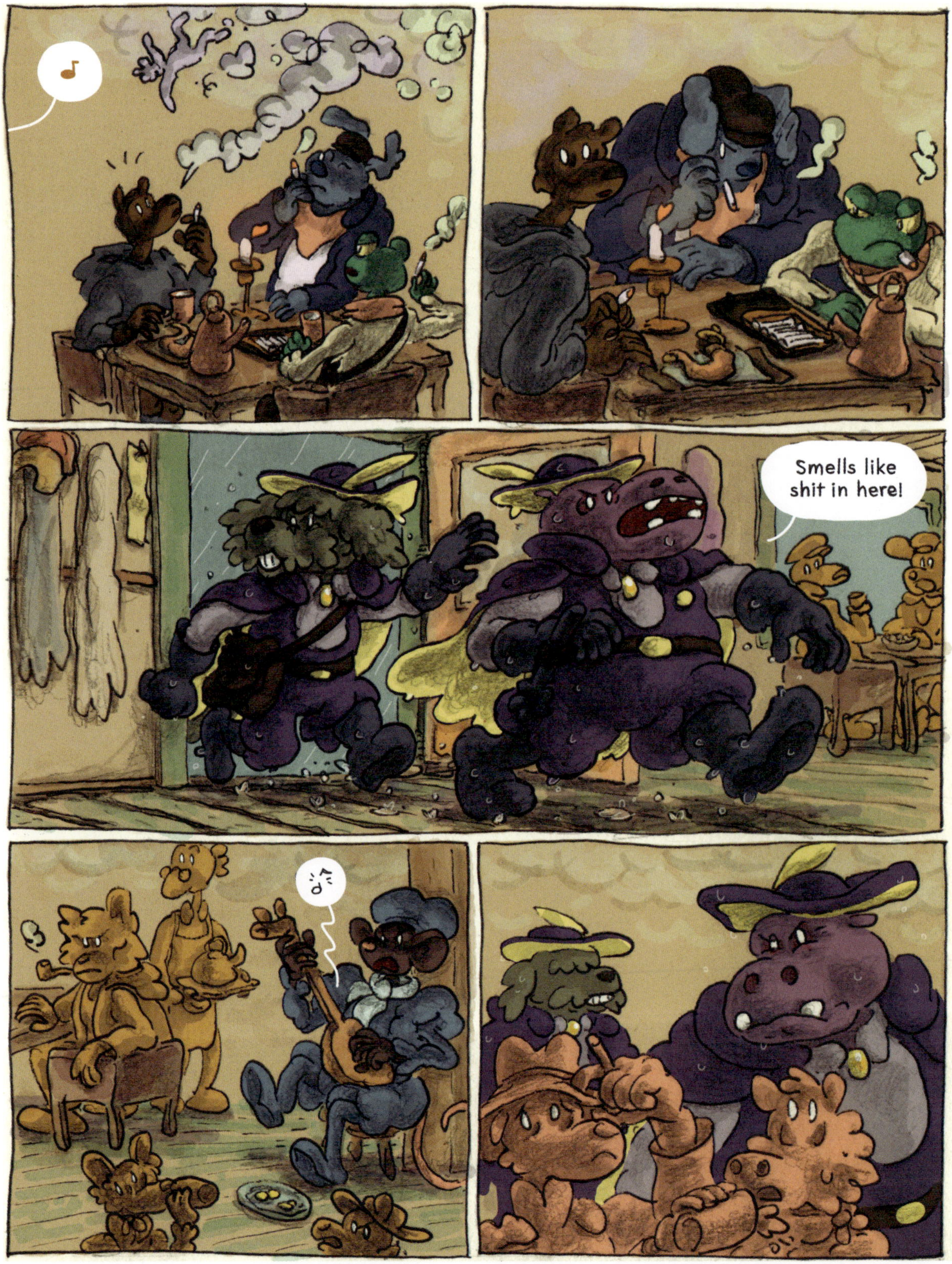
Smells like
shit in here!

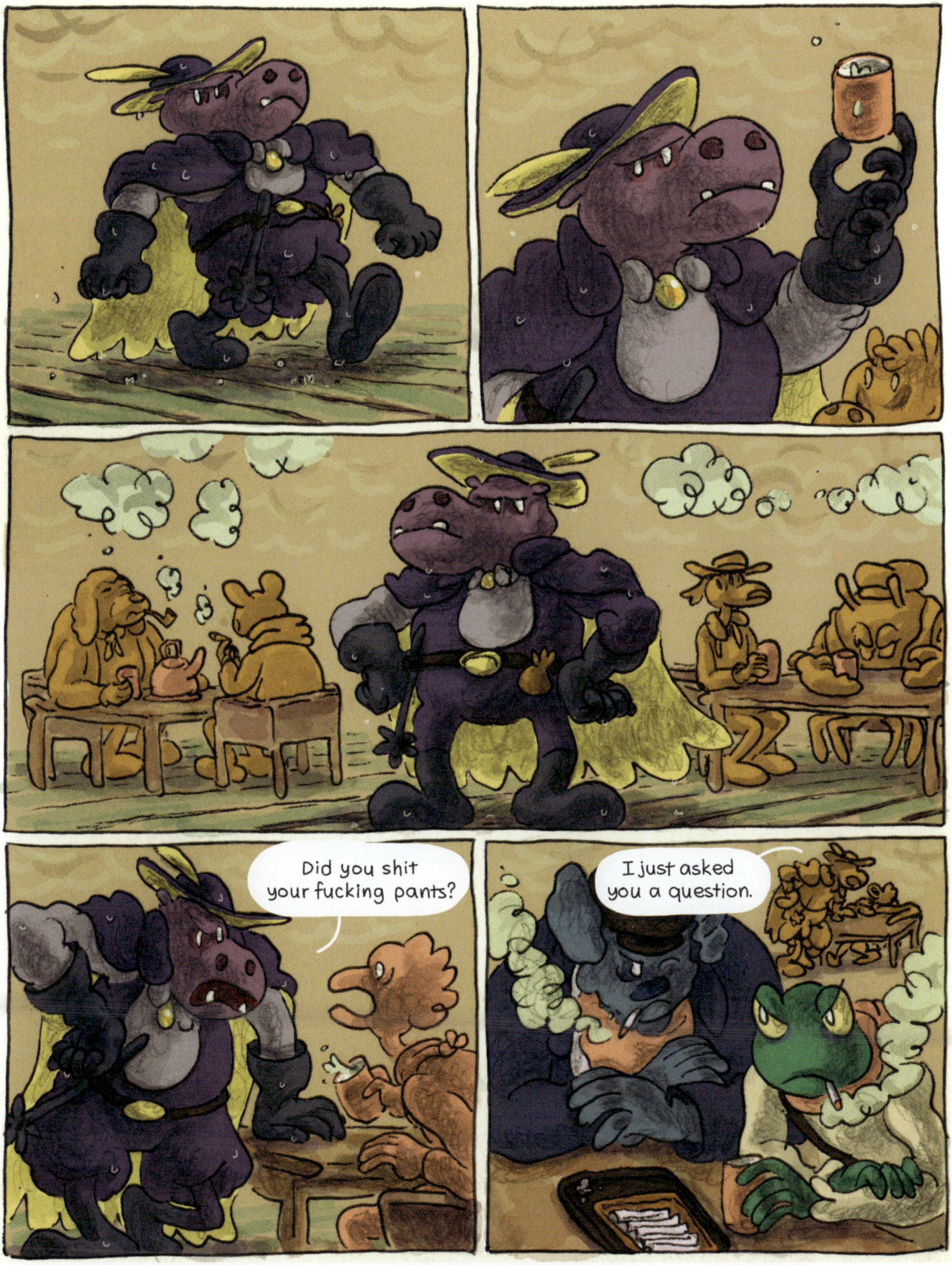
Did you shit your fucking pants?
I just asked you a question.

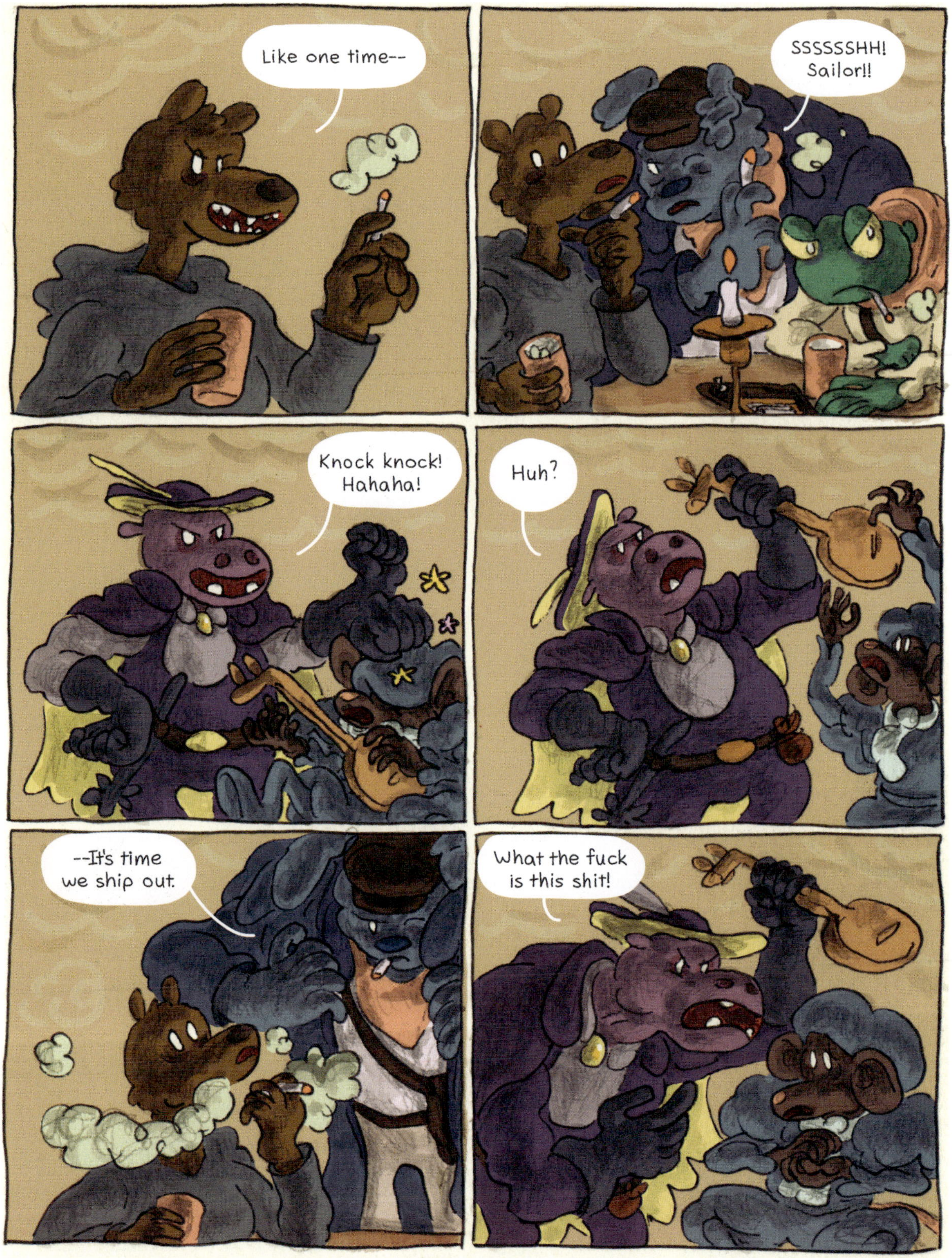
Like one time--
SSSSSSHH! Sailor!!
Knock knock! Hahaha!
Huh?
--It's time we ship out.
What the fuck is this shit!

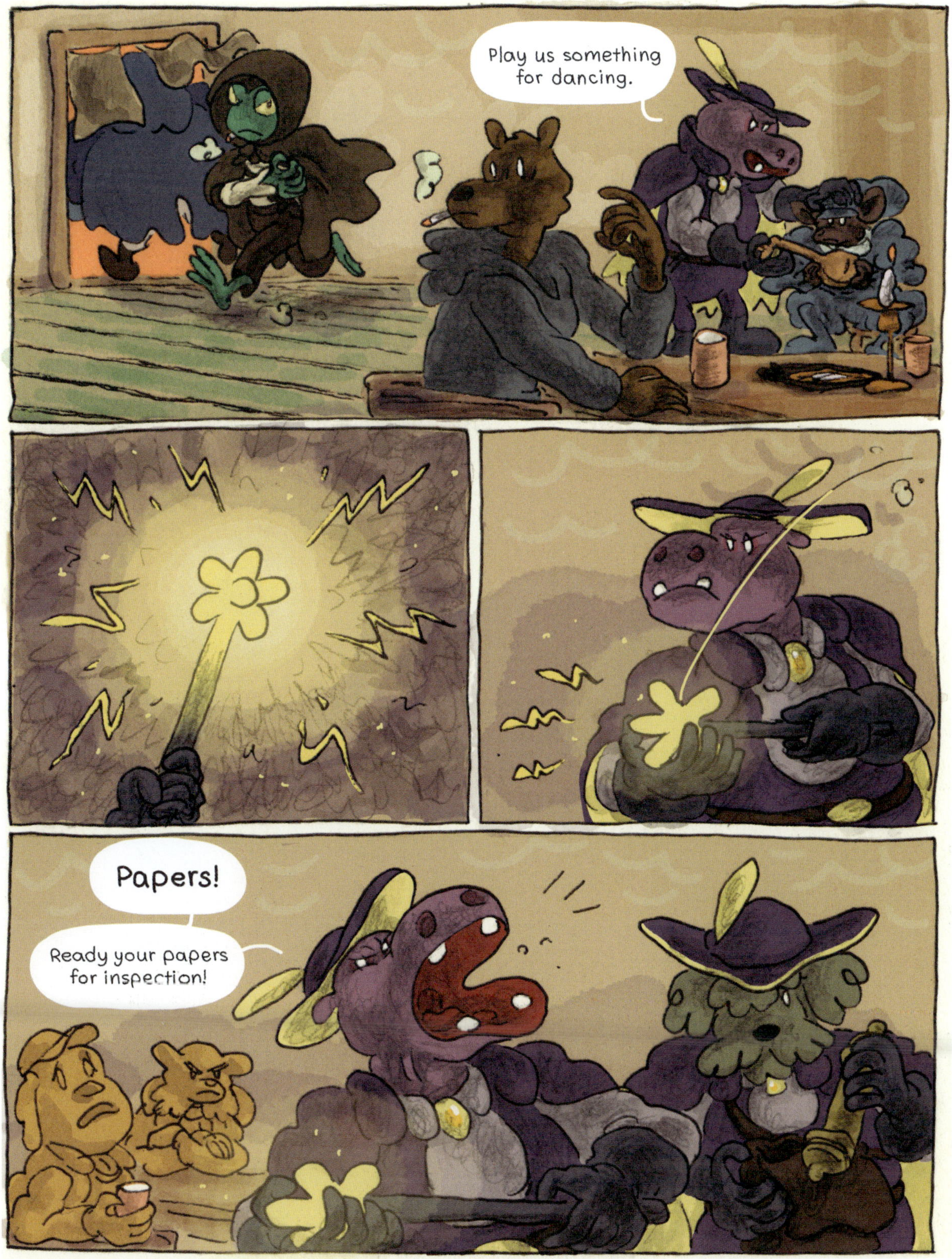
Play us something for dancing.
Papers!
Ready your papers for inspection!

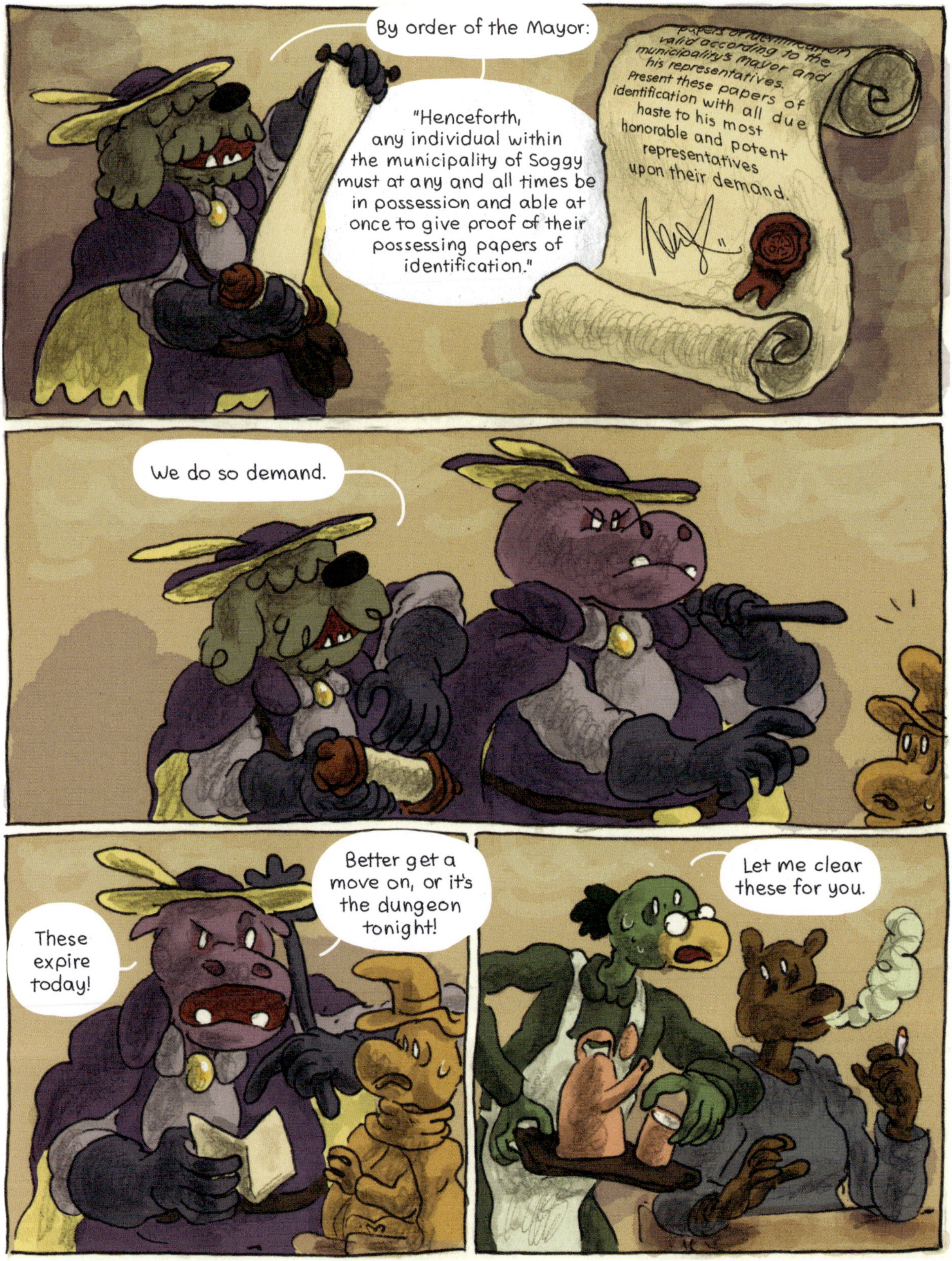

By order of the Mayor:
"Henceforth, any individual within the municipality of Soggy must at any and all times be in possession and able at once to give proof of their possessing papers of identification."
valid according to the municipality's mayor and his representatives. Present these papers of identification with all due haste to his most honorable and potent representatives upon their demand.
We do so demand.
These expire today!
Better get a move on, or it's the dungeon tonight!
Let me clear these for you.

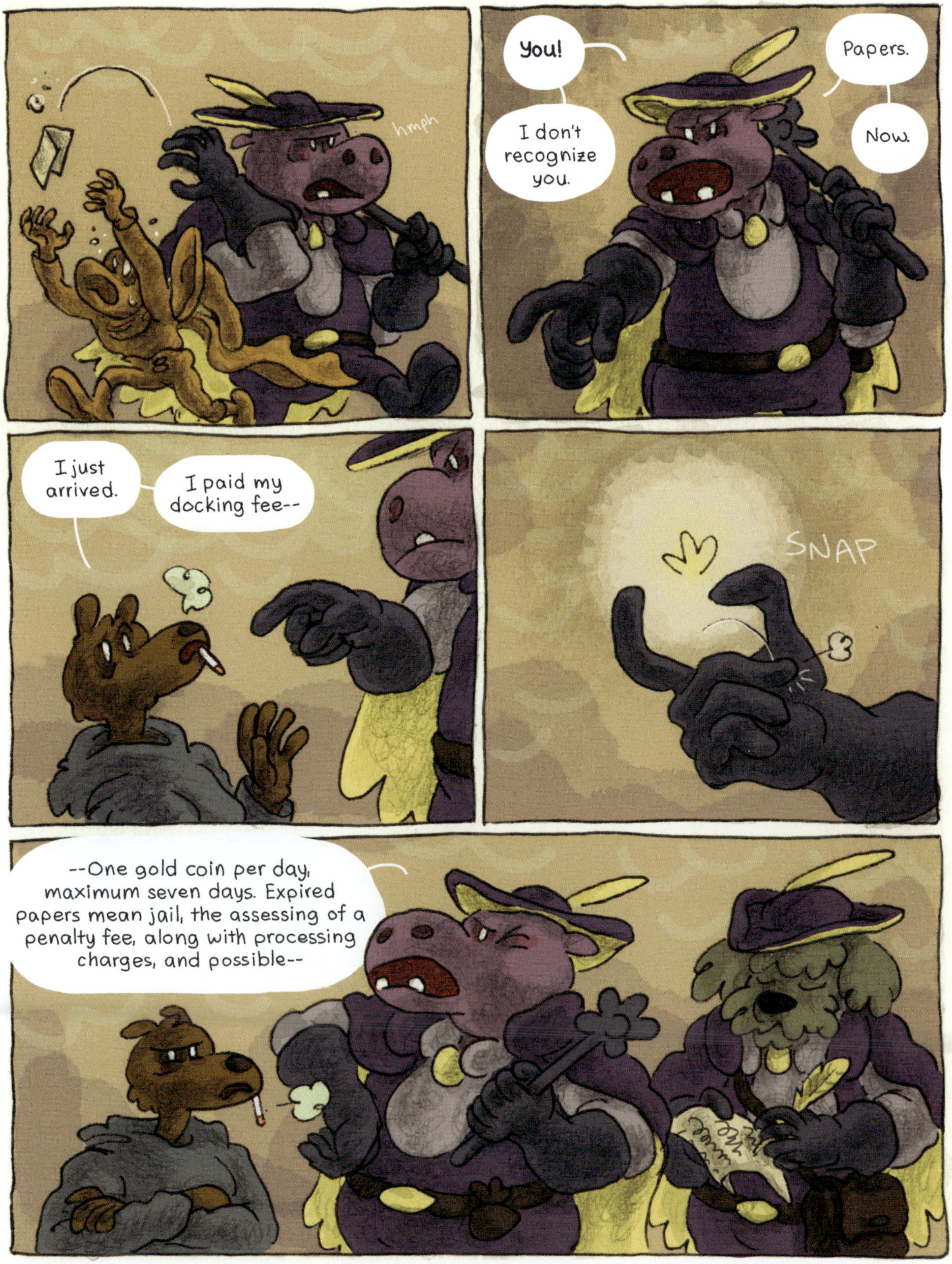
hmph
You!
I don't recognize you.
Papers.
Now.
I just arrived.
I paid my docking fee--
SNAP
--One gold coin per day, maximum seven days. Expired papers mean jail, the assessing of a penalty fee, along with processing charges, and possible--

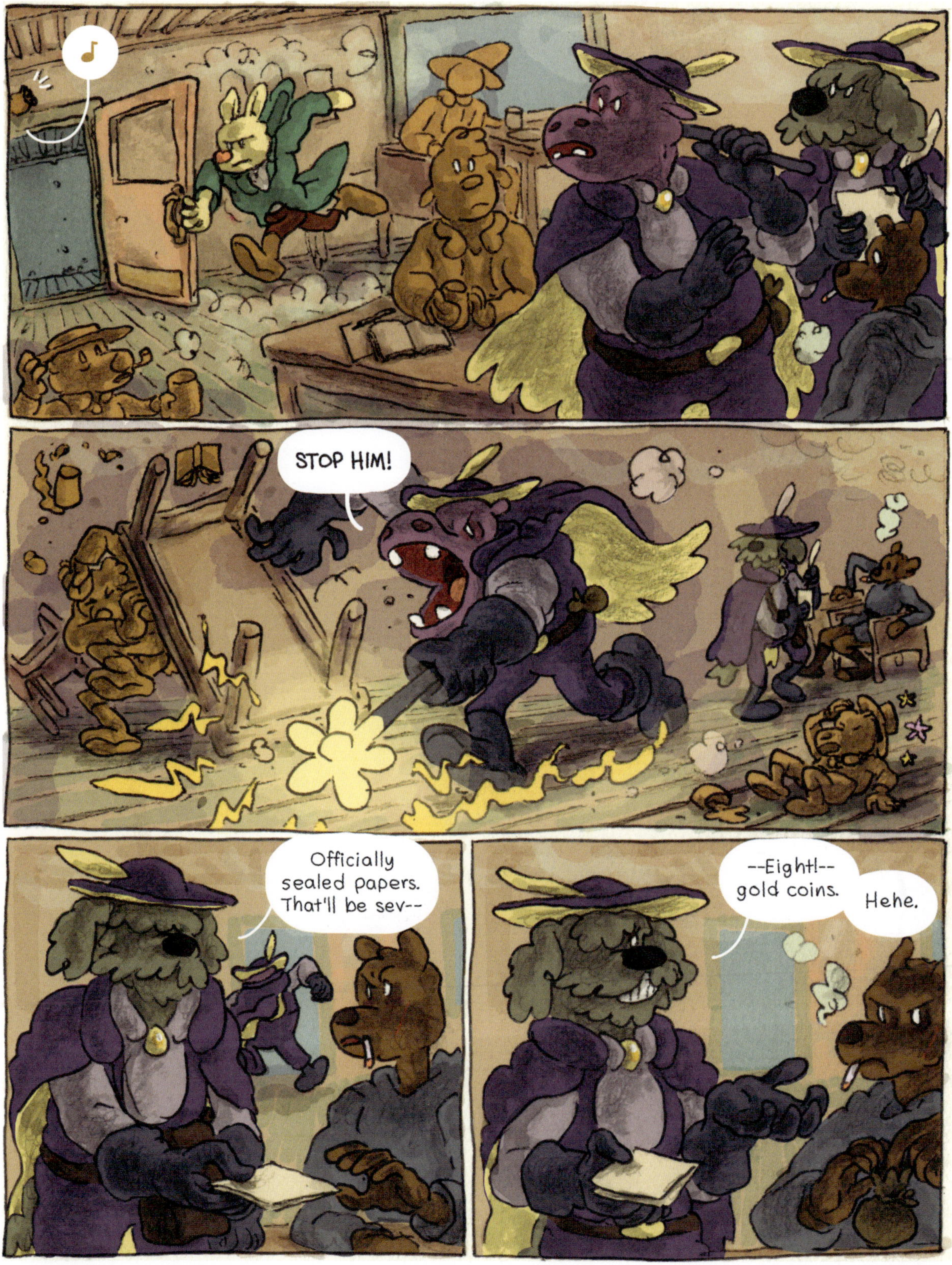
STOP HIM!
Officially sealed papers. That'll be sev--
--Eight!-- gold coins.
Hehe.

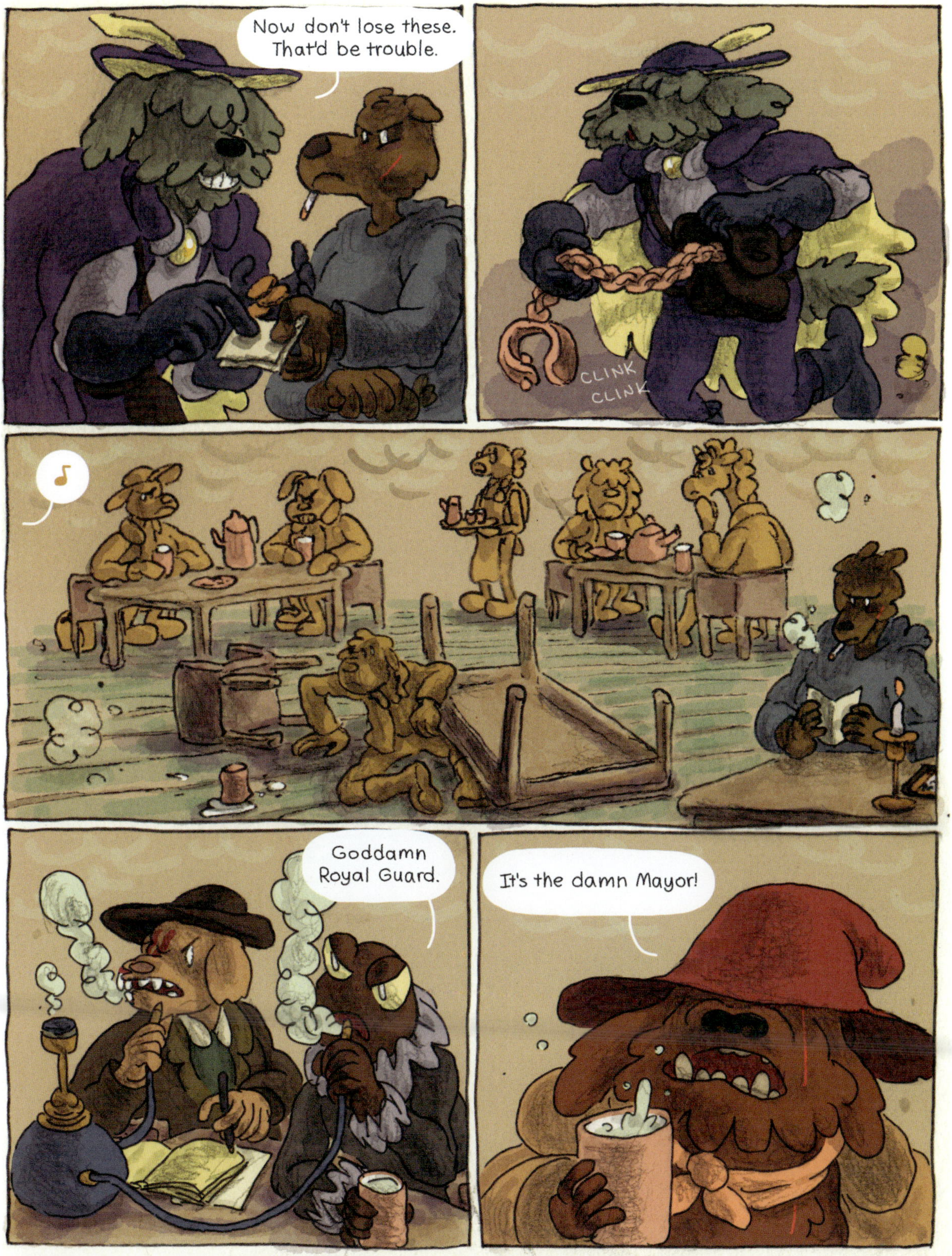
Now don't lose these. That'd be trouble.
CLINK
CLINK
Goddamn Royal Guard.
It's the damn Mayor!

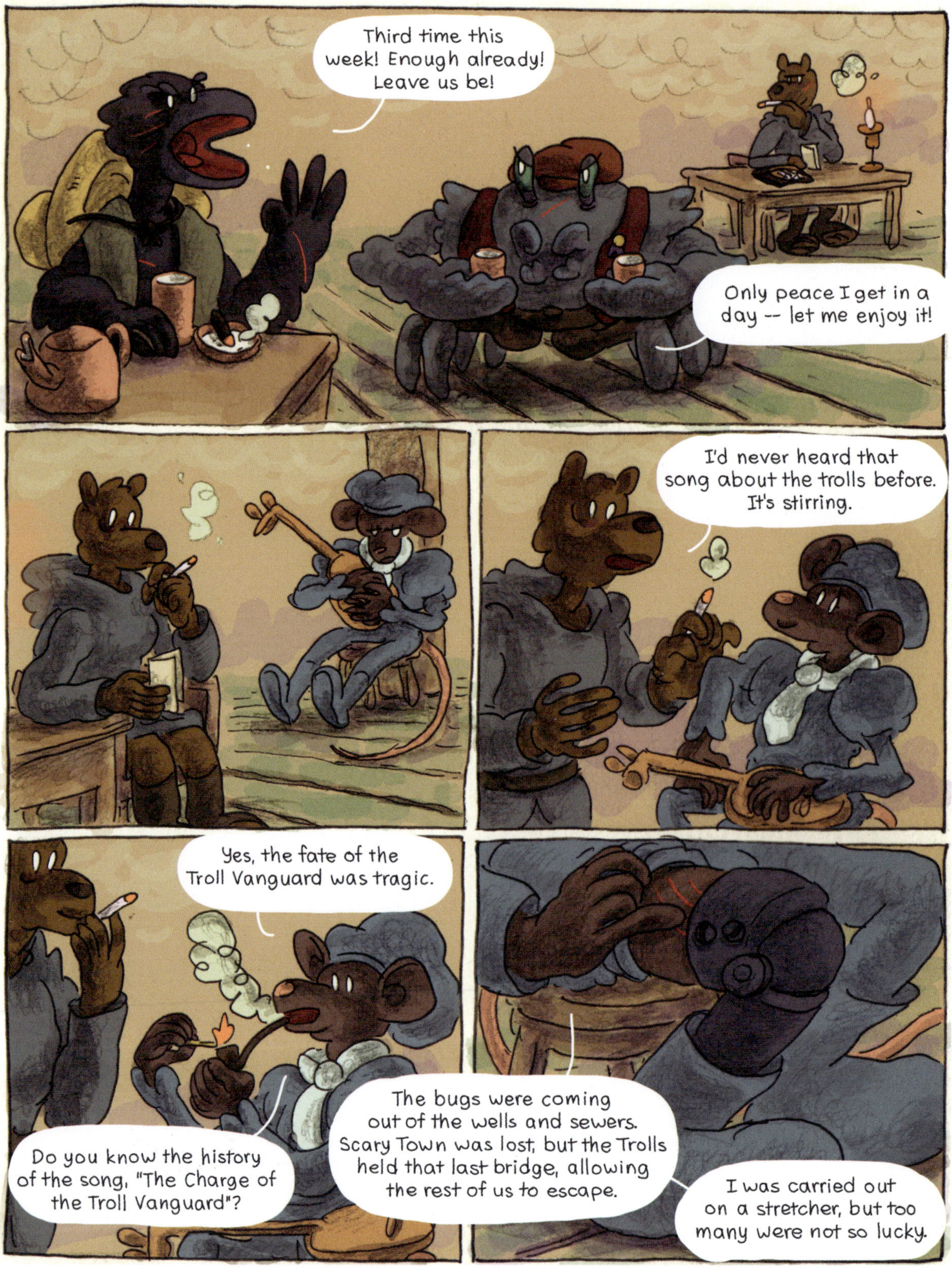
Third time this week! Enough already! Leave us be!
Only peace I get in a day -- let me enjoy it!
I'd never heard that song about the trolls before. It's stirring.
Yes, the fate of the Troll Vanguard was tragic.
Do you know the history of the song, "The Charge of the Troll Vanguard"?
The bugs were coming out of the wells and sewers. Scary Town was lost, but the Trolls held that last bridge, allowing the rest of us to escape.
I was carried out on a stretcher, but too many were not so lucky.

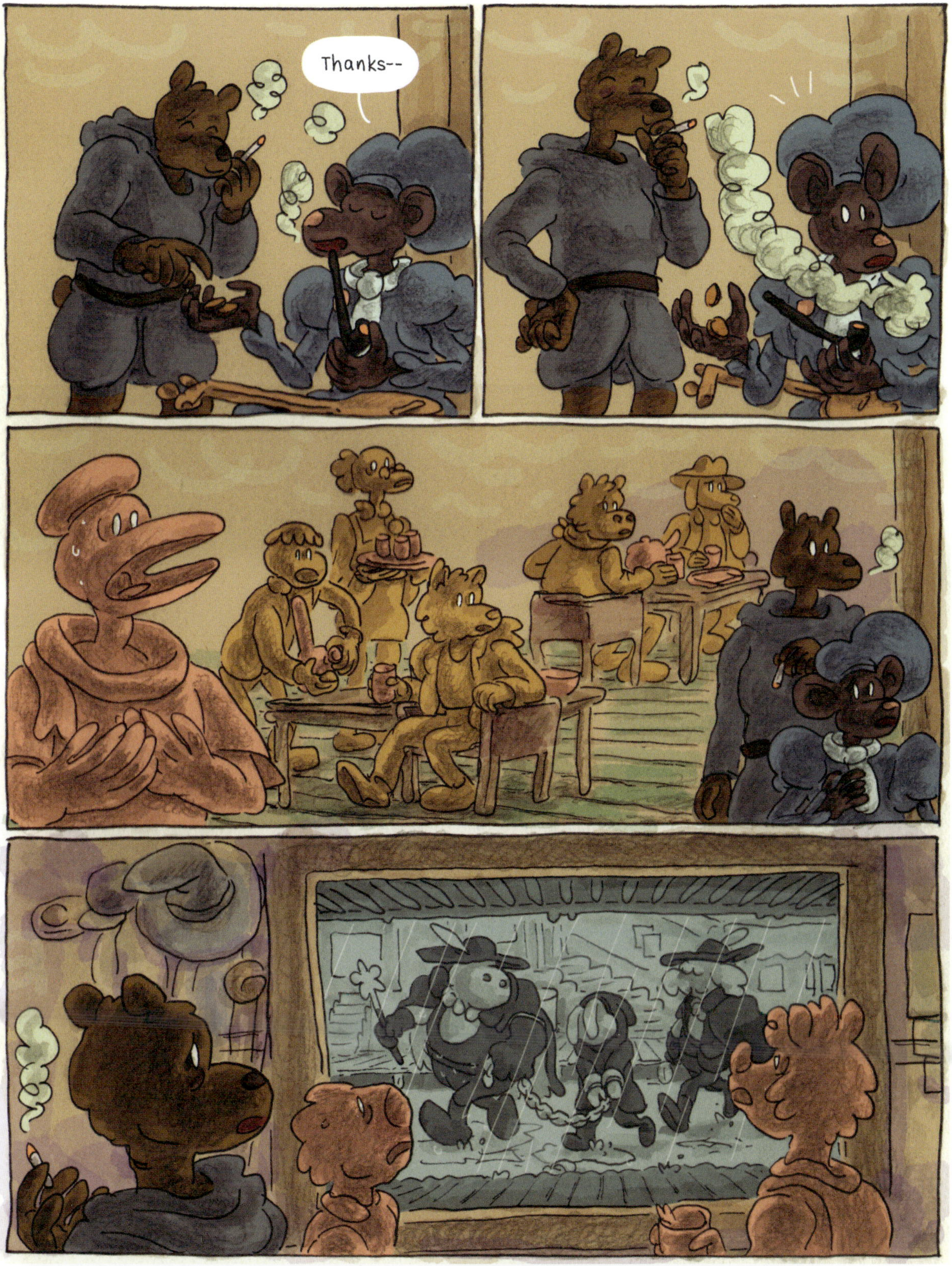
Thanks--

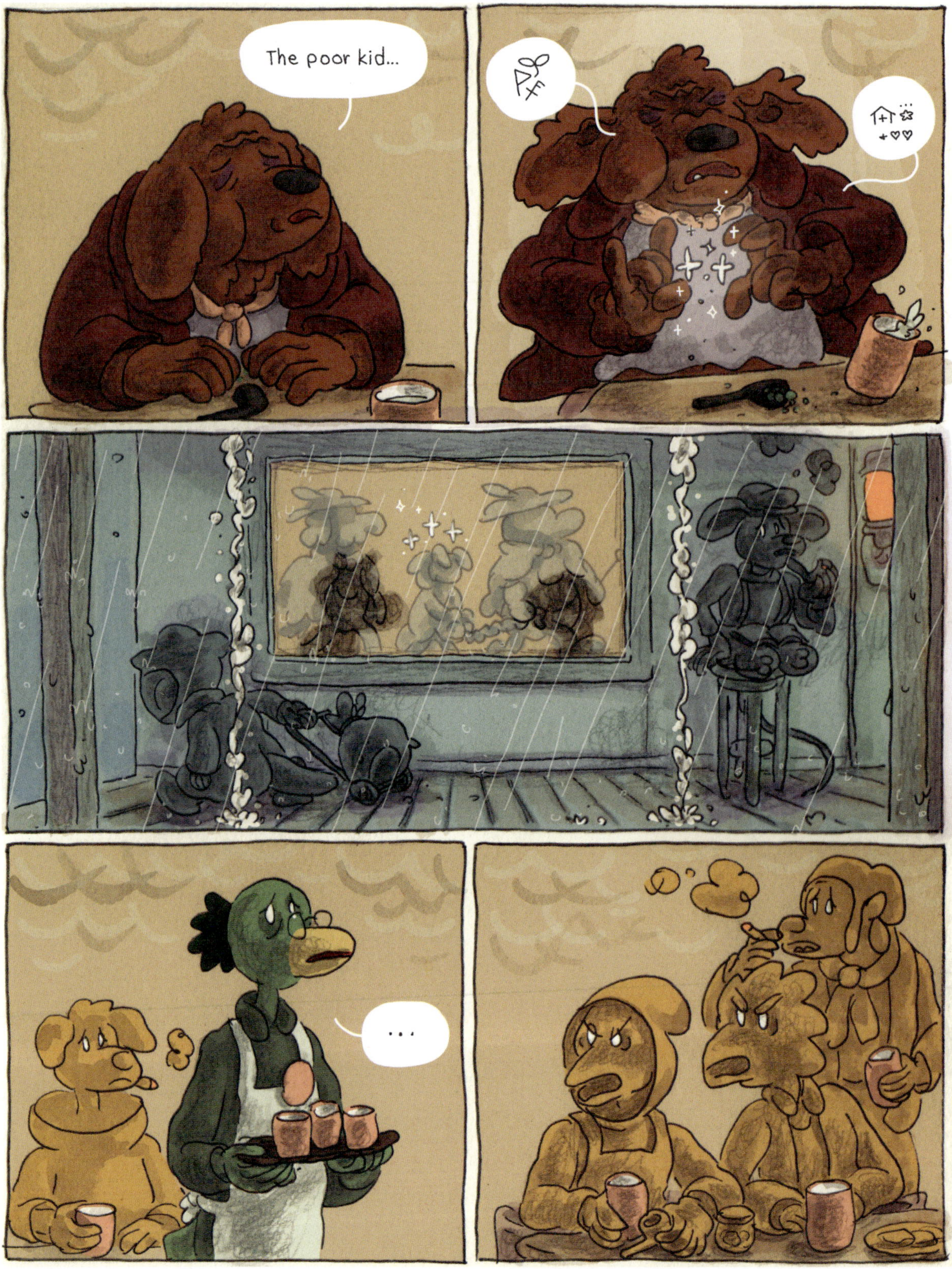
The poor kid...
...

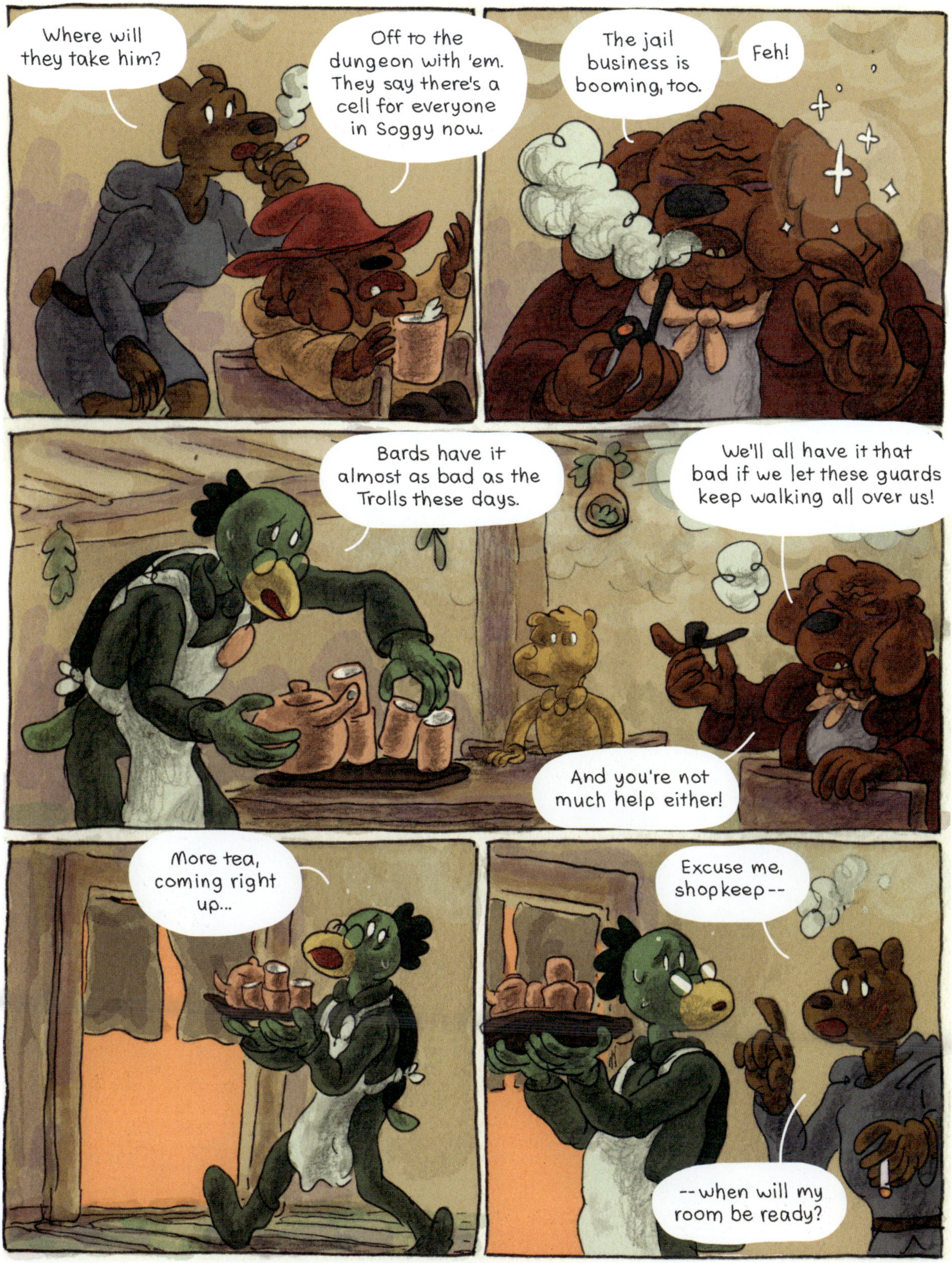
Where will they take him?
Off to the dungeon with 'em. They say there's a cell for everyone in Soggy now.
The jail business is booming, too.
Feh!
Bards have it almost as bad as the Trolls these days.
We'll all have it that bad if we let these guards keep walking all over us!
And you're not much help either!
More tea, coming right up...
Excuse me, shopkeep--
--when will my room be ready?

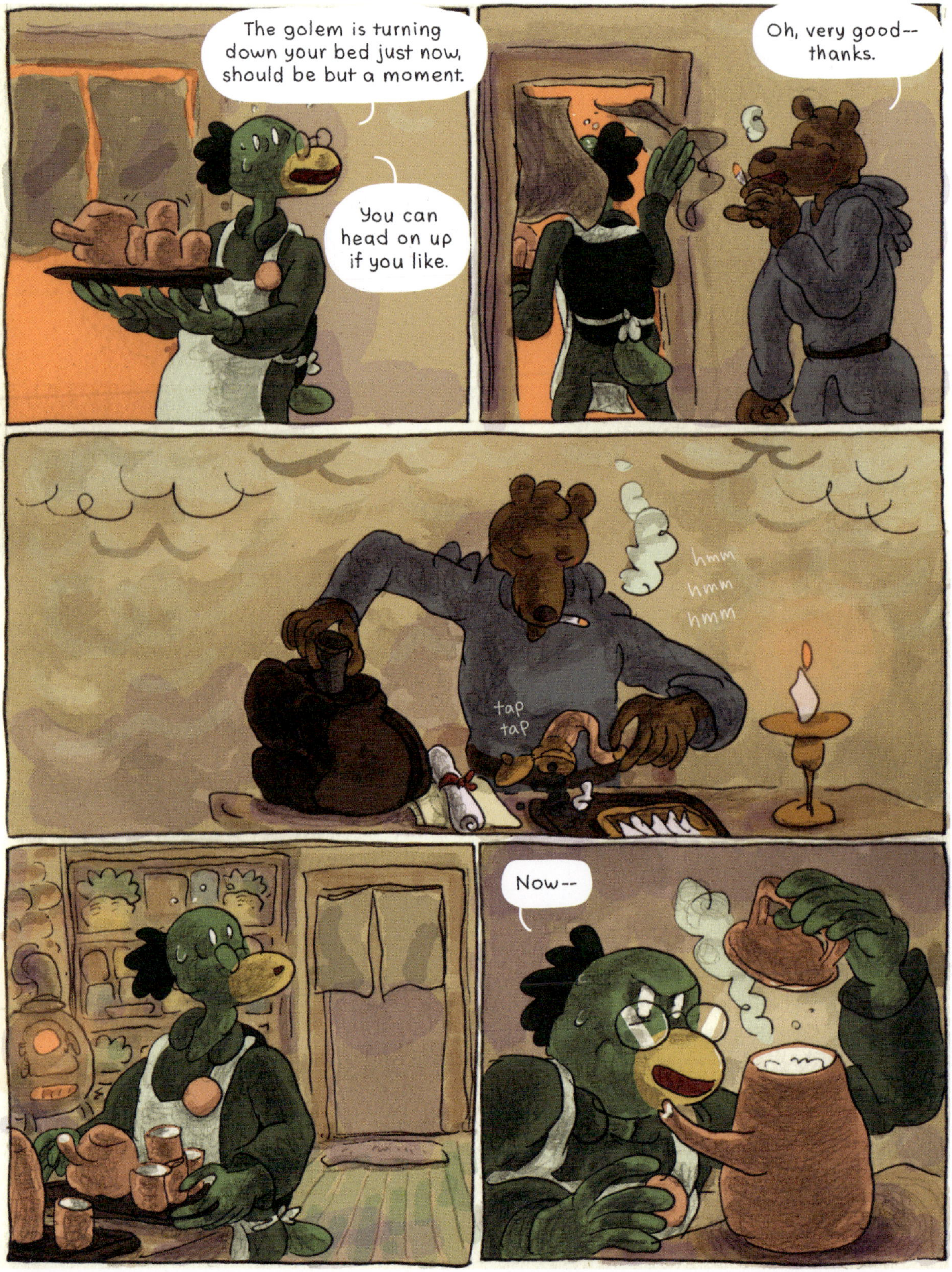

The golem is turning down your bed just now, should be but a moment.
You can head on up if you like.
Oh, very good--thanks.
hmm
hmm
hmm
tap
tap
Now--

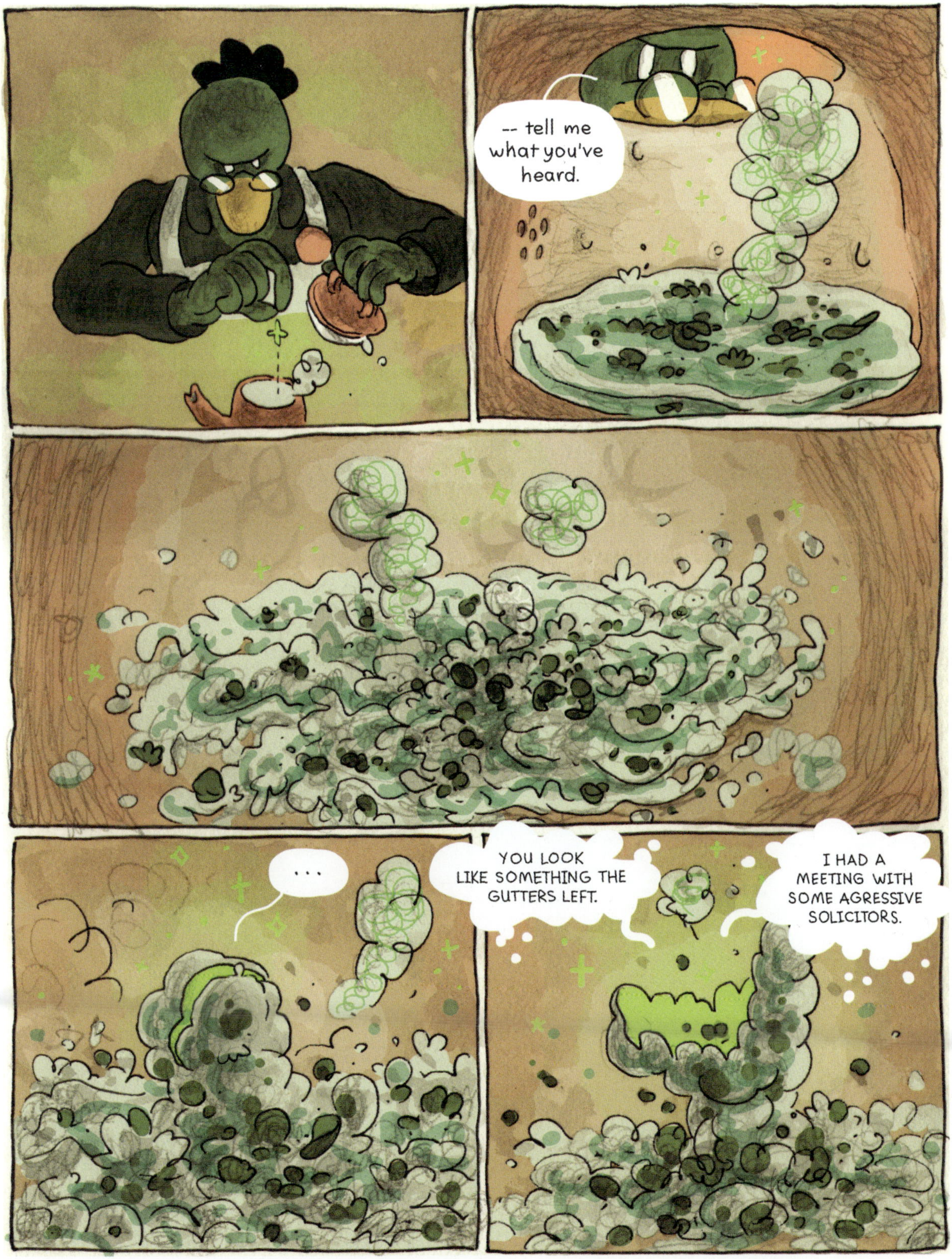
-- tell me what you've heard.
...
YOU LOOK LIKE SOMETHING THE GUTTERS LEFT.
I HAD A MEETING WITH SOME AGRESSIVE SOLICITORS.

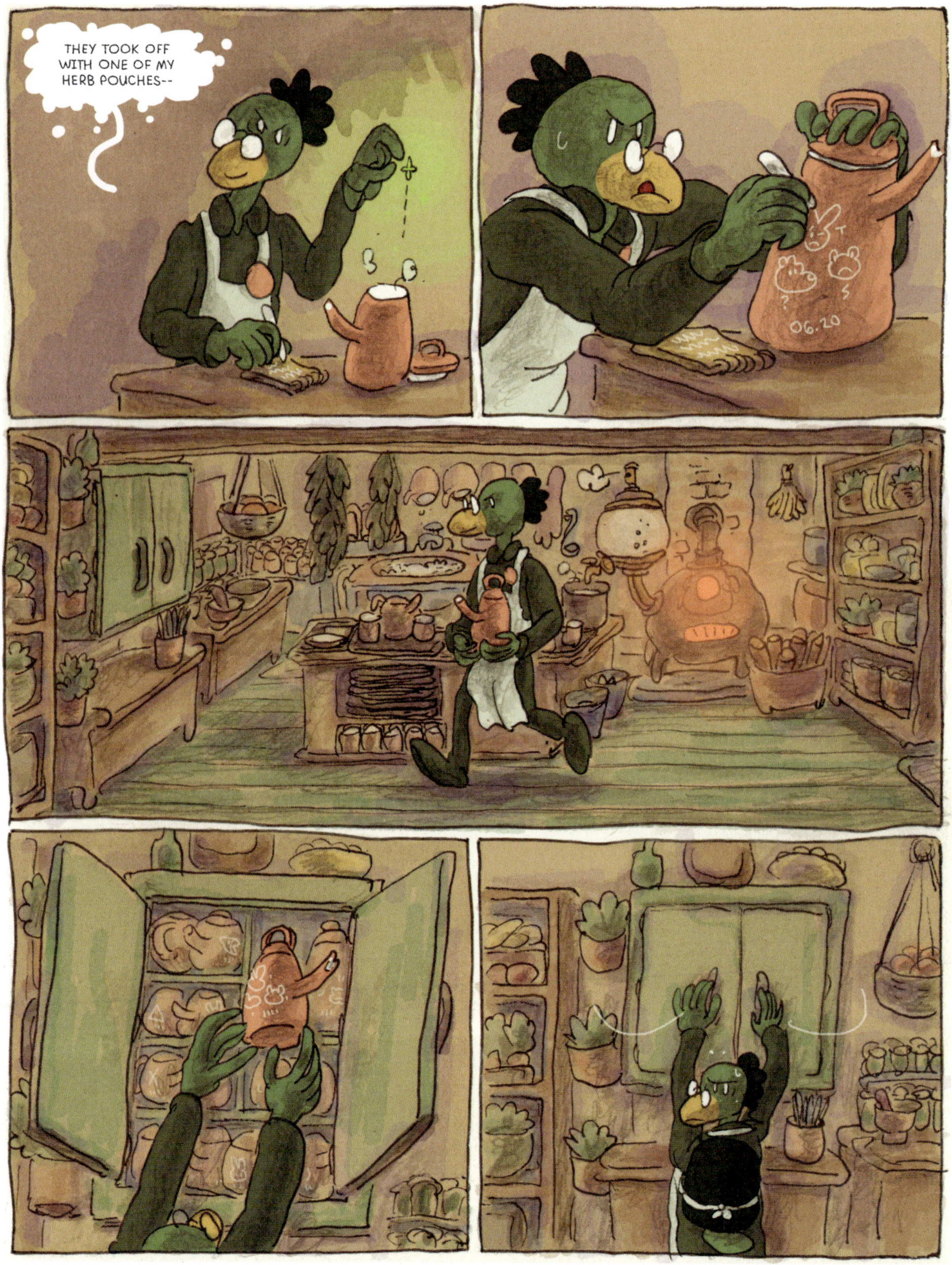
THEY TOOK OFF WITH ONE OF MY HERB POUCHES--
06.20

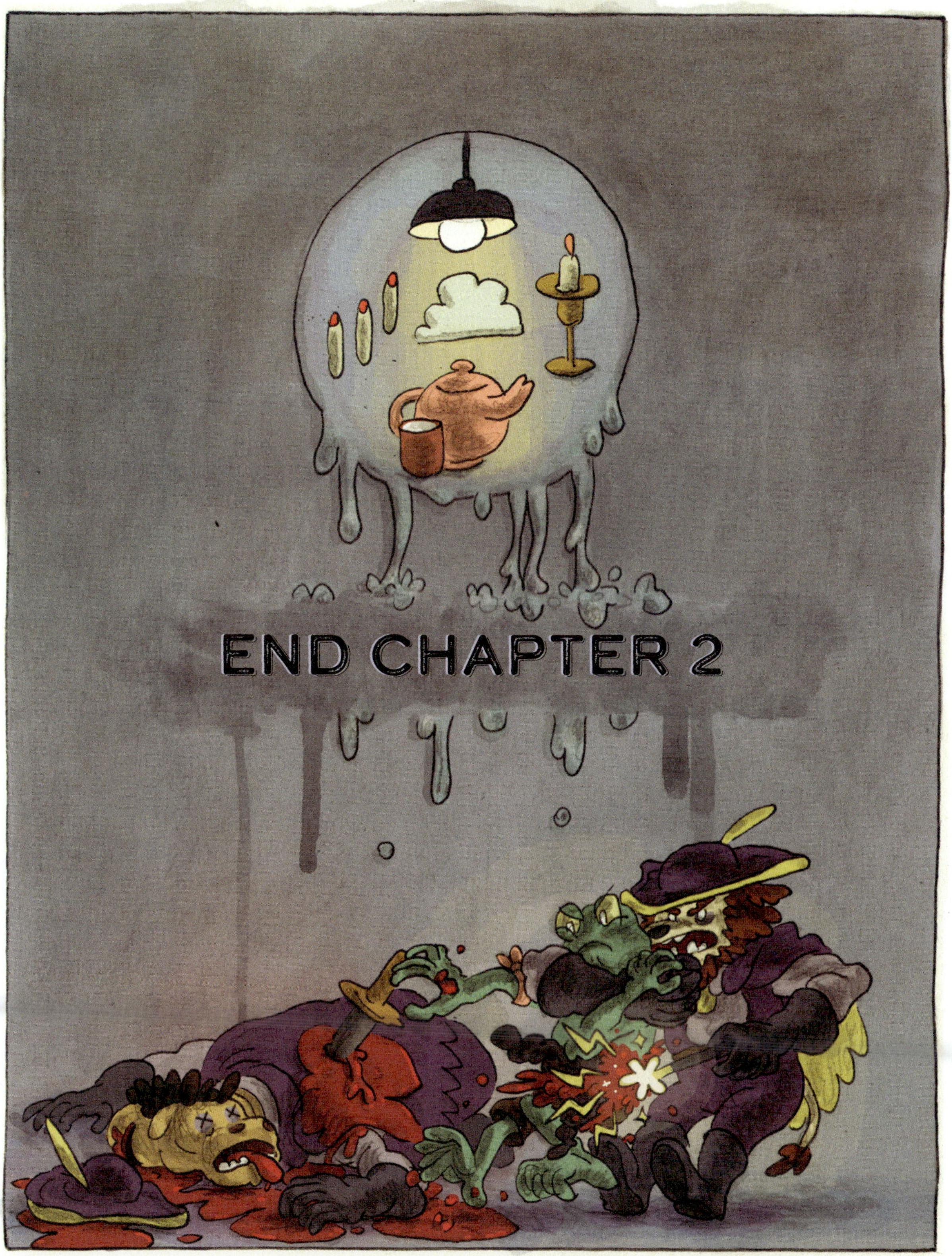
END CHAPTER 2

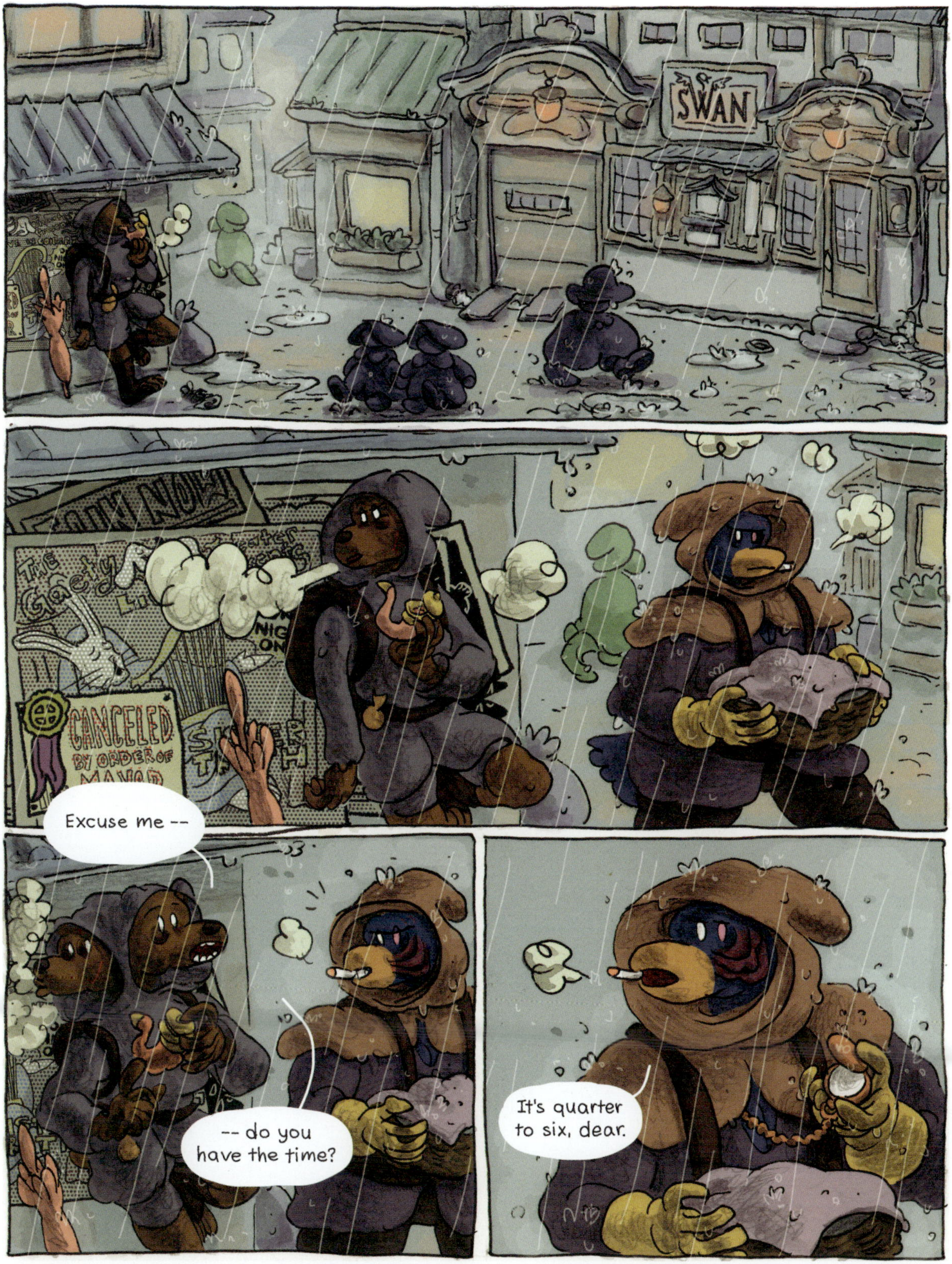
SWAN
The Gaiety
CANCELED BY ORDER OF MAYOR
Excuse me --
-- do you have the time?
It's quarter to six, dear.

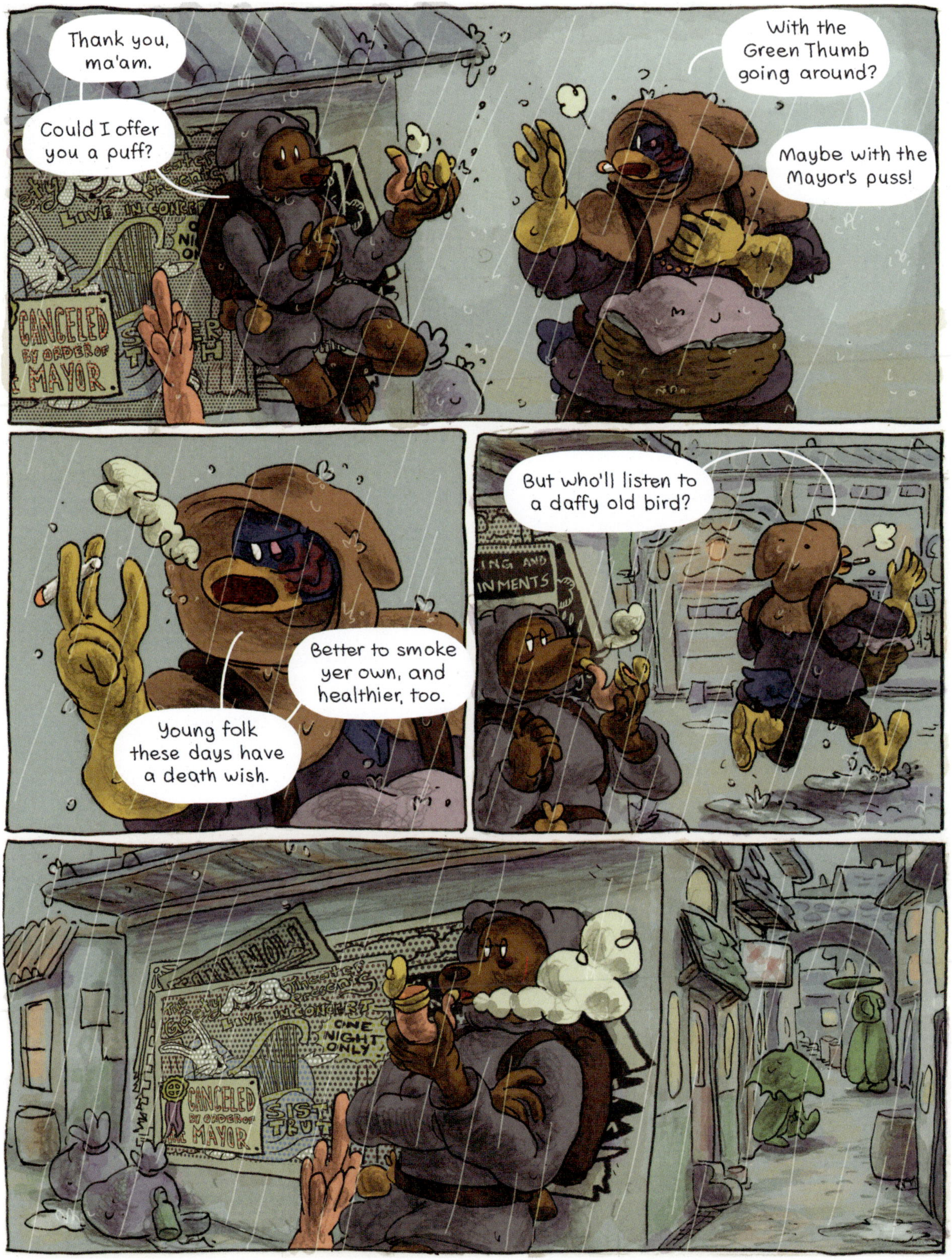
Thank you, ma'am.
Could I offer you a puff?
With the Green Thumb going around?
Maybe with the Mayor's puss!
CANCELED BY ORDER OF MAYOR
LIVE IN CONCERT
Young folk these days have a death wish.
Better to smoke yer own, and healthier, too.
But who'll listen to a daffy old bird?
ING AND
INMENTS
LIVE IN CONCERT
ONE NIGHT ONLY
CANCELED BY ORDER OF MAYOR

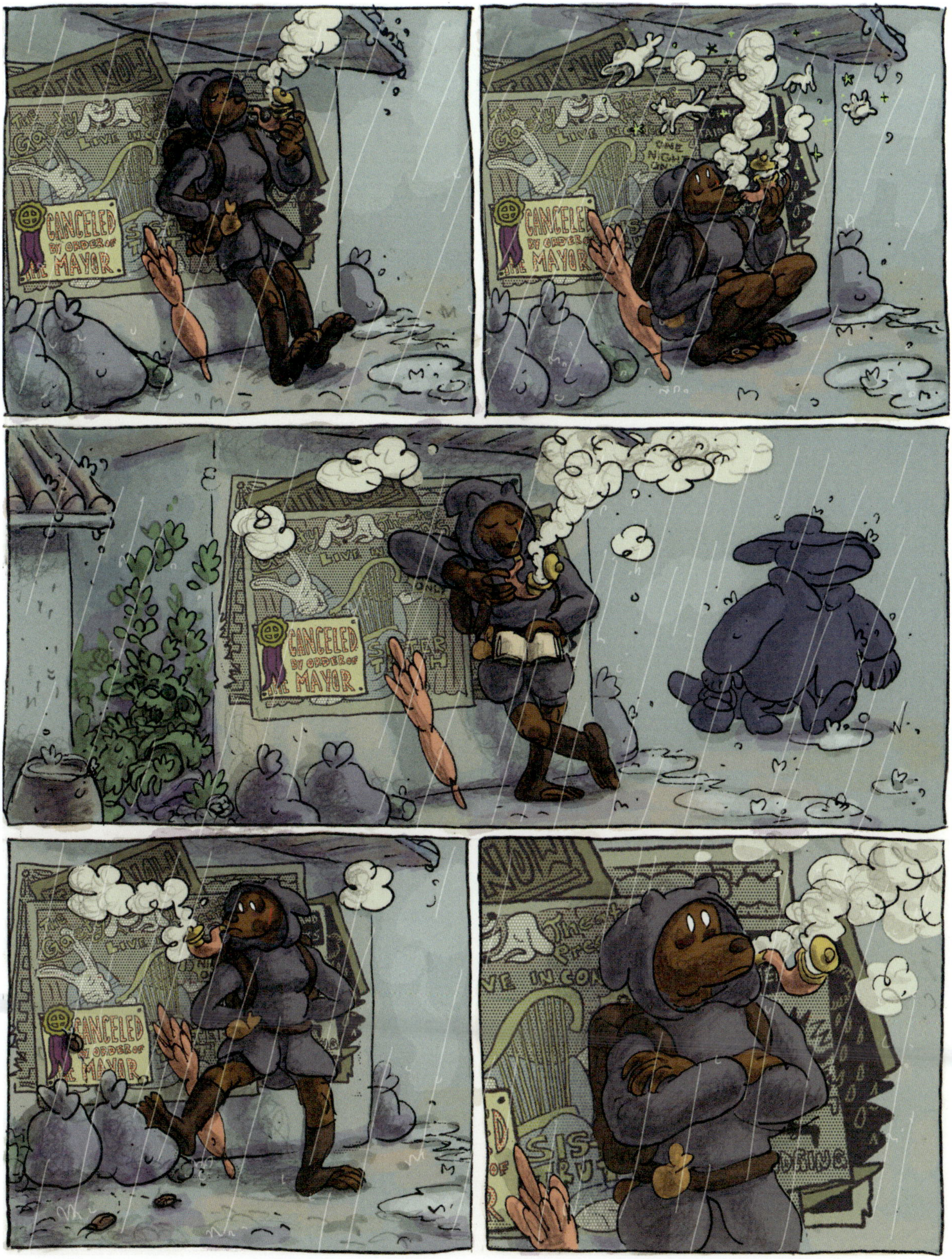
CANCELED
BY ORDER OF
MAYOR
ONE NIGHT ONLY

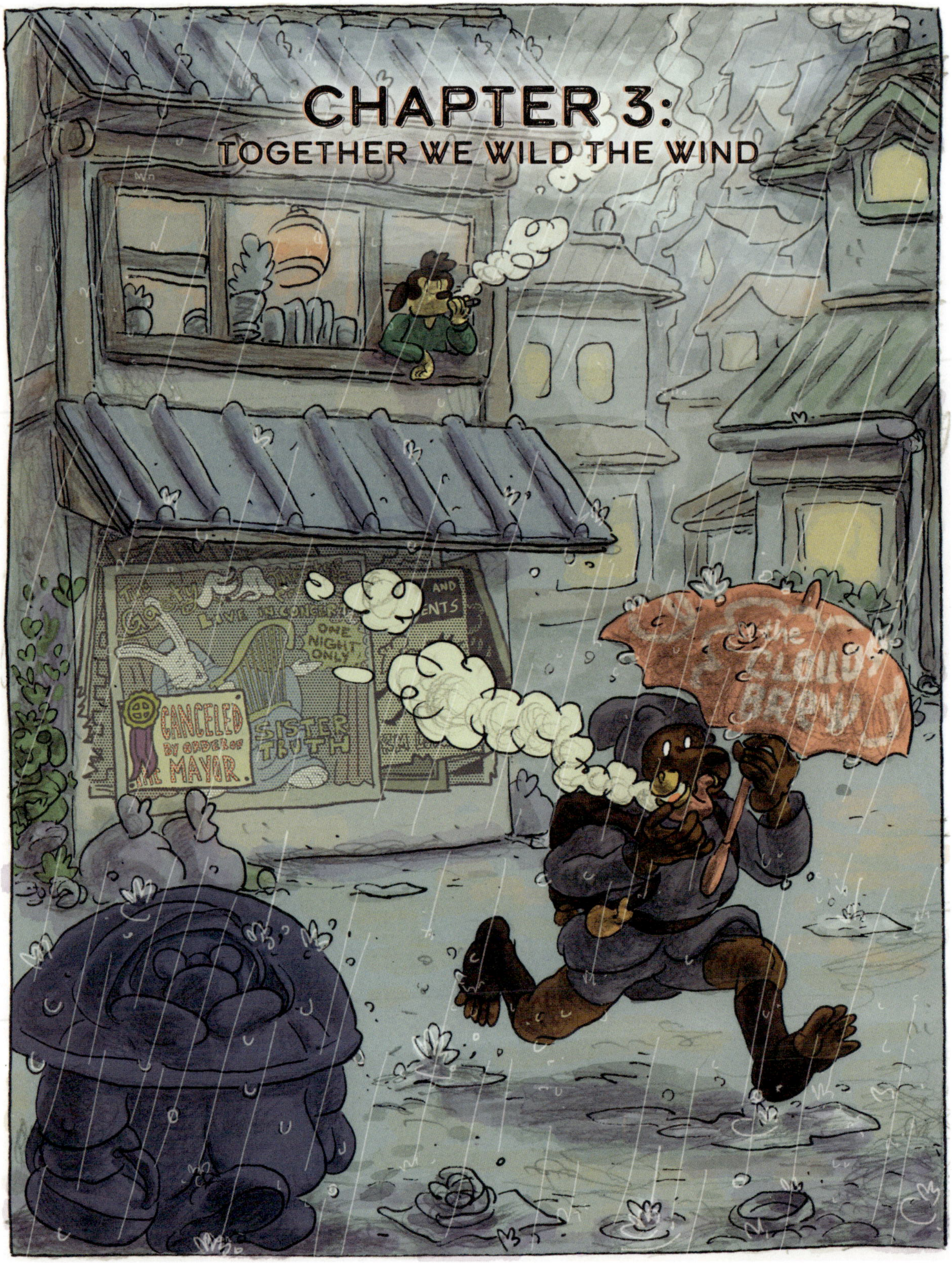
CHAPTER 3:
TOGETHER WE WILD THE WIND
LIVE IN CONCERT
ONE NIGHT ONLY
AND
ENTS
CANCELED BY ORDER OF THE MAYOR.
SISTER TRUTH
the CLOUDY BREW

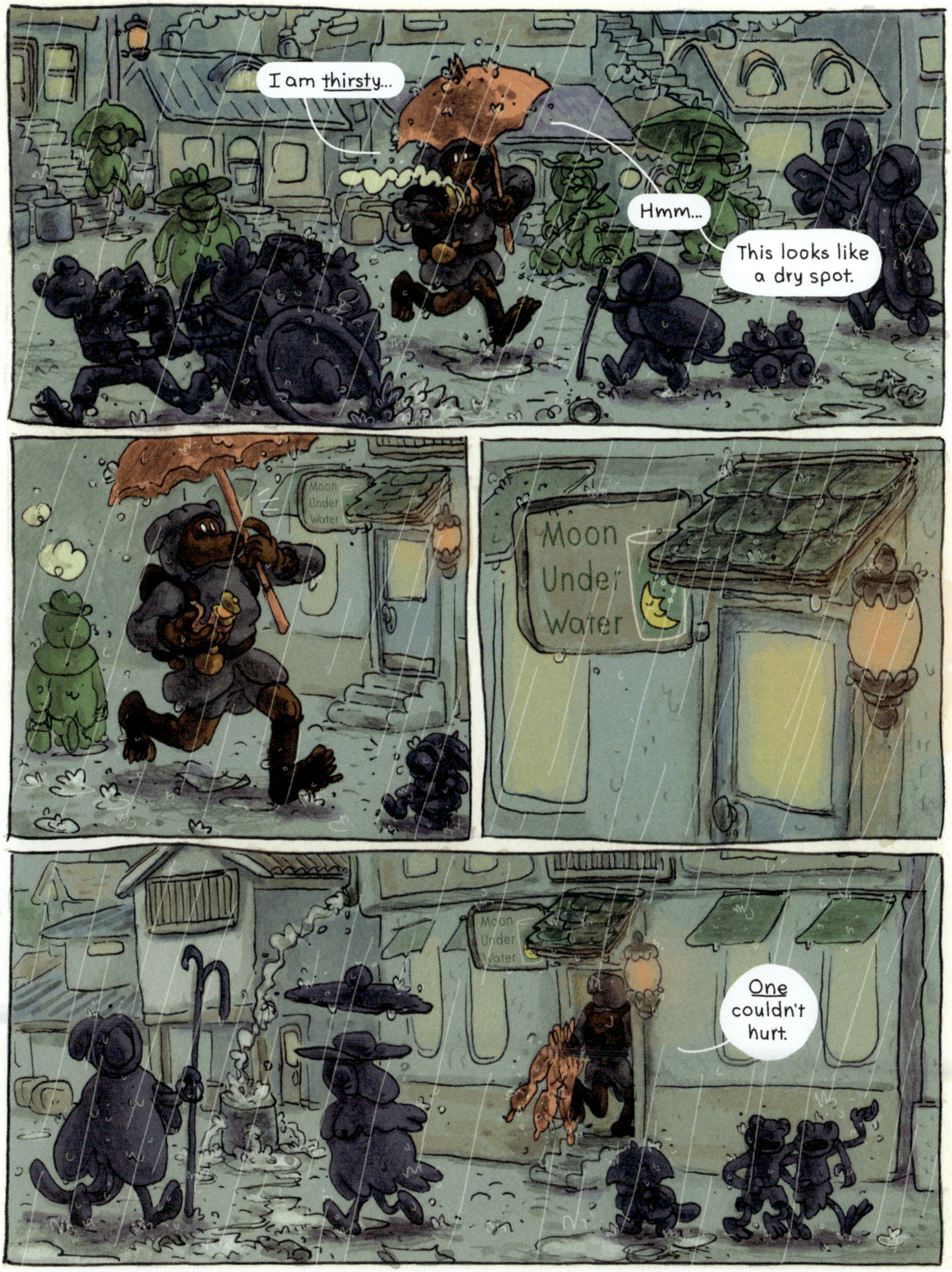
I am thirsty...
Hmm...
This looks like a dry spot.
Moon Under Water
Moon Under Water
Moon Under Water
One couldn't hurt.

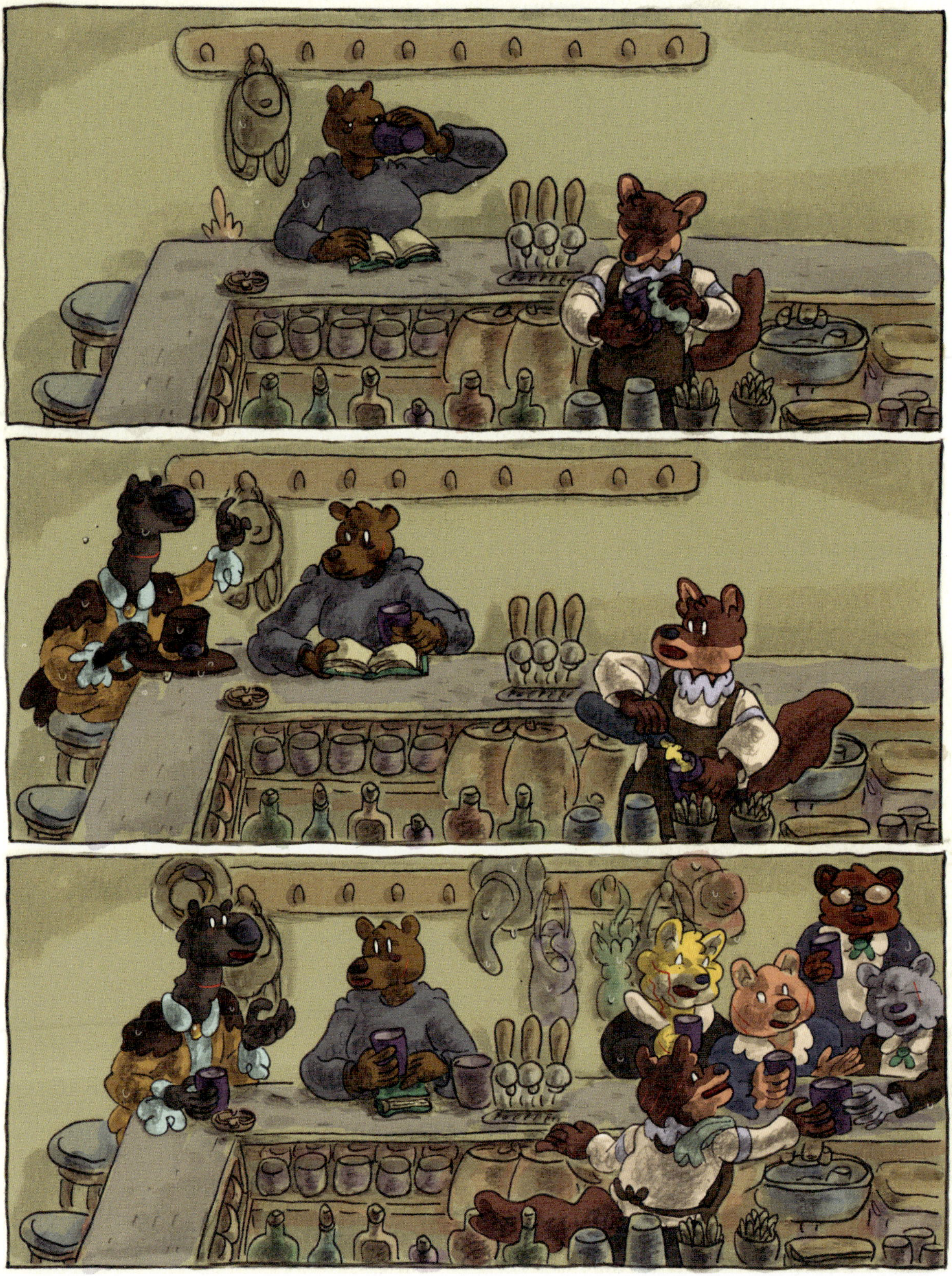

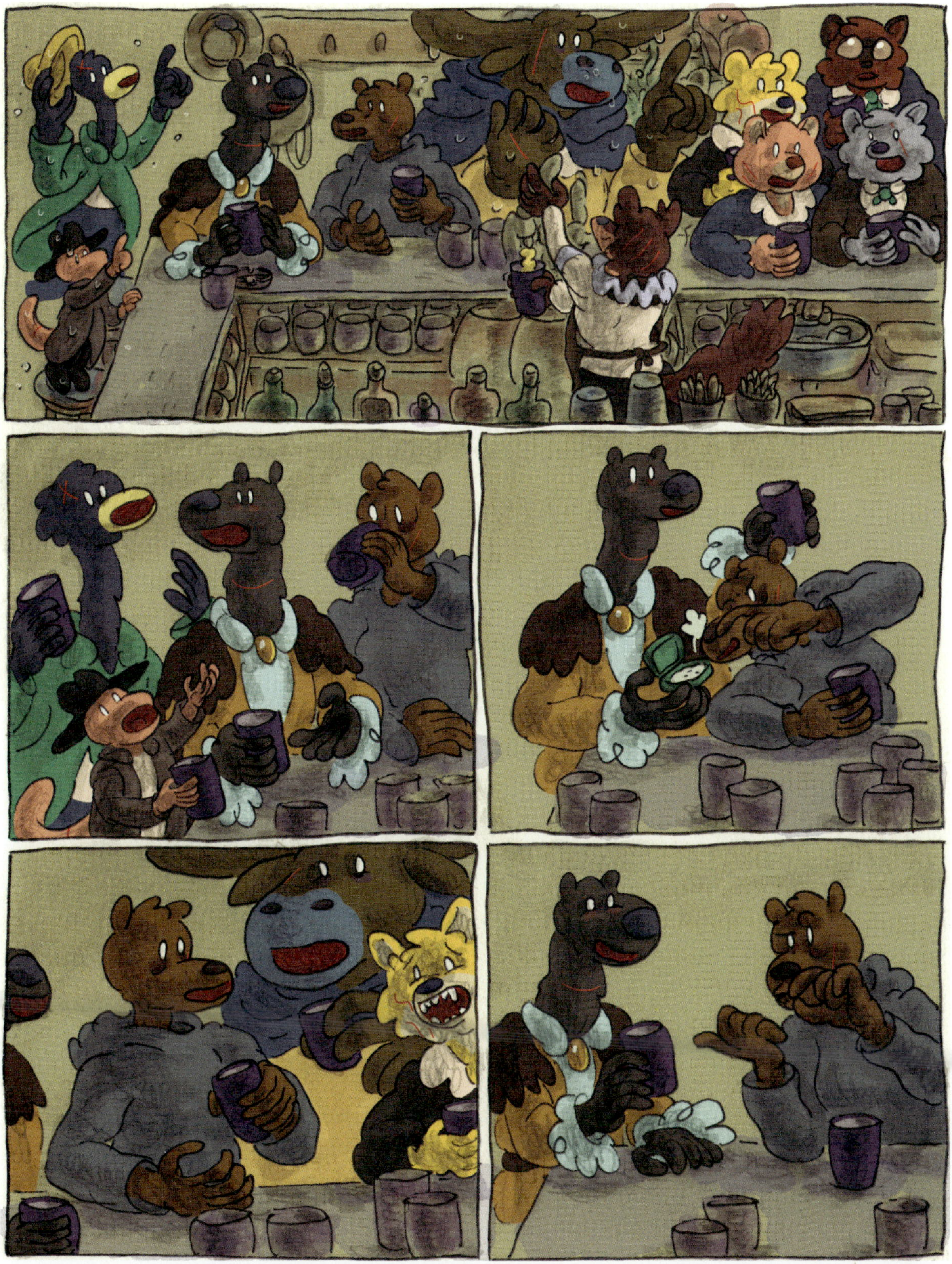

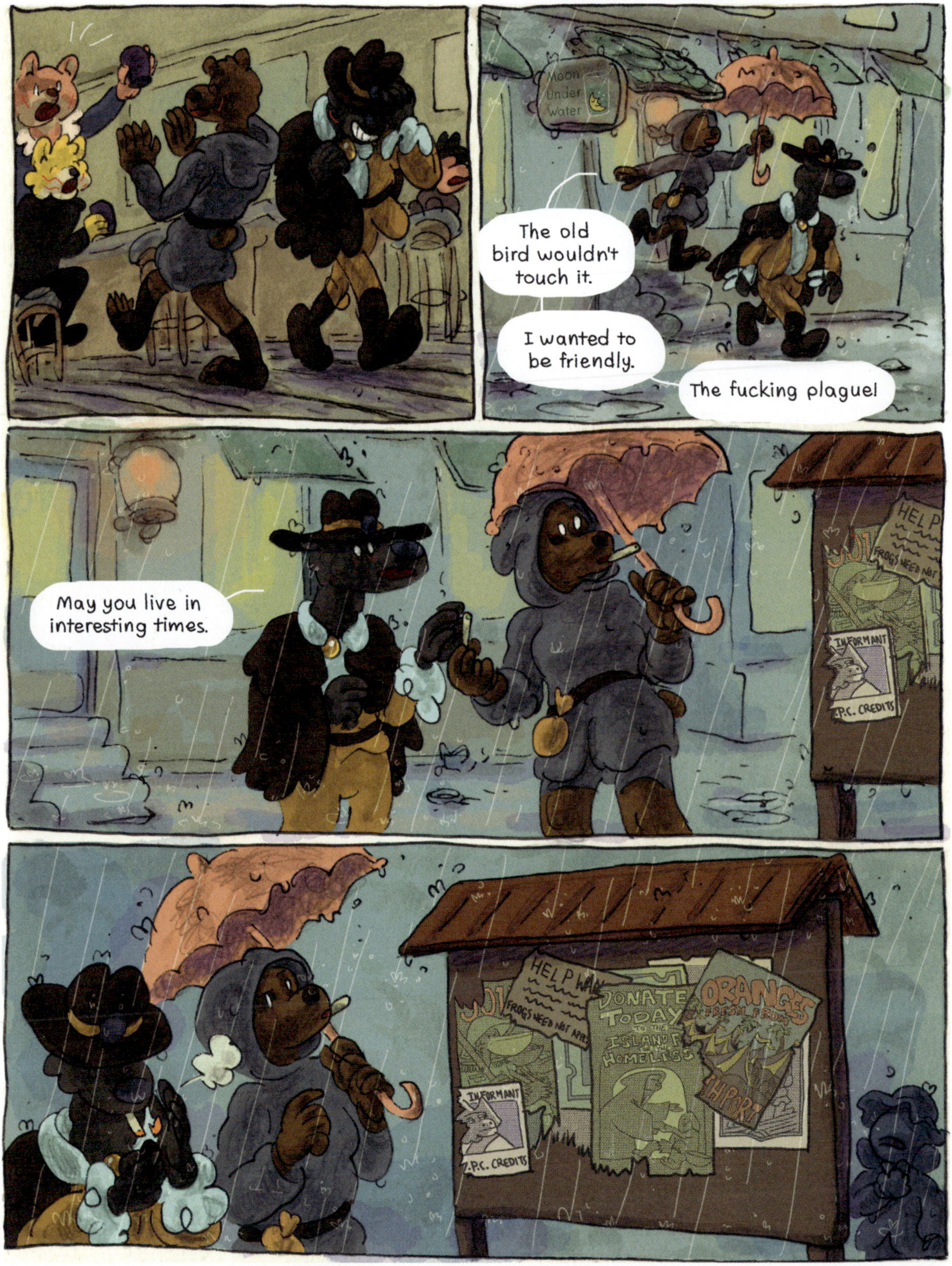
Moon Under Water
The old bird wouldn't touch it.
I wanted to be friendly.
The fucking plague!
May you live in interesting times.
HELP WA
FROGS NEED NOT APPLY
INFORMANT
P.C. CREDITS
DONATE TODAY TO THE ISLAND FOR THE HOMELESS
ORANGES FRESH FROM
IMPORT

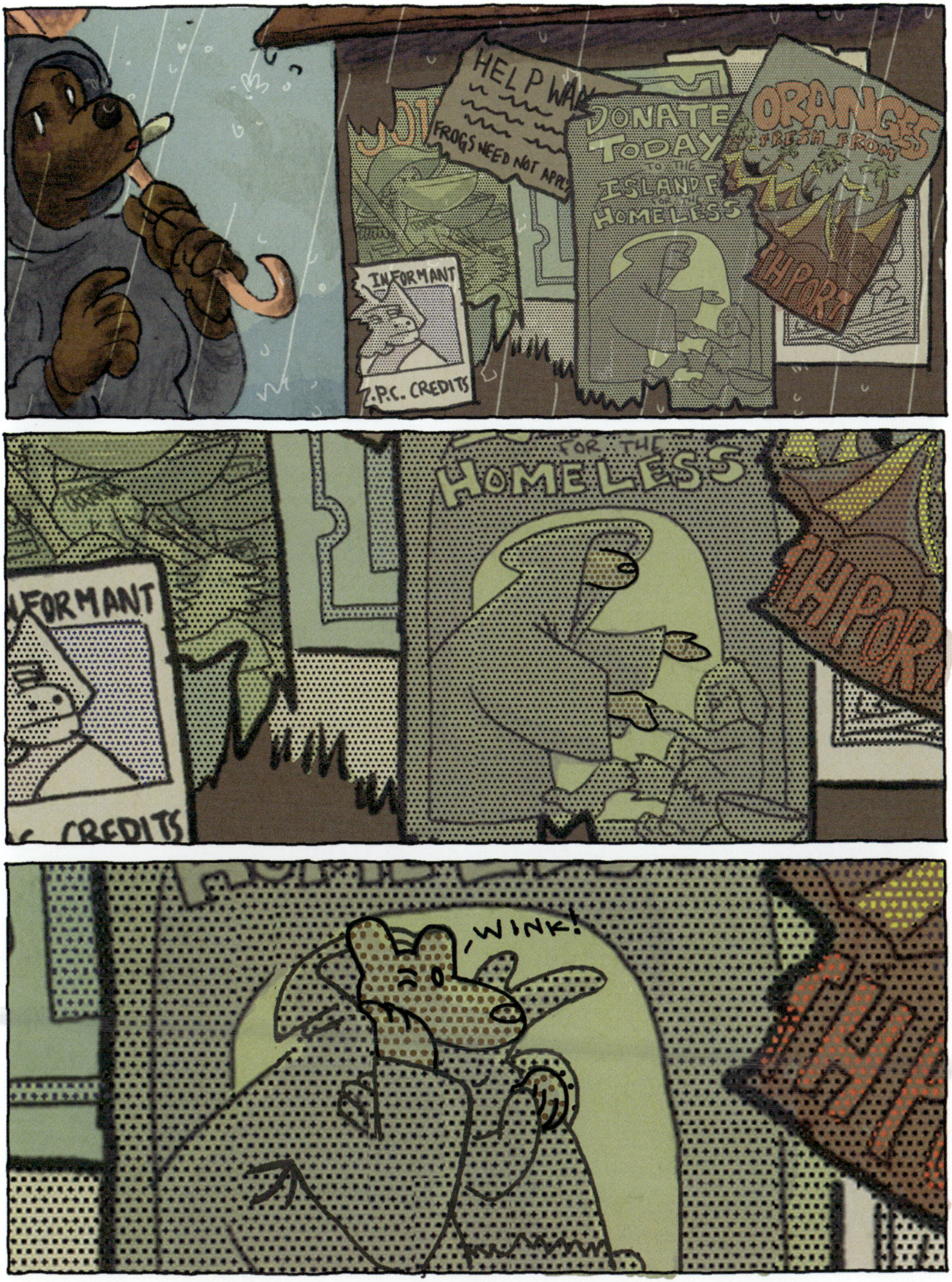
HELP WA
FROGS NEED NOT APPL
DONATE TODAY TO THE ISLAND F FOR THE HOMELESS
ORANGES FRESH FROM
THPORT
INFORMANT
.P.C. CREDITS
FOR THE HOMELESS
INFORMANT
CREDITS
THPOR
WINK!

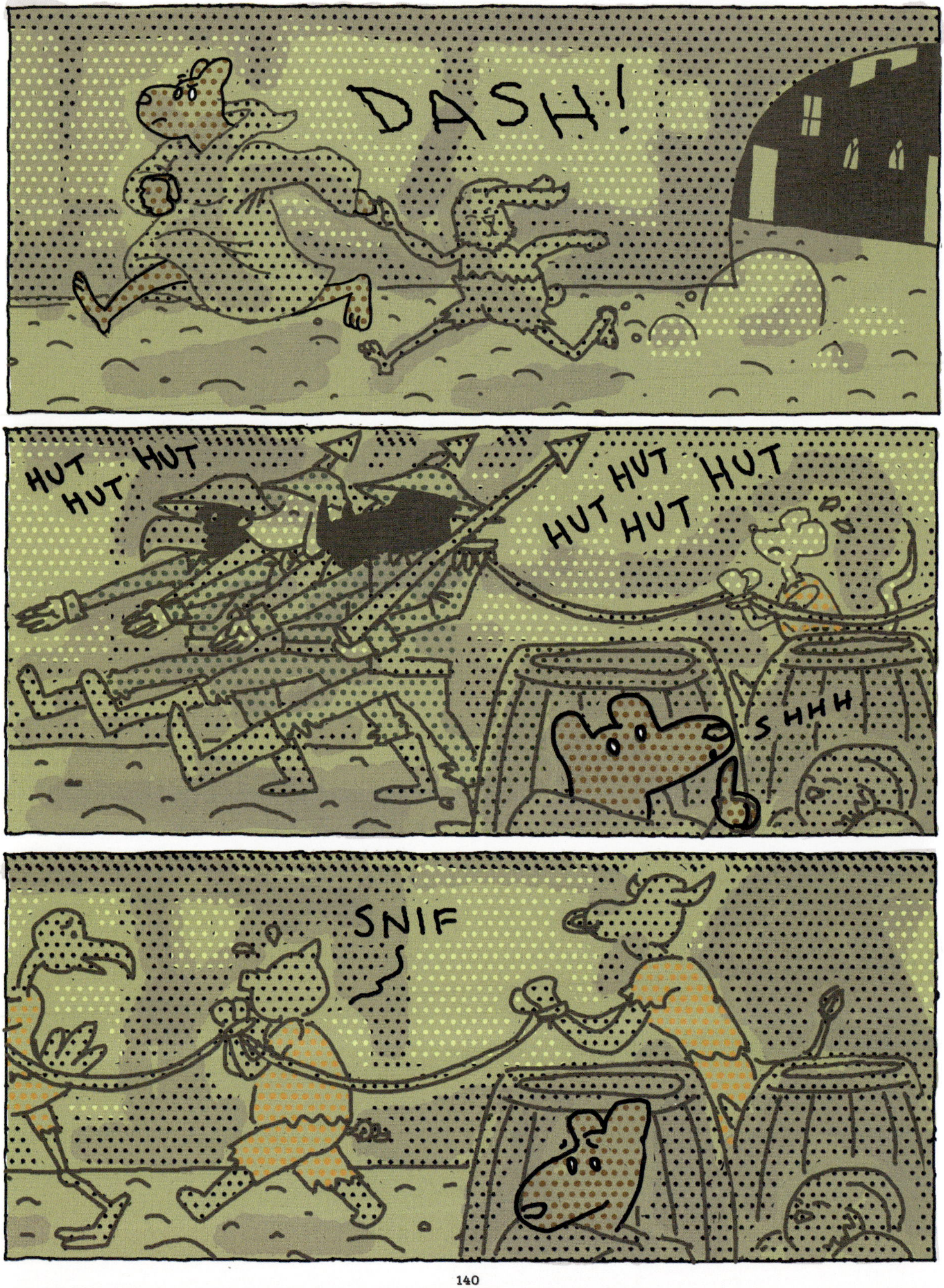
DASH!
HUT HUT HUT
HUT HUT HUT HUT
SHHH
SNIF

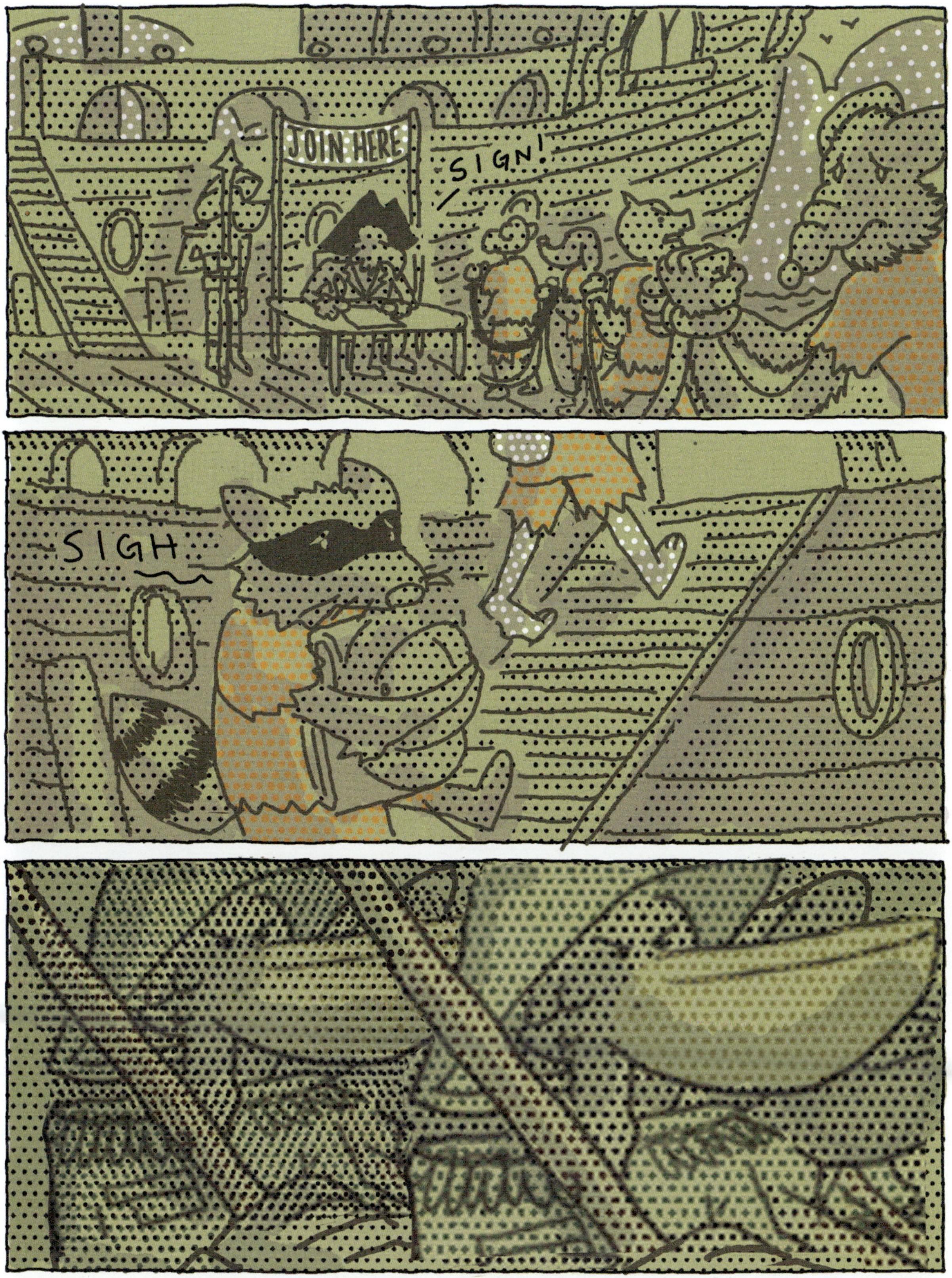
JOIN HERE
SIGN!
SIGH

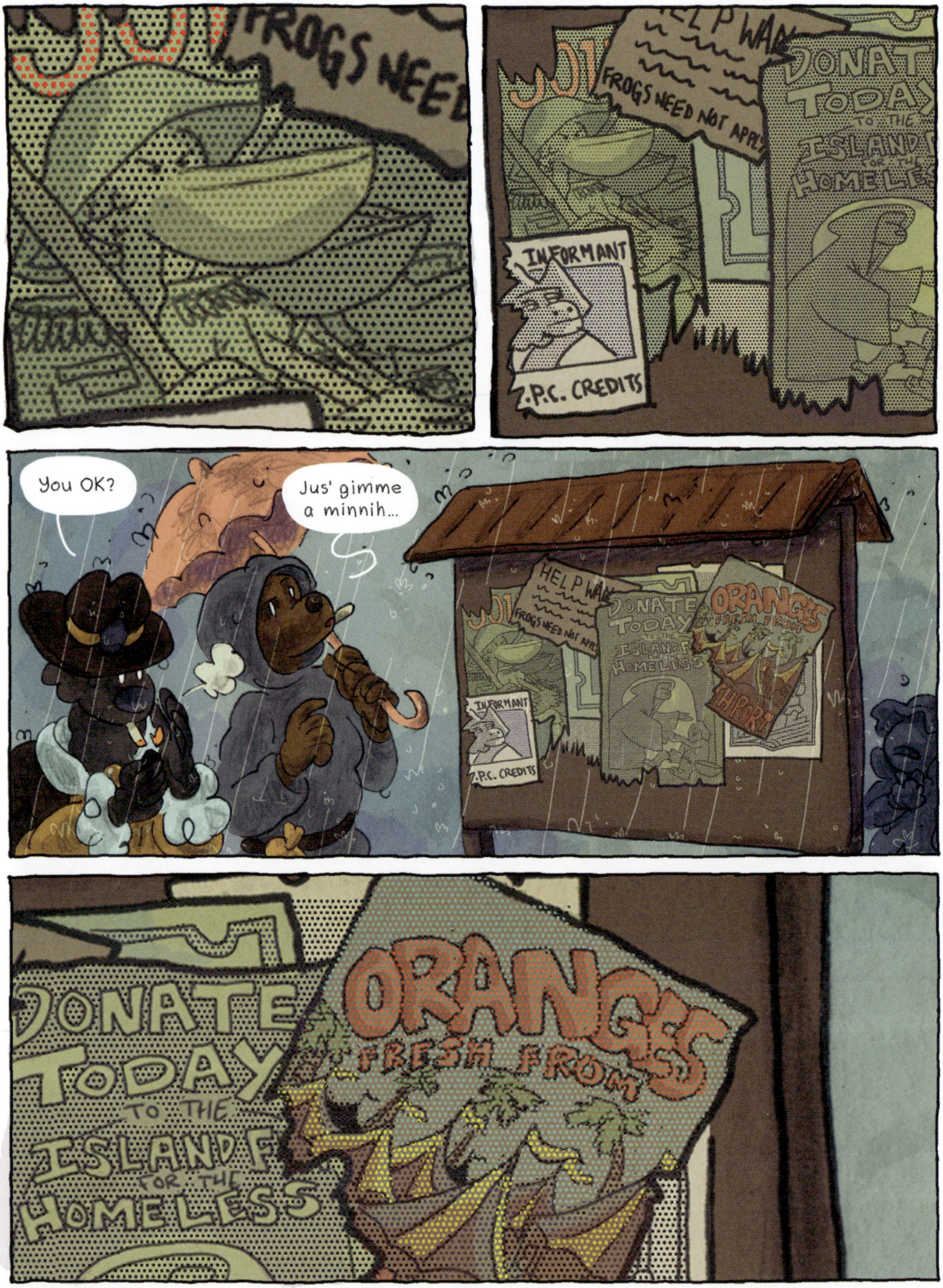
FROGS NEED
HELP WAN
FROGS NEED NOT APPLY
DONATE TODAY TO THE ISLAND F FOR THE HOMELESS
INFORMANT
.P.C. CREDITS
You OK?
Jus' gimme a minnih...
ORANGES FRESH FROM
DONATE TODAY TO THE ISLAND F FOR THE HOMELESS
ORANGES FRESH FROM

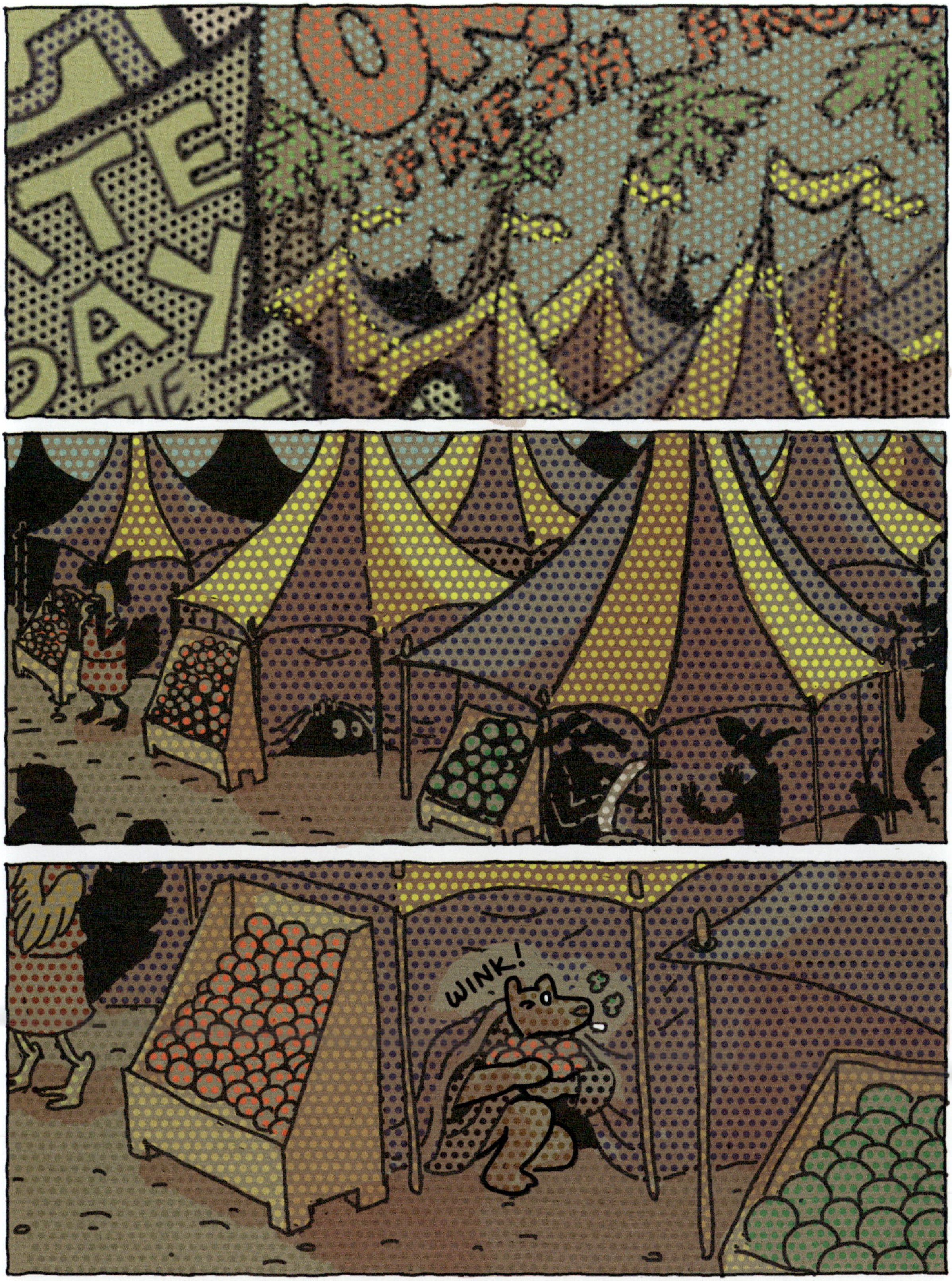
FRESH
WINK!

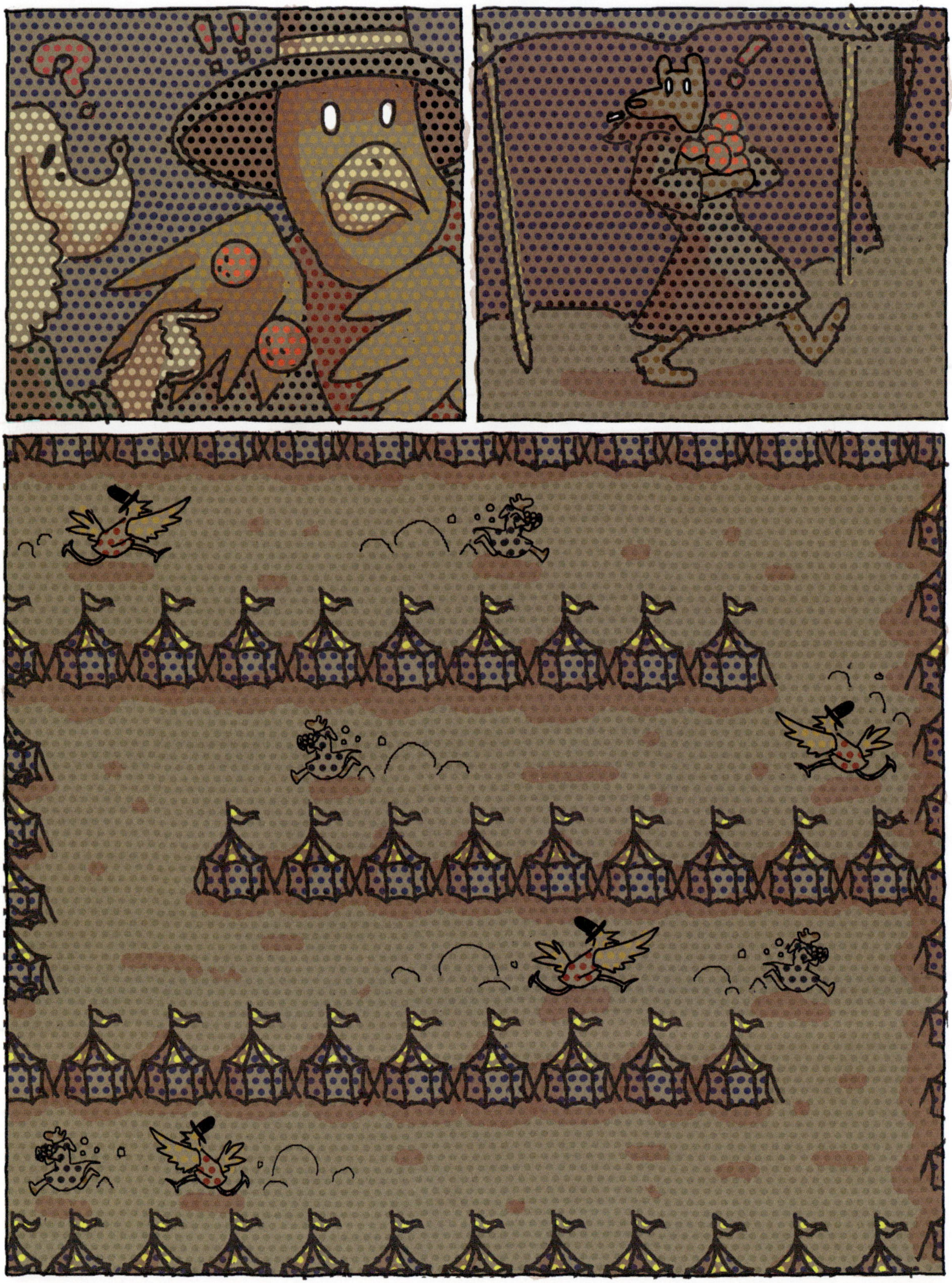

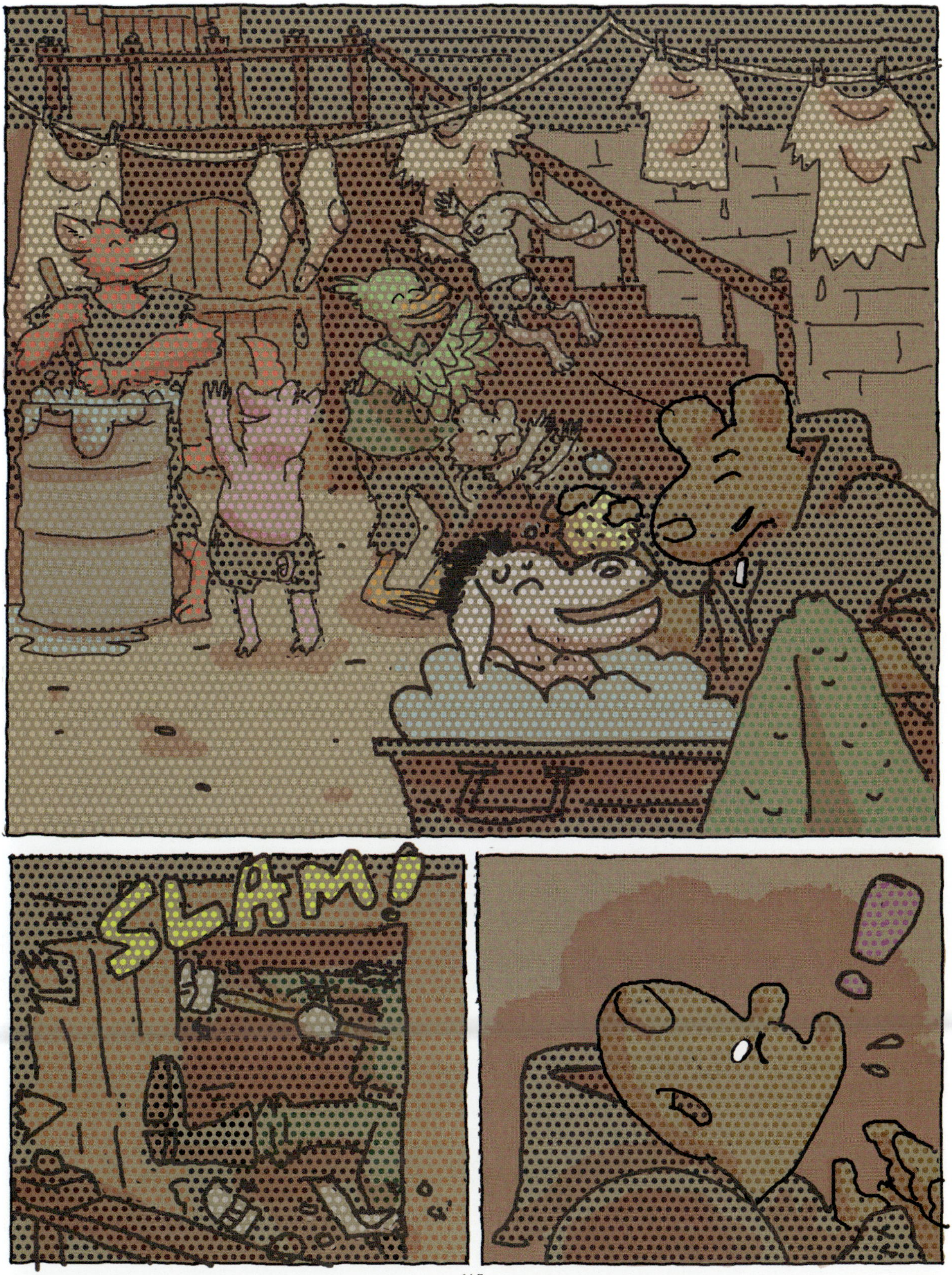
SLAM!

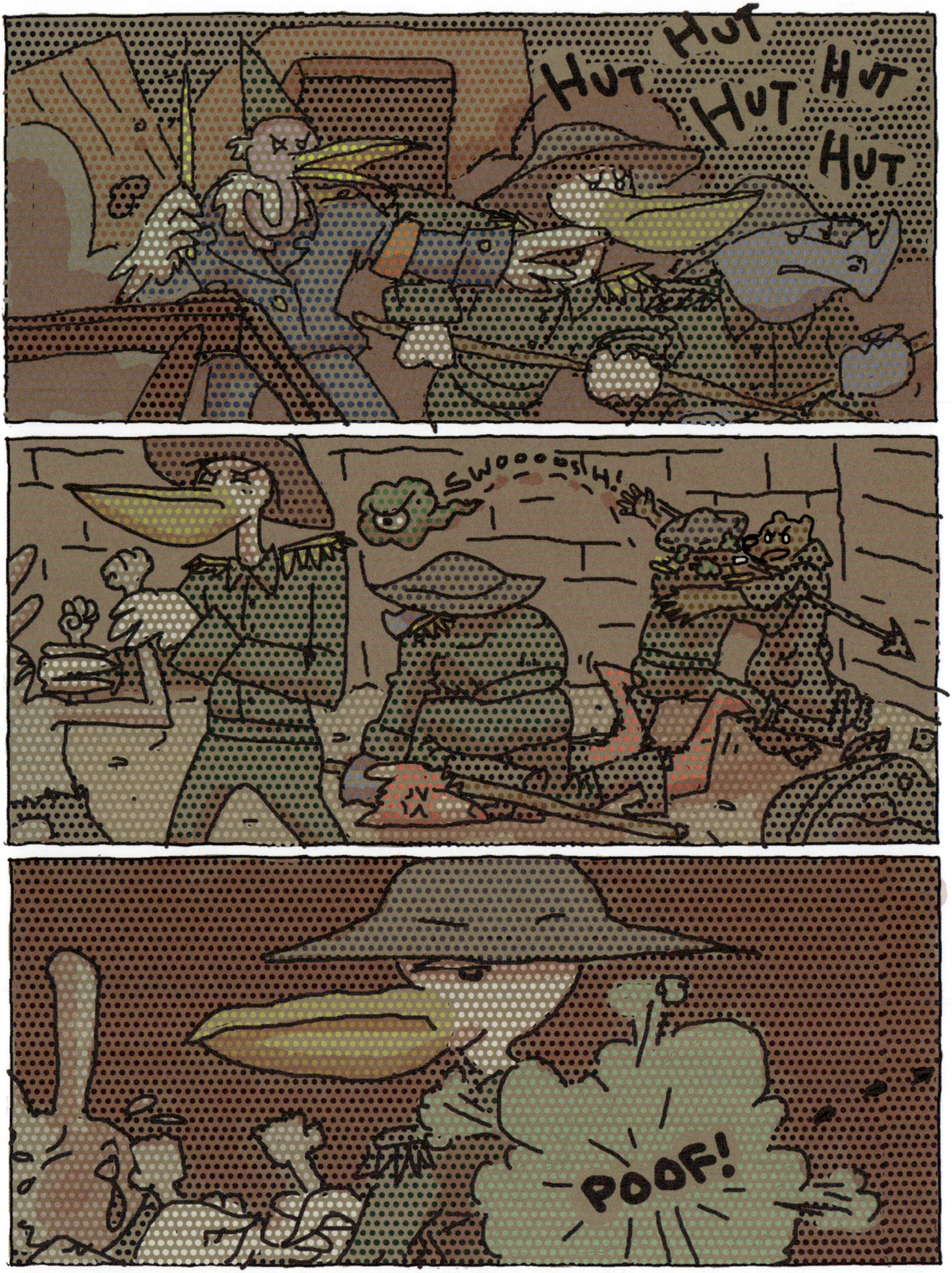
HUT
HUT
HUT
HUT
HUT
SWOOOOSH!
POOF!

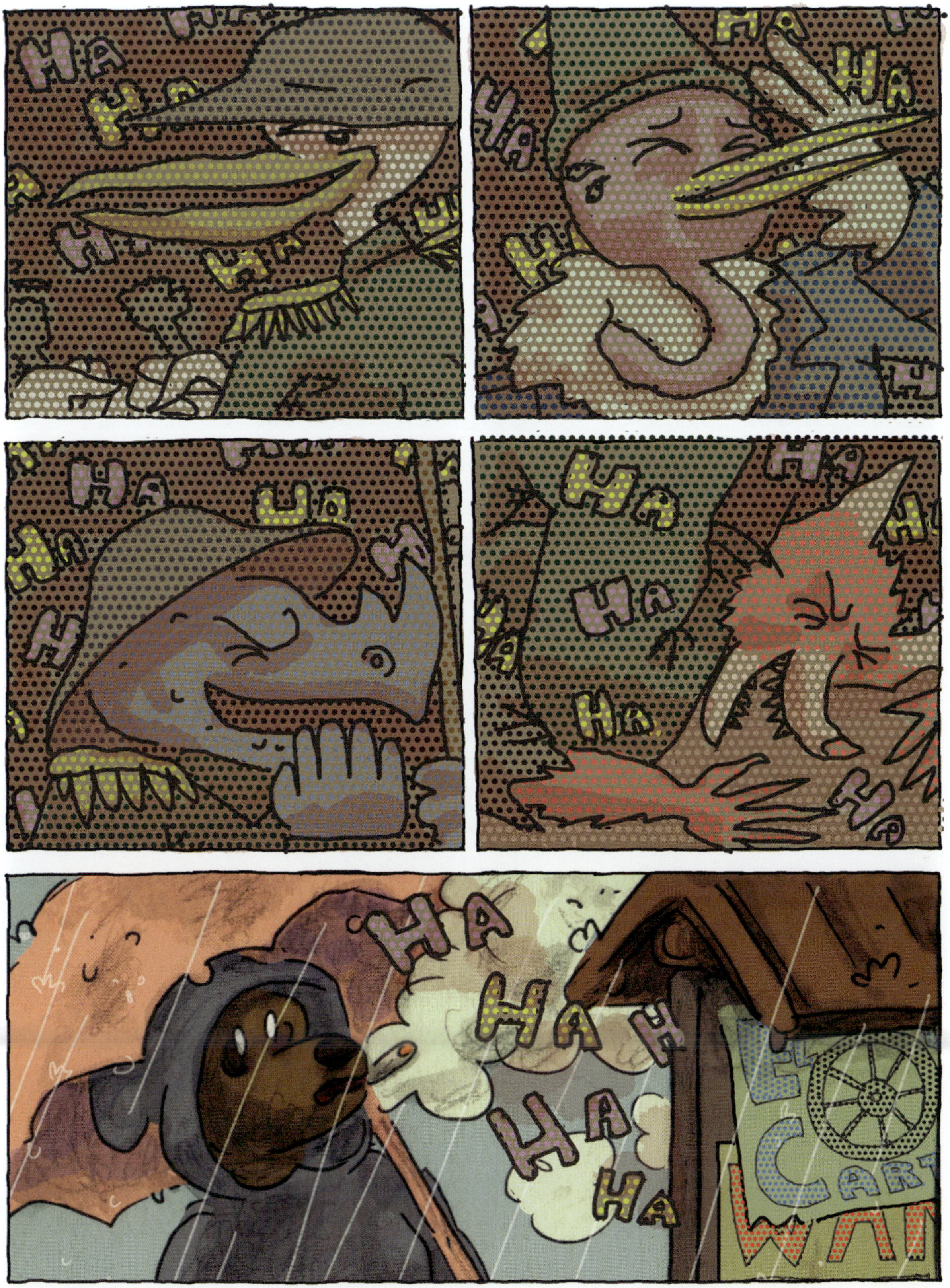
HA
HA
HA
HA
HA
HA
HA
HA
HA
HA
HA
HA
HA
HA
HA
HA
HA
HA
HA HA
HA
HA

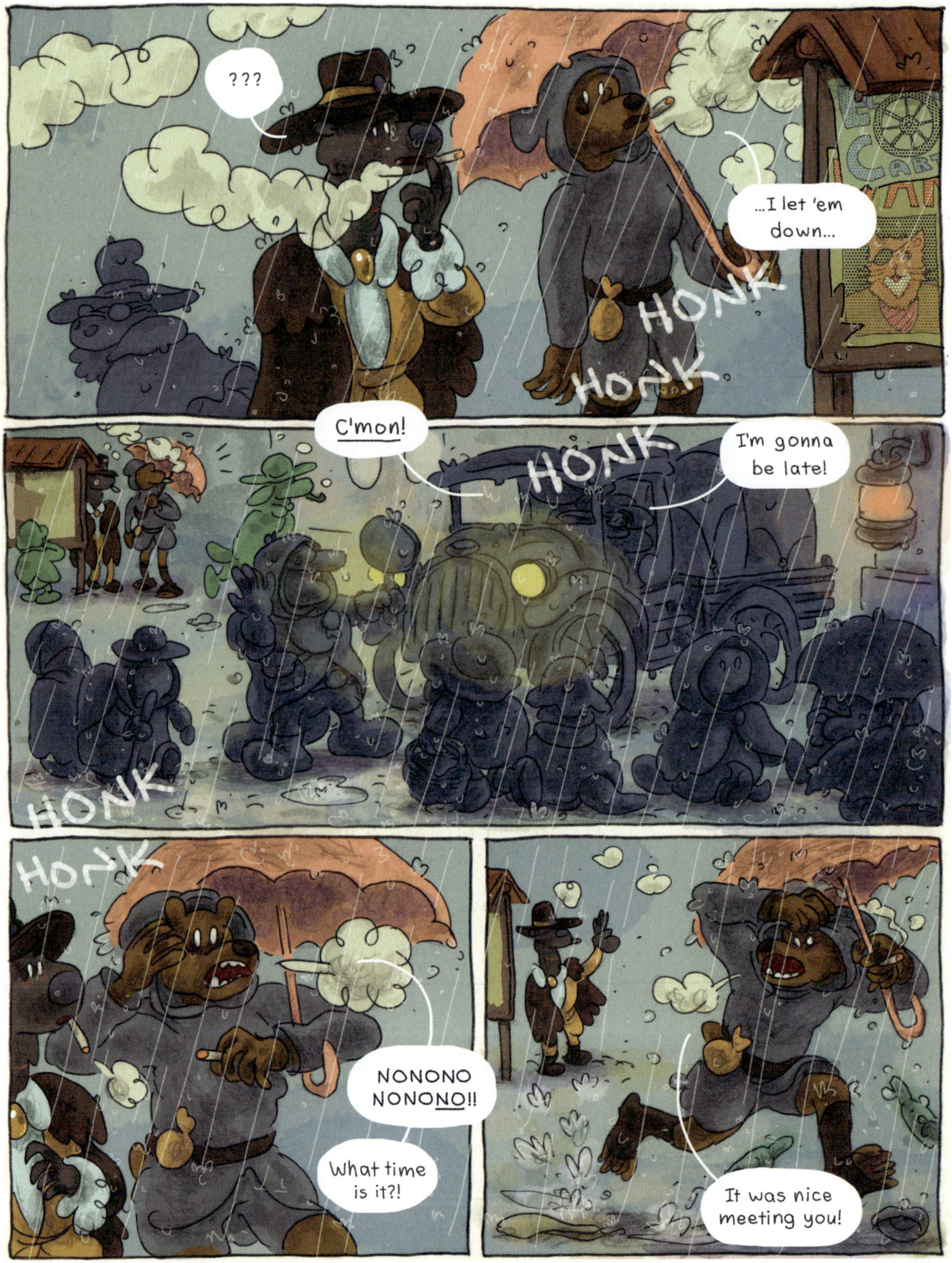
???
...I let 'em down...
HONK
HONK
C'mon!
HONK
I'm gonna be late!
HONK
HONK
NONONO NONONO!!
What time is it?!
It was nice meeting you!

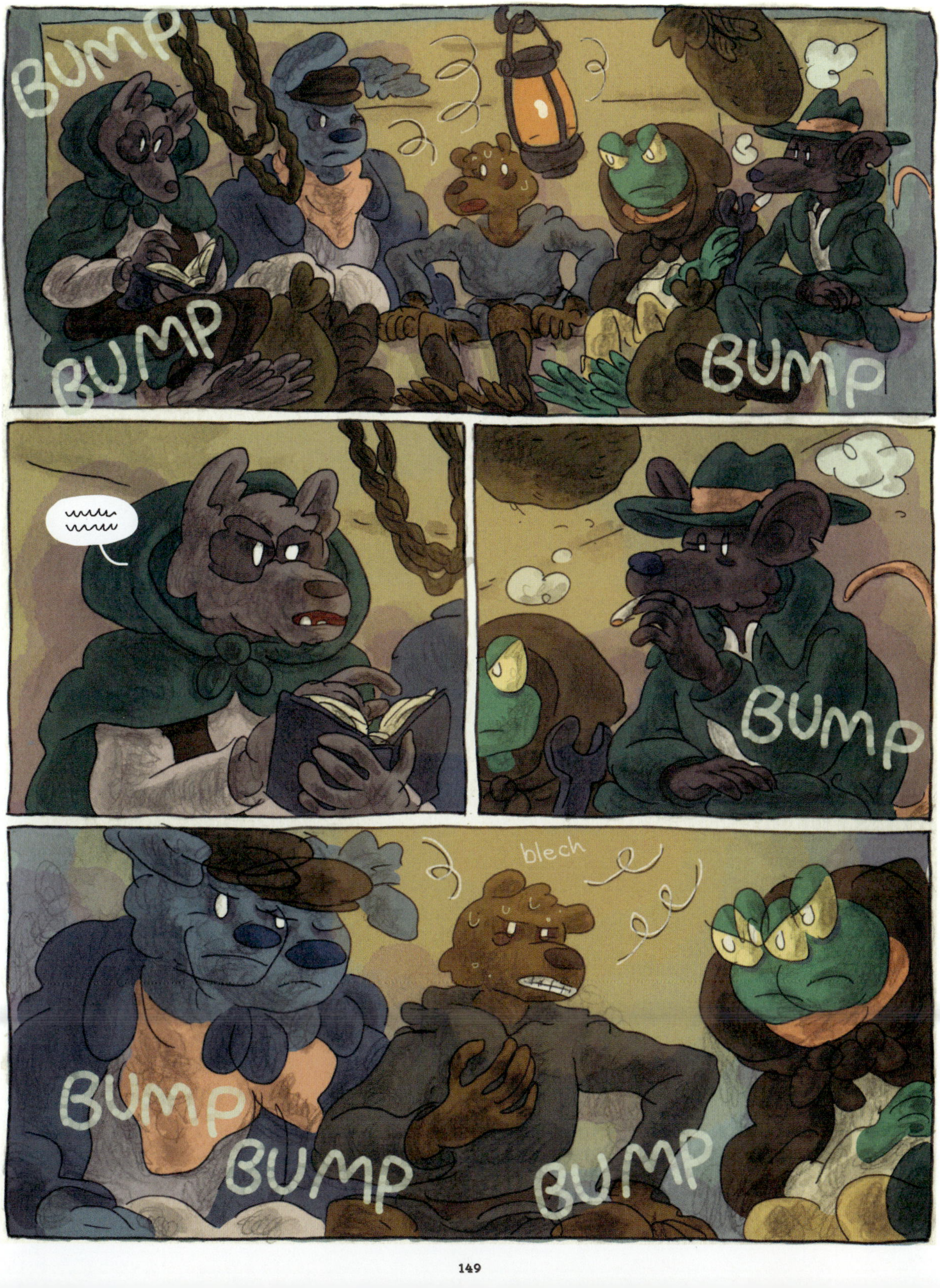
BUMP
BUMP
BUMP
BUMP
blech
BUMP
BUMP
BUMP

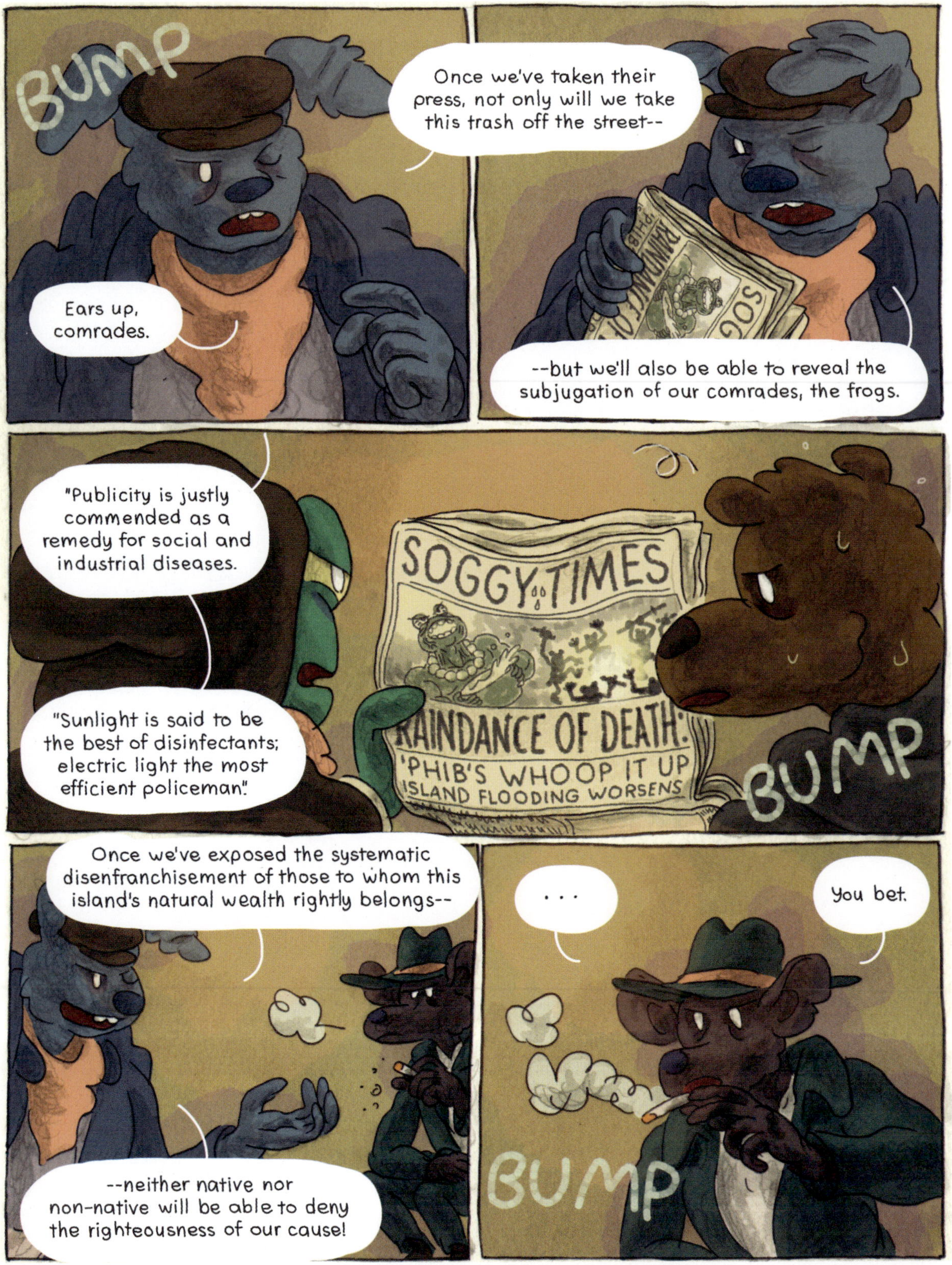
BUMP
Ears up, comrades.
Once we've taken their press, not only will we take this trash off the street--
--but we'll also be able to reveal the subjugation of our comrades, the frogs.
"Publicity is justly commended as a remedy for social and industrial diseases.
"Sunlight is said to be the best of disinfectants; electric light the most efficient policeman."
SOGGY TIMES
RAINDANCE OF DEATH:
'PHIB'S WHOOP IT UP
ISLAND FLOODING WORSENS
BUMP
Once we've exposed the systematic disenfranchisement of those to whom this island's natural wealth rightly belongs--
--neither native nor non-native will be able to deny the righteousness of our cause!
. . .
You bet.
BUMP

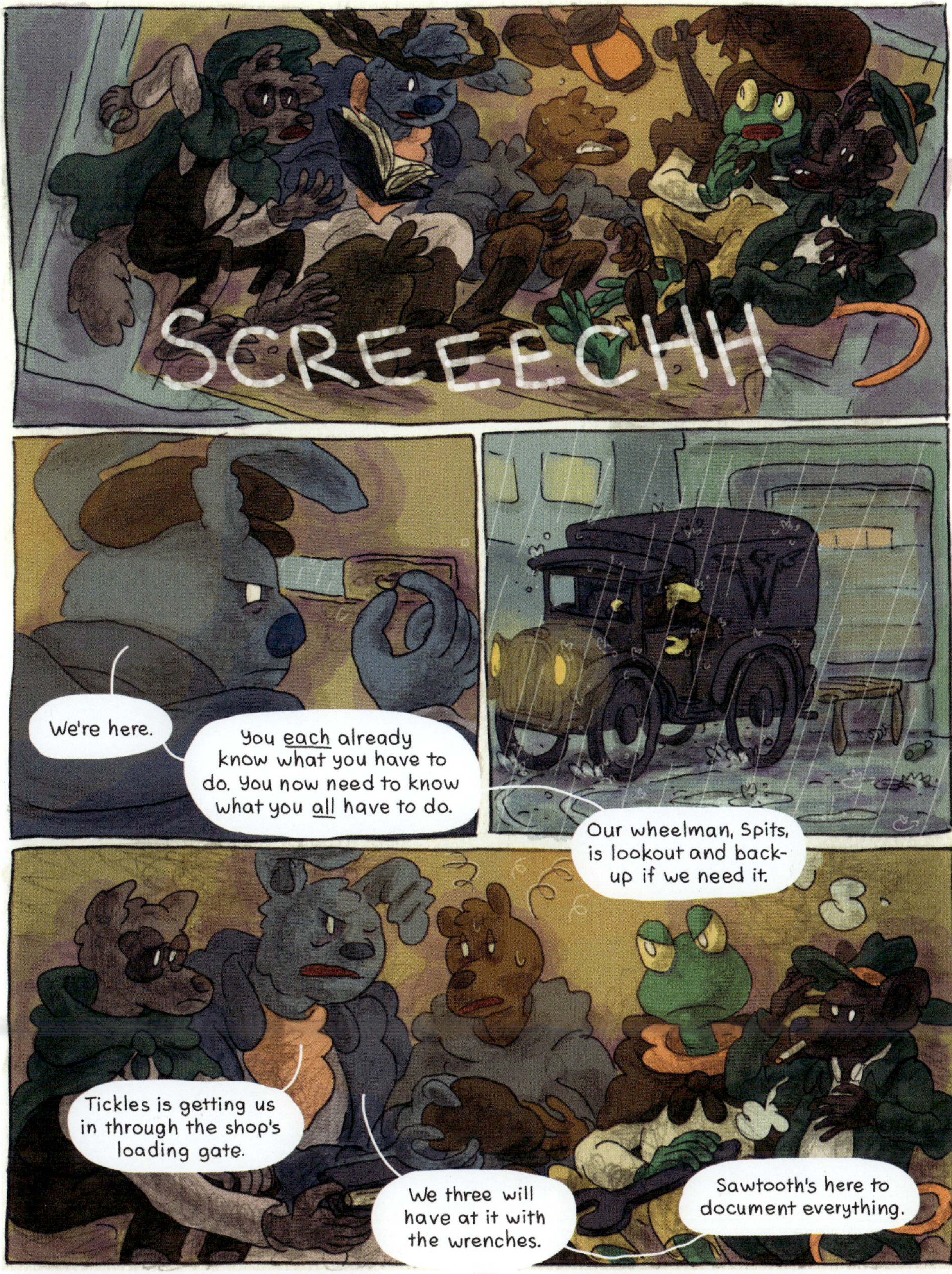
SCREEECHH
We're here.
You each already know what you have to do. You now need to know what you all have to do.
Our wheelman, Spits, is lookout and back-up if we need it.
Tickles is getting us in through the shop's loading gate.
We three will have at it with the wrenches.
Sawtooth's here to document everything.

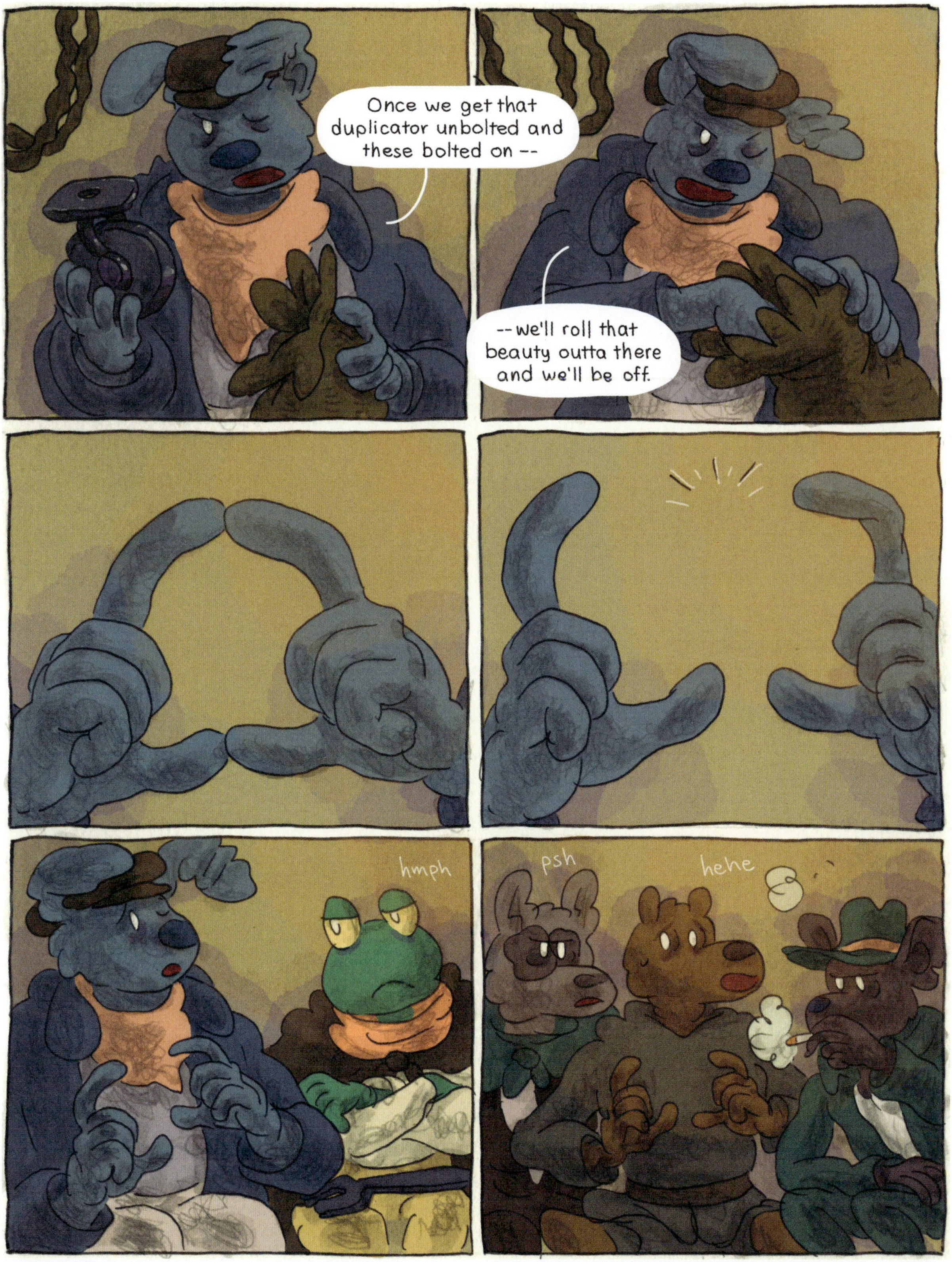
Once we get that duplicator unbolted and these bolted on --
--we'll roll that beauty outta there and we'll be off.
hmph
psh
hehe

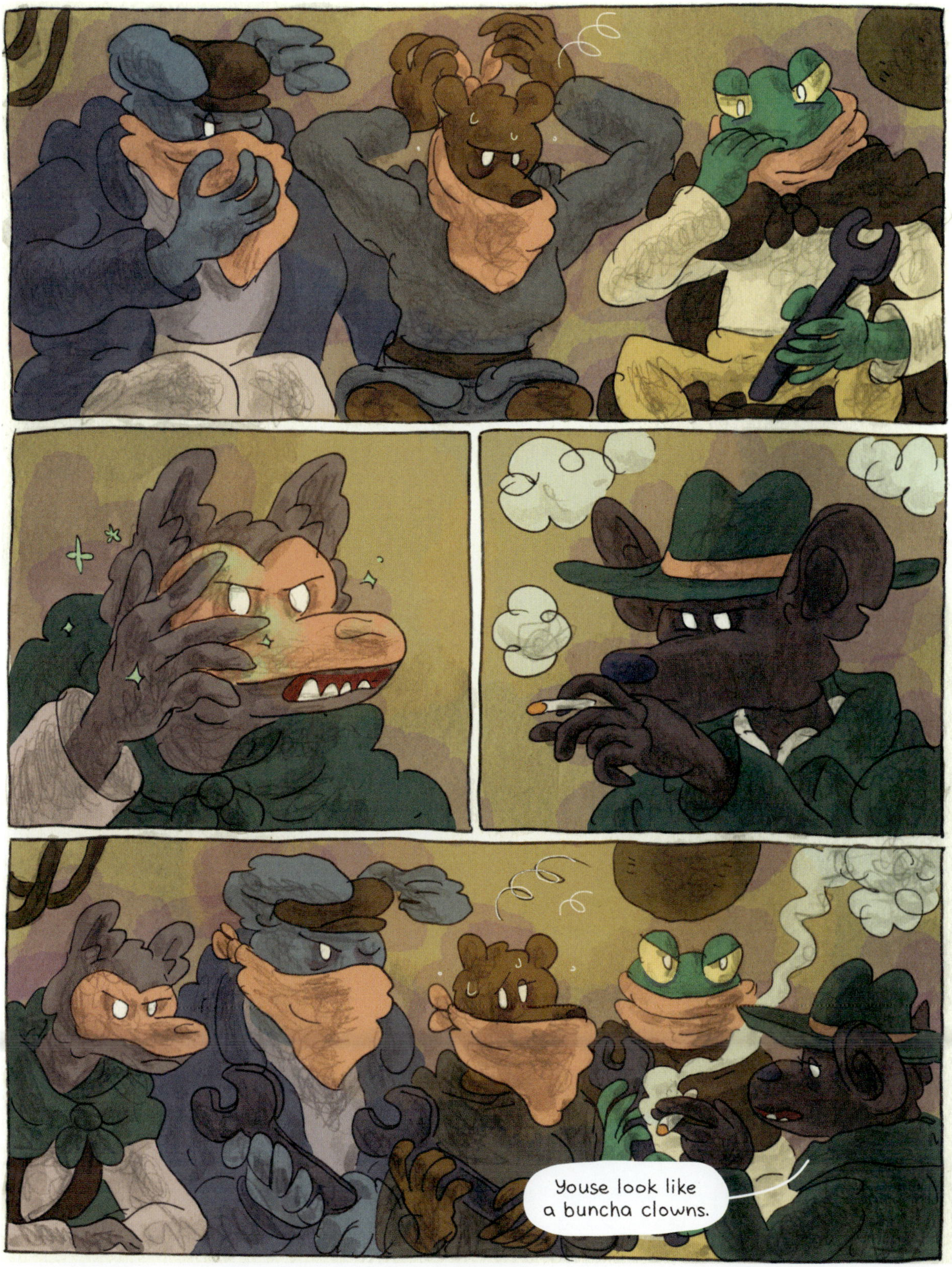
Youse look like a buncha clowns.

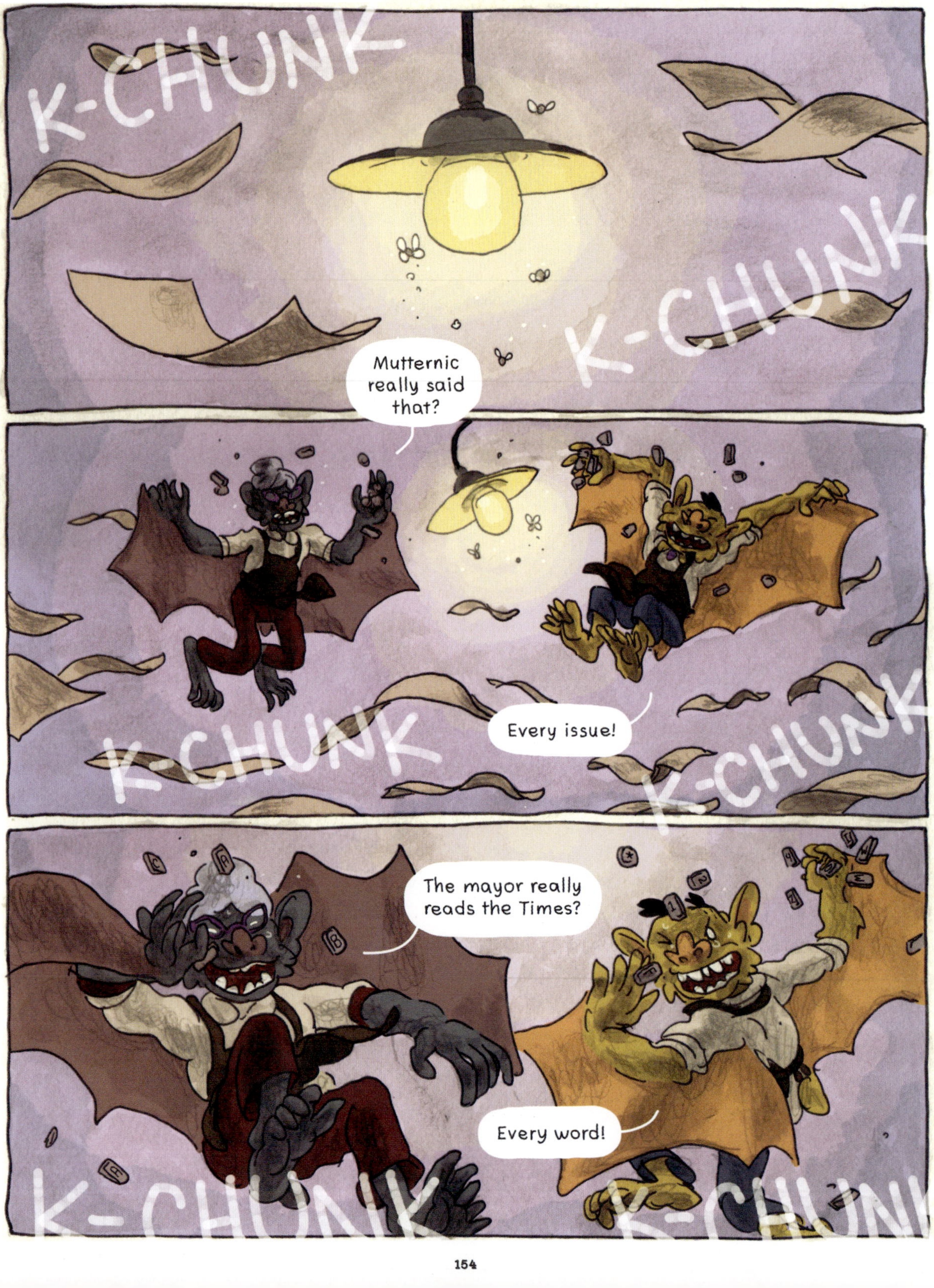
K-CHUNK
K-CHUNK
Mutternic really said that?
Every issue!
K-CHUNK
K-CHUNK
The mayor really reads the Times?
Every word!
K-CHUNK
K-CHUNK

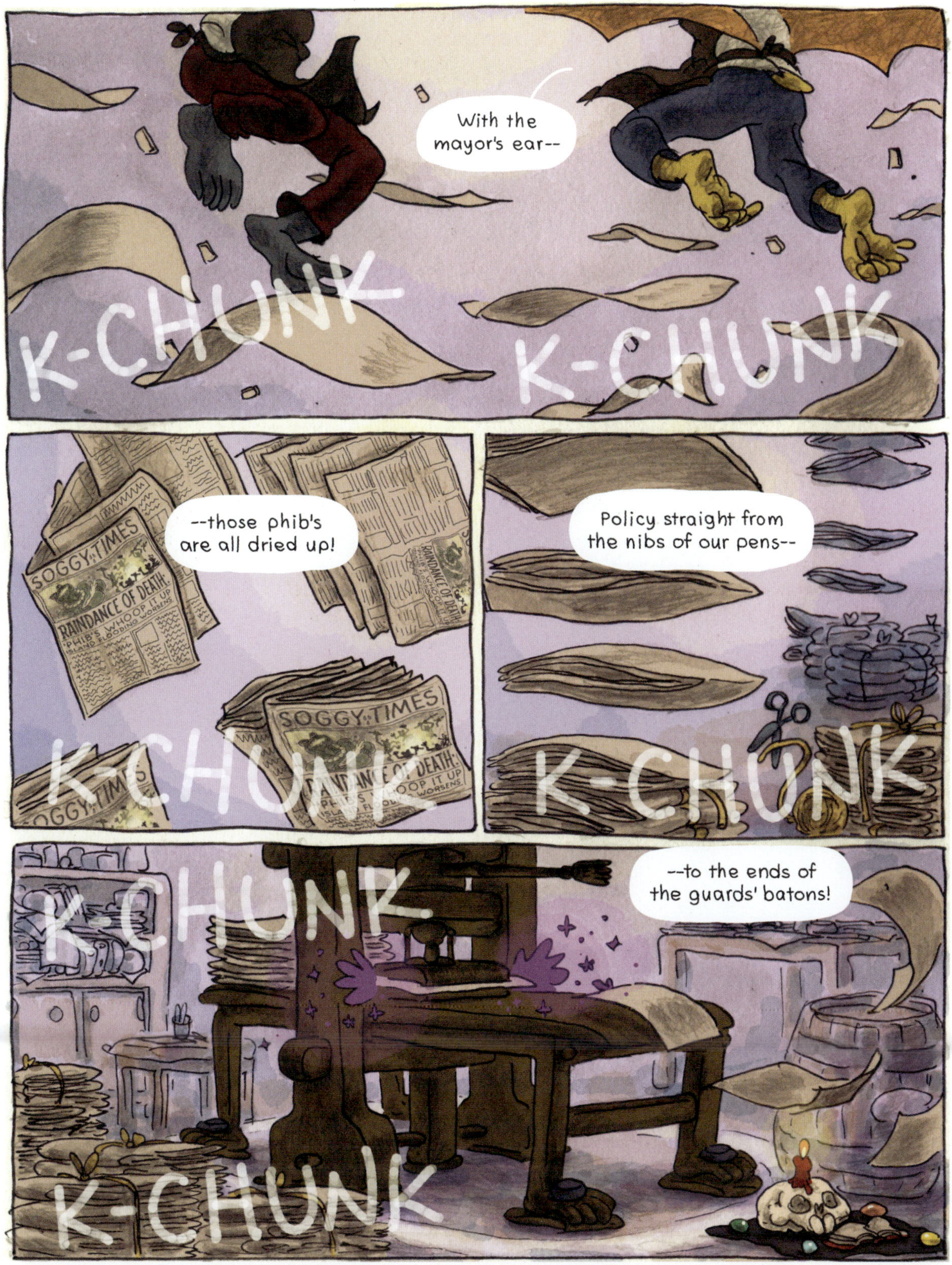
With the mayor's ear--
K-CHUNK
K-CHUNK
--those phib's are all dried up!
SOGGY TIMES
RAINDANCE OF DEATH:
PHIB'S WHOOP IT UP
ISLAND FLOODING WORSENS
K-CHUNK
Policy straight from the nibs of our pens--
K-CHUNK
K-CHUNK
--to the ends of the guards' batons!
K-CHUNK

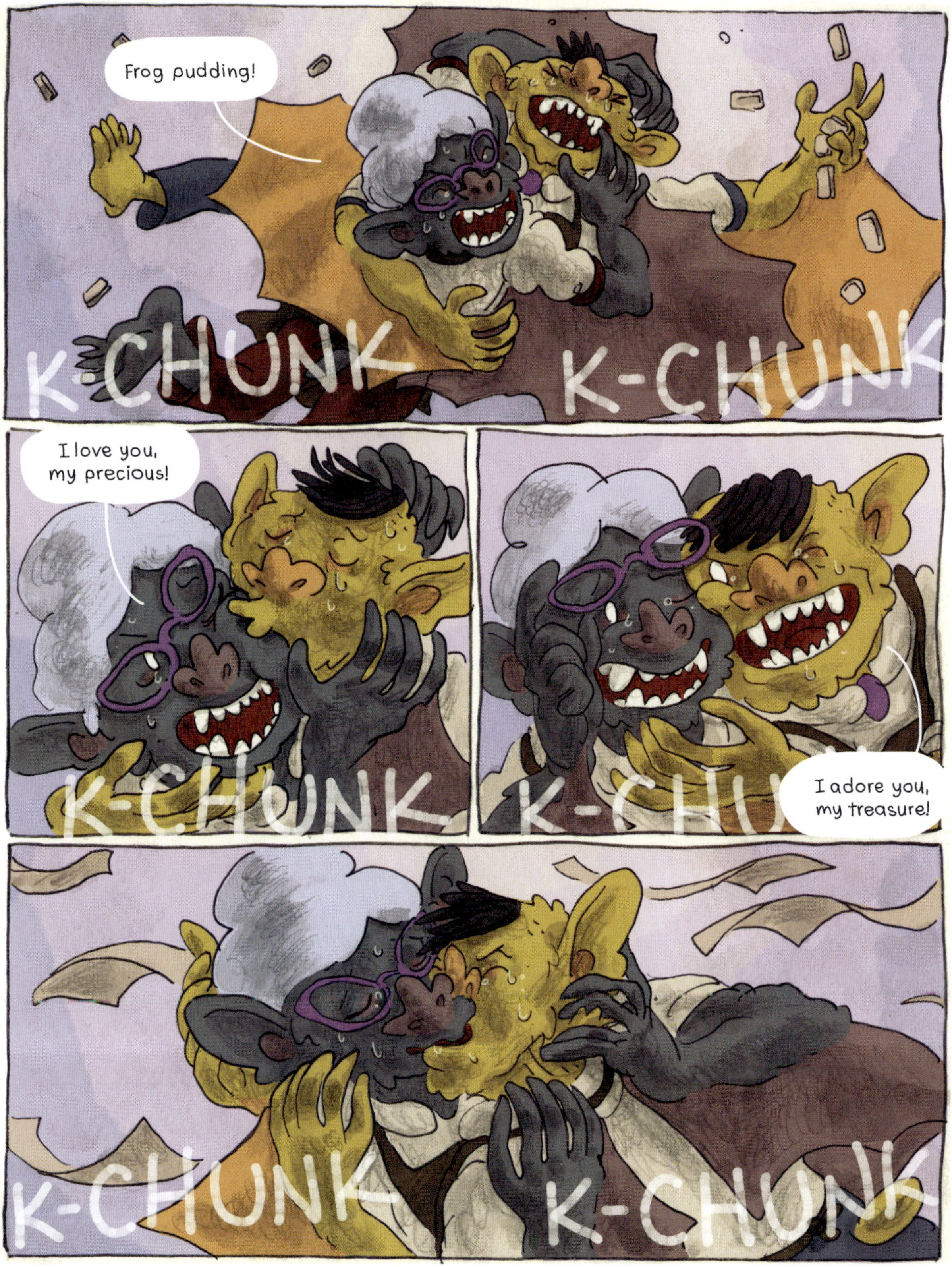
Frog pudding!
K-CHUNK
K-CHUNK
I love you, my precious!
K-CHUNK
K-CHU
I adore you, my treasure!
K-CHUNK
K-CHUNK

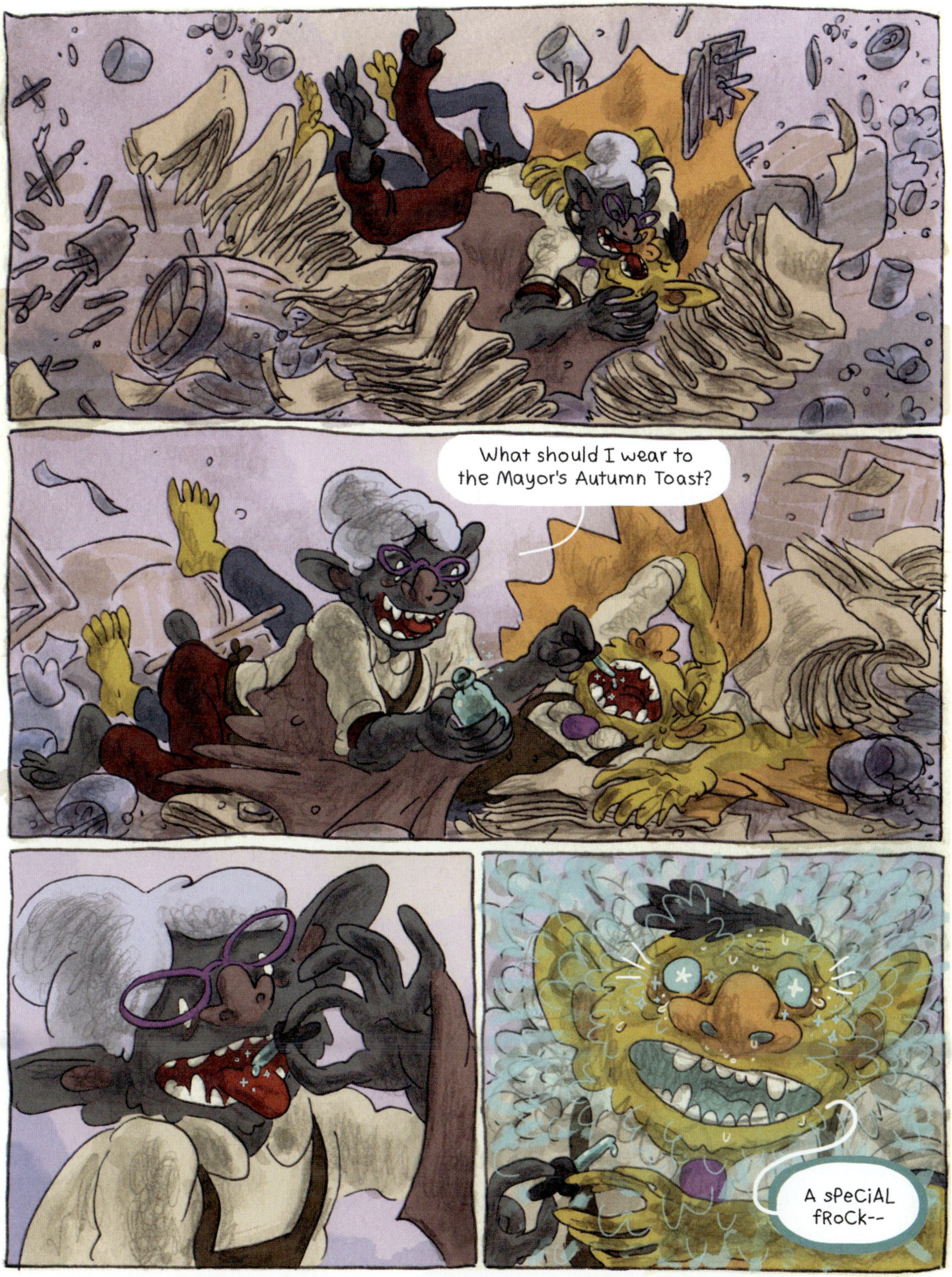
What should I wear to the Mayor's Autumn Toast?
A sPeCiAL fRoCk--

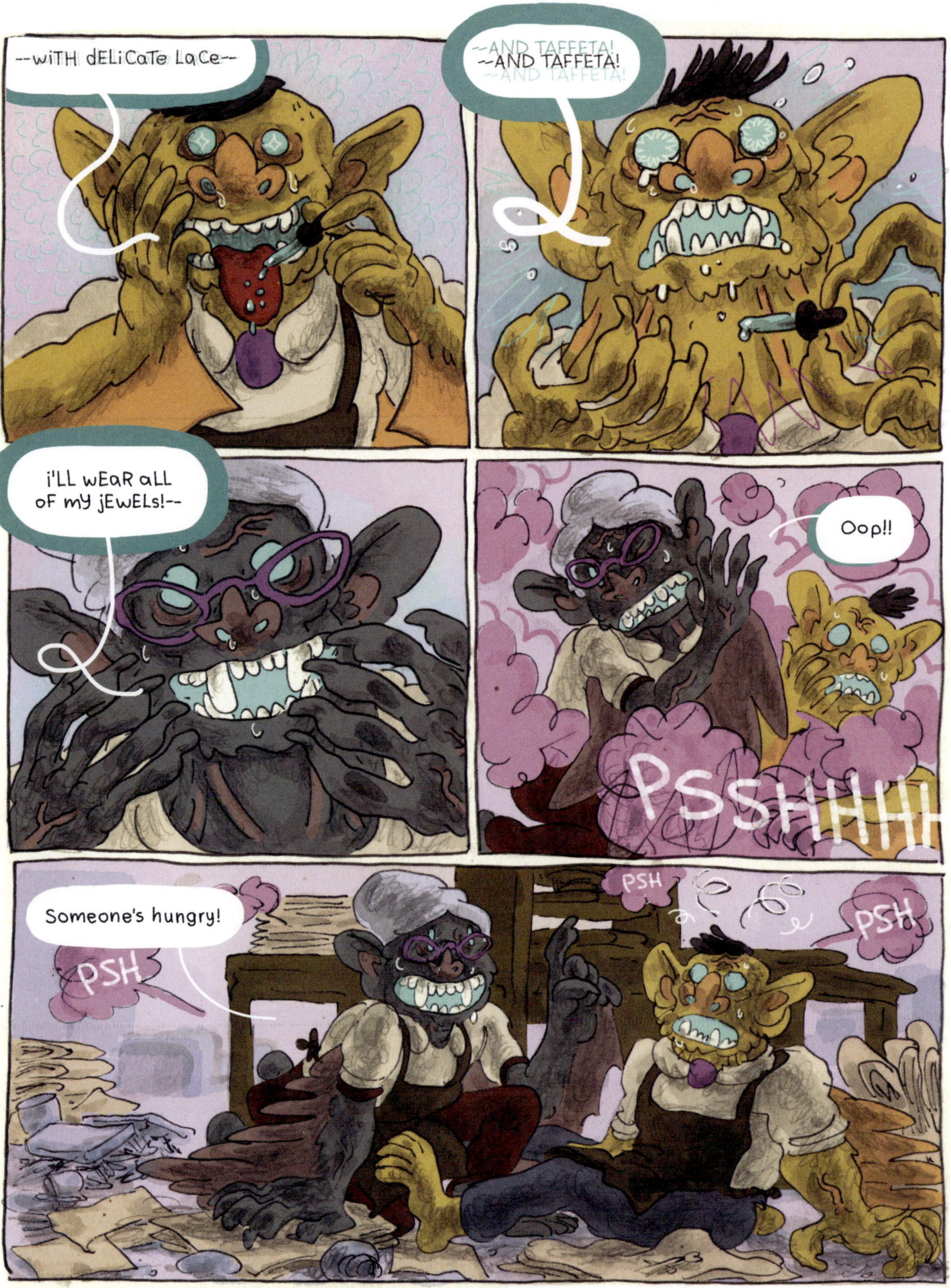
--WITH DELICATE LACE--
--AND TAFFETA!
--AND TAFFETA!
--AND TAFFETA!
I'LL WEAR ALL OF MY JEWELS!--
Oop!!
PSSHHHH
Someone's hungry!
PSH
PSH
PSH

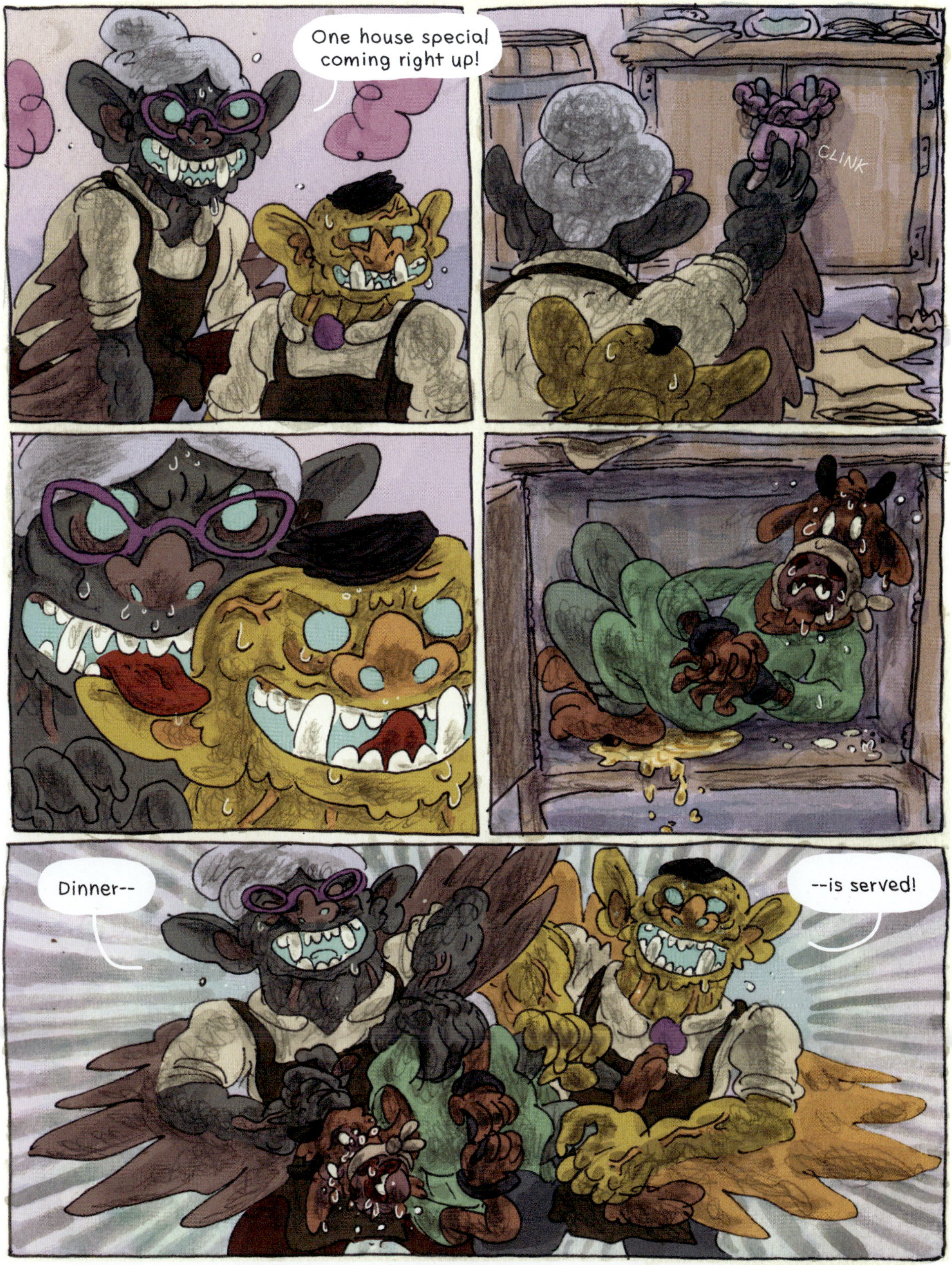
One house special coming right up!
CLINK
Dinner--
--is served!

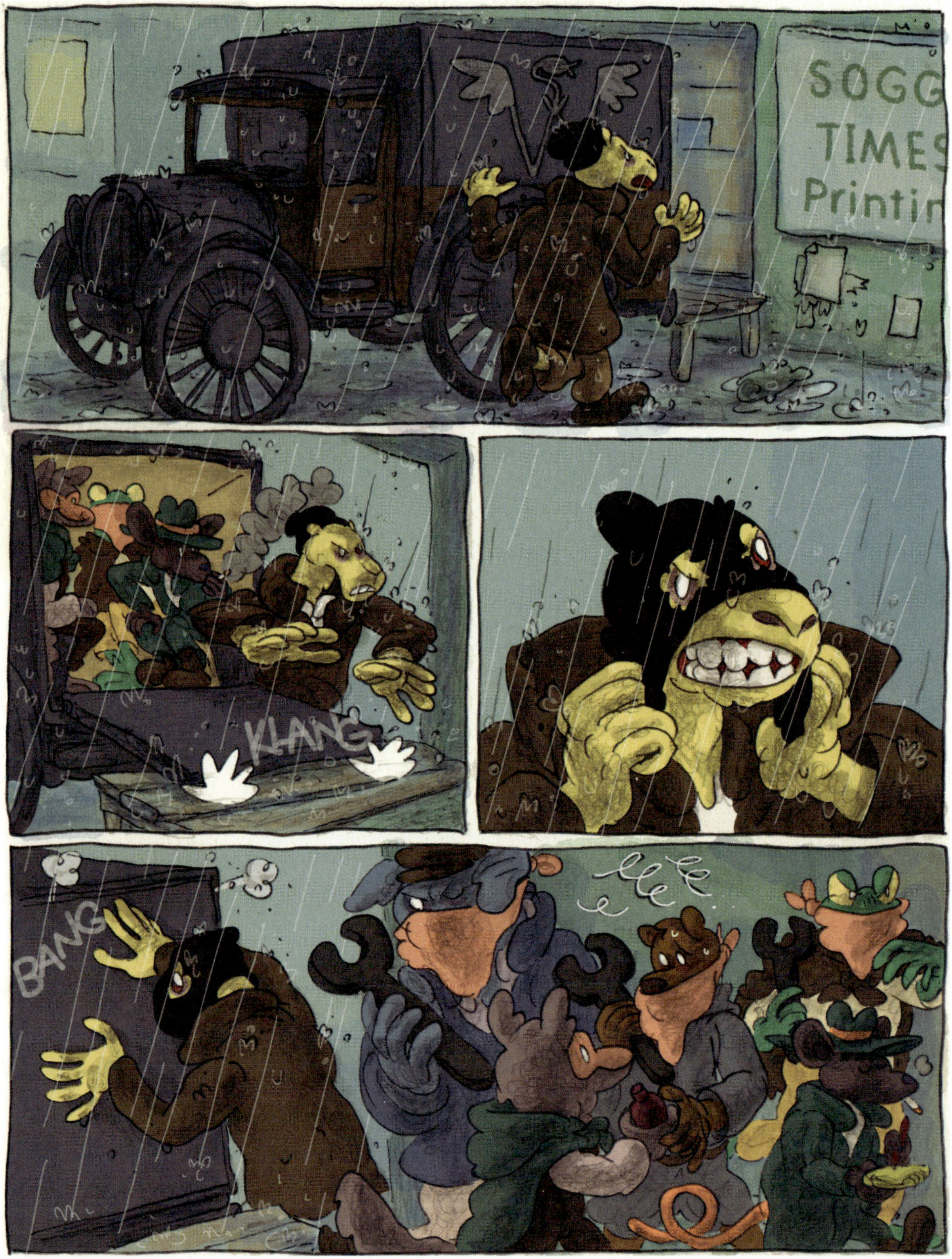
SOGG
TIMES
Printin
KLANG
BANG

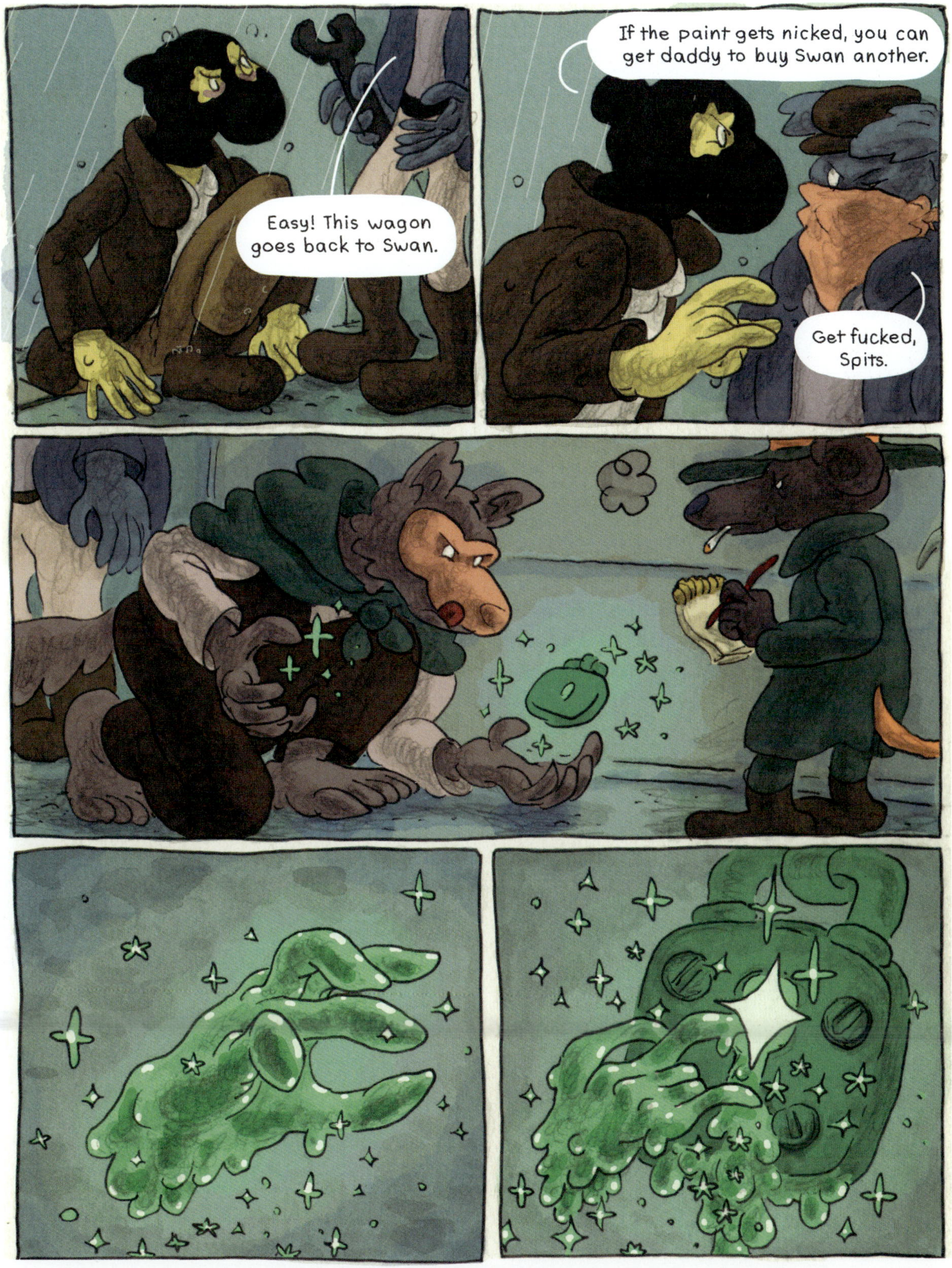
Easy! This wagon goes back to Swan.
If the paint gets nicked, you can get daddy to buy Swan another.
Get fucked, Spits.

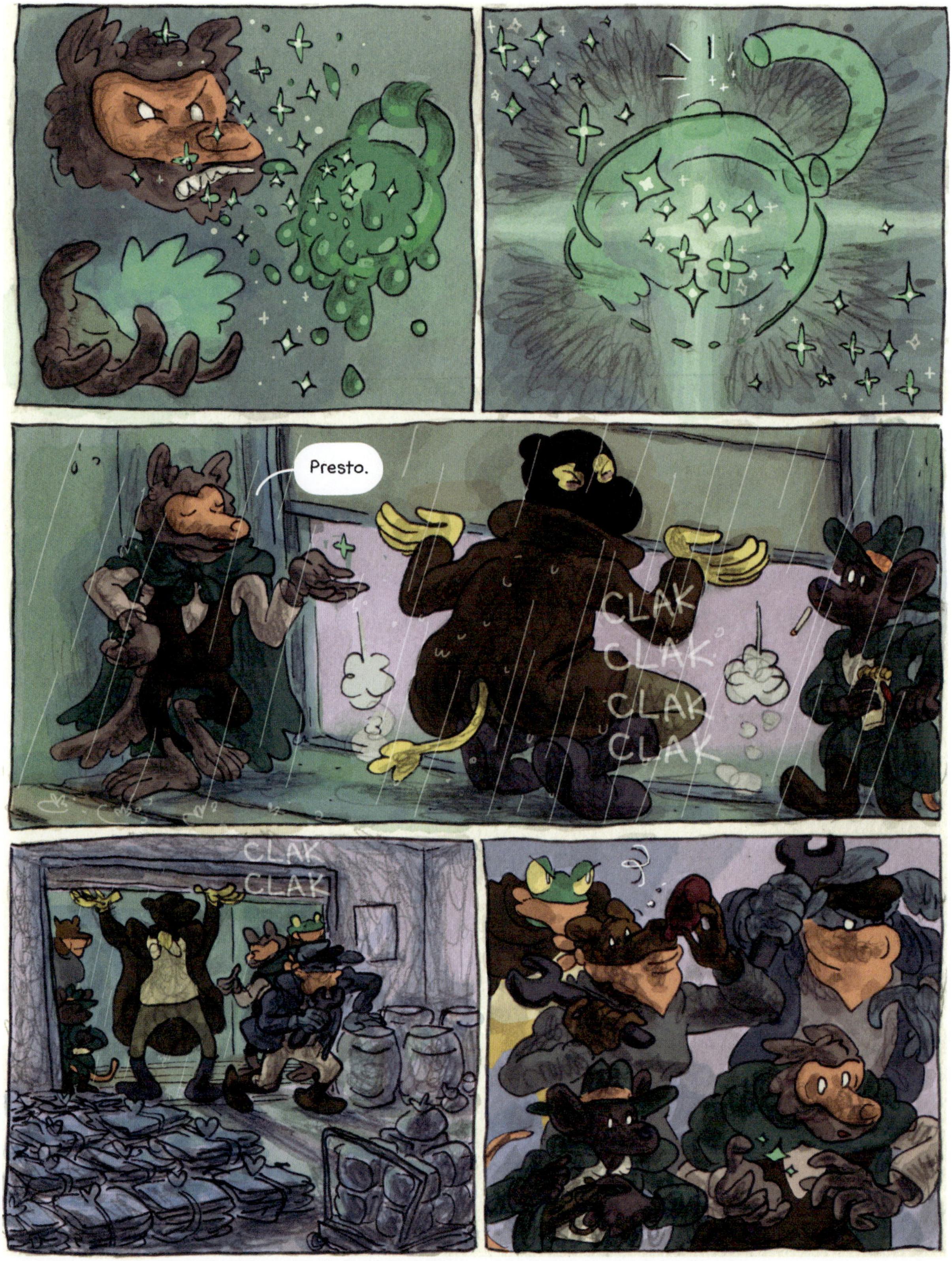
Presto.
CLAK
CLAK
CLAK
CLAK
CLAK
CLAK

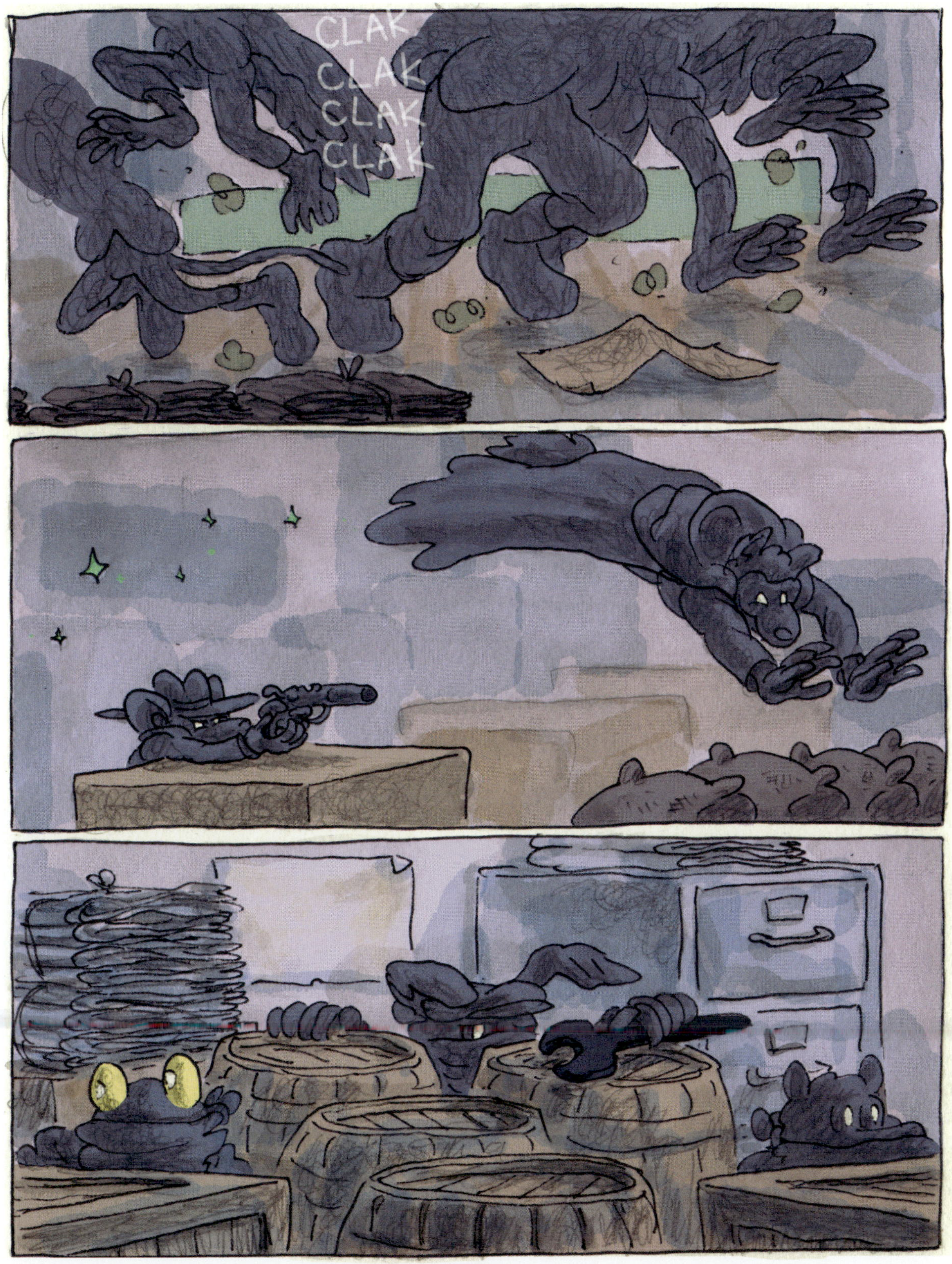
CLAK
CLAK
CLAK
CLAK

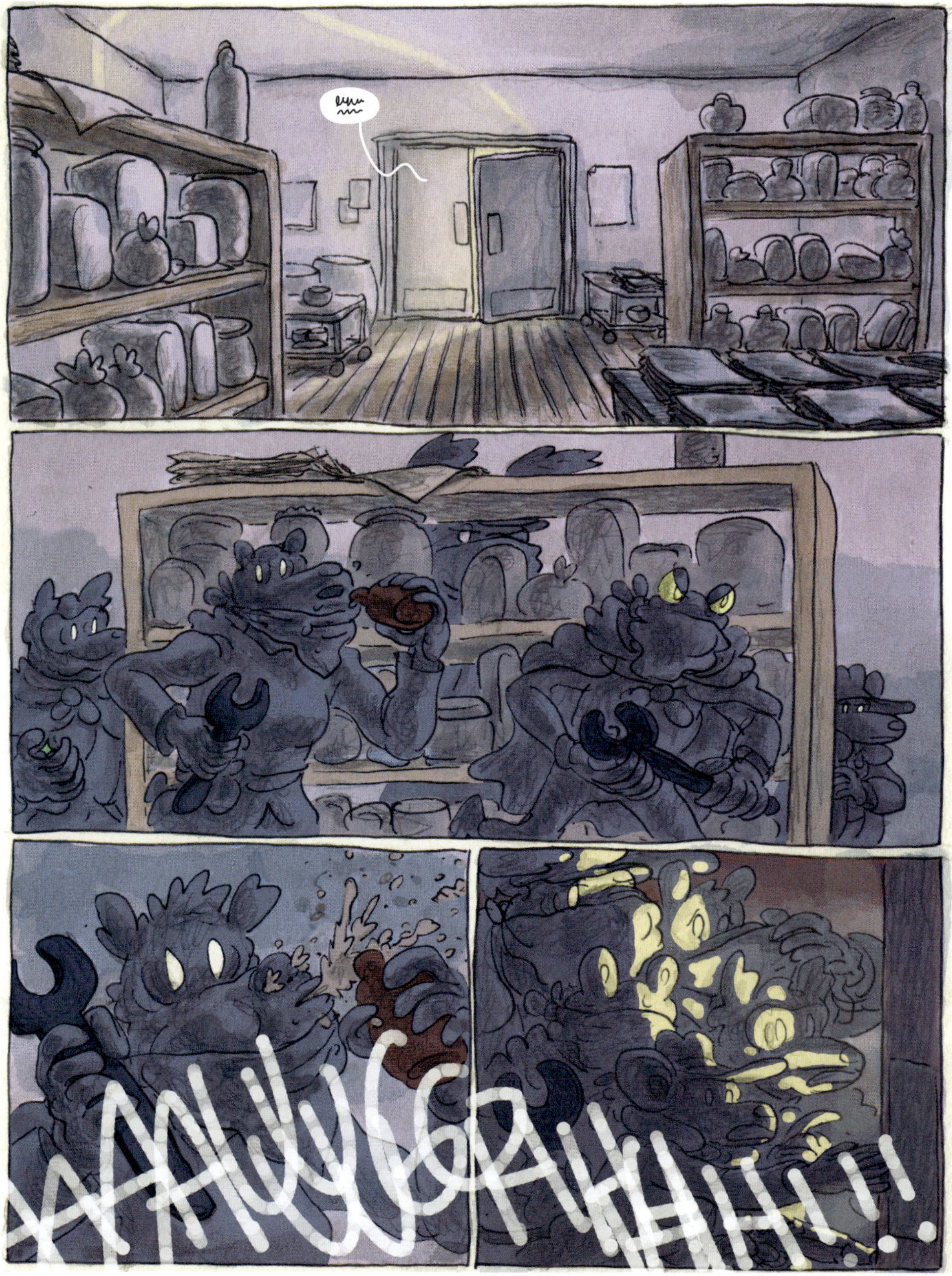
AAHUGRAHHHH!!

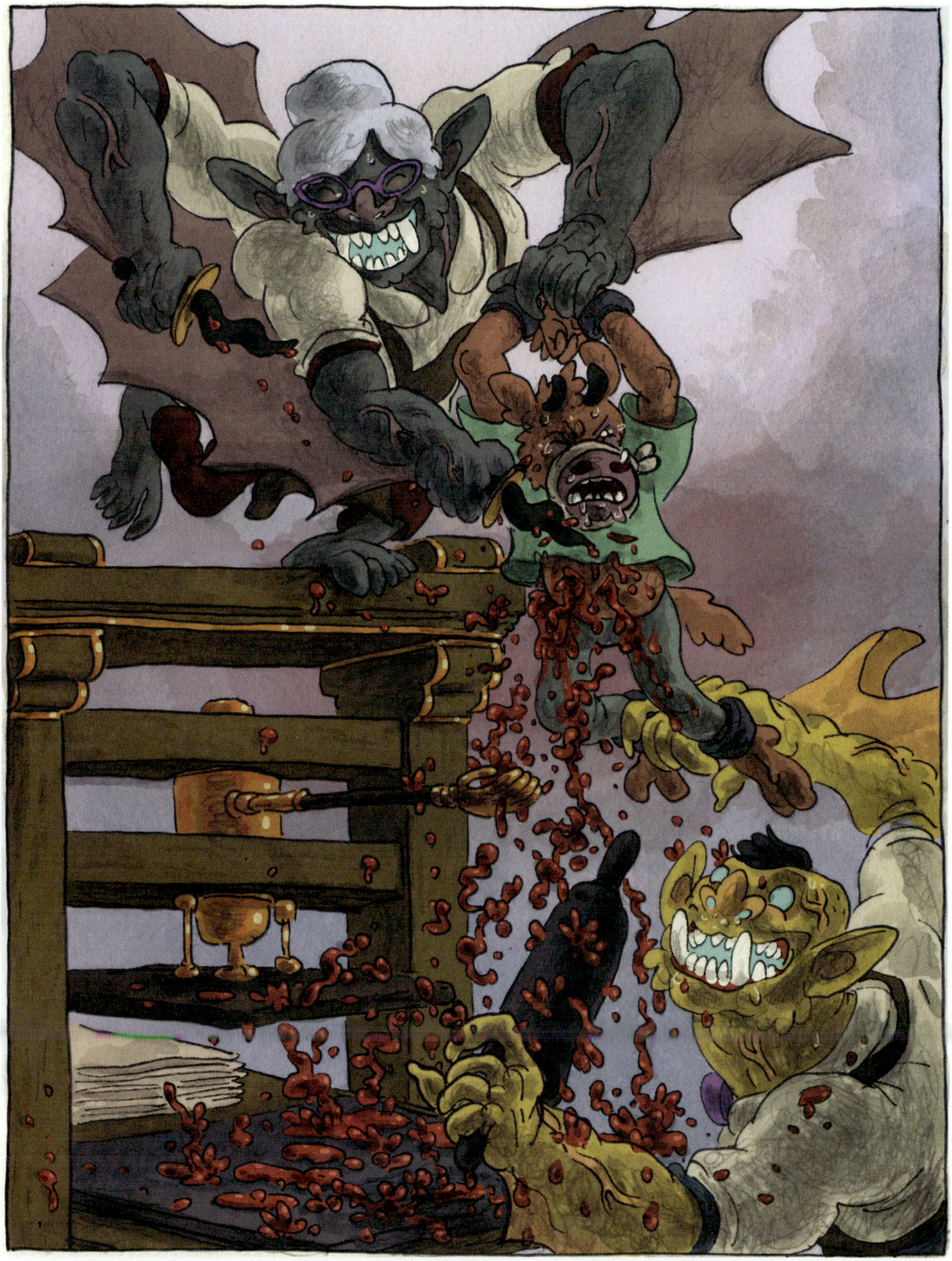

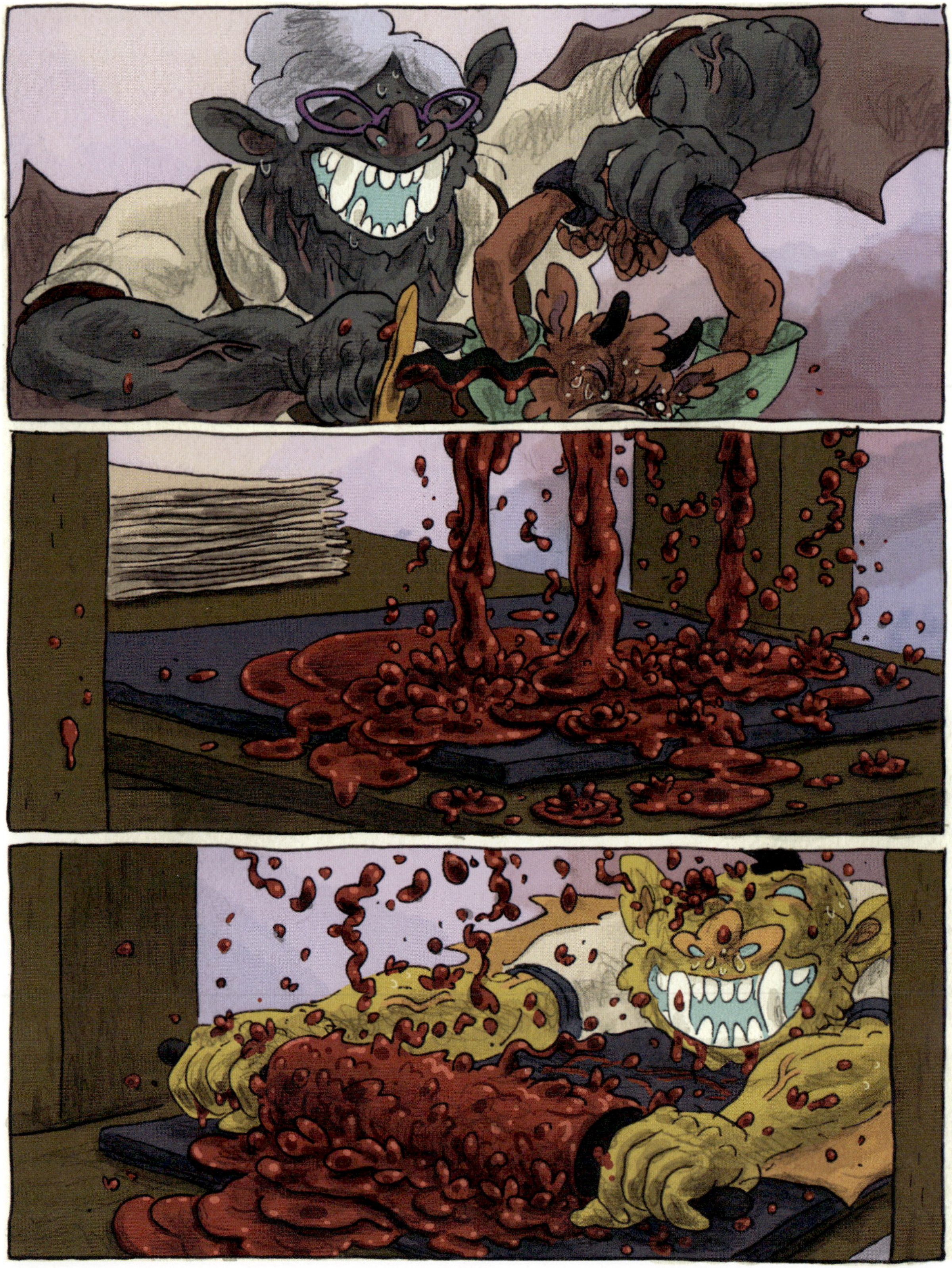

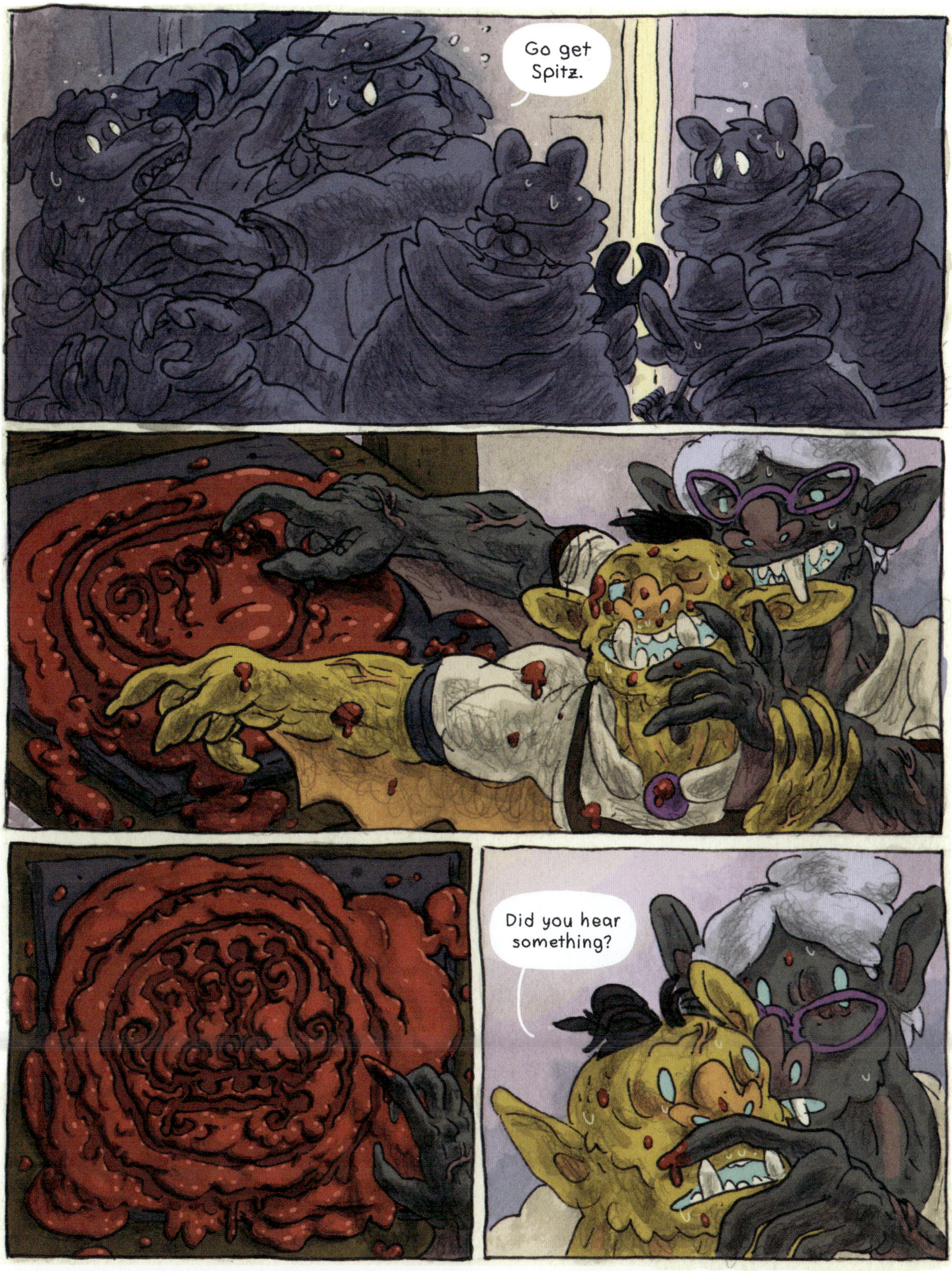
Go get Spitz.
Did you hear something?

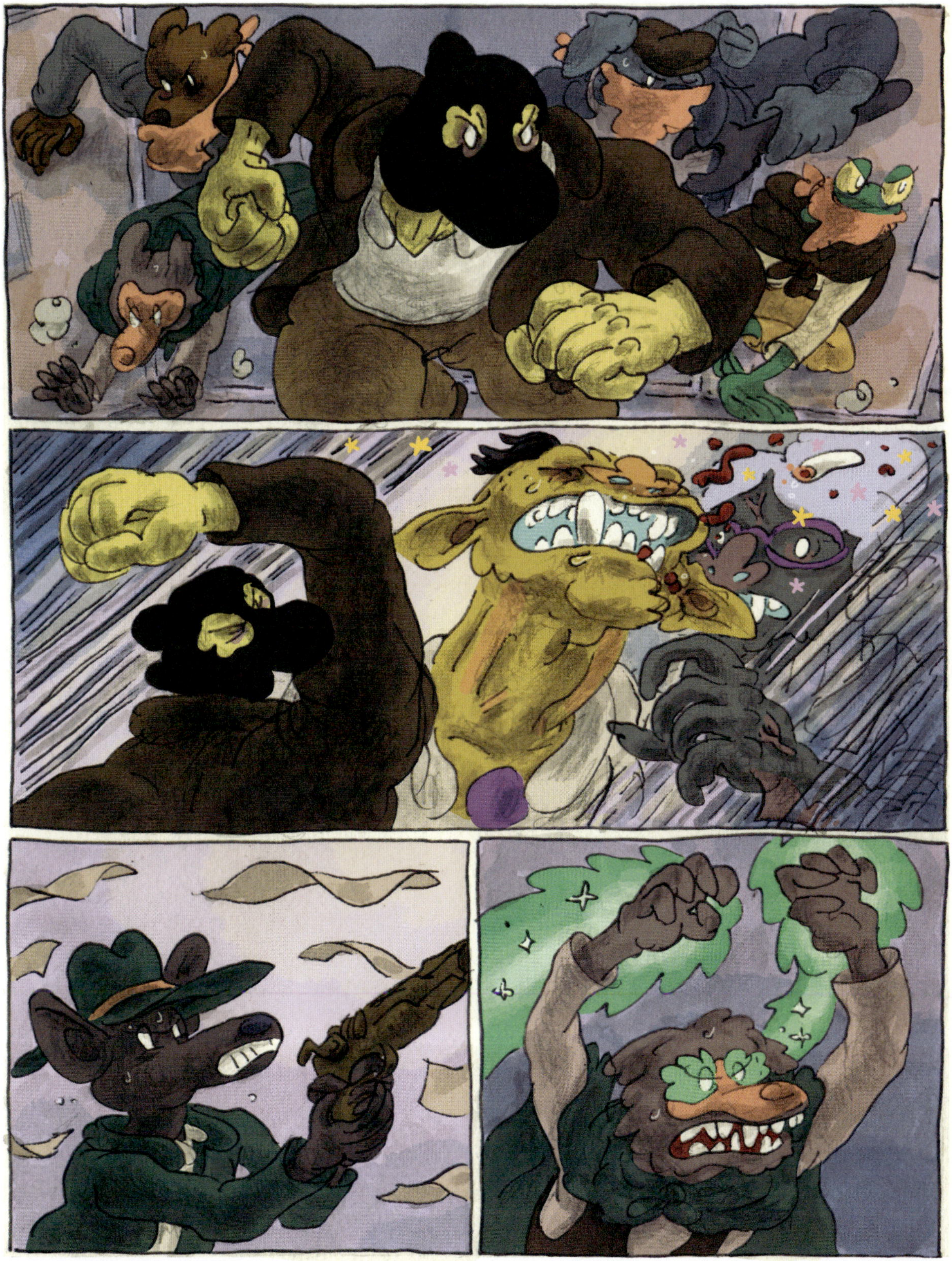

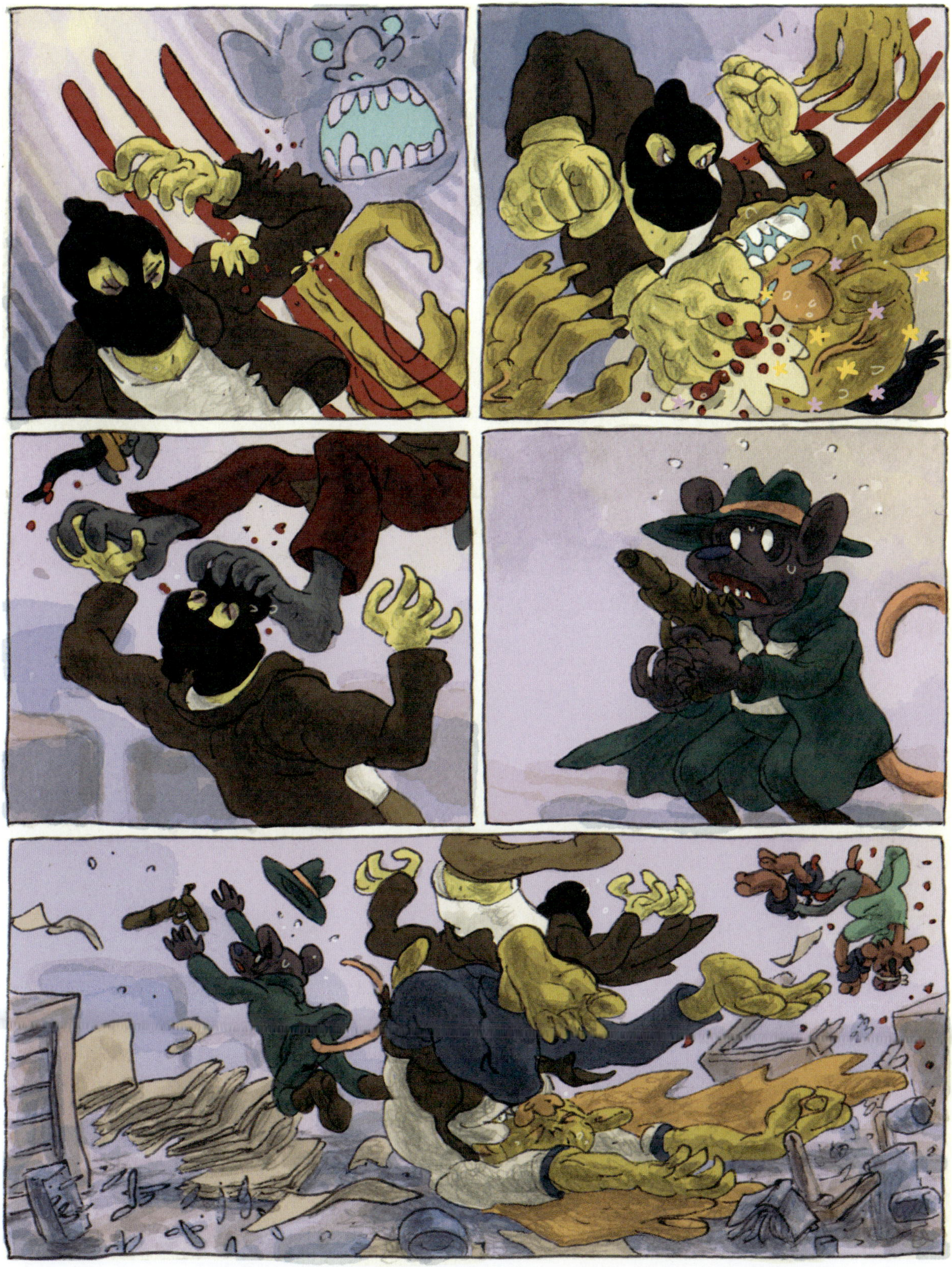

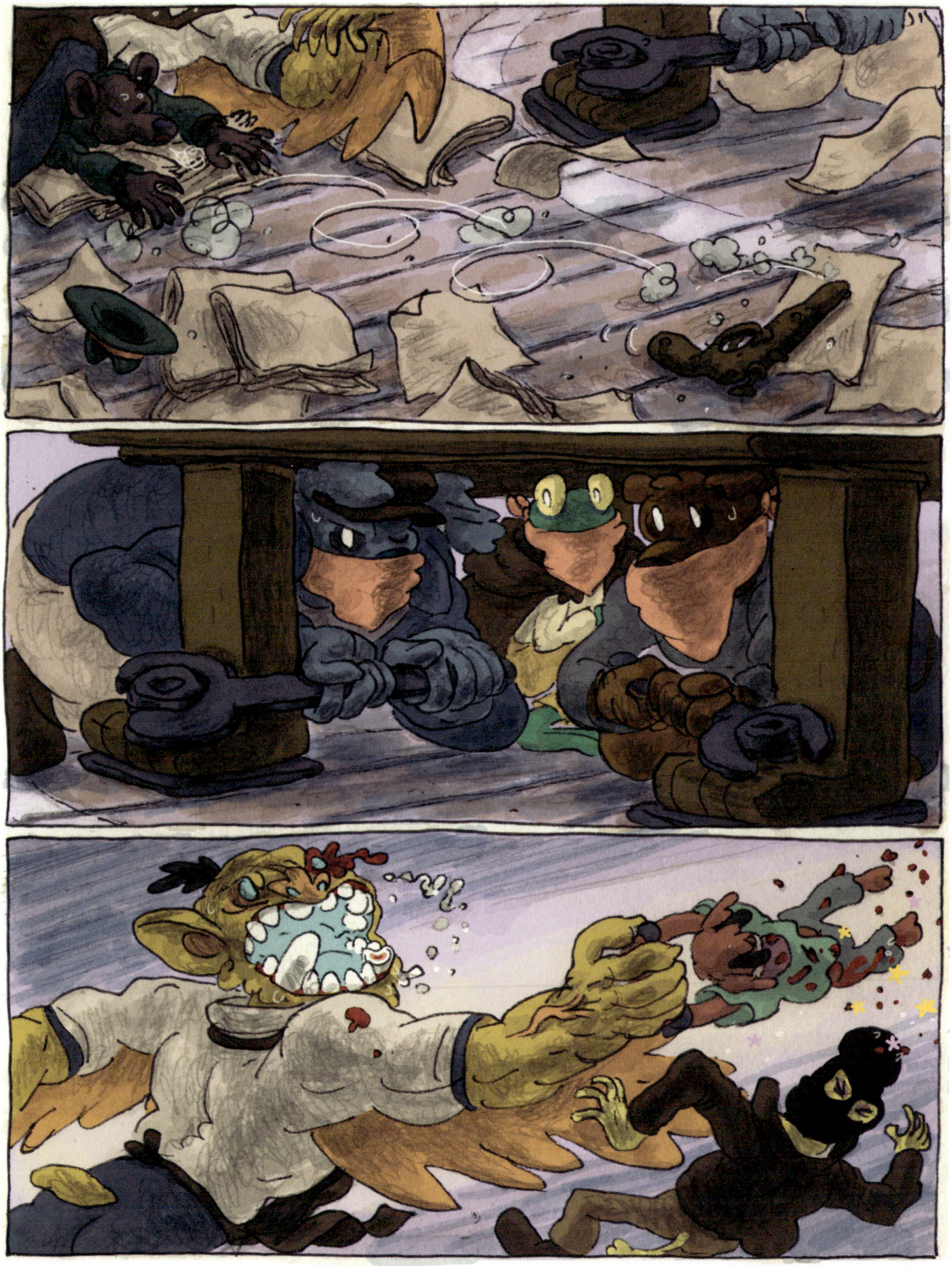

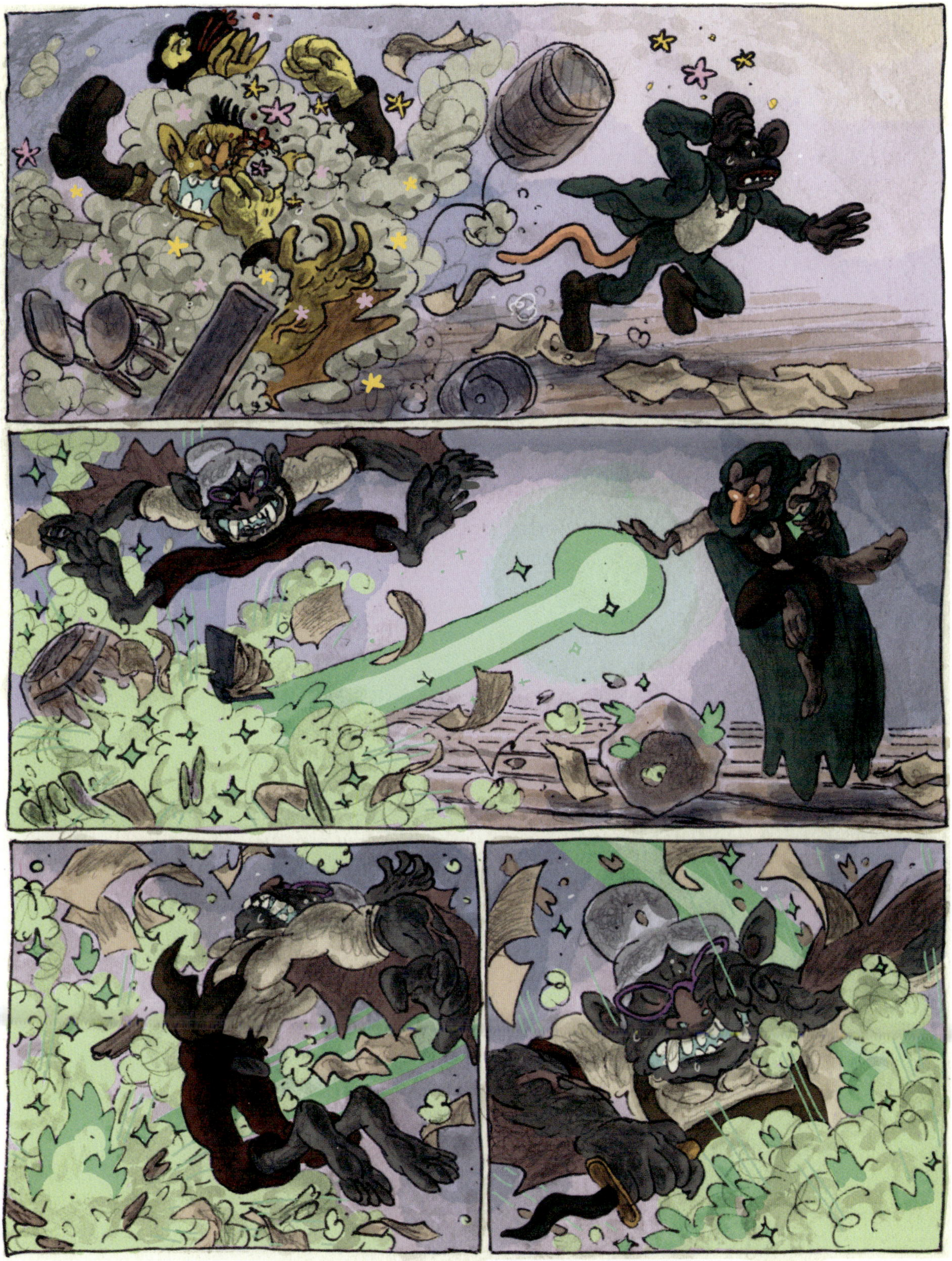

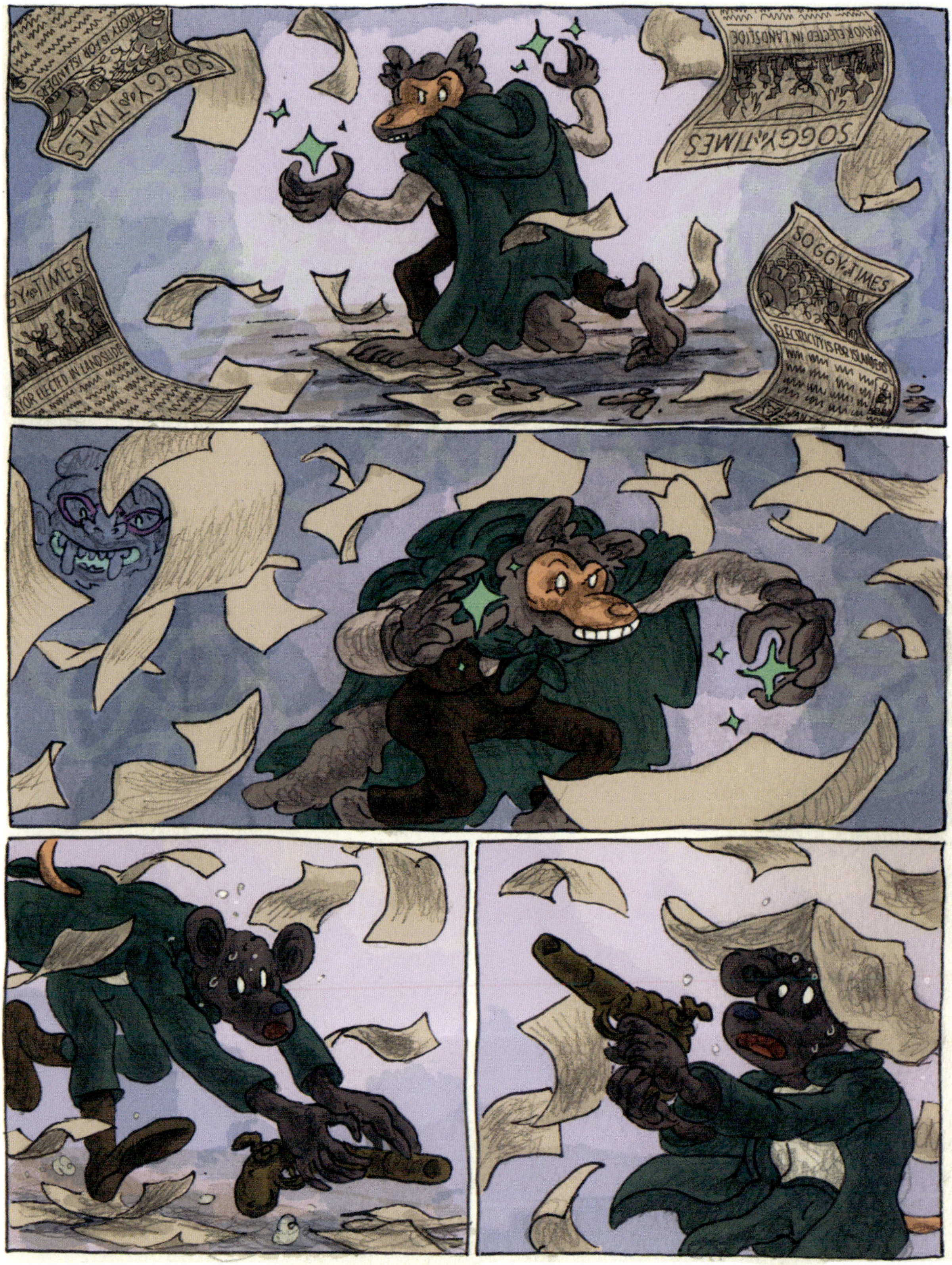
SOGGY TIMES
ELECTRICITY IS FOR ISLANDERS
MAYOR ELECTED IN LANDSLIDE

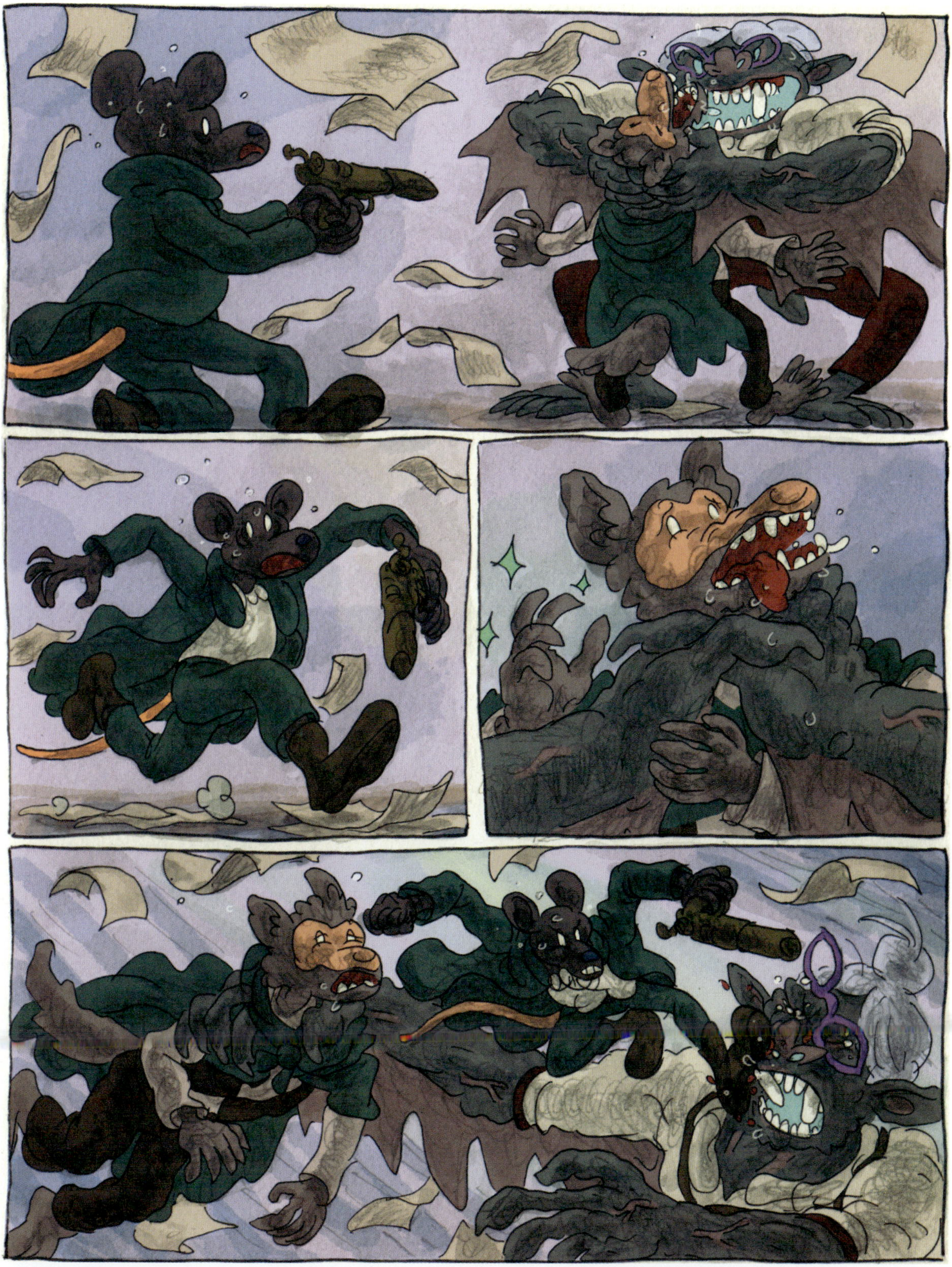

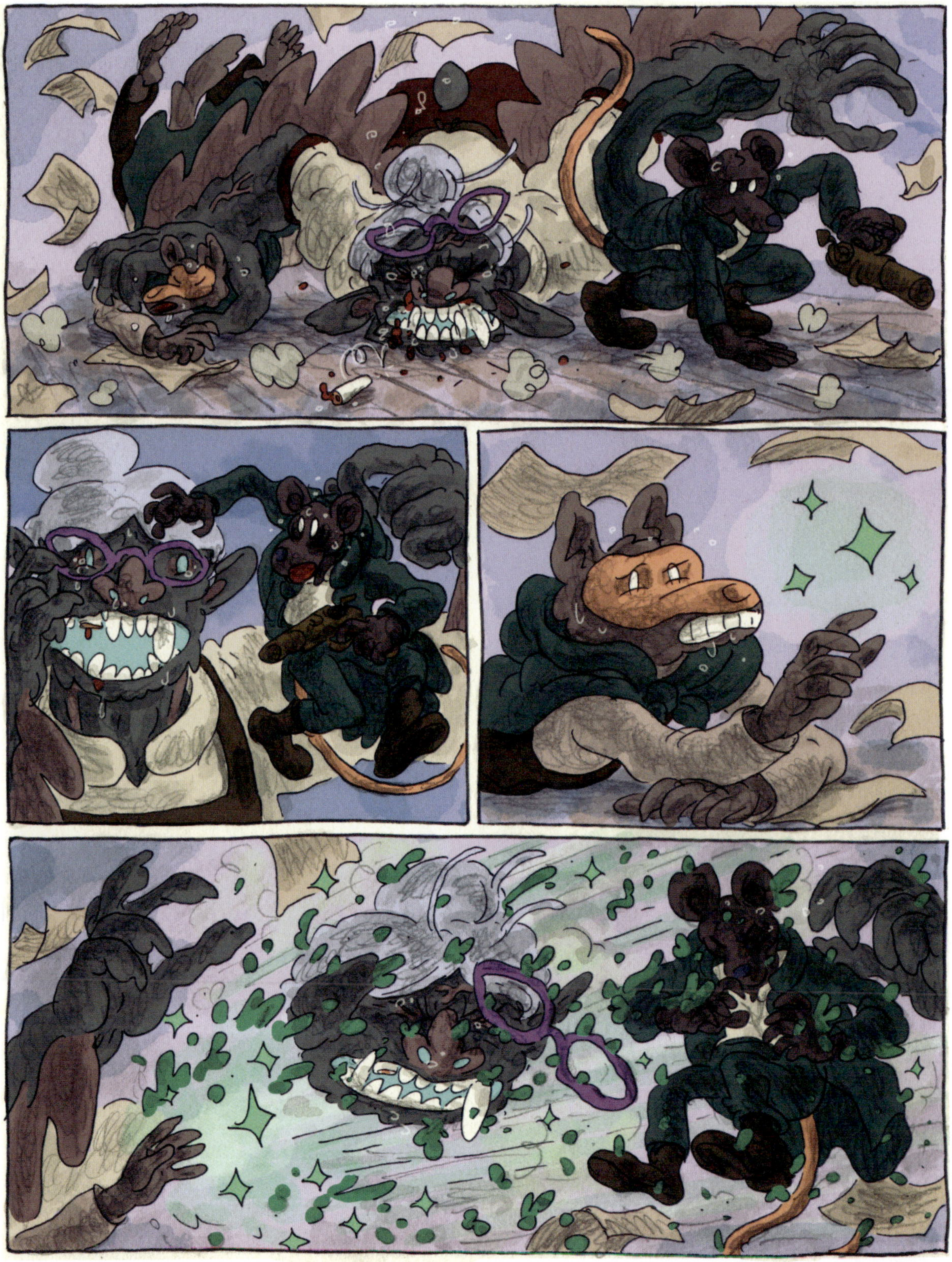

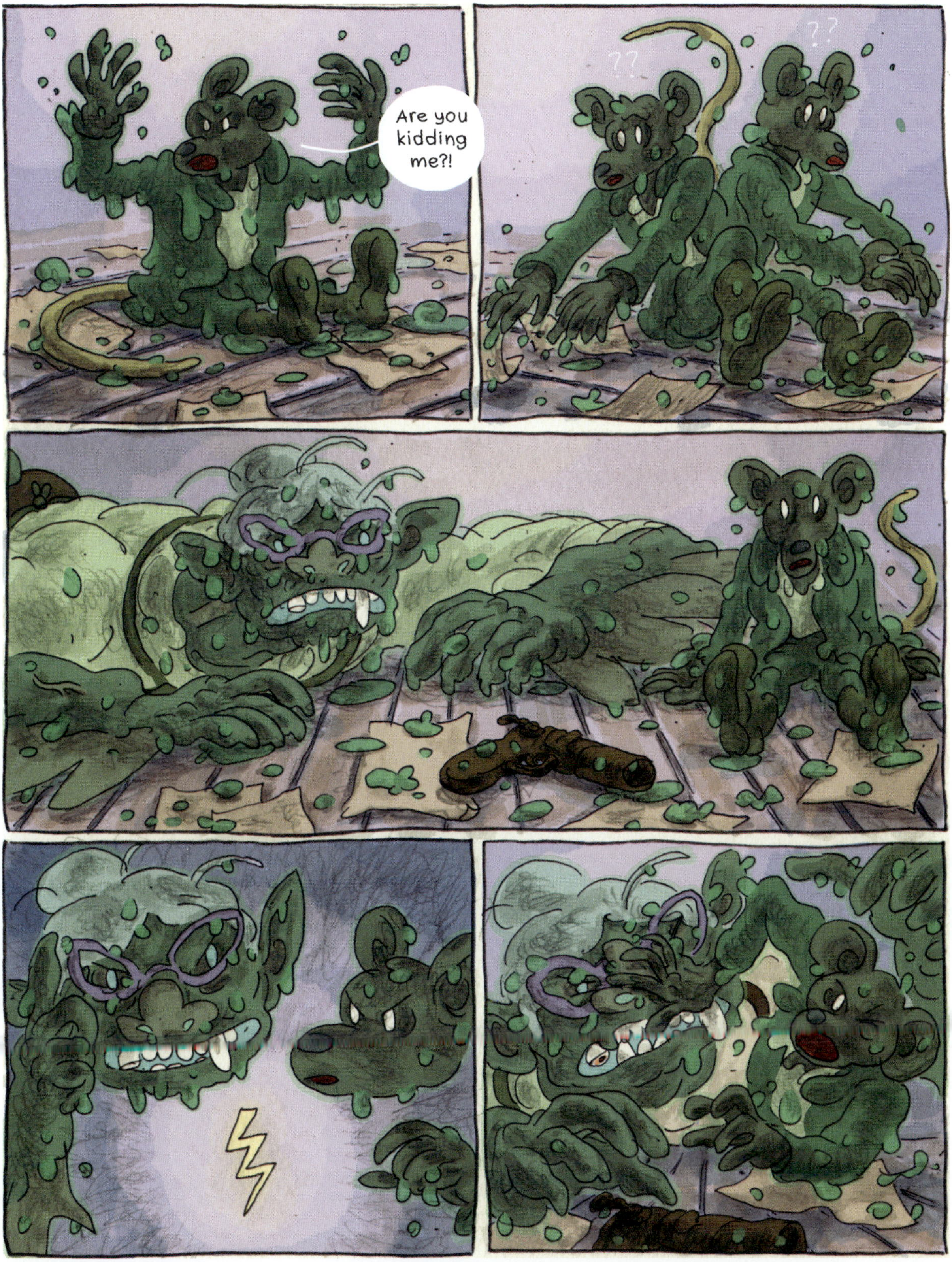
Are you kidding me?!
??
??

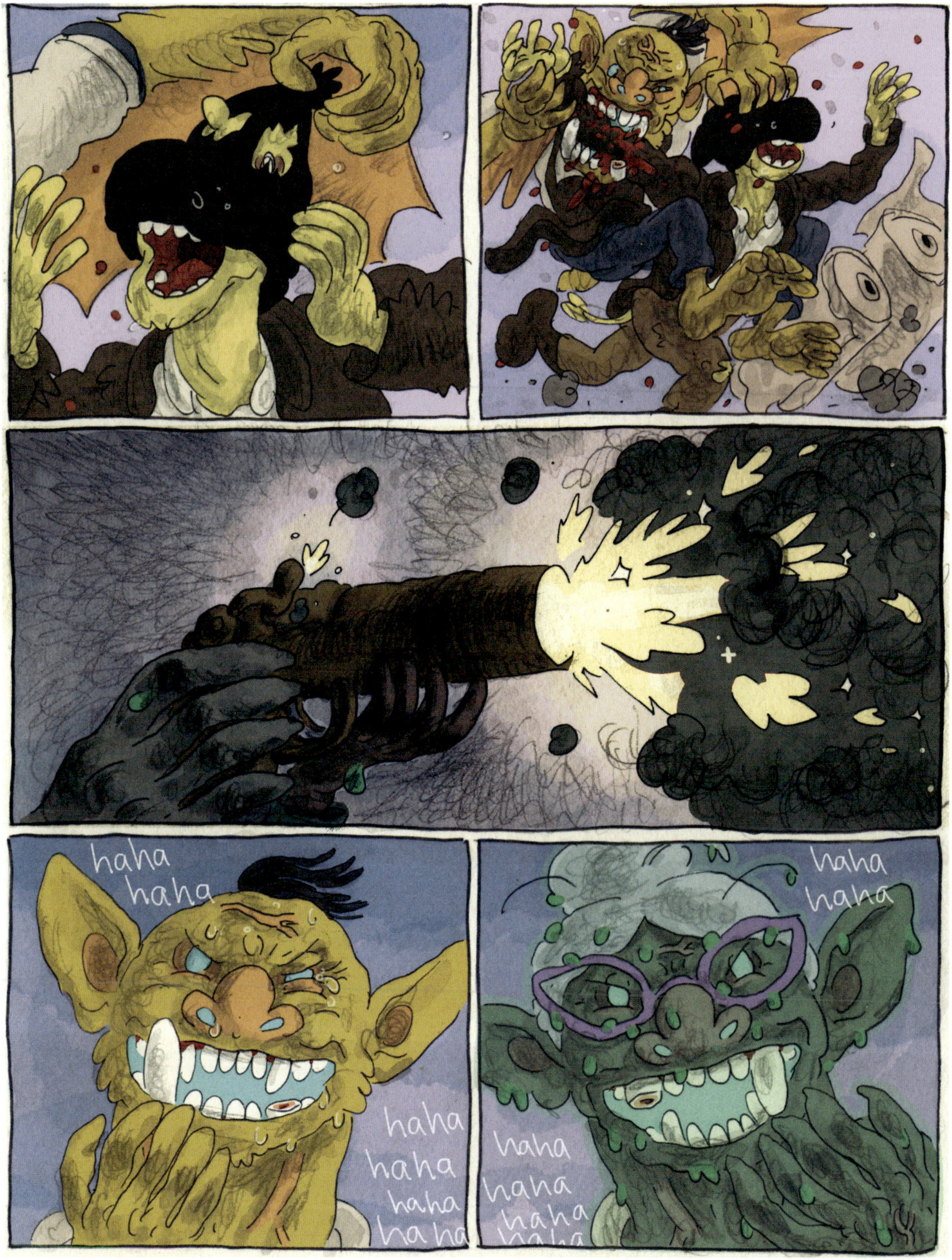
haha
haha
haha
haha
haha
haha
haha
haha
haha
haha
haha
haha
haha
haha

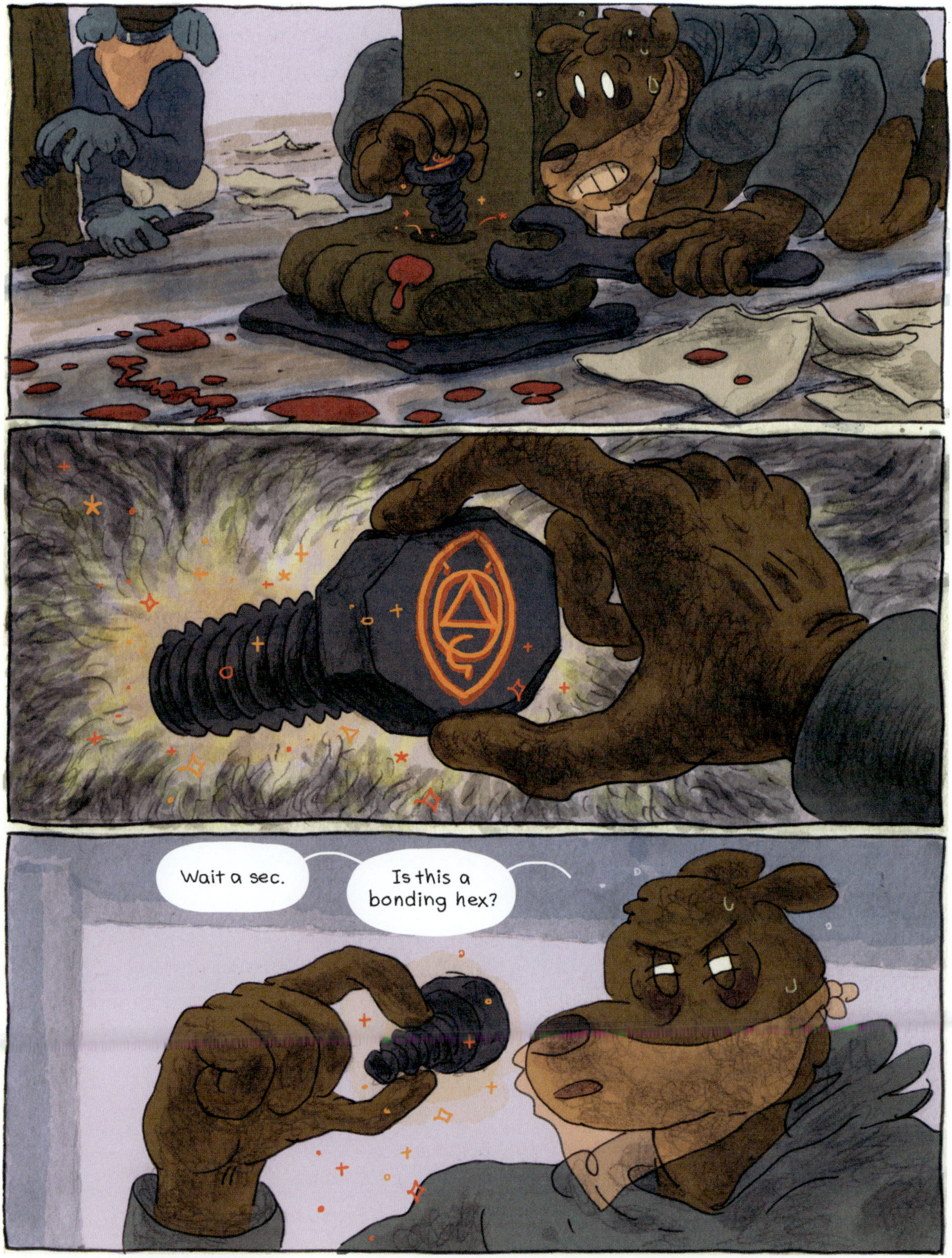
Wait a sec.
Is this a bonding hex?

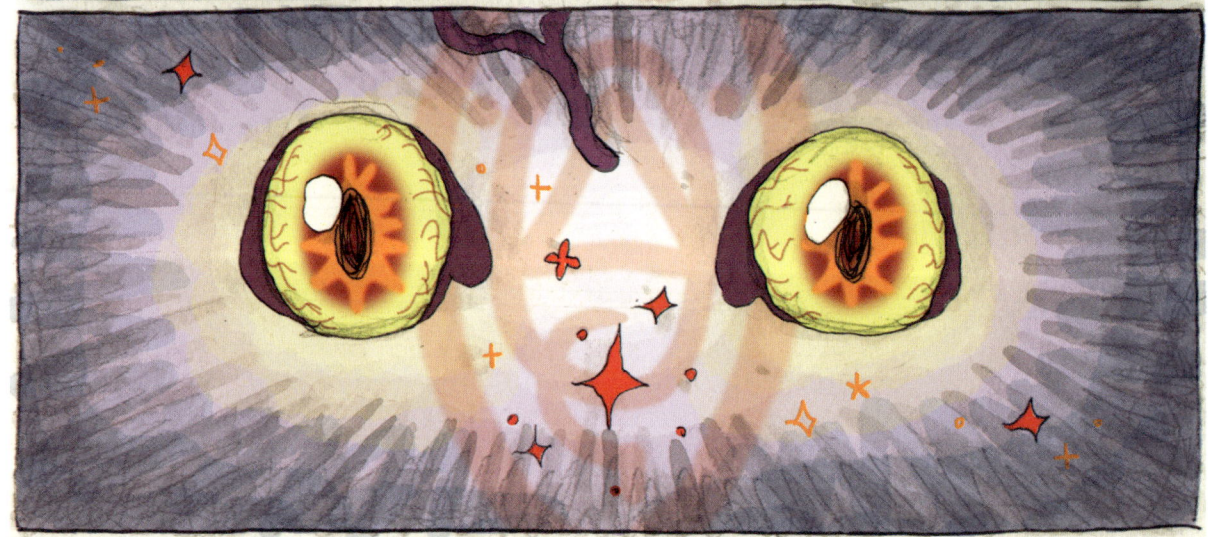

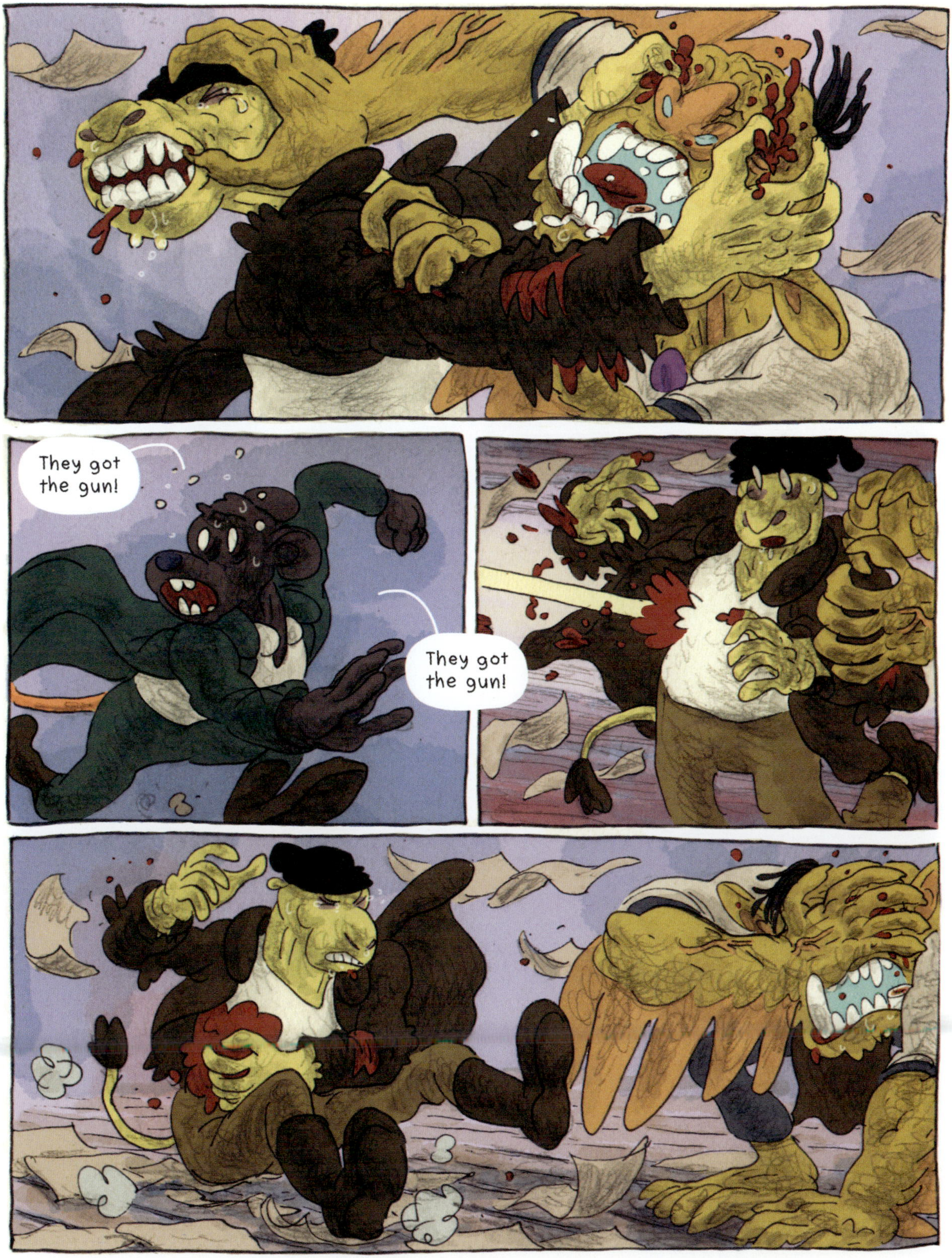
They got the gun!
They got the gun!

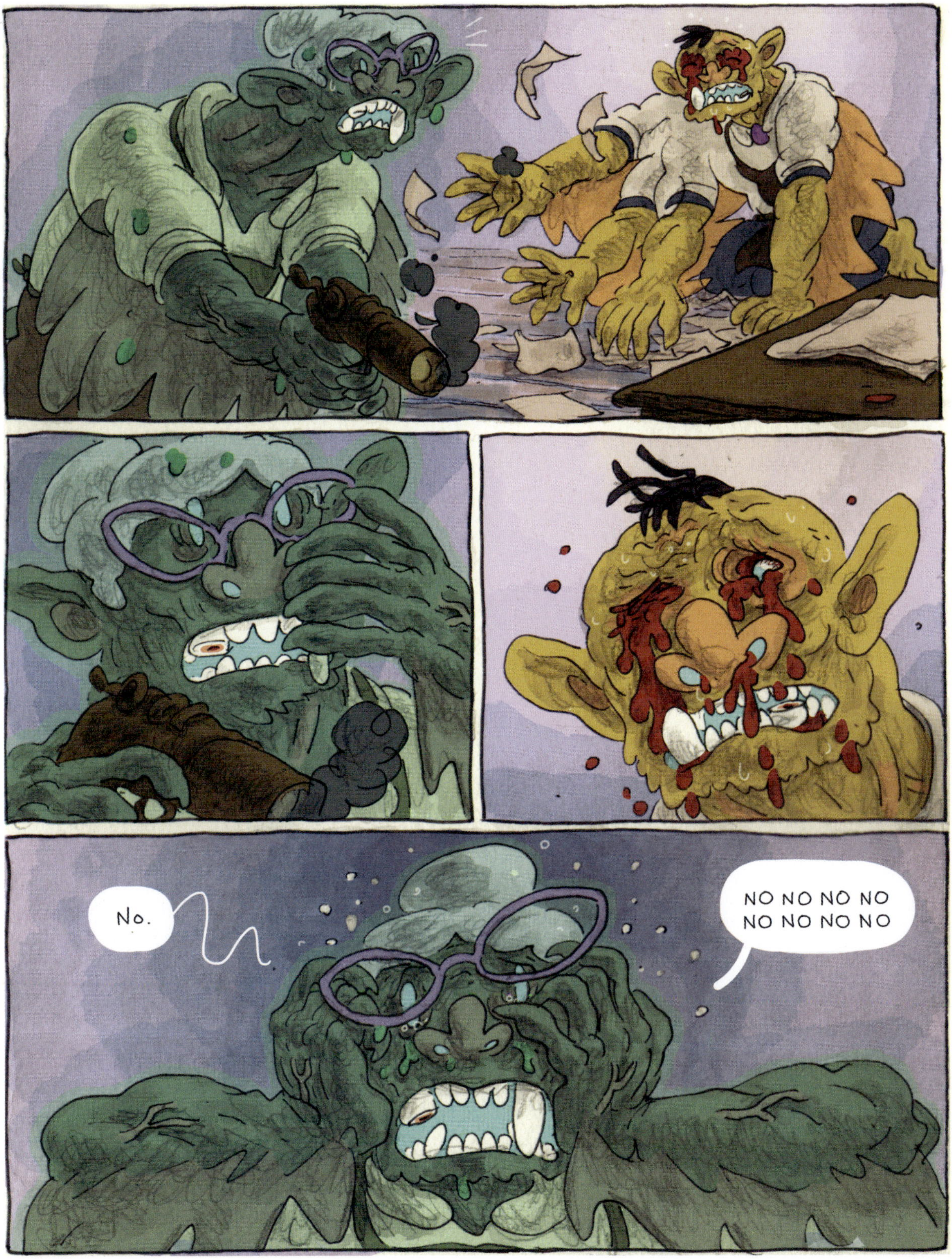
No.
NO NO NO NO
NO NO NO NO

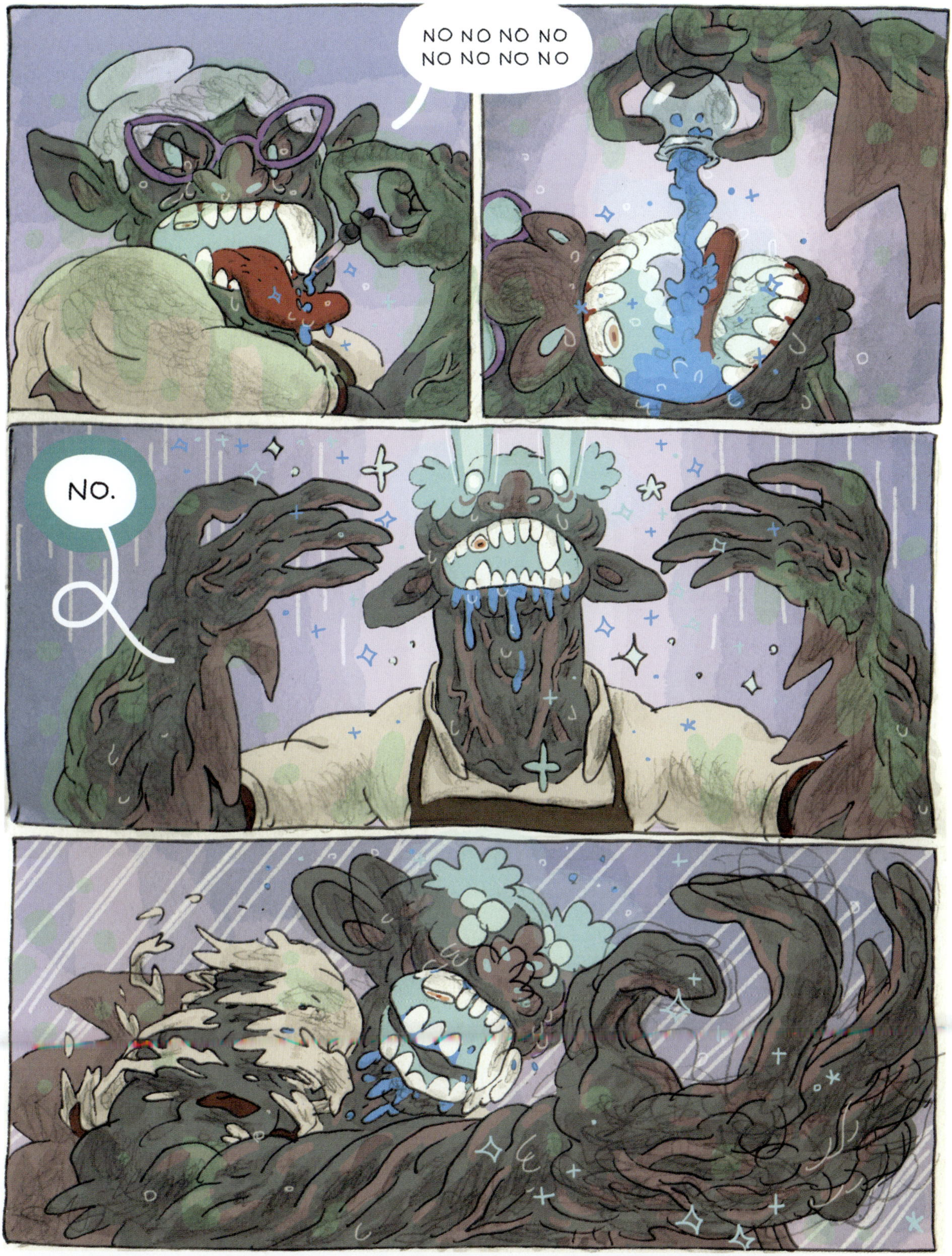
NO NO NO NO
NO NO NO NO
NO.

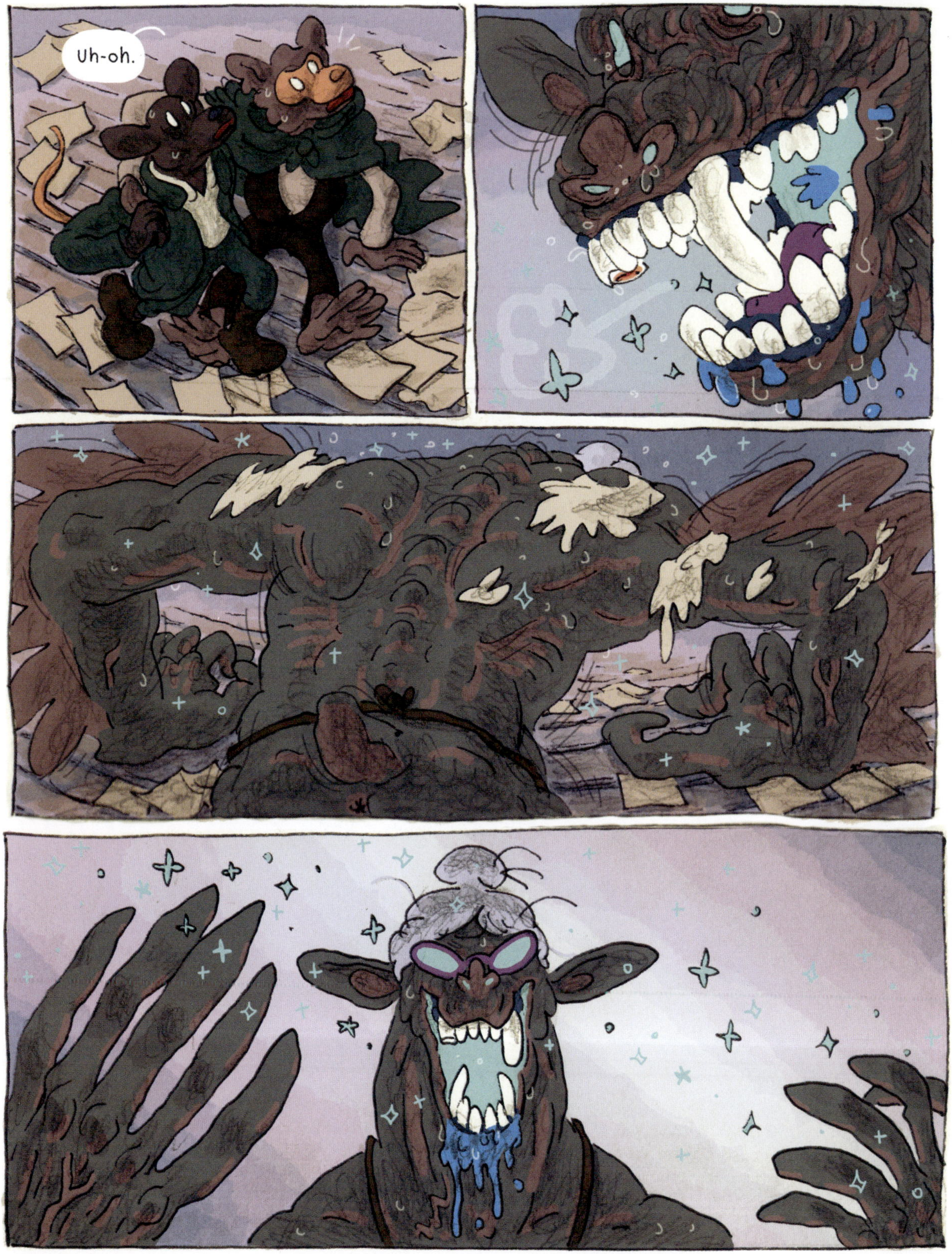
Uh-oh.

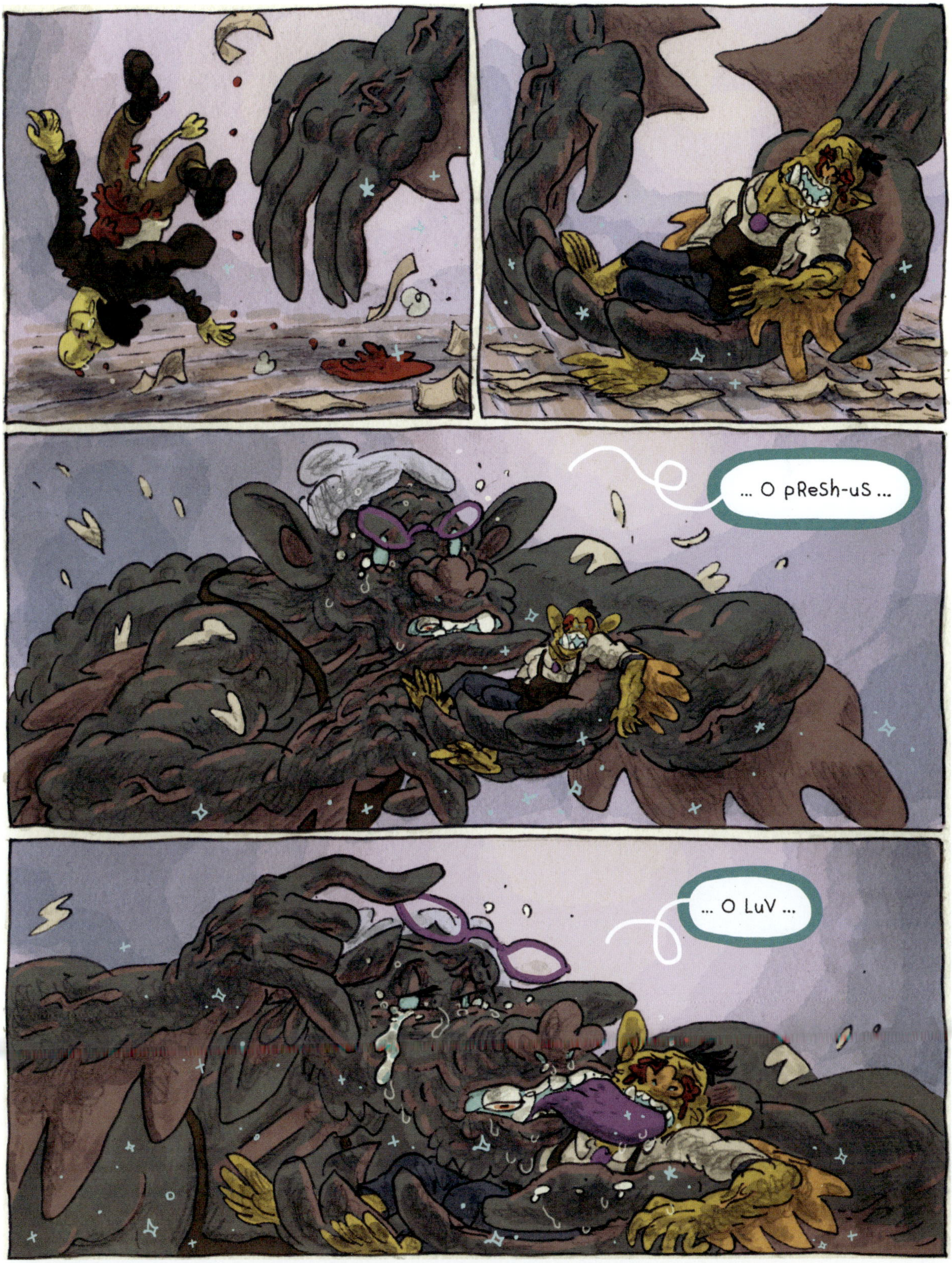
... O pReSh-uS ...
... O LuV ...

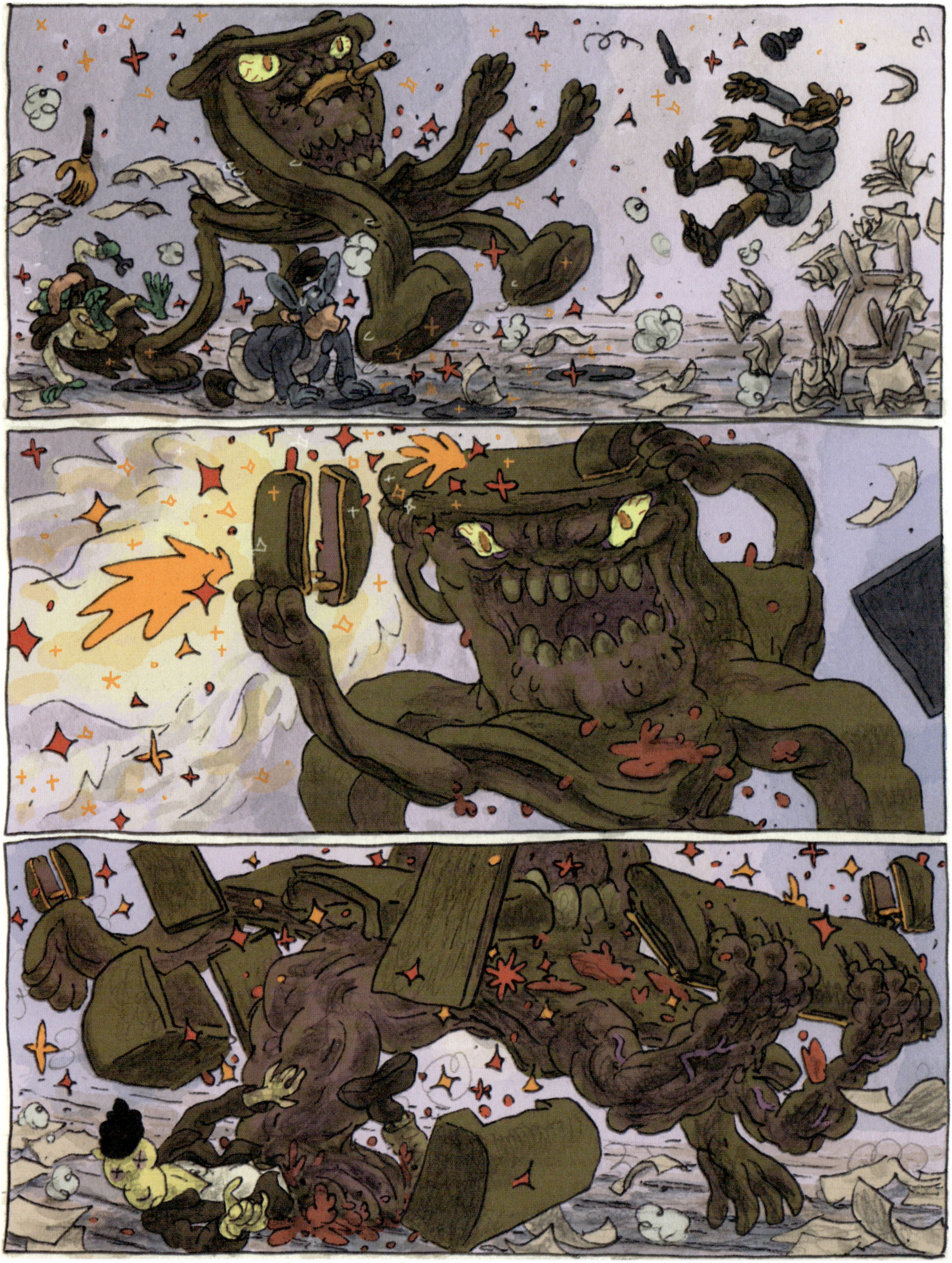

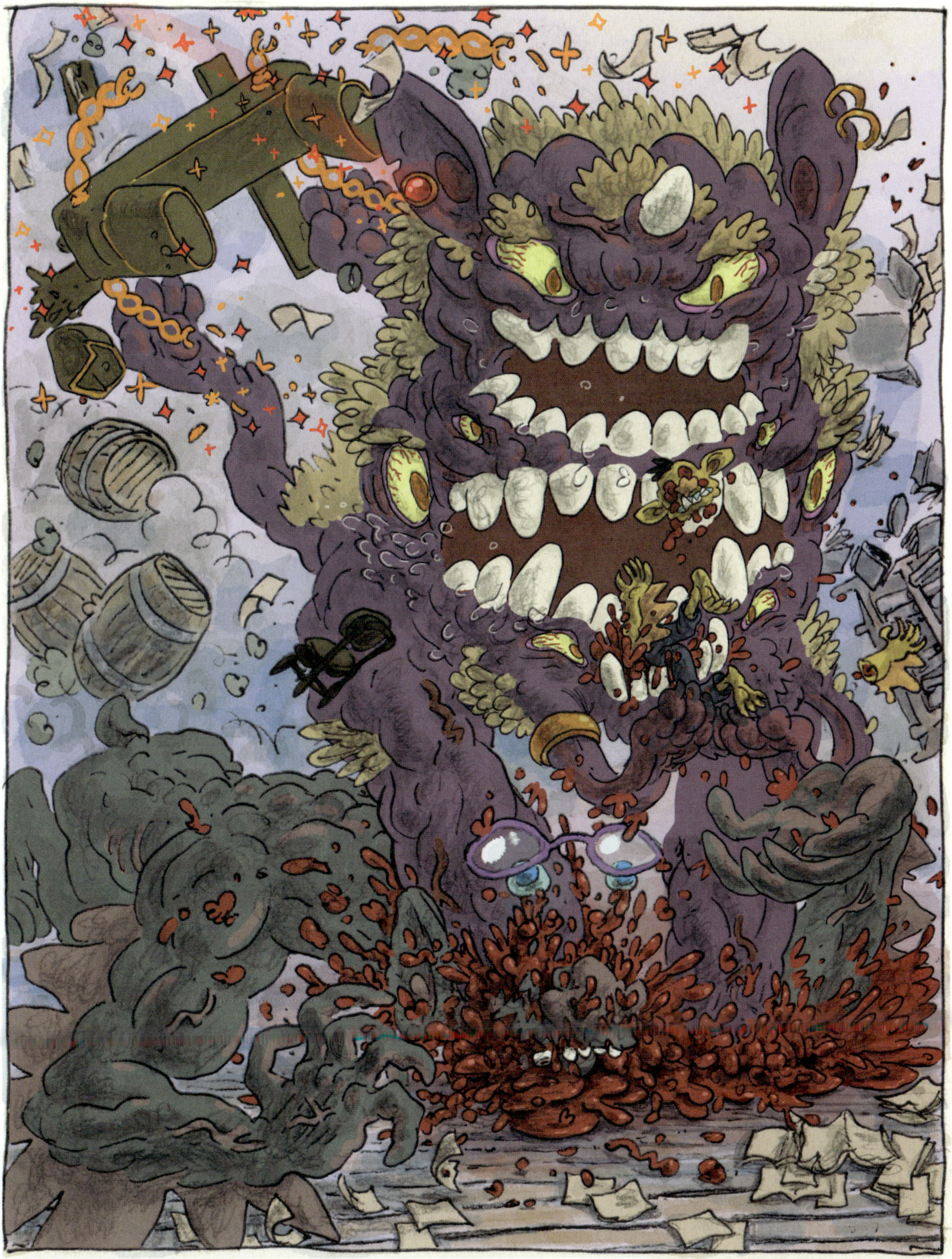

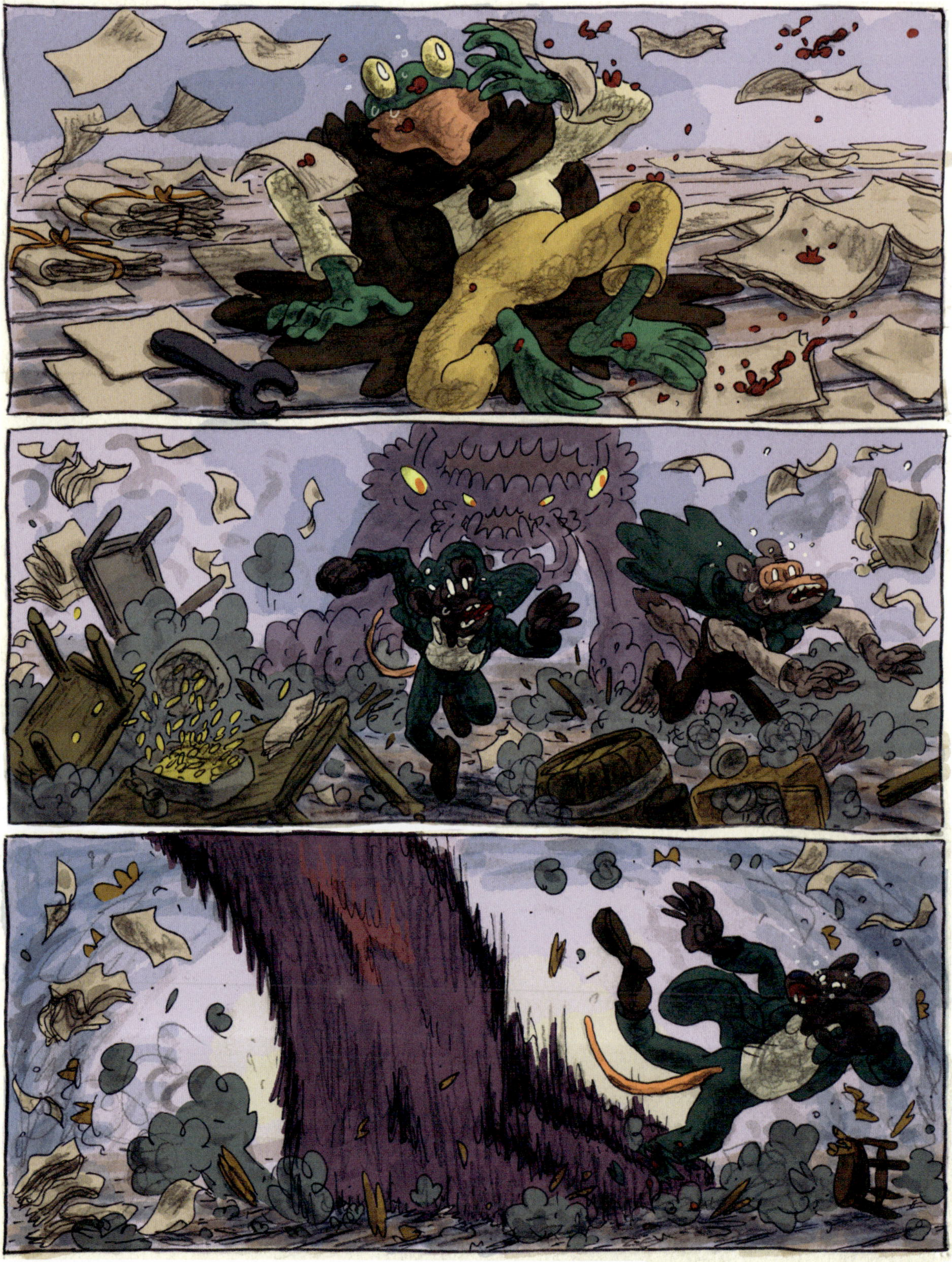

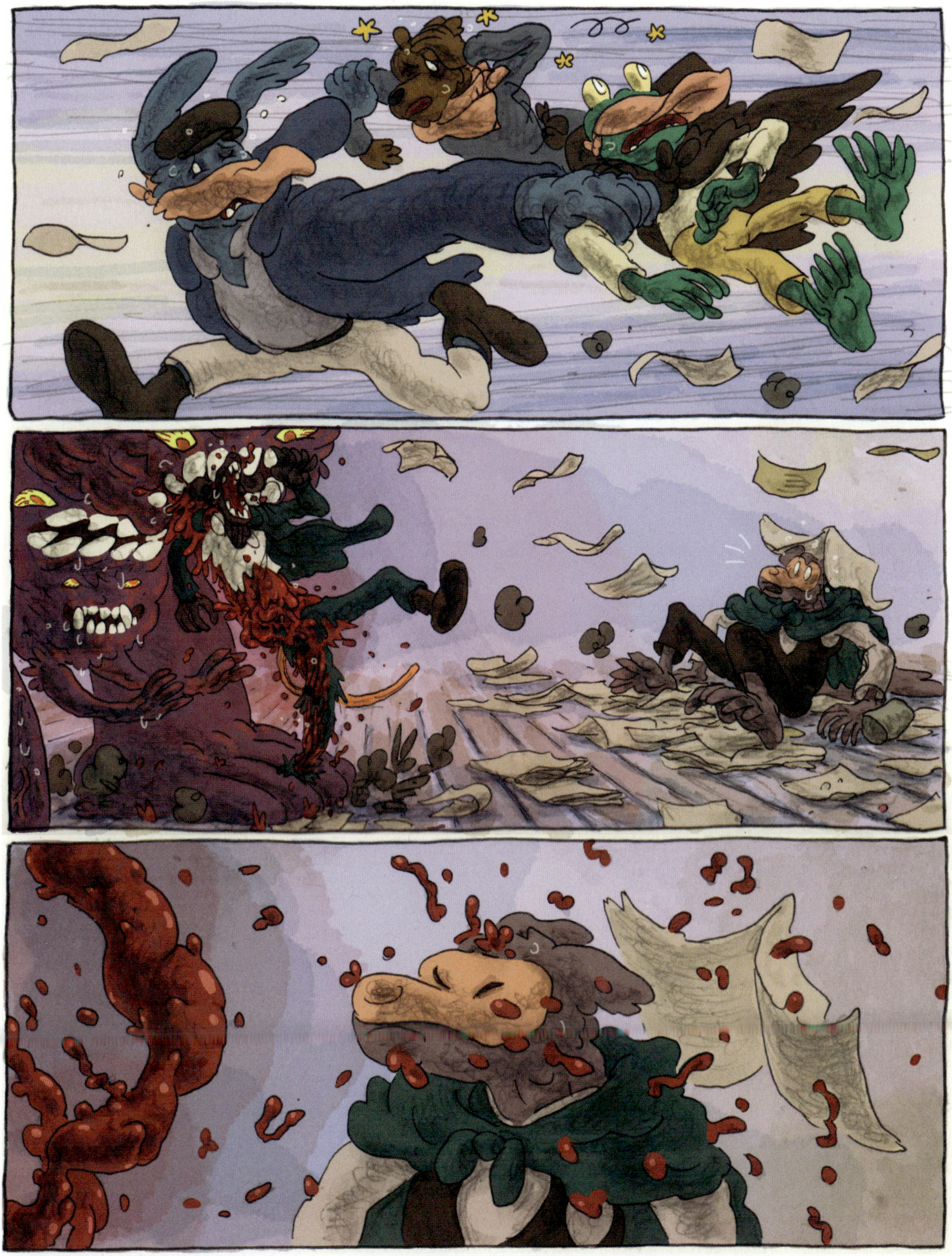

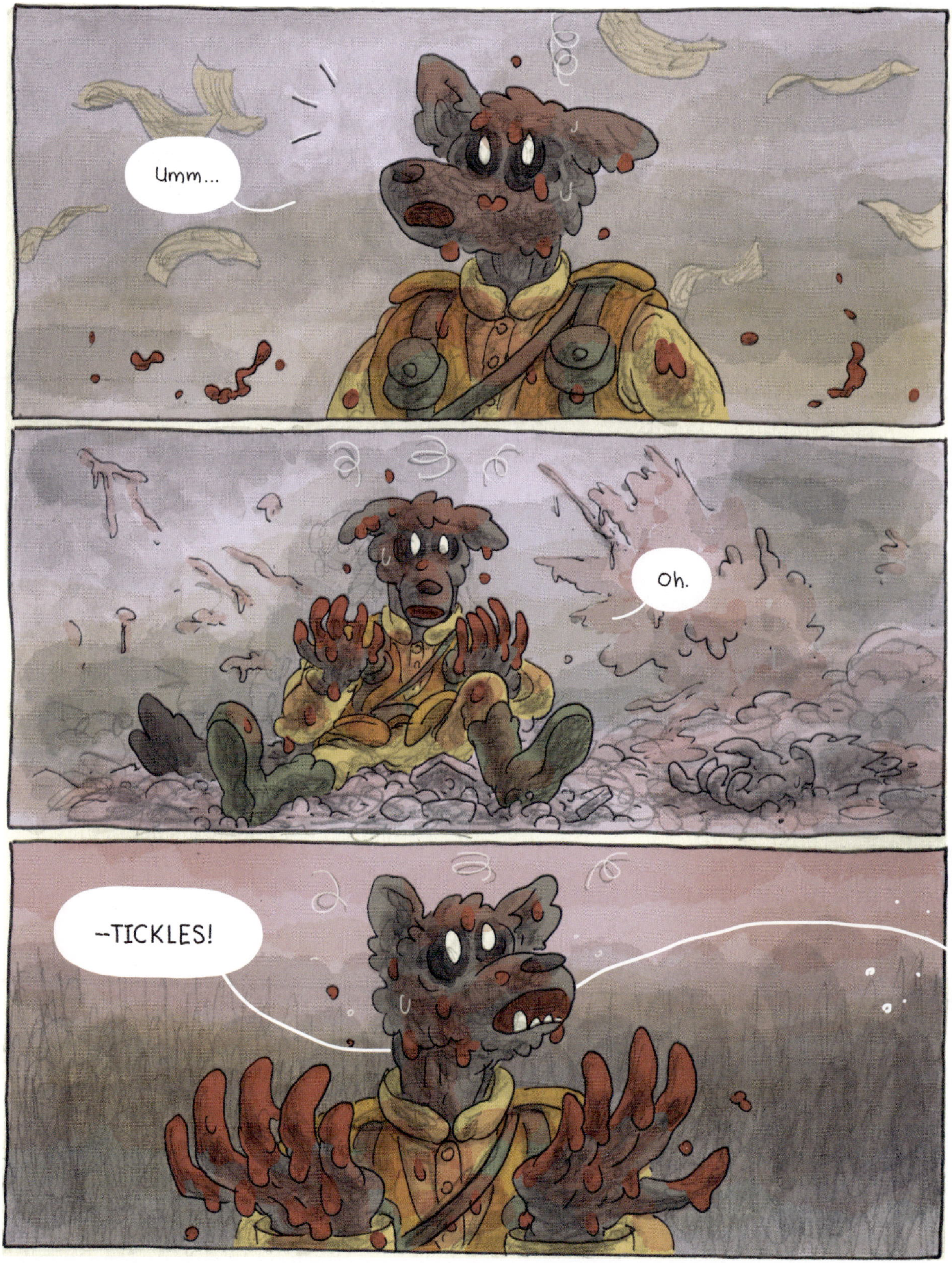
Umm...
Oh.
--TICKLES!

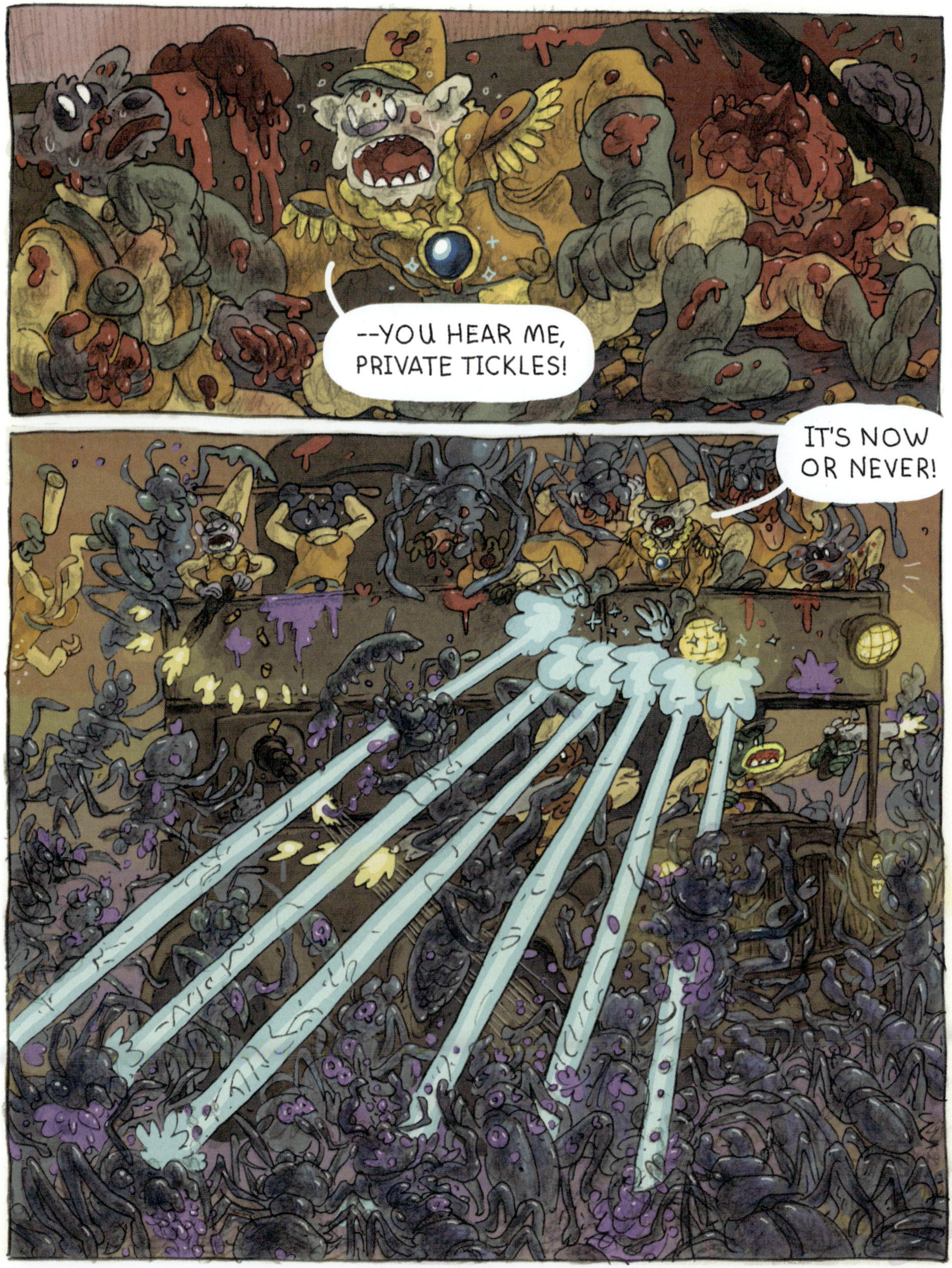
--YOU HEAR ME, PRIVATE TICKLES!
IT'S NOW OR NEVER!

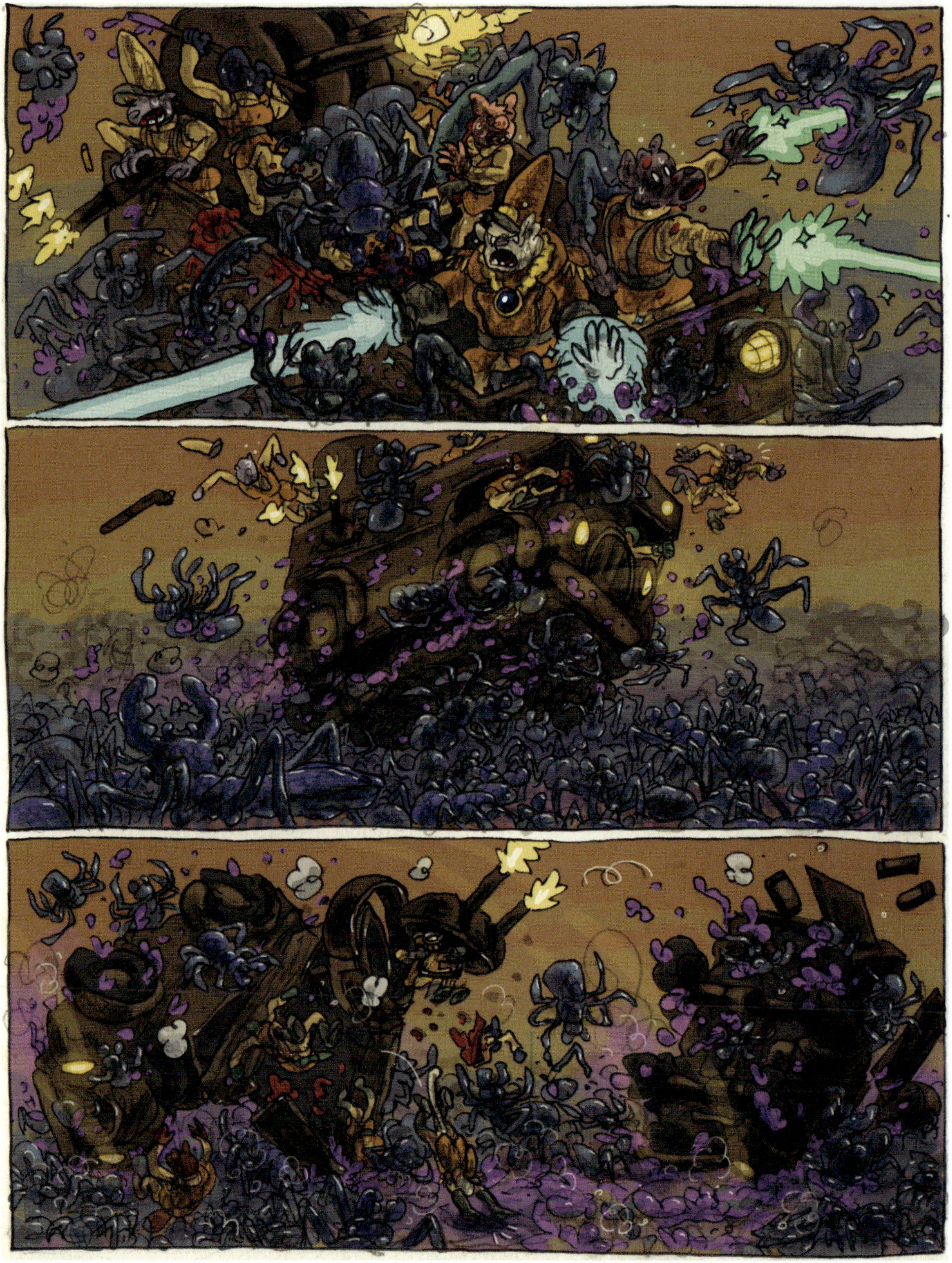

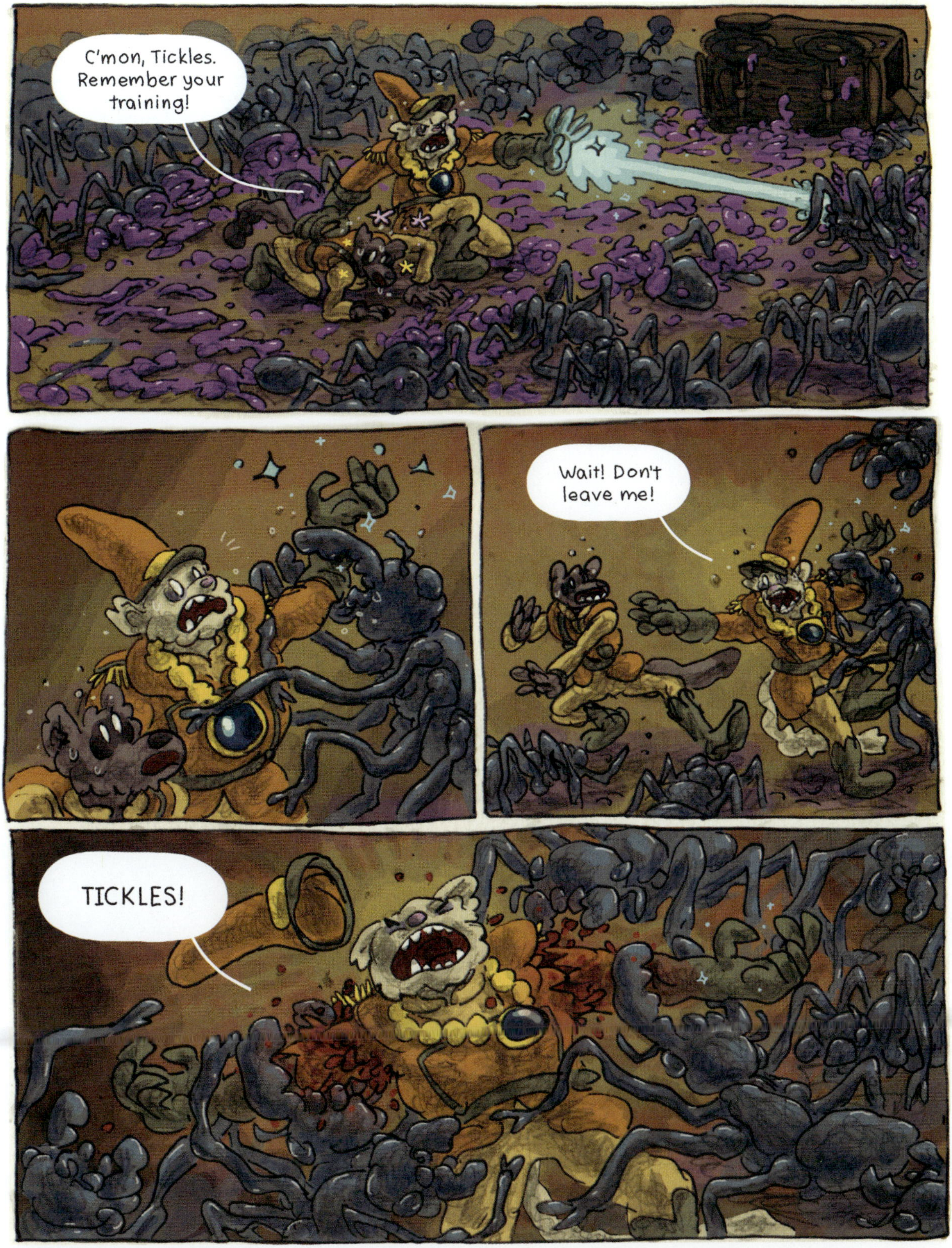
C'mon, Tickles.
Remember your
training!
Wait! Don't
leave me!
TICKLES!

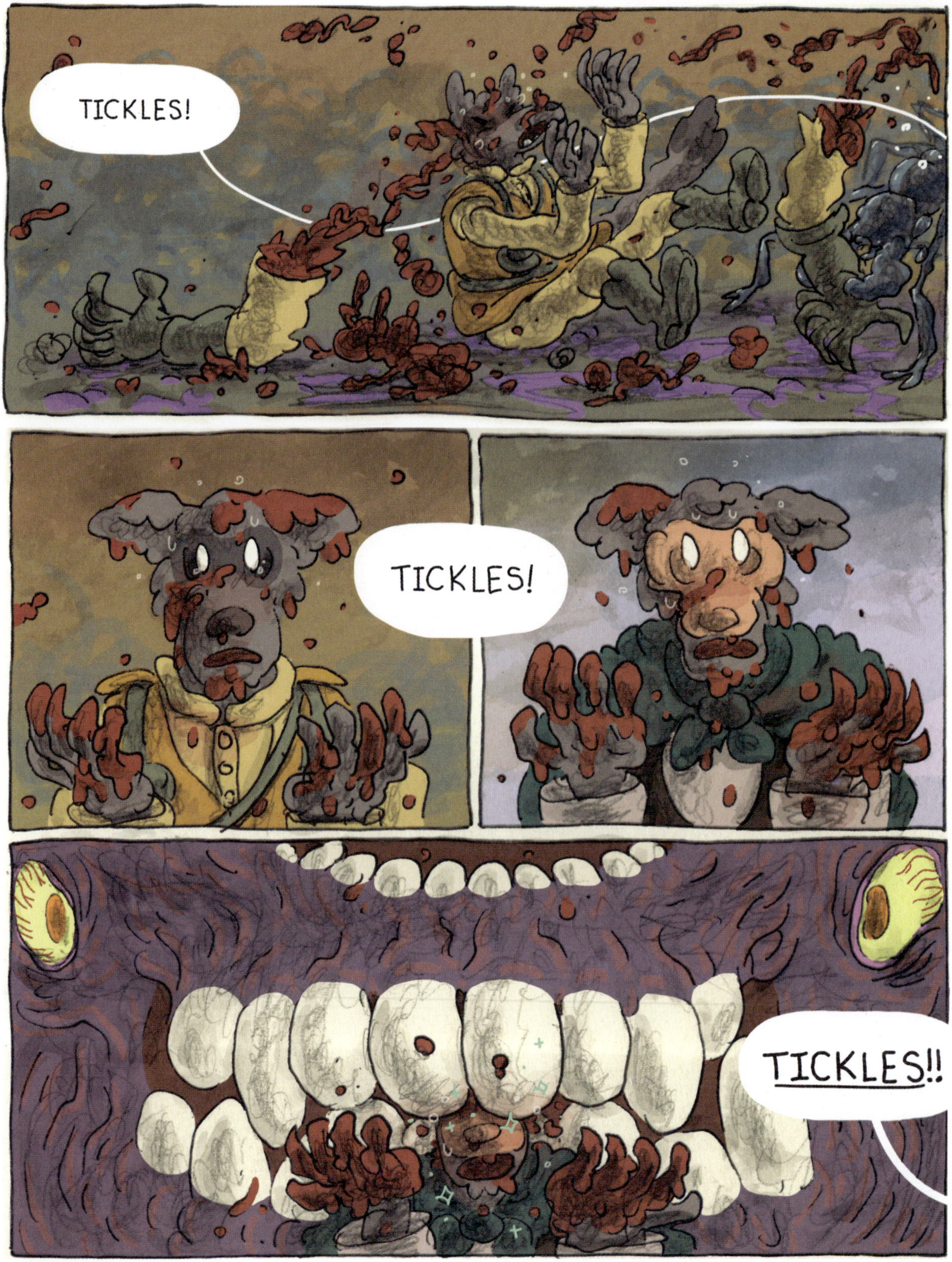
TICKLES!
TICKLES!
TICKLES!!

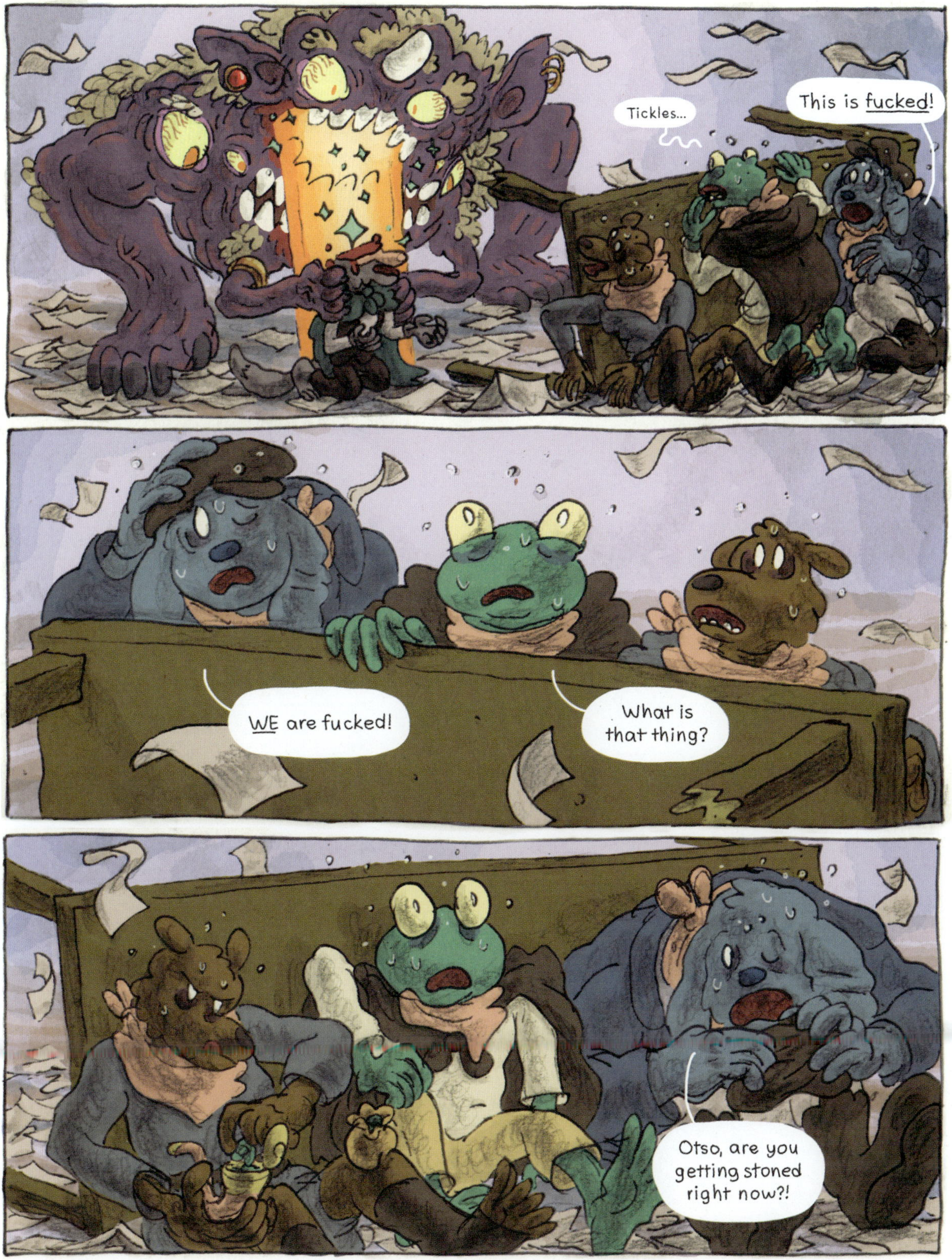
Tickles...
This is fucked!
WE are fucked!
What is that thing?
Otso, are you getting stoned right now?!

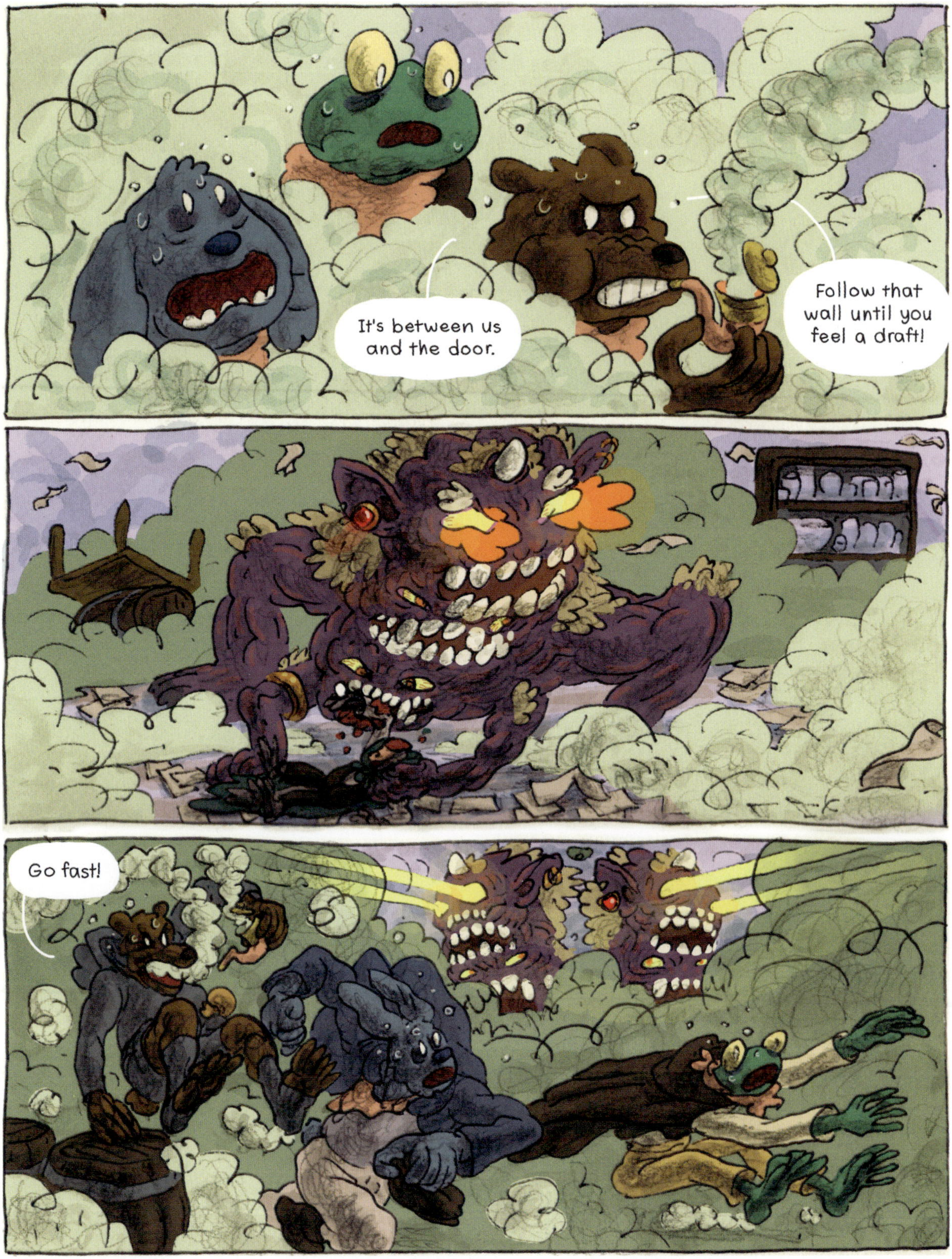
It's between us and the door.
Follow that wall until you feel a draft!
Go fast!

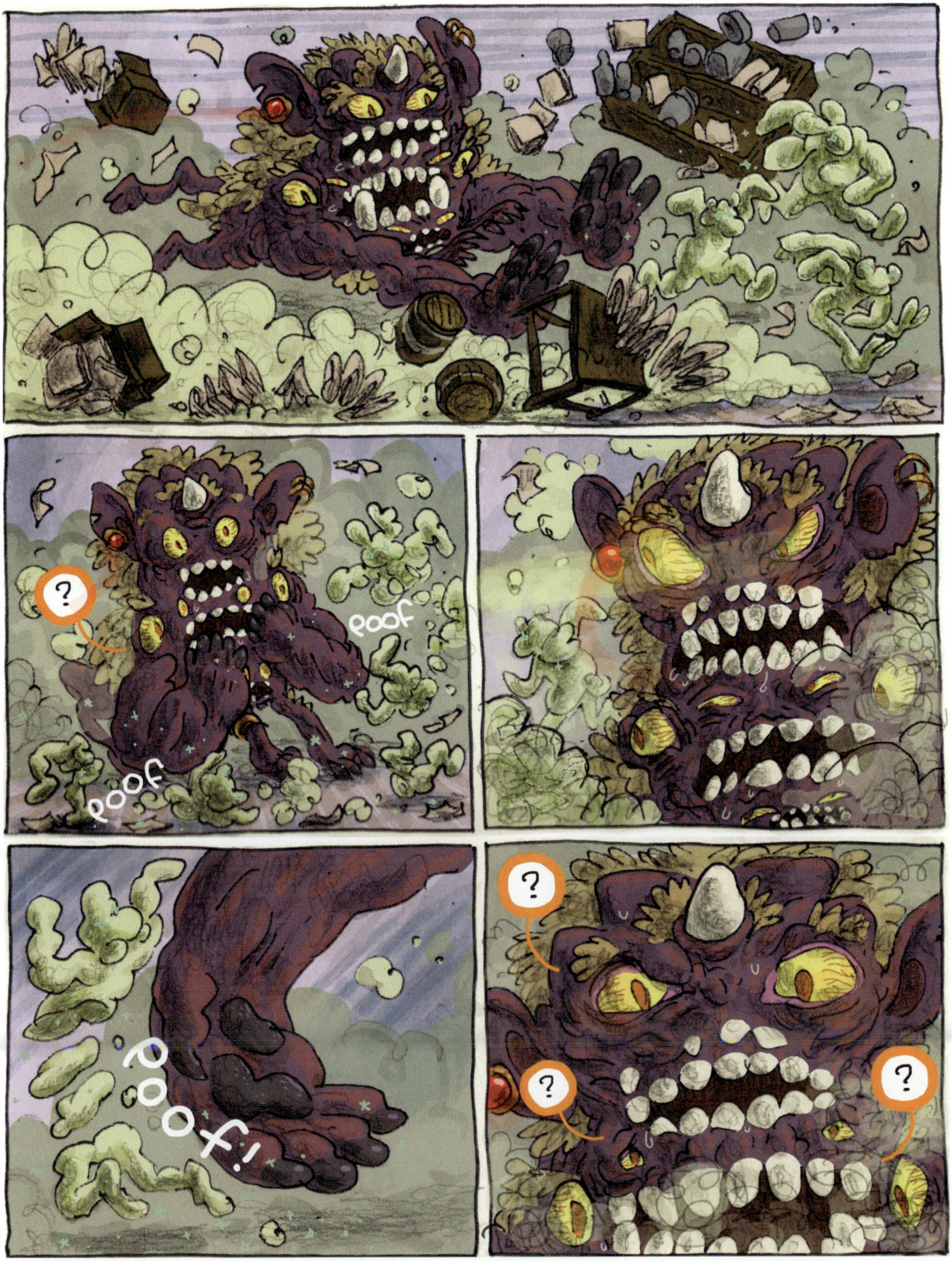
?
poof
poof
poof!
?
?
?

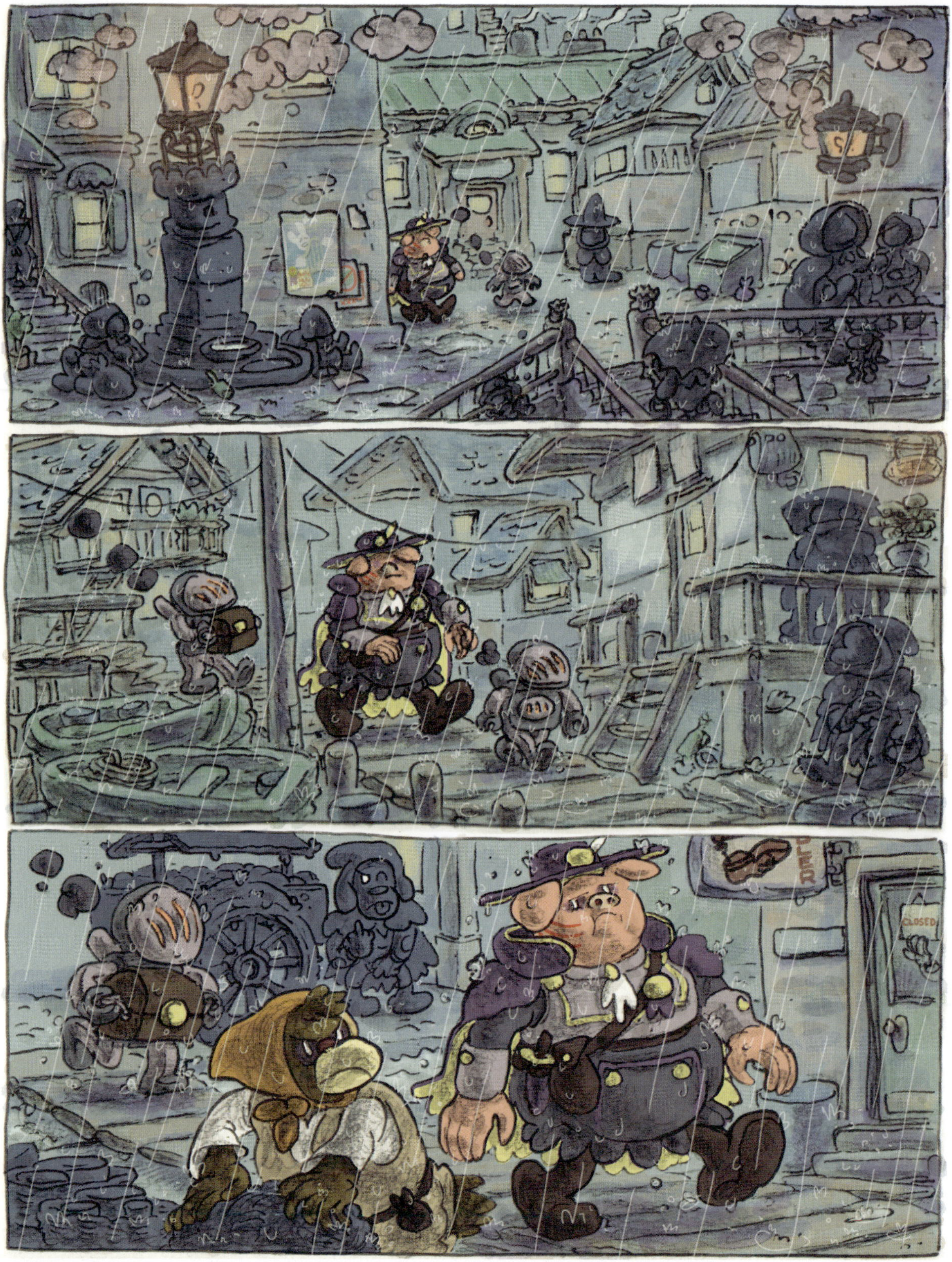
CLOSED

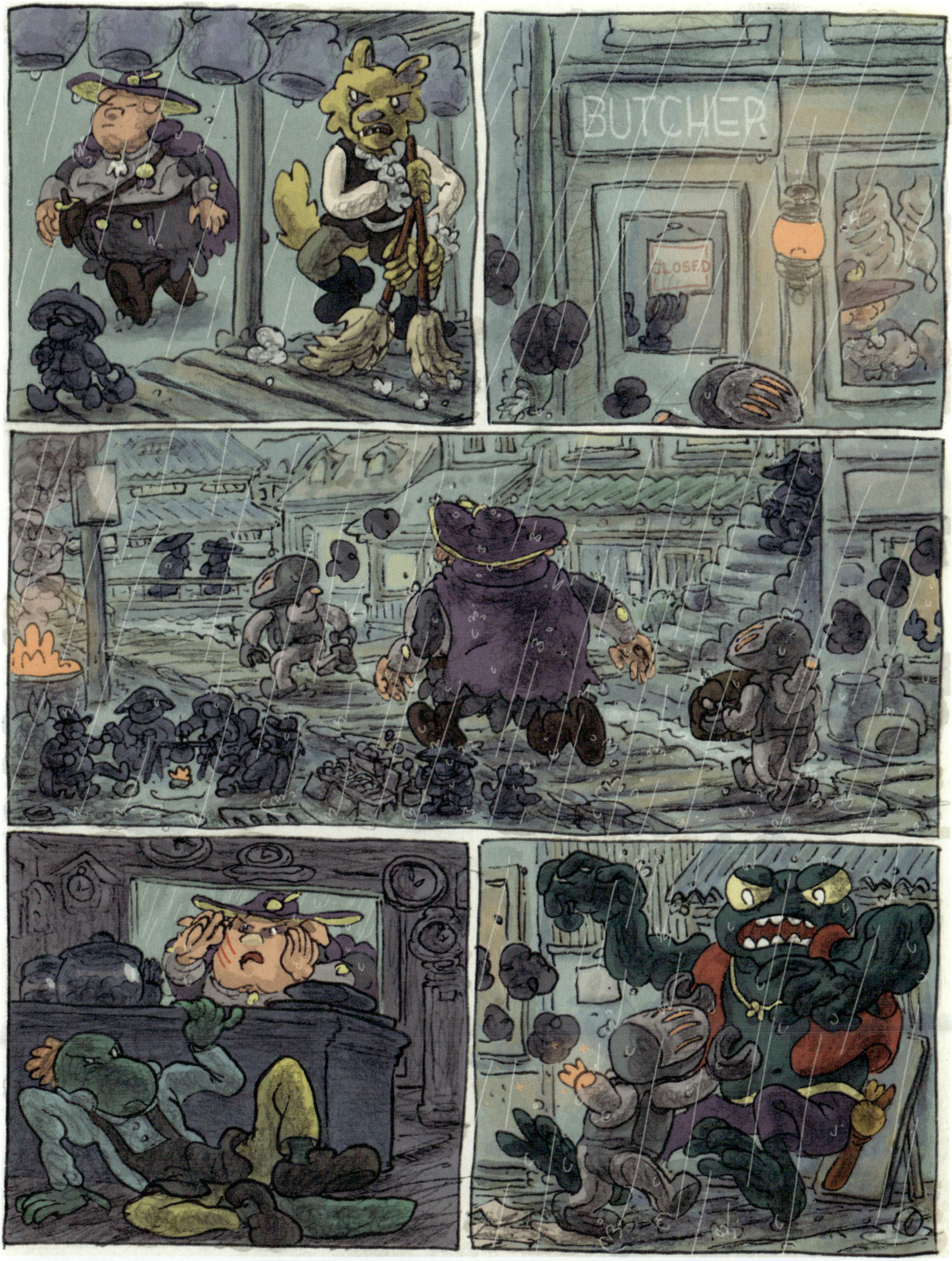
BUTCHER
CLOSED

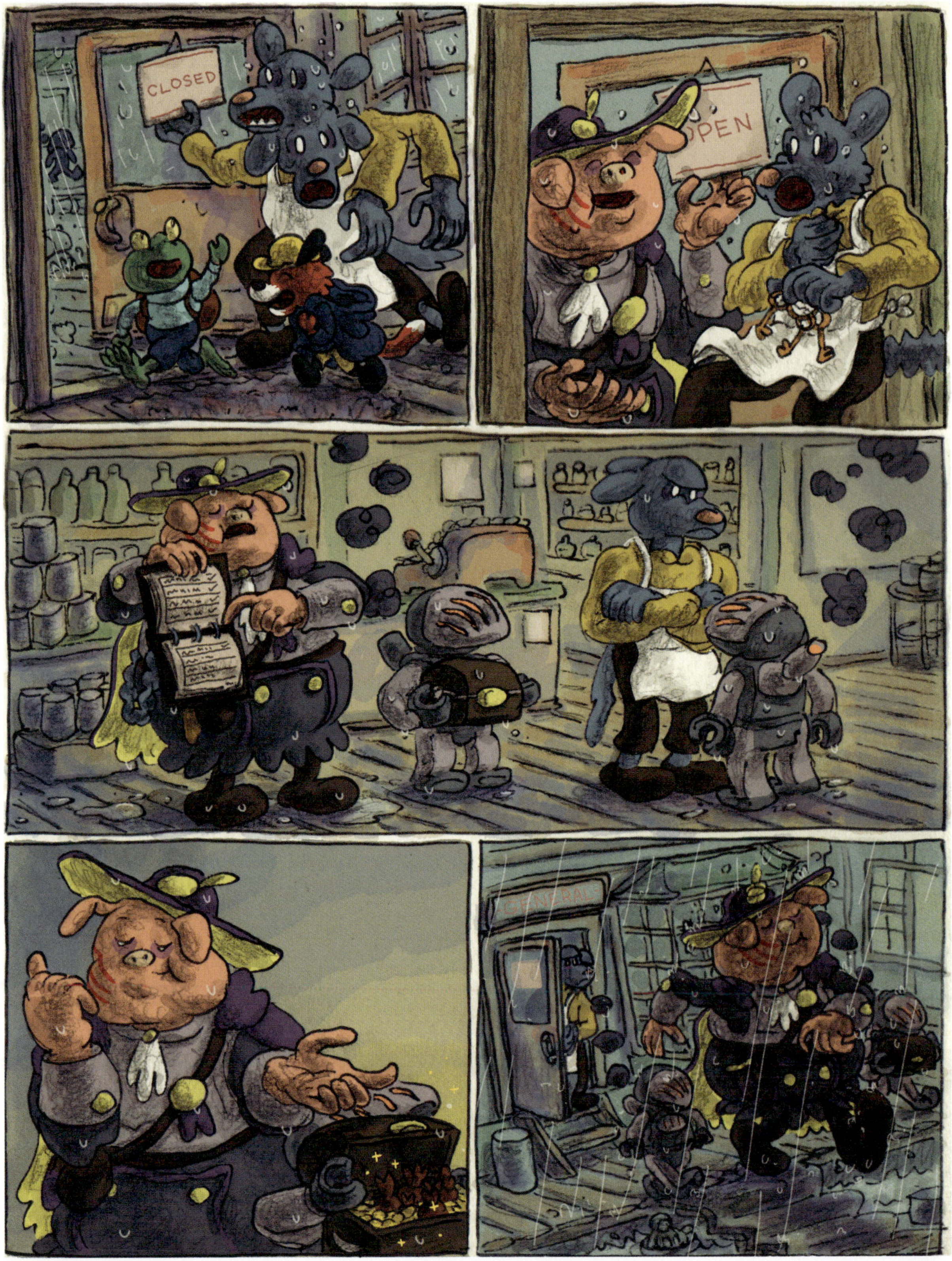
CLOSED

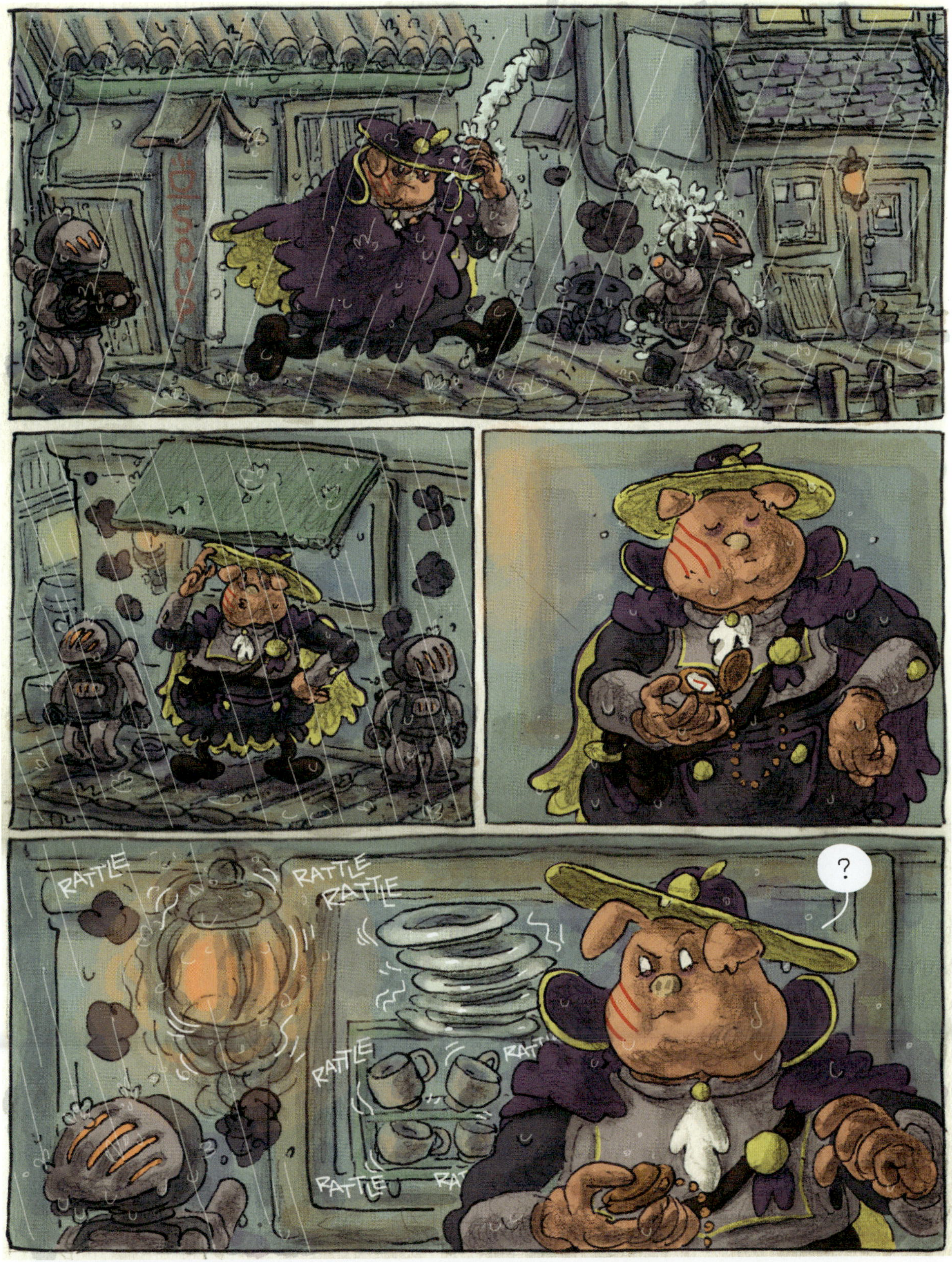
RATTLE
RATTLE
RATTLE
?
RATTLE
RATTLE

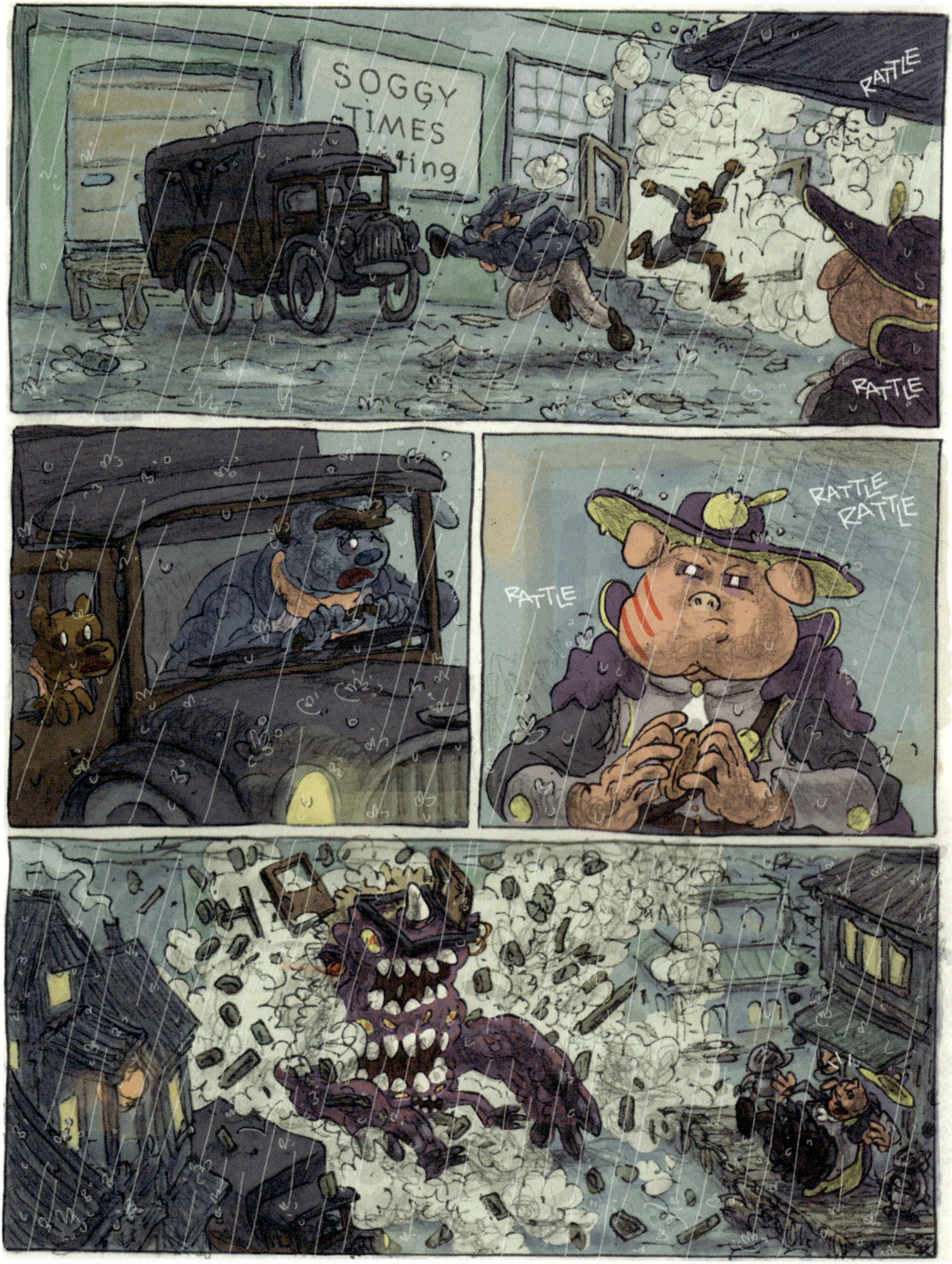
SOGGY
TIMES
RATTLE
RATTLE
RATTLE
RATTLE
RATTLE
RATTLE

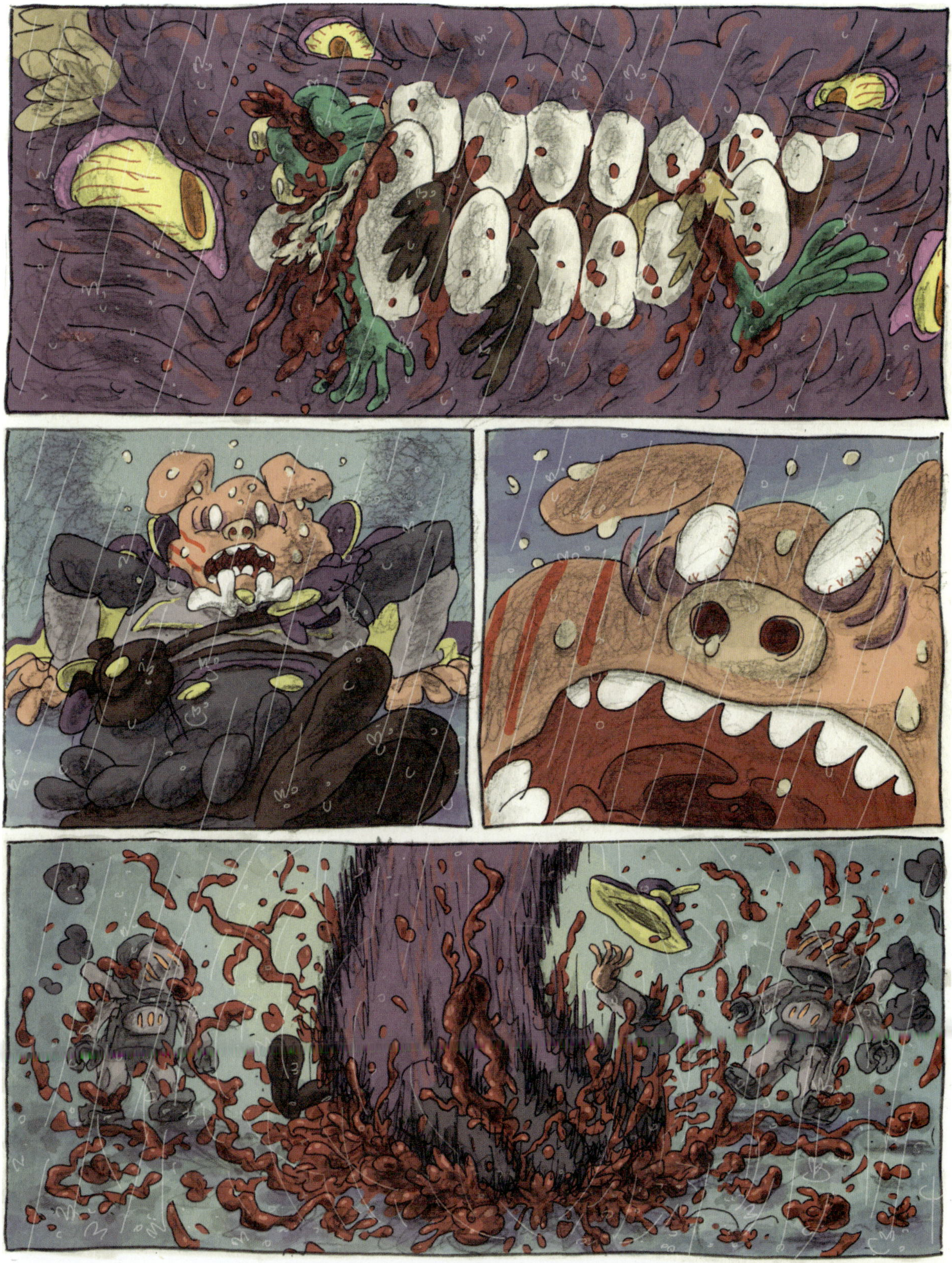

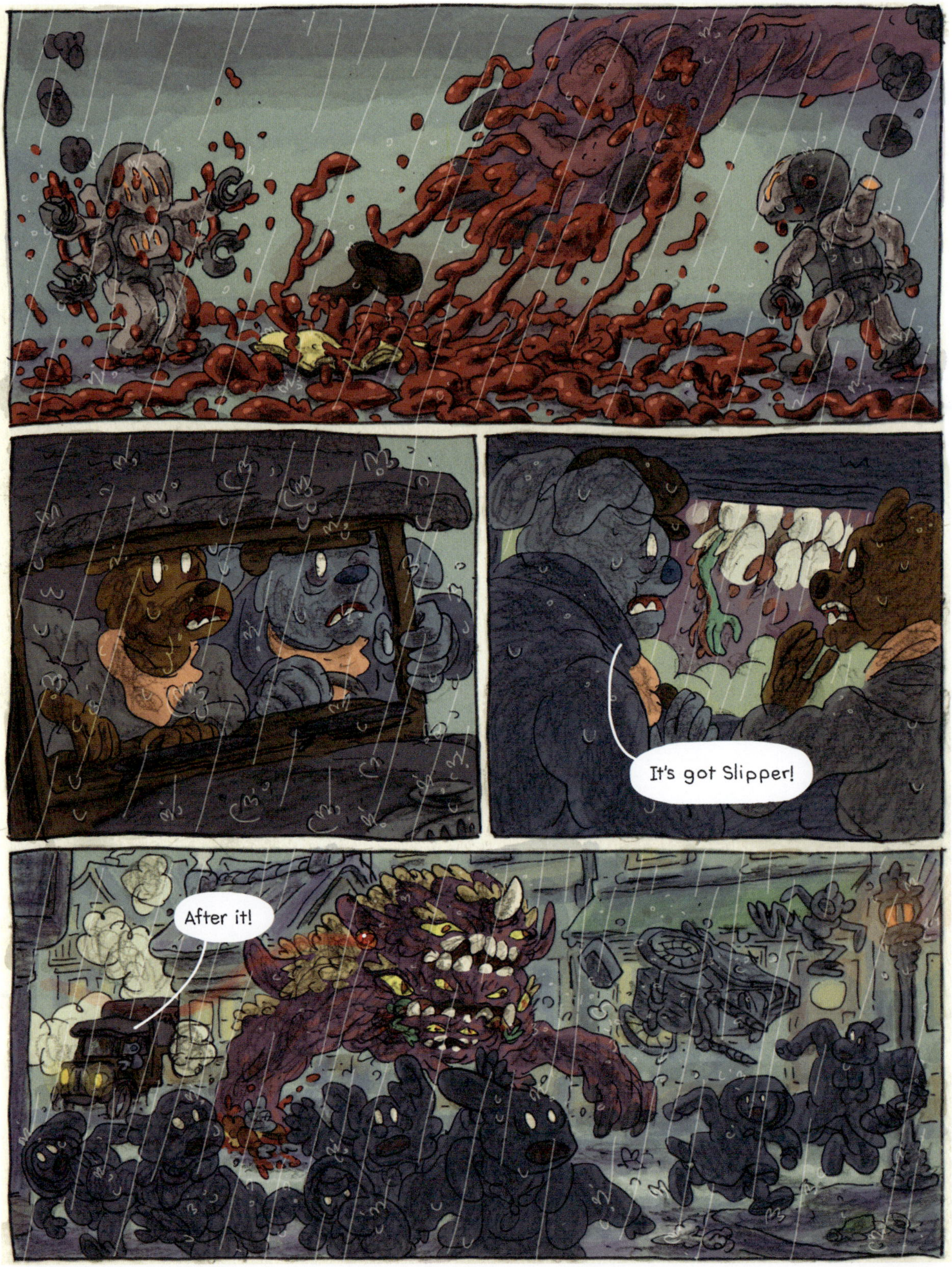
It's got Slipper!
After it!

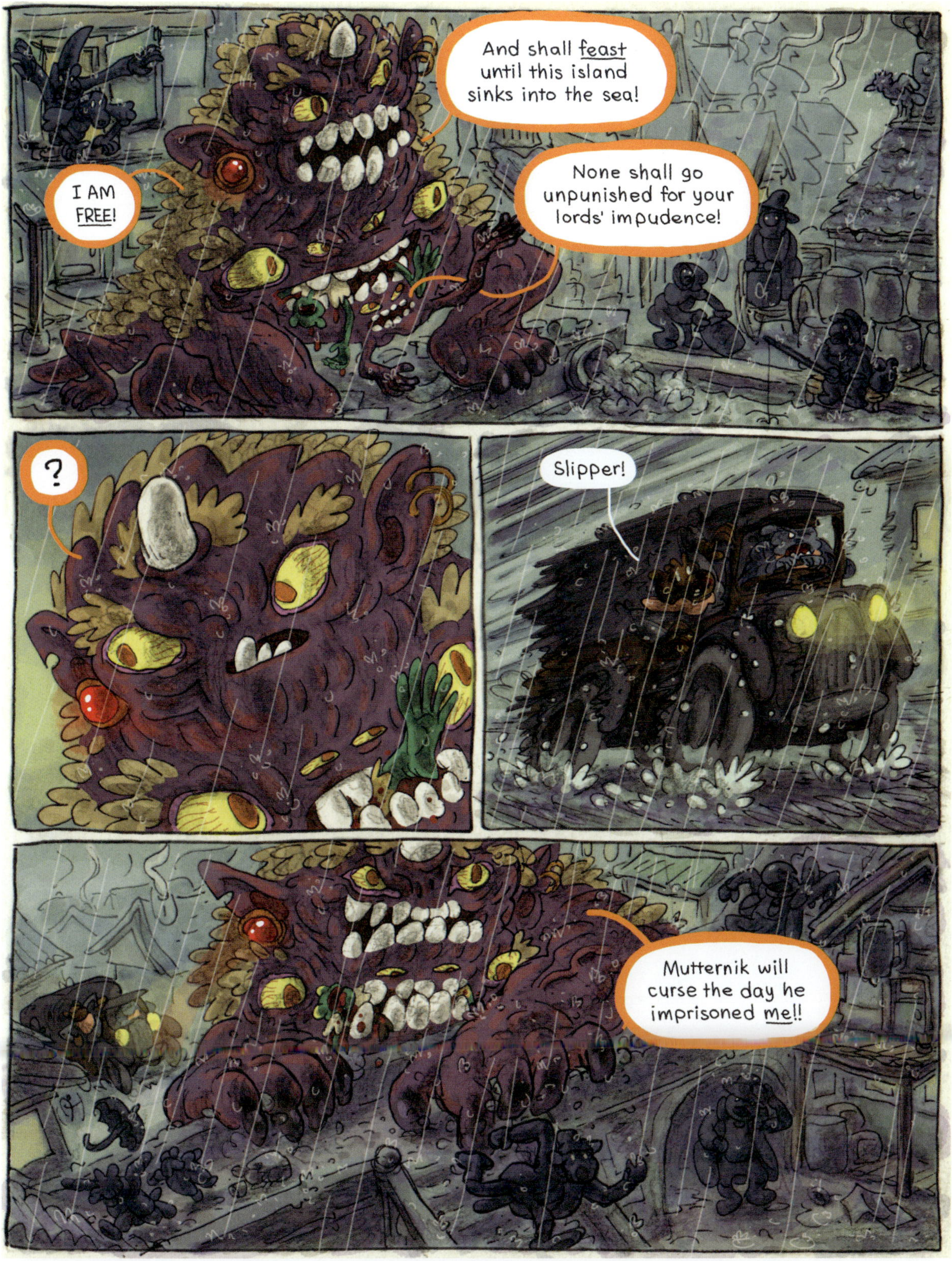
I AM FREE!
And shall feast until this island sinks into the sea!
None shall go unpunished for your lords' impudence!
?
Slipper!
Mutternik will curse the day he imprisoned me!!

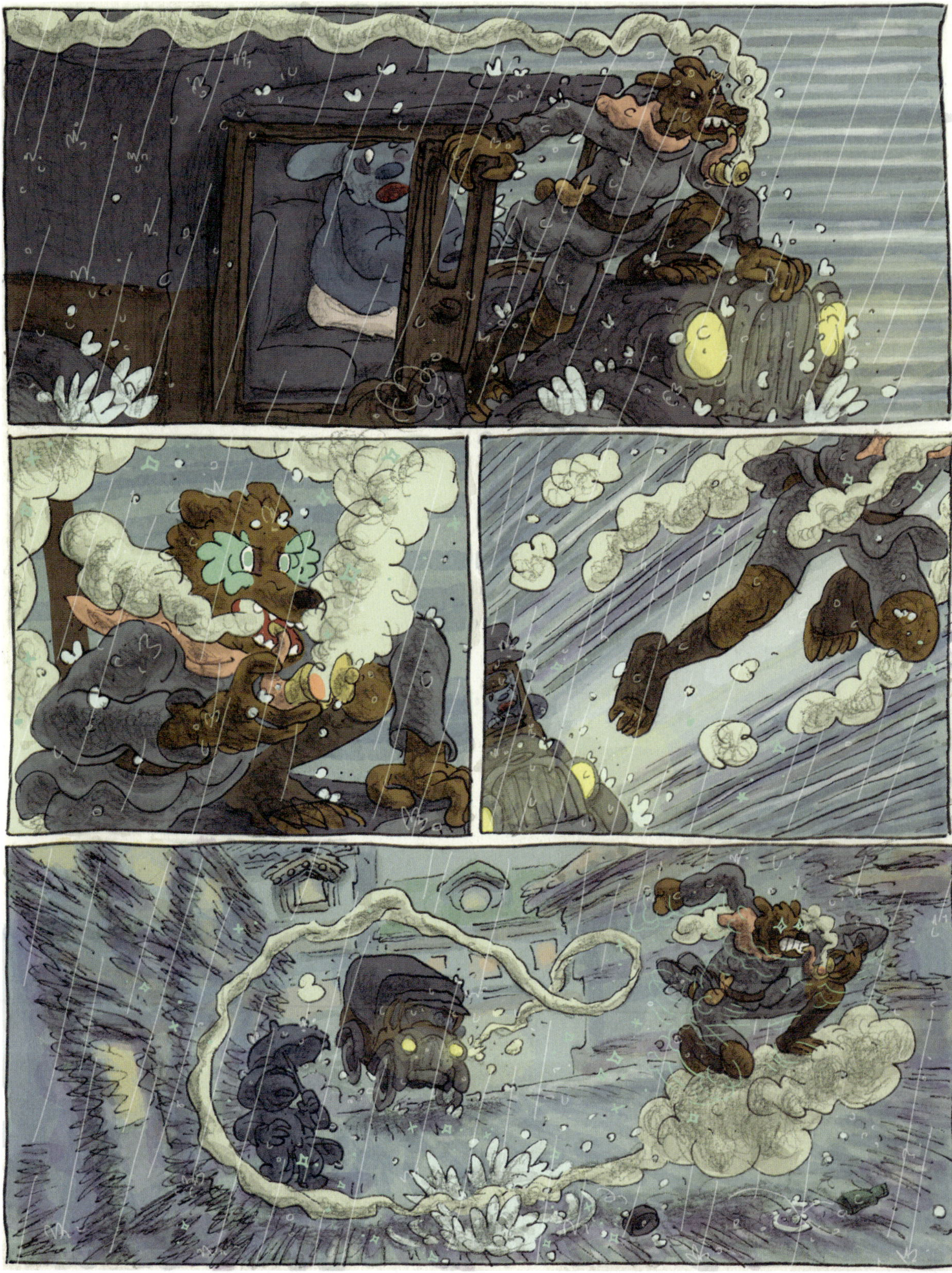

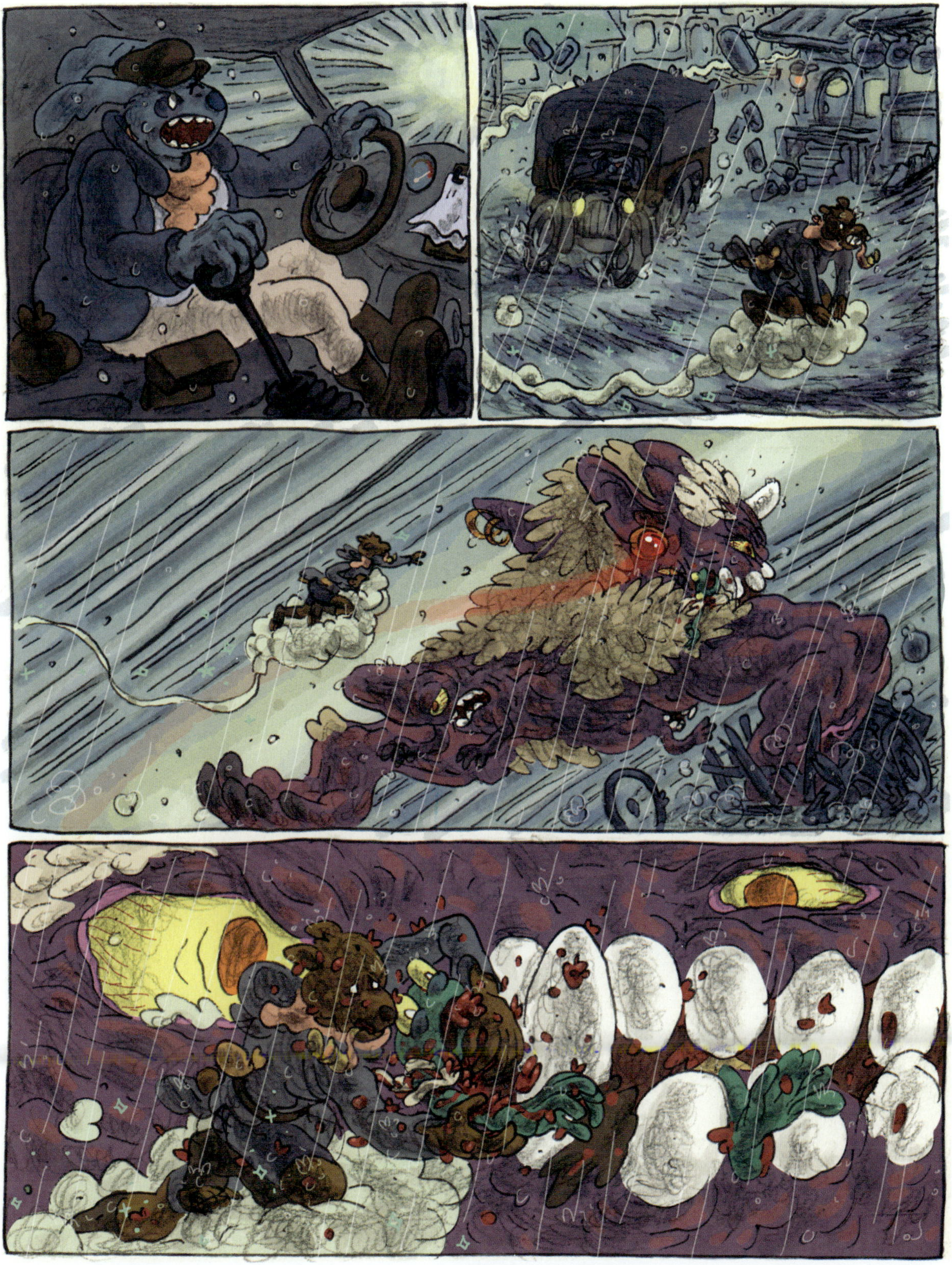

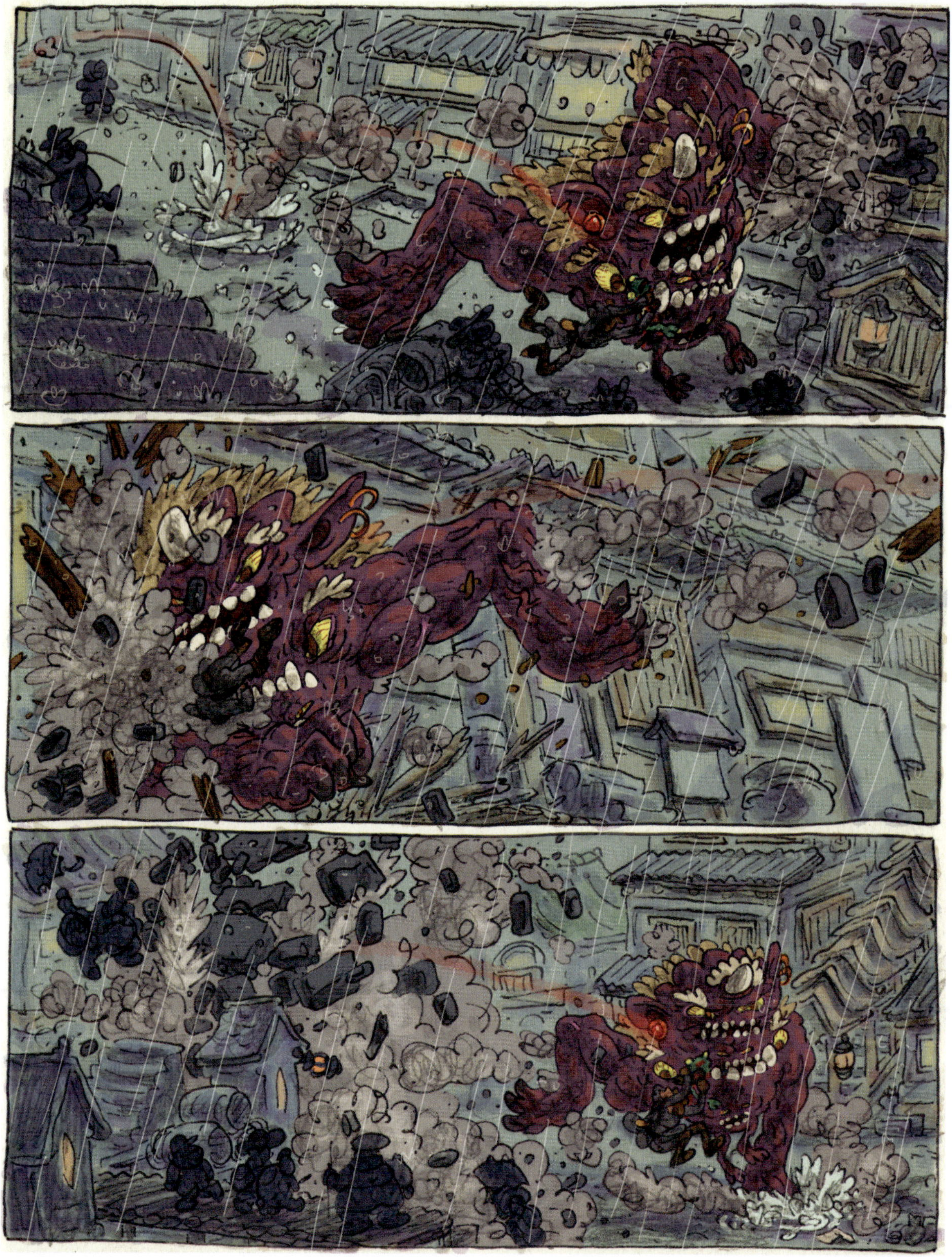

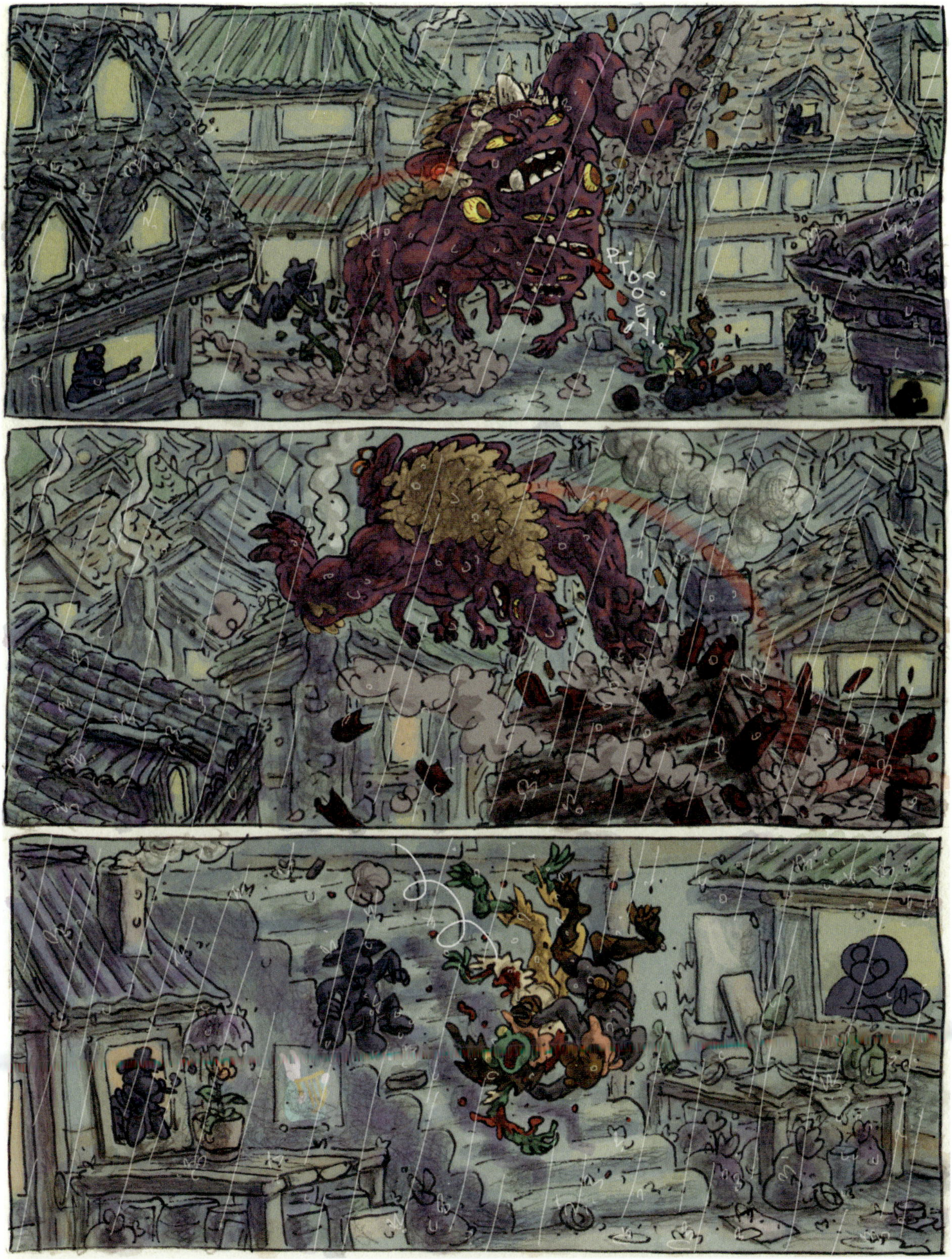
PTOOEY!

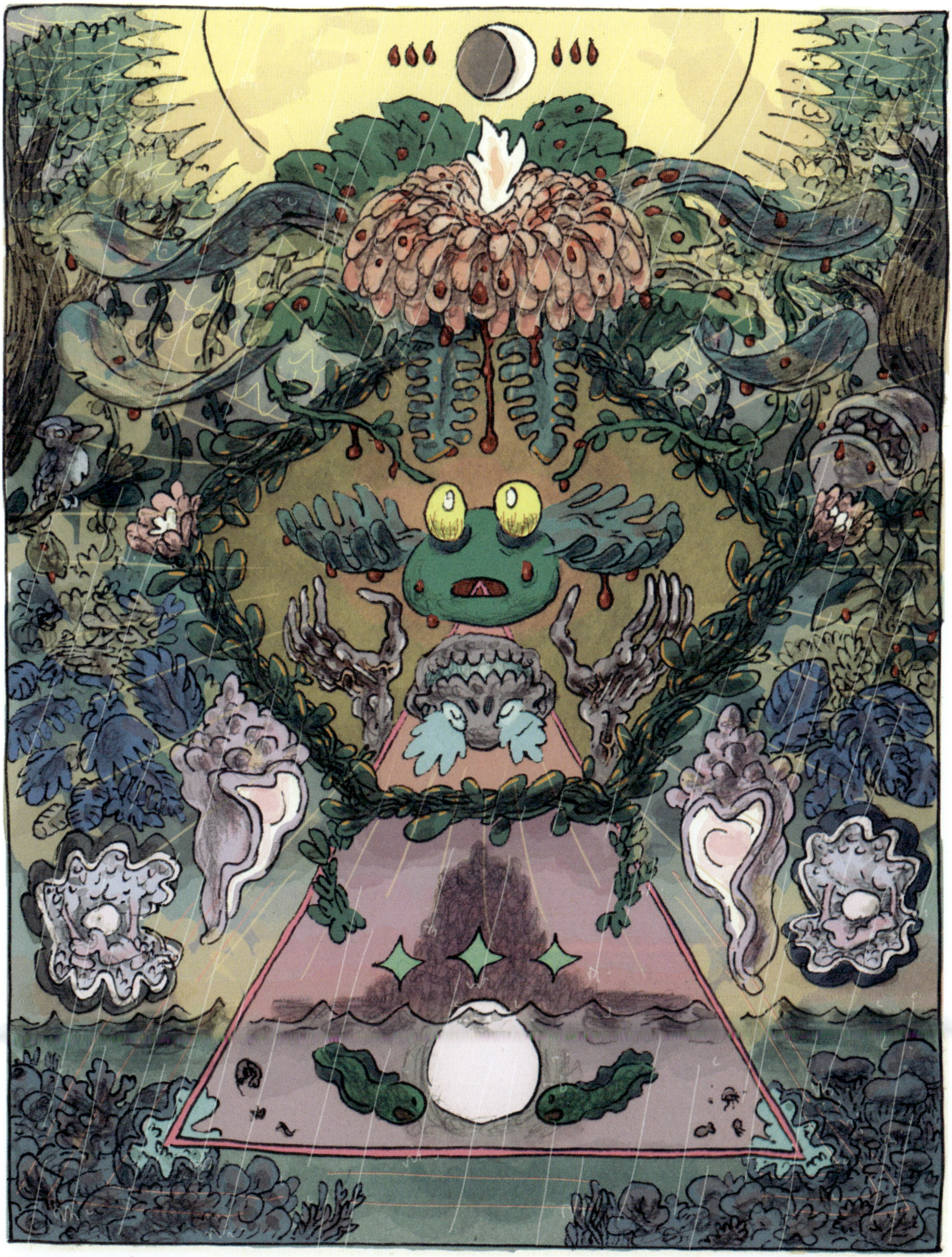

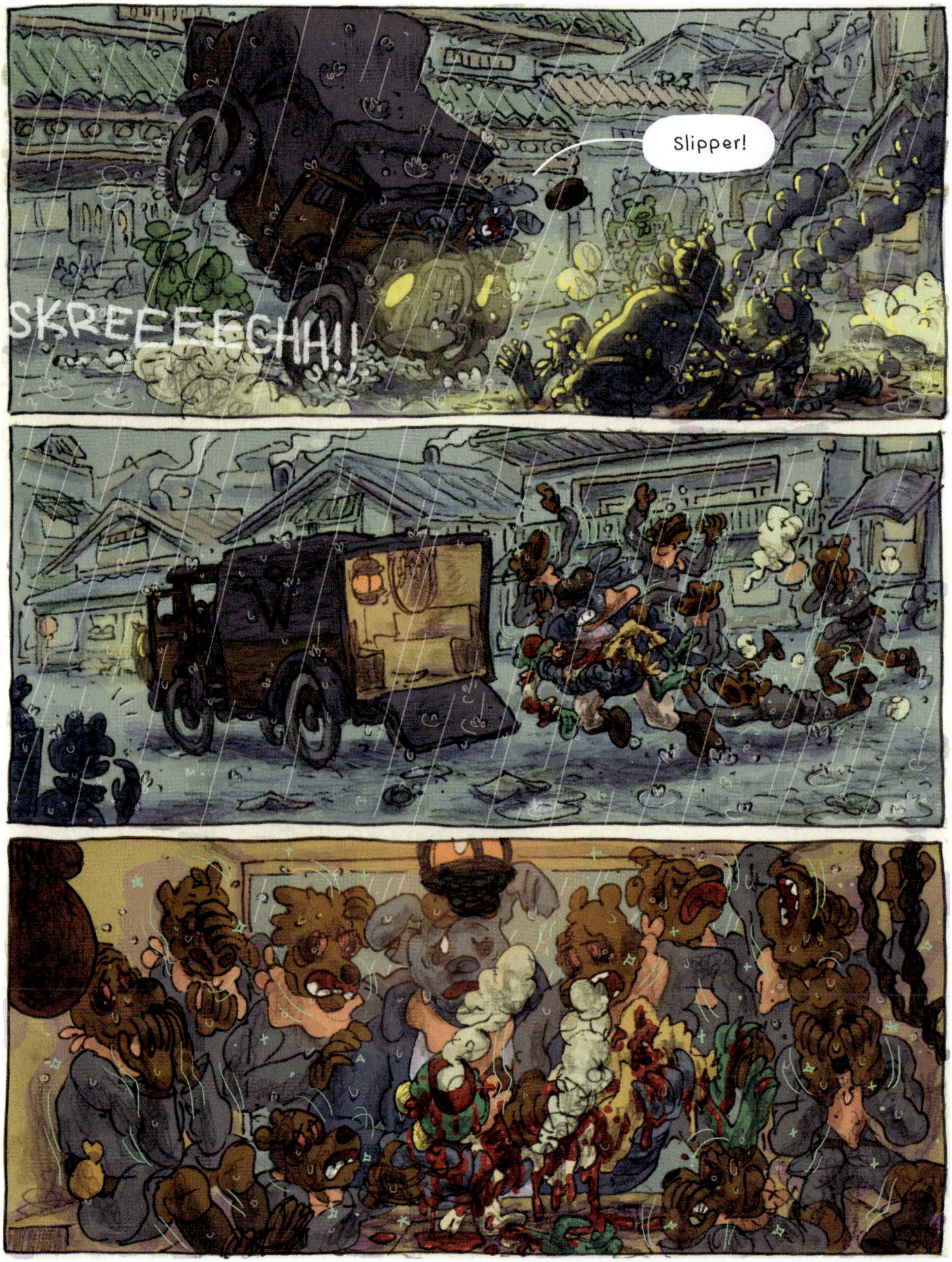
Slipper!
SKREEEEECHH!!

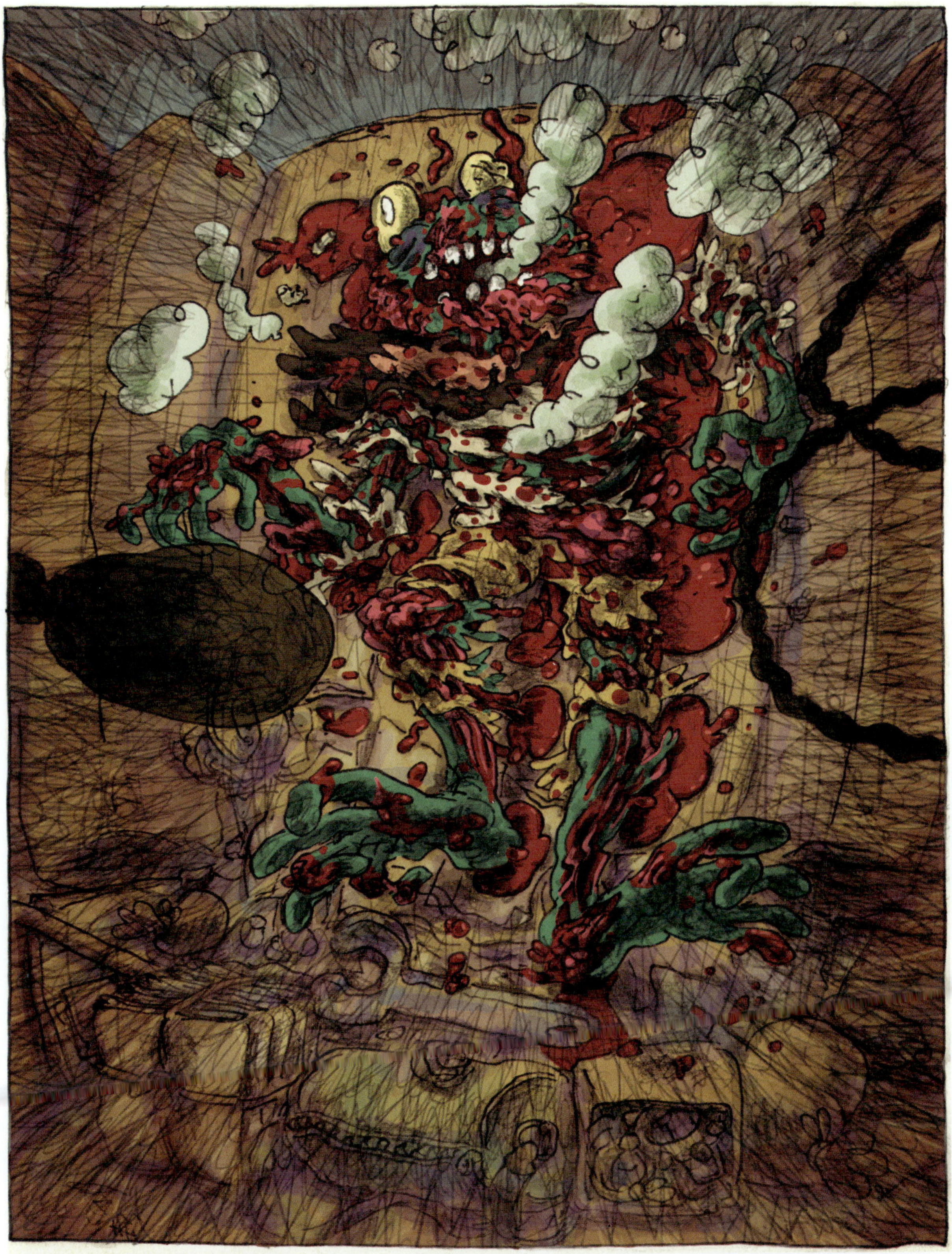

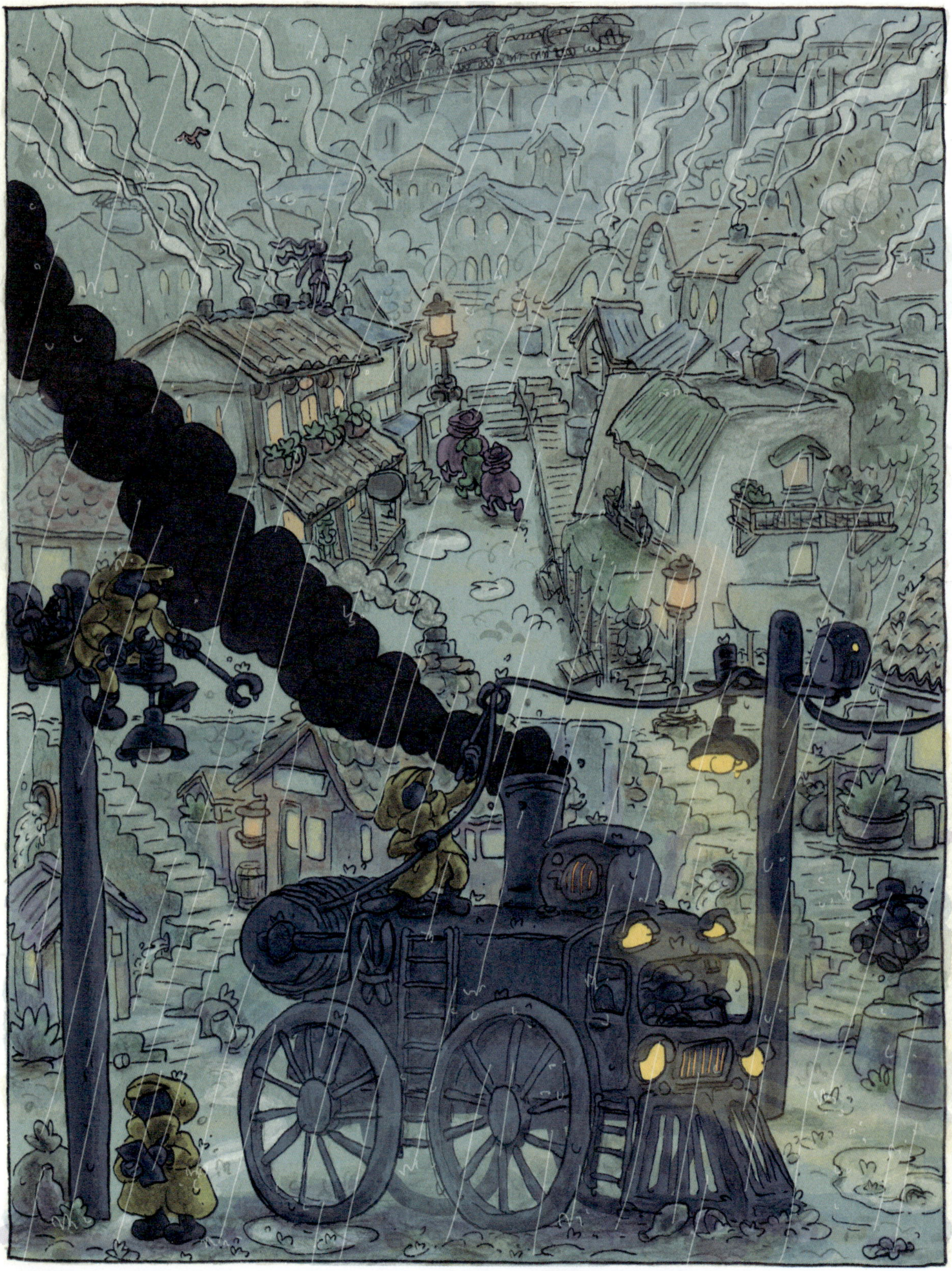

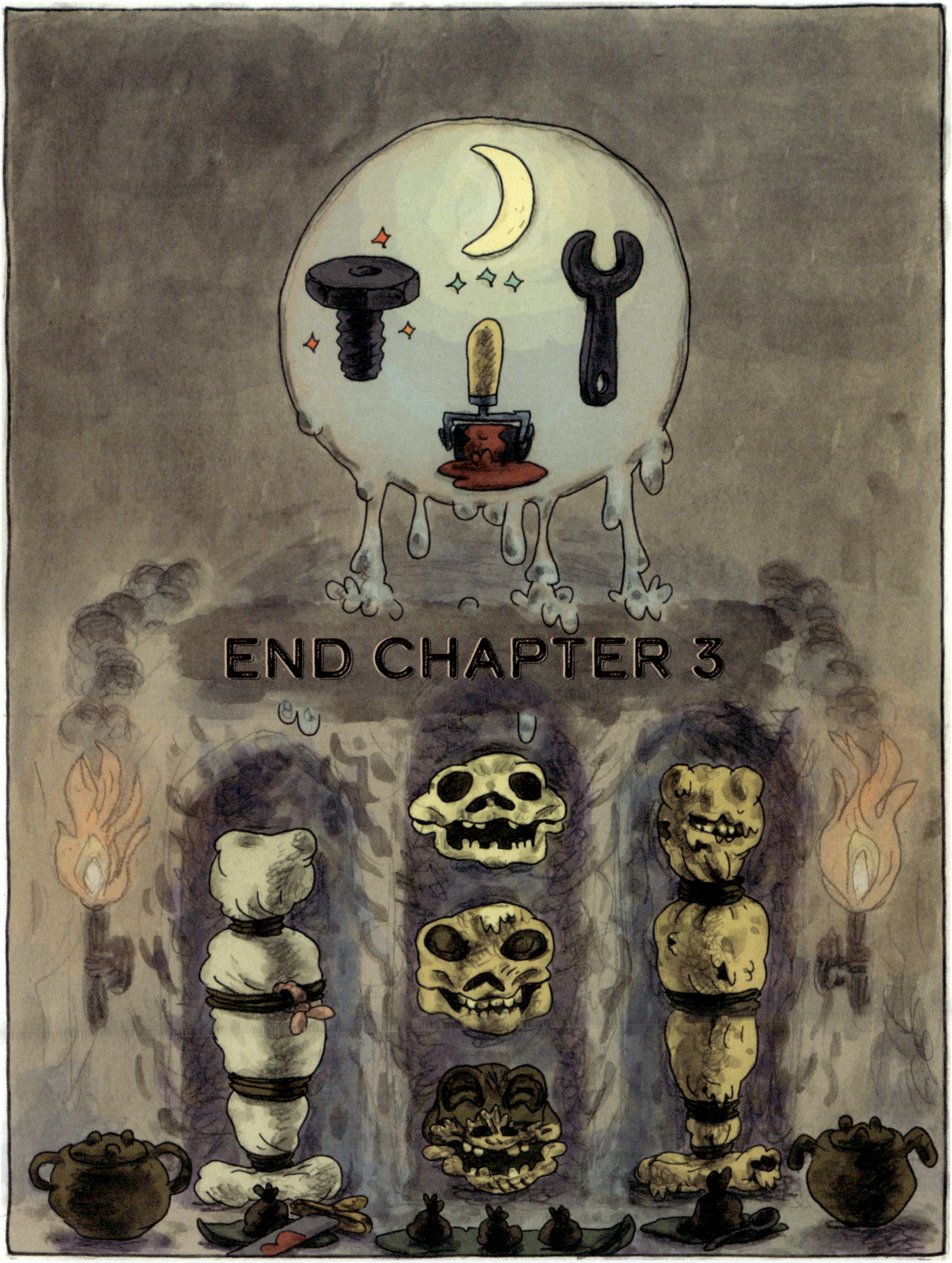
END CHAPTER 3